ONE LAST CHILD

TALLMAN'S VALLEY DETECTIVES

ANNI TAYLOR

bookish
COAST

Imprint: Bookish Coast

ISBN: 978-0-6484380-1-4

Dedicated to all who have been affected by the fires that raged throughout Australia in the last months of 2019 and early 2020, both people and animals.

A special mention to the communities of the Blue Mountains, where this story is based. In August 2019, there was snow. By January 2020, 80% of the Blue Mountains world heritage region was lost to the fires.

PROLOGUE

It was time to return the children.

Inside the van, the group of children—all blindfolded—sat obediently in their seats. Knees together, each clasping a toy in their hands. They had just been three when they were taken. Three-and-a-half years later, they were six, almost seven.

The driver gripped the wheel, keeping careful control on the steep descent. Stones skittered and rattled like bones in the van's undercarriage. Far below, the lights of Tallman's Valley were blinking on.

Twilight was coming in fast.

Sweat pricked the driver's hands inside woollen gloves. It was vital to stay hidden. Arrive in darkness and leave in darkness. Unseen by anyone but the children.

The returns would need to be swift and efficient. Each child back to his or her home.

All but for one child.

One child would not be returned tonight.

One child would never be returned.

1

NOLA HOBSON

The day of the abductions

The sky was cloudless, a sticky summer heat saturating the air. A blue haze hung over the line of distant mountains. To Nola, the edges of everything seemed smudged, as if nothing was distinct or completely itself.

She kept a watchful eye on the group of rowdy three-year-olds at *The Ponds* picnic area. Sometimes they almost merged with the dark spaces in between the trees. And they moved lightning fast. They were headstrong little humans, each with their own agenda.

Just then, the tinkling music of an ice-cream van slipped into the air. It wasn't there a moment ago. Or perhaps it had been, and she'd only just noticed it.

The music made her skin crawl and itch.

No, no. She couldn't allow her focus to slip. Because losing focus would put her job at risk.

Compulsively, she counted and recounted the children's nineteen little heads. *All there.*

The kids were her everything.

3

Her role as a nursery school teacher was the one bright spot in a life that was increasingly lonely. On the weekends, no one seemed to include her in their activities. On Sunday nights, she'd post photographs of her weekend on social media—pictures of a mountain hike or a cafe lunch—but she'd omit to say that she'd been all on her own. At just twenty-one years of age, she had the social life of an elderly recluse.

Little Ivy Wakeland zoomed in her direction with her arms outstretched and pigtails flying. Ivy was the daughter of a girl Nola had known from school, Abby. But Abby had barely noticed that Nola existed.

"Are you a bird or a plane, Ivy?" Nola called.

Ivy shot her a puzzled look and a shrug. "I'm just... *me*."

Nola tucked Ivy's words away in a keepsake box in her mind. The ability to switch off and just *be* was a gift.

Nola wasn't used to kids this age. It had only been two days since the director of the nursery school had moved her from the babies' group to the preschooler group.

And Nola wasn't used to the daycare workers in this group, either.

Justine, the senior teacher, was in her forties, with a permanently pursed mouth and pencilled-in eyebrows that didn't look right in broad daylight. She seemed nice enough, though Nola didn't doubt she was scrutinising her work performance today.

Kaylee was just sixteen and on work experience. She was sort of mousy and seemed happiest when given something to do.

The group of three-year-olds had a picnic at *The Ponds* every Wednesday. It was a grassy area—a bit overgrown if you asked Nola—nestled between a hill and a cool-climate rainforest. A shallow creek bubbled over a smooth bed of stone, with many tiny pools that gave *The Ponds* its name. A boardwalk wound through the rainforest and over the creek—the kids had been excited to spot frogs and birdlife from the boardwalk earlier. To the far left stretched a wide lake—distant enough that the children weren't lured by its ducks and glittering water.

The Ponds was just a block away from the nursery school. Nola, Justine, and Kaylee had walked the children down here an hour ago—the teachers wheeling trolleys of picnic food and rugs.

The children were dashing about on their tiny, stubby legs—throwing pinecones and gathering sticks.

This summer's theme was *wild bears,* and the children were certainly letting their wild sides out.

Justine checked her watch. "Goodness, eleven already! We'd better get the picnic started."

Kaylee took the cue and ran to get the rugs and baskets.

The music from the ice-cream van was drawing so close now that everyone heard it.

The children eagerly turned their heads, trying to locate the direction of the music. Their short heights prevented them from seeing much beyond the rise of the grassy hill.

Nola knew that the tune was *Greensleeves,* the same soundtrack that a lot of the older-style ice-cream vans used as they roamed the streets seeking children and families.

"Here," said Justine, tossing a headband to Nola that had round bear ears attached. "We're all koala bears today. Last week, we were grizzlies. Hopefully, being koalas will settle the kids down a notch. They were a bit feral last week."

Nola responded with a laugh, but the band made her head feel squeezed as she fitted it on. And her scalp was already sweating. The heat today was sucking all the oxygen out of the air. She couldn't wait for the picnic to be over, and then they could return to the air-conditioned nursery school.

Kaylee began placing containers of sandwiches, muffins and diced watermelon on the rugs. Nola's stomach turned at the sight of the food and she realised she felt ill. Maybe she was coming down with something.

The ice-cream van lumbered into view up on the street, pulling the droning *Greensleeves* tune with it. Nola waited patiently for it to go past, but it didn't. The driver parked the van right where they were about to hold the picnic.

The retro van was painted in pastel pink on the bottom half and cream on the top half, with oversize models of ice-cream cones adorning either side of the windscreen. An open servery displayed colourful images of all the ice-cream flavours that the van served. It was exactly the kind of van Nola remembered from when she was a child.

"I was told that we sing songs just before the kids have lunch, right?" Nola asked Justine, frowning deeply. "We're not going to be able to sing them with that racket going on."

Justine clucked her tongue in annoyance. "He usually comes by a bit later, after the kids have eaten. It doesn't matter so much then because we're packing up to go."

"I'll go tell him to clear off, if you like?" Nola suggested.

Justine flashed a big toothy smile, tucking her dark hair behind her ears. "You're a treasure."

Nola marched up the hill.

The driver looked across at her as she approached, his eyebrows raised in a question while he munched on a hot dog. The van's air-conditioner unit rumbled in noisy competition with the music.

A faint dizzy sensation circled Nola's head. She wanted to get out of the sun and return to the shadier spots at the bottom of the hill.

Her attempt to walk closer to the van was foiled as her legs refused to obey her. But she folded her arms and held her ground.

He could at least switch the damned music off.

Sweat dribbled from beneath her headband and down to her eyes. Her eyelids half-drifted shut as she tried to tune out the maddening sound. She could almost make herself believe there was a giant bumble bee in front of her, dancing to the maddening tune that repeated itself over and over....

She had the odd sense of time slipping from under her feet. Everything was merging.

The wheels of the van made a crunching sound on the road as it moved off.

Good, Nola thought, snapping her eyes open. She watched him drive away until his van was completely out of view.

As she returned down the hill, all was quiet. It wasn't just that the Greensleeves tune wasn't playing anymore, but the shouts and squeals of the children had gone silent. The smudged world she'd sensed earlier had erased all sound, as if she were viewing the scene through a soundproofed, hazed window.

The children were sitting obediently on the rugs with Kaylee.

Nola pulled the band off her head and held it so rigidly that she almost snapped it.

Something was wrong.

Justine was missing. So were some of the kids—Nola could tell that at a glance.

Justine might have taken a few of them to the toilet block, but there were too many children left behind—the rules were that you needed at least one daycare worker for every ten kids of that age group. And there were more than ten on the rug. Besides, Kaylee was just an inexperienced kid of sixteen.

She heard Justine's voice rising from the other side of the trees then, high and panicked. *Charlotte! Elijah! Ivy! Max! Olivia!*

Five names. Nola counted them off in her head, each one like a bullet firing.

Five of the children were missing.

2

KATE WAKELAND

A call flashed on my phone. From a police division that I didn't often deal with—*missing persons*. And from an officer I avoided dealing with whenever possible—Detective Sergeant Reagan Grimshaw. She wasn't exactly my favourite person in the world. The text message was cryptic, as was Grimshaw's style: *Five kids gone missing. School.*

A case of missing kids wasn't my area unless there was abduction and possible murder involved. As a senior homicide detective, I preferred being brought into such cases at the outset.

But five kids all at once? Unlikely anything serious was involved. They'd probably skipped classes to go play console games at someone's house.

I'd attend to the call when I was done with my current task. Right now, I was about to bring in a murder suspect. All signs pointed to a Mr Todd Dermott bludgeoning to death a friend of his, over a measly amount of $150. A senseless, brutal killing.

Todd had been a hard man to track down. But I'd suspected he was hiding out on an abandoned farm on Loft Hill. My partner and I were waiting him out, parked in a police vehicle on the ridge. The wait was tedious, but the second that Todd showed up, we had to be ready to move fast.

My partner slurped his coffee, shooting me a side glance that was partly apologetic but mostly *ehhh-what-can-you-do?* DS Jace Franco had been my partner in homicide for the past eleven years. He was forty-four now. At age sixty-one, I had seventeen years on Franco. He was like a younger brother to me, complete with idiosyncrasies that annoyed the living daylights out of me. The biggest thing that Franco and I had in common was a staunch refusal to be promoted out of the homicide division. That was the glue that'd kept us together as partners all this time.

"Wakeland," Franco said, resting his head back on the seat and sighing. "I decided I'm gonna do it."

"Buy better shoes?" I raised my eyebrows.

"Ask Martina to marry me."

"Send me the invite and then I'll believe it."

He'd been telling me the same thing for years. He always ended up backing out.

Shrugging, he began humming the *Here Comes the Bride* wedding march, pausing to sip his coffee every few seconds.

Ignoring the slurping noises, I focused on the view from the driver's window. Today, the mountain vista displayed the deep blue tint that it was known for. The mountains were on the outer reaches of Sydney—vast ranges that held back the urban sprawl.

I'd worked for the Blue Mountains Police Area Command for the past twenty years. Before that, I'd been with the state homicide squad, based in Sydney. I'd returned when I fell pregnant with my daughter, Abby.

I'd been glad to centre myself in the mountains again. It was a place like no other. The people warm, eclectic and close-knit, the seasons turning to severe winters and hot summers. Myths and legends here travelled as deep as the caves that veined the mountains. Sightings of panthers and lions, said to be escapees from circuses of many decades ago, were stories oft-repeated at the local pubs. There were tellings of ghosts and a mysterious lady in black. Real-life cults studded the upper mountains, together with the alternative lifestyle devotees.

Immediately below Loft Hill sat the town of Tallman's Valley. My town. Ten years ago, the houses here had been sparse and set apart from each other, arranged around the cleared sections of land near the lake. The houses had mostly been modest, with sweet-scented gardens of hydrangeas in summer and the whole place smelling of woodfires in the winter.

But when changes came, they'd been swift. A group of wealthy entrepreneurs had decided that Tallman's Valley was the perfect location to install a mini Silicon Valley. They said many of the best minds from around the world would be attracted to come live and work in such a place.

The idea had been sold to us as being a new, green city for families. Half of Tallman's Valley had remained as it was, with a massive, shiny development rising from the undeveloped land. People did come in from everywhere. Singles and families from America, Canada, the UK, India, Japan and elsewhere.

Everything gleamed in the new sector. An enormous technology centre housed hundreds of mysterious projects that were worked on night and day. The streets were newly paved and bicycle friendly. The houses solar powered and architect designed. Not a cheery woodfire in any of them. If you were offered a drink it was either organic coffee or chai or freshly squeezed juice. No one held a party there unless it was themed and catered. People had enormous kitchens that were barely used—dinners were ordered in.

The new Tallman's Valley was strange to me, but it had its positive aspects—I just missed the town of my childhood.

My biggest hope was that the new Tallman's Valley would offer enough for my daughter and granddaughter for their future lives, and then I might not lose them to urban Sydney. Abby had gotten pregnant with Ivy when she was just eighteen and she'd given up her studies to take care of her. This year, Abby had begun studying law at the local university. Abby was still living at home—an arrangement that both my husband Pete and I were happy with. Watching three-year-old Ivy run about the house was a daily joy.

Franco gulped the last of his coffee. "Someone's coming."

I checked the rear vision mirror. A battered SUV kicked up dust as it ascended the steep dirt road. It was Todd. He didn't seem to see us. He'd have to be eagle-eyed to spot us behind the bushes. As soon as the vehicle had passed us, I backed our car up and swung it onto the road.

The SUV stopped.

Inhaling a sharp breath, I stopped, too.

Todd might decide to reverse hard and ram us. Or spin his car in a 180-degree turn and attempt to get past. Or even jump out and run.

Instead, he surprised us by stepping out of his car and waiting there compliantly. His clothes were crumpled and his hair in greasy slicks across his forehead. I guessed he hadn't showered in days.

Todd's social media accounts—featuring himself as the tough gym junkie who was fond of calling the police *piss-weak dogs*—had made us believe that the last thing he'd do was to go quietly. We'd expected a fight.

Exiting our car, Franco and I approached Todd.

I flashed my badge. "Senior Detectives Wakeland and Franco. Homicide. You're under arrest for the murder of Oscar Waldon."

Todd met my gaze with dull eyes. "I didn't mean it. I didn't. We'd both been drinking heavy for hours. Things got said. I snapped."

I believed him when he said he didn't mean to kill his friend. That was how unremarkable murder often was.

Franco and I handcuffed Todd. As Franco moved him into the car, I answered the call from Grimshaw that I'd received earlier. Internally, I cringed at the prospect of speaking with her. Aged around fifty, she was a terse, ice-cold detective. She was hungry to get her cases solved, and she could be like a battering ram. Also not in her favour was the fact that she'd made a few snide comments about me choosing to hold off on retirement. It was none of her damned business.

"Wakeland," Grimshaw said, "you took your time."

"I'm in the middle of an arrest."

"Hmmm. Well, we have a group of missing tots on our hands. I'm down here at *The Ponds*."

"I know it," I replied, noting her use of the word *tots* and mentally recalibrating. I'd assumed the kids were young teenagers.

"The kids are from the Tallman's Valley Nursery School. My understanding is that one of the missing toddlers is your granddaughter."

"*Ivy?*" My heart squeezed up into my throat. Why were the children even at *The Ponds?* Then I remembered. The school held picnics down there each week.

"Yes. Ivy Wakeland," she confirmed.

"Did you say *five kids* were missing?"

"Correct. Five."

Five was good. One missing child could be an abducted child. But five altogether? They must have wandered off somewhere.

A new and terrible thought gripped me. *The lake.* They could have found their way there.

I gasped. "Oh God… that's close to the water."

"I've already organised a search of the lake. And of the bushland. I've got the forensic group on the way, too."

"Be down there in ten." Tremors raced up and down my body. Grimshaw must consider the situation serious to get forensics involved.

Franco took one look at my face and told me that whatever I needed, it was mine for the asking.

We drove to the station, where I left Franco with Todd Dermott.

Jumping into my own car, I drove down to the reserve, battling to keep my focus on the road. Mentally, I calculated the time that had passed since I first got the call from Grimshaw. At least twenty minutes. And there almost certainly would have been a similar amount of minutes lapsing between the time the kids had been noticed missing until the time the police were called. The preschool teachers would have searched before calling.

That was forty minutes gone already.

3

KATE

Waves of prickling fear burned my skin as I parked my car and hurried onto the reserve. The reserve was a wide strip of natural land and rainforest that ran for kilometres along the road. It was all bushland on the opposite side of the road, too.

I tried calling my daughter, but she didn't answer. I dashed off a text message to her.

There were no children here now. The rest of the group must have been taken back to the nursery school. I recognised a few of the children's parents—I'd dropped Ivy off at daycare many times. They were frantically searching, calling their children's names. Off to one side, three women stood together, their facial skin blotchy and their expressions almost frozen. I knew one of them—Justine. She was a teacher from the nursery school.

Police were dotted around the grounds. I couldn't spot Grimshaw. I raced up to the police officer nearest to me. I knew him from a previous operation that I'd been involved with. Senior Constable Cameron Vella. I liked him, an American who'd moved to Australia with his family ten years ago, as a teenager. He spoke fast in his Californian accent and seemed efficient.

"Senior, what's the story?"

He eyed me in confusion. "You're in homicide, right, Detective? Is there something I don't know?"

"One of the kids is my granddaughter. Ivy."

"Ah... hell." He nodded, sucking in a breath before exhaling forcefully. "Okay. The story is that the kids from the nursery school were having a picnic just there near that line of trees." He gestured towards the spot. "There were three daycare teachers. One of them went to tell the driver of an ice-cream van to move away because it was distracting the kids. That left two daycare teachers. While those two were setting up the picnic, five of the kids went missing."

"Where exactly were those five kids last seen?"

"The teachers aren't sure of the pinpoint location—the kids were all running about and playing. That's the teachers over there. Justine, Nola and Kaylee." He nodded in the direction of the three women. "Detective Grimshaw asked them to stay at *The Ponds* for questioning."

"So, the teachers have no idea which direction the kids might have run in?"

He shot me a grim look. "I'm afraid not, no."

"Thank you."

I scanned the grounds. There was a high concentration of police and parents in the rainforest area and along the boardwalk and creek. A couple of child-sized headbands with bear ears were lying discarded on the grass.

I sprinted away to the lake.

There was a hospital up this end—a hospice for terminally ill patients and also a dementia ward. The lake was further away from *The Ponds* than I'd remembered, and that was a good thing. Above, a helicopter swept in and began executing a slow circle of the water.

Reaching the lake, I began searching with the other police, running, calling Ivy's name. I gulped the hot air, my throat dry and tight. The thick smell of mud and rotting reeds rose from the shoreline.

Police had already spanned the edges of the lake as far as I could see. The children weren't here, or they would have been found.

Grimshaw had things under control, at least. She was bombastic, but she was thorough.

I caught sight of her up ahead. Tall like myself, with dark auburn hair in a neat shoulder-length style, she was giving instructions to a group of officers. The officers left in different directions.

She turned to me as if she sensed I was behind her.

"I'm sending a team to door knock the nearest streets," she told me. "Might get someone who saw something odd."

"Good. Which locations have been searched?"

"Any place small tots could conceivably run to," she told me. "The rainforest and up around the top of the hill. We've also spread out to the hospital and around the edge of the lake." She gestured towards the water for emphasis.

I kept my gaze averted from the lake's surface, not wanting to think too hard on that possibility. "It seems to me there's a good chance that the children *did* run up that hill and along the street. Chasing the ice-cream van maybe?"

"Maybe," Grimshaw said. "But one of the teachers swore they didn't go up the hill. And no one at the hospital saw them. It's a real puzzle."

"What about CCTV? There's got to be cameras here."

"Unfortunately, not many. The council doesn't have any surveillance cameras that are aimed at *The Ponds*. The hospital would have cameras, of course. I'm going to take a look at their footage. For the moment, the priority has been to find the kids quickly."

My head felt faint as I recalculated the time that the kids had been missing. Almost an hour now. I instructed myself to breathe. "Has anything been found? Socks, shoes?"

"A few things, but they could belong to any of the nineteen children. It's going to be a process to find out what belongs to who."

Panic wheeled inside me. "If they didn't reach the water and they're not anywhere, what's the alternative? Someone led them away. And if that's what it's come to, then we need to work out *who*."

"Yup. But the daycare workers didn't see anyone in the area. Hard task to lead five tiny tots away quietly, too. Like trying to get a bunch of monkeys out of a tree."

"What about the driver of the van? He—or she—?"

"*He,*" Grimshaw cut in. "Mr Brent Cole. We've already caught up with him. There were no children on board."

I tried to absorb the pieces of information that I had so far. "He might have made a stop somewhere before your officers got to him." It was a long shot, the driver taking the kids. But if he had, the sooner we found out, the better.

"Well, we'll cross that bridge when we come to it," she replied, not seeming to share my concern. "Have you contacted your daughter—Abigail? We've been able to contact all the parents of the missing five so far, except for her."

"I'll try Abby again." I tried to think where she'd be. It was Wednesday. Abby would be at one of her uni lectures today. The worst thing would be for her to hear on the news that Ivy was missing.

Angling herself away from me, Grimshaw answered a call that had come through on her phone. "Yup, the Forensic Services Group are on their way. Dog squad, too."

As soon as Grimshaw ended the call, another call came through for her. Justine—the senior teacher—had found a button on the hill at *The Ponds*.

Alongside Grimshaw, I rushed back to *The Ponds* area.

Justine was standing there waiting, gingerly holding the button on the palm of her hand, as if it were a tiny bomb. "I'm fairly certain this belongs to Ivy. It was at the top of the hill."

I peered at the tiny bee-shaped button in her hand, tears immediately pricking my eyes. "Yes, that's Ivy's."

Ivy had a pinafore dress with a bee motif on the front pocket and decorative buttons shaped like bees on each strap. Taking the button from Justine, I tucked it safely into my hand.

The other two daycare workers stood at a short distance away. One looked like a teenager, her hair in two plaits. The other, who looked in her early twenties, had her arms crossed tightly over her chest. Dressed in overalls and a striped T-shirt, she resembled a large child.

"Nola," Grimshaw bellowed at the older girl in the striped shirt. "Didn't you tell me the kids couldn't have run up the hill when they went missing? Because you were at the top of the hill at the time, right, and you would have seen them?"

Nola walked up to us, looking as if she were going to be sick. "Yes, that's right. But Ivy was rolling on the hill earlier, and maybe that's when she lost the button."

Grimshaw frowned. "But they weren't on the hill at all? Isn't that what I was told earlier?"

Justine nodded, throwing Nola a perplexed glance. "Yes, they're not meant to be. I don't recall seeing any of them there. And they certainly didn't play at the *top* of the hill. We keep them in the picnic area. That way, we can see them all."

Nola pushed her hands into her overall pockets, her elbows sticking out at awkward angles. "No, they didn't play on the top of the hill. And when we arrived, we walked down the path."

"And yet," Grimshaw said tautly, "a button was found where it shouldn't be."

Nola cringed as if Grimshaw's words had burned her.

"Hi, Nola," I said, softening my tone. "I'm a detective, and I'm also Ivy's grandmother. Kate Wakeland. Is it at all possible that the children followed you when you went to speak to the driver?"

"No. I definitely would have seen them," she said stubbornly, her gaze briefly flicking to Justine. "And I know who you are. I went to school with Abby."

I made a quick study of her face, but I didn't remember her. My job hadn't given me much time to hang around the schoolyard after the bell during those years.

"Oh, I wasn't one of Abby's friends," Nola hastened to add. "I... I wasn't one of the popular kids."

"I'll probably remember in time," I responded. "Do you remember seeing anyone hanging about?"

"No," she said. "There was just... the ice-cream van."

Grimshaw exhaled as if this was old news and it was bothering her. "Yes, we've established that there was a van."

Timidly, the youngest of the daycare workers stepped over.

"This is Kaylee," Justine told me. "She's doing a daycare course and is with us on work experience."

"Hi," I greeted the girl. Privately, I wondered how on earth five children managed to get away from these three workers.

"I don't know if this is of any use," Kaylee told me. "But I took a little video of the kids playing. For the parents to see later."

"For the love of—" snapped Grimshaw. "You have *video?* Why didn't you tell me that before?"

The girl's expression crumbled. "I don't know. I didn't think."

Grimshaw and I quickly examined the clips that Kaylee had taken. There were only two of them and only a few seconds long each. I spotted no one except for the kids and Justine. The sight of Ivy in one of the clips made my chest tighten.

I raised my head to Kaylee. "Where was Nola at the time you took these?"

"She went to tell the driver to leave. Look, I'll switch the sound on. You can hear the music." Kaylee turned the sound up.

The tinkling ice-cream van music entered the air.

Justine watched the video clip intently, while Nola turned her head away, looking ill.

I eyed Grimshaw. "This must be just before the kids went missing."

Grimshaw nodded, narrowing her eyes and studying the footage. "We'll get this back to the station and look at it on a large screen. I want to see every square centimetre."

Nola gestured towards the road. "There's Abby now."

I whirled around.

A slim girl dashed onto the reserve, her long, dark ponytail swinging behind her.

I ran to meet her.

She was breathing hard, her eyes huge. "What happened? Where's Ivy?"

"Oh, honey, this is just terrible." I tried to hug her, but she grabbed my arms and held me back, her face flattening with fear.

"You mean they haven't found her yet? Not *any* of the kids?"

"Not yet," I tried to say as gently as possible. "But they will."

Her hand reached across her mouth, tears springing in her eyes. "The lake! They could be—"

"They don't think they got that far," I broke in. I couldn't promise that the kids hadn't, but I couldn't bear to tell her that.

"Why weren't they being watched properly? How did they let *five* kids out of their sight?" She cast an angry, despairing gaze across the reserve at Nola.

Nola dropped her head, staring straight down.

Grimshaw cut towards us. "Abigail! I need your signature. I need all the parents' permission to put photos of the kids front and centre in the news. The sooner the better."

My daughter cast one last desperate look at me as she stepped away with Grimshaw.

A van pulled up on the road.

I watched the forensics group exit the vehicle in their plastic jumpsuits and plastic-covered footwear. They'd soon be combing the area for shoe impressions in the ground, pieces of clothing or hair caught in twigs or bark. Unfortunately, any shoe impressions of the missing kids were probably trampled by now.

Please, find something. Find something that leads us straight to the children.

4

KATE

24 hours after the abductions

Marching into Superintendent Andrew Bigley's office, I approached his desk. "Andrew, I want onto Grimshaw's team."

The five children had been missing for a whole day. The entire town was looking for them. Still, not one child had been found. The possibility of them reaching the lake had been ruled out. The shores of the lake had been damp, but there were no fresh, child-size footprints. And CCTV footage from the hospital didn't show the children coming up that way. Police had tracked the route that the ice-cream driver had taken yesterday. They hadn't found a viable space of time in which he could have taken the kids somewhere, but he also hadn't been ruled out as a suspect.

Abby, Pete and I had been searching the reserve and surrounds in a state of relentless shock, looking for any clue to the children's disappearance.

Grimshaw had flatly refused to take me onto her team. I was going over her head, trying to override her. She was currently working with Inspector Jeffrey Zimmerman to establish a team to work on the case of the missing children. They were selecting from the constables and detectives Grimshaw normally worked with, while also bringing in people from the state Homicide Squad and the state Child Abuse and Sex Crimes Squad. Grimshaw herself was based in the Blue Mountains Police Area Command, and she specialised in missing person cases.

I waited as a moment of surprise crossed Bigley's face. He flexed his shoulders back into his chair, expelling a tight breath. "You know I can't put you onto the team."

"You *can*. There isn't a specific rule against it."

"Kate, it's not good practice. As a close relative of Ivy's, you'd be personally involved, and that can lead to bad places."

"I know where the lines are, and I know better than to cross them. The best way I can help is to be put on the case. Grimshaw doesn't want me but you can override her."

"If I did, and then you put one foot wrong, you could get yourself fired."

"I'm sixty-one, Andrew. You can't scare me with that."

"You don't want to go out in disgrace. Over the years, I've had to let too many good detectives go because they lit their own fuse."

"I'll keep myself under control. Grimshaw's team could use me. You've agreed with me before that we should be sending out our best homicide detectives to missing person cases. There's a good argument to say that many times, we should be first on the scene."

"Right. Agreed. But Reagan didn't mess around. She covered all bases. She even got forensics out there first thing. I've got faith in her. She's a one-woman machine, and she's damned good at what she does."

"I'm not calling her into question. I know she's good. But the team will be even better with me on it."

"Kate, be reasonable. You've got open homicide cases."

"Two of them are in the hands of forensic analysts now. Active police investigation is at a halt until the results come through. And the results are predicted to take months. But it's not a case of *if*, it's a matter of when. We've already got our guys. All we need is the bulletproof evidence and then we'll be staging the arrests. The third case—Harper Rawlings—is at a standstill. We've got no leads left to follow. You know me, though, I won't rest until we've got her killer."

Harper, aged just twenty, had died in a car parking bay at night. Months ago. She'd sustained seven blunt force blows to her head and then strangulation. Her lovely face had been covered in dark bruises. With her long dark hair and small, pointed chin, she'd reminded me so much of Abby that I'd almost vomited at the scene. The case had frustrated us so far. Without CCTV footage, without witnesses and without DNA evidence— we virtually had nothing. Either her killer had planned her murder with precision, or they'd gotten extremely lucky.

I swapped from a determined tone to a tone that was almost pleading. "But I can still pursue Harper's case while I'm on Grimshaw's team."

"Kate... there's another matter."

"What's that?"

"You tracked down the three childcare workers and interviewed each one of them."

"Those weren't interviews. I just wanted to talk to them and find out if something had been missed." Ivy had been missing for hours at that point. I'd been frantic then, and I was even more frantic now that a night had passed.

"You also approached Brent Cole in the street."

I nodded in silent confirmation. I'd walked up to the ice-cream van driver after he'd come out of a bank, and I'd thrown questions at him. I'd already run my own research on him and knew his life history. He'd briefly been in trouble with the law when he was a teenager. He grew up in the Blue Mountains, on the same street as his cousin. I'd put his cousin in jail twenty-three years ago for the murder of another man.

"You can't go jumping down the throats of persons of interest in this case," Bigley said. "Not in your capacity as a detective. Not unless you're officially on the case."

"I know," I said. "But if it was one of your grandkids who'd disappeared, you'd understand."

Bigley gazed at me from beneath weary, hooded eyes. "I understand completely. And that's why I can't put you on the team. I'm sorry. This is non-negotiable."

"It wouldn't be the first time a detective has been personally involved in a case."

"That's rare. And there's been nothing like this. What you're doing is going to compromise the case. Kate... if you persist, I'll have no choice but to take legal action against you."

I wanted to shake him. Just pick him up and shake him.

Instead, I hit the desk with an open palm before I turned to exit. That was exactly the kind of display that I'd warned myself away from before I'd entered his office. Because if I showed the rage and desperation I felt inside, that would only give him more fuel for deciding against me.

"Kate," he called.

I stopped short but without turning my head.

"You can sit in on the team meetings. You'll know everything they do. You just can't take part in the active investigation." I heard the squeak of his chair as he shifted his weight. "They're forming the strike force team right now. In the meeting room off Zimmerman's office."

Before I kept walking, I gave a quick nod.

I realised at that moment that the superintendent had been expecting me. That resigned expression on his face when I'd walked in should have told me everything. He'd already known what I was going to ask for and he'd already had the chance to work through all his objections.

There was nothing I could do from here.

I strode down the dim hall to the meeting room, an angry heat radiating from my skin.

Inspector Jeffrey Zimmerman and DS Reagan Grimshaw were in the meeting room with a group of two dozen or so detectives and constables.

Grimshaw raised her chin as I entered, shooting me a sharp questioning look.

"Bigley sent me down here," I explained, my throat too tight to put any nuance into my words. "I'm just sitting in."

"Okay," said Zimmerman. "I've got no problem with that. Everyone, get seated."

Zimmerman was short for a man, his head so bald it was shiny, his nose beaklike. He had a presence that dominated a room—which was saying a lot for any space that also had Grimshaw in it.

I knew that Zimmerman didn't have much to do with the day-to-day operations of the missing persons unit. Grimshaw was the lead detective in that unit, and that role rested squarely on her shoulders.

I took a seat next to a couple of familiar faces—Constables Cameron Vella and Ella Valletti. I liked both of them. Both were in their twenties and smart as whips.

Inspector Zimmerman began the case summary without ceremony.

"Reagan and I are still building our team," he said. "But we know who we want. We're not waiting to get the team established before we start. As you know, some of our team are missing as they're already out in the field. I'm sure you can appreciate the serious nature of this case and the fact that we have to move quickly." He cleared his throat. "Over to you, Reagan."

Grimshaw nodded at him.

"You all know the story from the media reports," Grimshaw began. "This is the official police version. Yesterday, five kids vanished from a reserve, under the watch of three childcare workers. Let me set the scene. The spot is called *The Ponds*. The land slopes upward from the road in a hill and then down to a flat, grassy area. The grassy area is a strip of land between the hill and a small rainforest area. A boardwalk winds through the rainforest and across a shallow creek. The road bends around to meet the other end of the boardwalk. Due to the recent spell of dry conditions, the grounds were damp but not wet, with the creek barely running."

She walked to a large white board and began drawing a map of *The Ponds*. "This is where the nineteen children from the Tallman's Valley Nursery School were playing that day."

She drew an X. "And this is where two of the three childcare workers were positioned at the time the children went missing. Justine Farina and Kaylee Mortensen."

She made two X marks in the picnic spot. "And this is where the third childcare worker was. Nola Hobson." She drew an X at the top of the hill.

"The time the kids went missing is between 11.00 a.m. and 11.15 a.m. At this time, there was an ice-cream van parked here."

She drew yet another X not far from Hobson, at the roadside kerb. "Hobson had gone to ask the driver of the van to move, as the music was distracting. The driver complied with this request and drove off. Hobson walked back down the hill. Meanwhile, Justine Farina was searching for the missing five children while Kaylee Mortensen waited with the remaining fourteen."

Cameron drummed his knuckles lightly on the desk. "Could the kids have seen the ice-cream van and gone to check it out without the childcare workers noticing?" Cameron always spoke fast but while stressing certain vowels in a particular west coast American way. He claimed to speak unusually quick for what he called a *Los Angelino*.

"The kids couldn't see the van over the hill from where they were," Grimshaw informed him. "Three-year-olds are on the short side. But, yes, they did hear it."

"So, is that the scenario we're working towards?" asked Constable Ella Valletti. "It could have been relatively easy for the driver to lure the kids into the van."

"It's one of the scenarios," answered Grimshaw. "Something that helps that story is that a button belonging to Ivy Wakeland was found on the hill, right at the top. The spanner in the works is that Nola Hobson swears she would have noticed if the kids came up that way."

I cleared my throat, trying to relax the tight feeling. "What if the driver drove off, but stopped just a little way around the bend, just out of view? The kids might have run up the hill to the extreme left-hand side, out of Nola's view."

Grimshaw twisted her mouth, looking vaguely annoyed that I'd spoken. "Yup, that's a possibility. In that scenario, the driver has done nothing to lead the children away—they've come to him, hopeful for an ice-cream. It's then a crime of opportunity."

Detective Sergeant Liz Booth clicked the end of the pen she was holding. "Or, he planned it," she said. "In which case, he might have had someone else waiting somewhere to help him, at some point along his route."

DS Liz Booth was from the state Child Abuse and Sex Crimes Squad. I'd met her on a few occasions before. Grimshaw must have brought her in especially for this case. Booth always looked half-put together, like a school kid running for the bus with their hair unbrushed and their books spilling from their bag. But she was good at her job from all I'd heard.

"Yes, but that seems remote." Grimshaw furrowed her brow. "He couldn't predict that any of the tots would come up that way, especially unseen."

Booth shrugged. "He was stopping there every week, right? He might have been trying his luck."

I considered that possibility. "He doesn't have a history of child offences, but you never know."

Grimshaw inclined her head, giving me an odd look. "You ran a search on him? We're doubling up. I already ran an extensive one."

I ignored her stab. "Do we have a list of the people who knew that the kids would be at *The Ponds* that day?"

The reply came swiftly from Grimshaw. "We're working on it."

Ella looked from Grimshaw to me. "So, someone who knows the kids might have planned to take them?"

"Maybe," said Grimshaw, raising her voice a notch to turn Ella's attention back to herself. "But it's extremely unusual that anyone would want to take five children all at once. There's no precedent for this."

Cameron Vella, as if remembering something, leaned forward, nodding. "There was a case not far from where I grew up. Chowchilla, California. It was a long time ago, way before I was born, but a whole busload of kids got kidnapped."

"Late 1970s," I said. "The kidnappers were after a ransom."

"Yeah," Cameron said. "The bus of kids got buried with the kids in it. But the bus driver got the kids out from the roof of the bus. They all survived."

"Not relevant," Grimshaw snapped. "True, ransom is the most likely reason for the kidnapping of five children. But if it's a ransom-style kidnapping, then something went hideously wrong. We don't have any ransom demands turning up."

"Maybe he—or she—got spooked?" Cameron suggested. "If that's the story, then it's a matter of finding the kids while the kidnapper is working up the courage to contact us."

Grimshaw crossed her arms. "When kidnappers get spooked, they kill their victims. The most compelling scenario is that it's our ice-cream guy. He might be a secret paedophile. If it's him, then he's hiding the kids at some location we don't know about. And there's a high probability a paedophile kidnapper will kill their victims, spooked or not. Part of the thrill."

"Jesus," muttered Cameron under his breath, glancing at me. "That's harsh. I'm sorry, Detective."

Ella glanced at me with large, worried eyes.

"It's okay," I said quietly. "I can deal with it."

The truth was, I couldn't deal with it. Grimshaw's words had felt like a knife slicing straight through my heart.

Zimmerman looked uncomfortable, pacing across the front of the room and gazing around at us. "Okay, people," he said. "This team needs a name. Any ideas?"

Cameron cast a sideways glance at me, but I shook my head. I didn't care what it was named.

Cameron raised two fingers. "I was sent to the nursery school yesterday to confirm some specifics with the director. I noted they've got different rooms there for the different groups of kids, going by age. Wait a sec." Turning his phone on, he checked his notes. "They've got the *Brushtail Possums* for the babies, the *Squirrel Gliders* for the toddlers, hmmm... the *Green Tree Frogs* for the two-year-olds... ah, looks like the *Flying Foxes* is the room for the three-year-olds." He shrugged. "Just an idea."

Zimmerman gave a nod to Grimshaw. "That'll do."

Grimshaw wrote the name in large capital letters at the top of the board.

STRIKEFORCE FLYING FOX.

5

KATE

One week after the abductions

Ivy was still missing.

All five children were still missing.

Superintendent Andrew Bigley hadn't relented on his decision not to let me join the strike force. Instead, he insisted I have some compassionate leave from work. I didn't want compassionate leave. I wanted to be in the thick of things.

But I wasn't allowed to take part in the active investigation. I couldn't interview anyone or conduct my own initiatives.

Strikeforce Flying Fox had been in operation for six whole days—seven if you counted the day before it was properly formed.

There'd been no sleep for Abby and Pete and me those first six nights. We'd spent each day and night looking for the kids. And never stopped. Because there was the possibility—*the very slight possibility*—that the kidnapper had decided that five children were too much trouble and they'd simply put them out of the car somewhere.

My mother stayed at our house in our absence. I worried for her, too.

Her health had already been frail. And now she was shaken with worry about Ivy and the children.

The police and volunteers searched for the children in ever widening circles. The sounds of people calling out the children's names and the whirr of police helicopters punctuated our days.

We caught quick naps in our cars, with phones in our hands, tensed and ready for any incoming call.

Abby had alternately raged her anger at the world and sobbed in a tight ball on the ground.

"Mum," she'd said. "I can't go home and leave Ivy out there somewhere. I can't ever go home again. Not until she's found."

But by the end of the sixth night, we'd finally crawled home and into our beds. Exhausted and empty. I could hear Abby's heartrending sobs from down the hall.

We didn't know who or what we were dealing with. No search had produced a single hair, sock or shoe of the missing children. All we had was the original button of Ivy's that had been found. With each passing hour, a part of me steeled itself against news of the discovery of small bodies. Discarded on the bank of a river or forest track.

I'd attended every meeting of the strike force, and the cold ball of fear and frustration in my gut had grown larger with each dead end they'd run into.

I was dreading tonight. A committee of Tallman's Valley residents was going to hold a vigil for the missing children. They'd decided on holding it today to mark the fact that the kids had been missing for a week. And the location they'd chosen was the picnic area from which the kids had vanished.

It was a thoughtful gesture, but I knew Abby wasn't ready for it. I worried for her. She'd become fragile looking overnight, her shoulders always crumpled and her eyes with that open stare of terror.

Again, we spent the day joining the search. And again, the search was fruitless.

The clock sped to twilight.

I didn't think Abby would go to the vigil, but she had a change of heart at the last minute.

The roads leading to *The Ponds* were jam-packed.

Pete found a spot and parked his SUV. As we emerged from the car, I hugged Abby close. "We don't have to stay long," I said softly. "I know this is going to be hard for you."

Her voice was tight and flat. "Maybe I should just go. I can't deal with the crowd."

"It's up to you," I told her. "You don't have to do anything you don't want to."

She nodded, her eyes wet. "I'll give it a try. The other parents are coming."

With Abby in the middle, the three of us walked to *The Ponds*.

People were spreading blankets on the hill and holding solar candles. Some were just hugging their children close. Everyone had packed in tight —no one was bothering with personal space tonight.

Down on the flat ground, a giant screen had been erected on a high stand. I'd seen a similar projector screen before—in the Tallman's Valley village square. It might be the same one. The screen had been used for happy occasions, ceremonies, sports and open-air movies. Never for anything like this. Next to the screen was a podium and a small platform.

The night was clear, still. No breath of wind. The air was cool, with a humid undercurrent. Overhead, purplish-grey clouds were clumping together just like the people below.

I caught sight of Nola Hobson, the nursery school teacher who'd been there the day of the abduction. Her face was half obscured with the hood of her yellow zip-up top. It seemed she didn't want anyone to recognise her. But I was good with faces, recalling features from the slightest view of a face. I knew that the head teacher, Justine Farina, had lost her job. She'd been responsible for the children that day. Nola wasn't put under the same scrutiny. The teenage work experience student, Kaylee Mortensen, simply went to complete her work experience elsewhere.

Pete found us a clearing among the crowd, and I spread out our picnic blanket. Abby sat and hugged her knees to her chest. She seemed so lost and small.

Music began filling the air. A small group of guitarists and singers was performing down near the giant screen. The music helped fill up the void— the vast empty night that stretched in front of us.

The music ended as the Blue Mountains mayor stepped up to the podium and gave an address. He read a carefully written speech about how the whole community had come together in shock and grief. The next to speak after him was DS Reagan Grimshaw. Her message was quick and dry. She told the gathering that the police had formed a special team named Strikeforce Flying Fox, and they were following up on all available leads. Grimshaw injected about as much emotion into her words as she would if she were speaking about lost property.

The music started again, and the big projector screen blinked on.

Five photographs scrolled across the screen. The faces of the missing children. I knew their names off by heart by now.

Charlotte Hinton. Elijah Parrish. Max Foster. Olivia Crane. And our *Ivy.*

Abby cried openly as soon as she saw Ivy's face appear on the screen. I was barely holding it together myself.

The screen then displayed videos of all the children, including Kaylee's video from the day they vanished. People held their solar candles high in the air, swaying and softly singing along with the music.

I was surprised to feel a sense of solidarity. I'd thought I wouldn't. I knew that people cared—of course they did. But tonight, I really felt it. I glanced at Abby, hoping her spirit was just a little strengthened. But it was hard to tell with her. She kept her thoughts so close to her chest. Pete put his arm around her while looking straight ahead and murmuring the words to the song. Pete always knew better than I did how to relate to our daughter, at least, since she'd hit her mid-teens.

A group of people shuffled towards the podium now, a video of them relayed to the large screen. They were the parents of the missing children. I hadn't expected them to talk tonight. They all looked nervous, holding each other's hands and glancing at each other for support.

I'd briefly spoken with the parents at a press conference that had been held four days ago. And I knew all their specific details from the police files on the case—the files that Grimshaw allowed me access to, anyway.

Lori and Sean Hinton were Charlotte's parents. Lori was a forty-five-year-old systems analyst who worked for a large data company. Everything about her, from her well-styled bobbed hair to her expensive shoes matched. Sean was an accountant of the same age as his wife. Charlotte was their only child.

Nick and Marcy were Elijah Parrishes' parents. Both in their thirties. The Parrishes, consisting of the two parents, three daughters and the missing Elijah, were a black American family from Fort Lauderdale, Florida. Nick had almost come to the end of a project here in Australia as a computer programmer. The family had been preparing to return home when Elijah had gone missing. It was an easy guess that they wouldn't be leaving anytime soon.

Penny Foster was the thirty-four-year-old mother of Max. She'd worn her ash-blonde hair back in a ponytail every time I'd seen her, as if her hair was just an annoyance. Her pale face bore almost no makeup. She worked in sales at a large baby goods store. She was divorced, with Max her only child.

Roxanne and Rhys Crane were Olivia's parents. Both aged around forty. Roxanne worked in the fitness industry and had a large Instagram following. She'd had a lot of cosmetic work done on her face and body, the details of which she openly shared with her followers. Rhys worked in a sports shoe shop. They had two children besides Olivia. The family was apparently under severe financial distress.

Lori stepped up to the microphone at the podium, shielding her eyes from the glare of the stadium lights on the hill. "I want to express our gratitude," she said. "You've all come out here tonight for five children who are missing from our community. You've searched with us, you've wept with us, and now, tonight, you've wrapped your arms around us. Thank you."

Lori's voice cracked, and she took a moment to compose herself. "There is one more parent who is yet to join us down here. Ivy's mum... Abby

Wakeland. Abby, I've heard that you're up there on the hill. Please, come down and join us." She extended an arm out to the crowd.

Abby buried her face in her father's shoulder. "I can't."

"Honey, you don't have to," Pete told her quietly.

Penny Foster took the microphone. "Please, Abby," she begged in a gentle tone. "We need to stick together."

Reluctantly, Abby rose and threaded through the crowd. I knew it was the last thing she wanted to do tonight. She'd always hated the spotlight. The recorded image of her making her way to the podium appeared on the large screen. She had her head down.

Taking Abby's hands, Lori and Penny drew her in between them.

Lori took the microphone again. "This is all of us now. The parents of the missing children. We stand united. And united we ask, if anyone knows or suspects anything, then, please, come forward. Let us know where our children are. This isn't right... or fair. My house is no longer a home. It's empty and silent. I miss hearing Charlotte's little feet on the stairs and having her glitter and glue all over the kitchen table. I need her back. We need all our kids back."

Lori handed the microphone to Roxanne then.

"Please," said Roxanne, pushing her thick hair back from a face of heavy makeup, "if you've got our kids, anyone out there, you've gotta do the right thing. Don't keep our kids. It's bloody heartless."

Penny Foster looked as if she were close to vomiting as she took the microphone from Roxanne, her face pasty with high spots of colour in her cheeks. "It takes a lot of courage to stand here before all of you. Raw and exposed. This is us, without our skin. But we wanted to show ourselves as we are now. Because if this—tonight—prompts anyone to tell what they know, then it will be worth it. And—" She shook her head, suddenly too overcome to continue. She handed the microphone to Abby.

Abby stood rigidly with the microphone, as if she were frozen in time. When she spoke, her voice was so low everyone strained to hear. "Ivy is my everything," she said. "She's my sun, my moon, my stars. I just want her to come home."

She handed over the microphone to Nick Parrish, looking relieved that her speaking part was done.

Nick cleared his throat. "Please join us in prayer for the safe return of our precious little ones. There are five children missing from our town. We want those children back with their families. We want them in our arms and not just in our hearts. Lord, hear our prayer."

"Lord hear our prayer," the crowd responded.

A woman that I didn't know spoke prayers in different religions and languages and included the appropriate response for everyone to follow at the end—in French, German, Hebrew, Indian, Sudanese and others. Due to the Tallman's Valley tech village, we were home to more people of different nationalities and religions than most places.

Abby kept her head low, her hair hanging about her thin face. I'd never felt sorrier for her than at that moment. I saw her the way everyone else was seeing her. A young, broken mother who was only just hanging on by a thread.

I should have taken a mental snapshot of that image of Abby and burned it into my mind, because it would come back to haunt me. But I was focusing too hard on Ivy, and I let Abby slip away from me.

6

KATE

One month after the abductions

The results of the extensive testing of every square inch of Brent Cole's ice-cream van were back. Not one hair or scrap of DNA of the children had been found inside. CCTV footage of his trip from *The Ponds* to his next destination seemed to check out. He'd gone nowhere except for where he claimed to have gone.

If Brent Cole was the abductor, he must have planned things with military-like precision. He remained a suspect, but without evidence, he couldn't be charged with anything.

The most viable theory was that the children had run up the hill when they heard the music, without Nola seeing them. Ivy had lost her button at this point. And then while Nola was walking back down the hill, the driver of another vehicle took the children.

If the theory was correct and the abductions had been a crime of opportunity, then finding the person responsible would be like finding a needle in a haystack.

I stood in my kitchen, overwhelmed by what felt like an enormous grey void.

Staring from the kitchen window, I surveyed the parkland before me, memories flooding in.

Our backyard looked out over a large circular park—Prescott Playground. A hundred or so houses stood around the perimeter of the park. We lived in the older part of Tallman's Valley, where many of the houses were postwar red brick homes of the 1940s and 50s. When Abby was little, she used to tug me from the house and out to the yard and then down to the gate. She'd push the gate open and then count each step that led down to Prescott Playground.

Those were happy days. The children who lived on the park's perimeter all got to know each other. I'd often sit with the parents on the grass while we watched our kids dart about on the climbing frames and slippery dips.

I thought I had life worked out, then. I took a year off work after Abby was born. After that, Pete and I managed our workloads so that we both got to spend precious time with our daughter. We hadn't intended having children. It was never in the plan. I'd been close to forty when I fell pregnant. But once we absorbed the shock, it seemed to make sense. Our baby had happened for a reason. We'd both been working in Sydney at the time. Me in the homicide squad and Pete in finance. We moved back to Tallman's Valley and bought this house. My mother had been ecstatic to have us back in town and even more ecstatic that I was having a baby.

As I washed this morning's coffee cups in my kitchen, I watched children zooming about in the park and felt nostalgic for those simpler days. My relationship with Abby had fallen off a cliff the year she had turned fourteen, and it had never recovered. And now Ivy was gone. Ivy had been gone for thirty terrible days.

There was no recovering from this. Our lives had already been fractured, but now they'd splintered into a thousand tiny pieces.

Abby was also watching the kids play in the park—she was sitting on the swing in our yard, letting it shift aimlessly back and forth. From the back view, with her hair half-spilling from her ponytail, she looked just like she had when she was a teenager. Back then, she'd stay out there on the swing after school, moody and silent.

Drying my hands with a tea towel, I stepped out of the house and up to Abby. "I'm about to make lunch. Salad sandwiches. How do you want yours?"

"I don't want one." She didn't bother to turn around.

"You haven't been eating enough," I said.

She didn't answer.

I felt a vague rush of irritation. I'd had too many sleepless nights to keep my emotions in check the way I usually did. All the while, I'd been trying to stay on top of an investigation that I wasn't officially allowed to join.

Rather than say anything more, I walked back inside. Pete had taken over in the kitchen, slicing the tomatoes and Spanish onions. He glanced out the window at Abby. "She certainly seems in a bad way today. I couldn't get a word out of her."

"Same. She's barely talking."

He sighed heavily. "She's got nothing left to give right now. Maybe this is what she needs to do. We've all run ourselves ragged over the past weeks."

Pete was always a voice of wisdom.

I sat at the kitchen bench with him, eating sandwiches that felt dry in my throat. "I can't bear this... this *waiting*. If I were on Grimshaw's team, at least I'd have things to do. I feel so helpless."

"I feel it, too." Pete's eyes looked haunted.

In some ways, it was worse for him. He didn't have a job to keep him distracted. He'd been retrenched four years ago, when he was sixty.

"Bigley made the wrong decision in not letting you in," Pete said. "It's selfish, because I worried that joining the team would destroy you, but I wanted our little Ivy back. And I knew you'd be like a dog on a bone."

"Pete, where do we go from here? How do we even live? I can't..." My eyes welled with tears.

"We keep hoping," he said, but his expression betrayed his thoughts.

Hope was fading.

———

Sipping my coffee, I hurried along the corridor of the Tallman's Valley police station. I had some work to do on my homicide cases, then I planned on catching up on what was happening with Strikeforce Flying Fox.

I almost bumped straight into a young woman crossing my path at the intersecting corridor. Raising my head, I was surprised to see Abby.

Abby was pale and red-eyed, her cardigan draped in loose folds from her shoulders.

"Abby! What are you doing here?"

"I was asked in," she told me stiffly. "I just got questioned by three detectives about everyone I've ever known. Including that Grimshaw woman. Apparently, all the parents got questioned, trying to find out if we know someone who might have taken the kids. It's rubbish. They're caught up in busywork, trying to justify their paycheques. They still don't have a single clue about who took Ivy."

"I'm sorry they put you through the wringer. They're just making sure they're not missing anything. Uncovering every stone they possibly can."

"Mum, can you stop sounding like the police? For just one second? This is *Ivy* we're talking about. I don't want to know about police procedures. I want them to tear this town apart and find out who the hell took the kids."

"I didn't mean to sound like that. Ivy means the world to me. You know she does."

The muscles in her thin face tightened. "It's your fault she was even at that nursery school. You kept pushing me, telling me that I was wasting my life just staying at home with her. You insisted that I go study."

I recoiled. "That's not fair, Abby. I never said you were wasting your time. I was just thinking of the future for you and Ivy. You'd wanted to study law since you were at school and I thought it would be a good time to get back on track. There's no way I could have known what was going to happen."

"Well, I should have stayed at home with my daughter," she said coldly.

"Watching her grow. Keeping her all to myself. Now, all that's been snatched away from me."

The coffee I'd just had was bitter on my tongue. "Let's talk at home. Tonight, when I'm done with work."

She shook her head. "I'm moving out. I can't stay there anymore."

"Don't do that. You'd have to pay rent. Surely you don't want to have to do that right now?"

"I just need my own space."

She hurried along the hall, exiting through a sliding glass door and onto the pavement. With my heart in my mouth, I watched her run across the road without even a glance at the oncoming traffic.

I wanted to sprint after her. But it was obvious I was the last person she wanted to talk to.

The things that she'd said burned in my mind.

You kept pushing me.

Had I really done that? I'd thought I was doing the right thing. Helping her to make a future for herself. She'd had her heart set on becoming a lawyer since she was about twelve—and she'd excelled in legal studies in her final year of school. Pete and I had been shocked when she chose not to continue onto university. Instead, she'd taken waitstaff jobs in clubs and restaurants, earning just enough money for a plane ticket somewhere overseas, and then she'd be off. One of those times, she returned home pregnant. The father of the baby was in Ireland and wanted nothing to do with it. Abby had been eighteen then and she'd decided to keep the baby. When Ivy was born, Abby had become super-protective of her. She said she'd never leave her with anyone—and she'd stayed true to her word.

Overnight, Abby had gone from a restless person who wanted nothing better than to keep travelling the world to someone who barely left the house. She'd seemed over-vigilant with Ivy. At the same time, Abby was also very sensitive to the noise that Ivy made, at times yelling at her to stop singing or quit bashing wooden spoons on the pots. Pete and I had tried to convince Abby to see a psychologist. But Abby had refused, saying we were treating her like she was crazy. Pete and I had trodden a fine line, not knowing whether we were making things worse. Slowly, Abby seemed to get better on her own.

When Ivy turned three, I began suggesting to Abby that she go to uni and study law. She'd liked that idea. She'd begun studying part time at the brand-new university that had opened up in Tallman's Valley. That was when Ivy started at the nursery school. Finally, it'd seemed like things were getting on track.

Until the day of the abduction.

When everything burned to ashes.

7

KATE

Three months after the abductions

"Ease up, Kate." Pete folded his arms tightly, crinkling his brow at me in concern.

Too puffed to answer, I completed five more chin ups before dropping to the floor of our gym room.

Pete handed me a small towel. "Let the war go on without you for a while."

"Thanks." Blinking the sweat from my eyes, I patted my face with the towel.

It was our routine to work out each morning and three afternoons a week. Pete and I had the bottom floor converted into a gym soon after we'd bought this house, and we'd always done the workouts together. But lately, I'd been coming down here alone, before Pete was even awake. I woke around five every morning with an image of Ivy in my mind.

"I need this," I told Pete. "Keeps me sane."

"Won't help if you end up killing yourself." Crossing to the middle of the floor, Pete began some warm-up exercises.

I knew what he was referring to. I'd had a couple of bouts of increased heart rate and dizziness over the past couple of months. My doctor told me it was stress related. I'd tried resting, but the thoughts crowding my head were relentless. Keeping myself physically occupied was the only thing that calmed the demons.

Three whole months, and still none of us had any idea as to what happened to Ivy. No trace had been found of the children.

Abby had packed up and moved out two months ago. We didn't know where she was from day to day. She'd been couch-surfing at friends' houses. At first, she'd called me for daily updates on Strikeforce Flying Fox, but she was calling less and less often now. She'd met with her father for lunch twice, and I guessed he'd given her money.

In the past three months, I'd gained five new homicides on my case load. DS Jace Franco and I had solved all five cases quickly. The suspects had been in clear sight. There'd also been one murder suicide, and that had been more of a matter for forensics to confirm what we already knew from the scene. Two of my previous homicide cases had also come to an end—conclusive evidence had come back from months of forensic work, and Franco and I had finally been able to make the arrests. The only cases I was working on now were cold cases, the most recent of which was the Harper Rawlings murder. The Rawlings case was intensely frustrating. We'd still been unable to uncover any solid leads. I desperately wanted to be able to give her parents a resolution, but we had nothing.

"Have you heard from Abby at all?" Pete asked me.

"Not a peep," I replied with a shrug.

"That's two weeks, then," he said. "She's just... disengaging. Kate, I'm worried. When she sold her car, she told you she was going to use the money to rent her own unit, and then get a casual job. But she didn't do either of those things."

"She's not answering any of my messages." I felt a flash of anger. The last thing our family needed was for Abby to start behaving like this.

Pete's forehead indented with a deep frown. "She would have gotten at least ten thousand from the sale of her car. What's she doing with it? And who is she hanging out with? People will do bad things to people for money."

I stared at him. I'd stopped thinking about Abby. My job and Ivy were taking up all the available space in my mind. But Pete was right to be worried. I'd forgotten Pete had told me she'd sold her car. "Maybe we should check to see what's going on with her. Who's that girl she's supposed to be living with? Chelsea?"

"Yeah. Chelsea. I dropped Abby off last time she came to lunch, just at the local shops. She didn't want me to know where she was living. But it has to be within walking distance of there."

"I'll do some digging and find out who Chelsea is. That's if Abby gave you the right name."

I headed upstairs to my office and opened my laptop.

It took me all of one minute to find a list of local people named Chelsea on social media. I narrowed the list down to a girl named Chelsea Dawson. I couldn't see her birth date—she had the good sense to hide that—but I could see lots of information about her. She was the same age as Abby—twenty-one. I could see birthday notices from friends. She'd attended the same school as Abby. She worked at a hairdressing salon just around the corner from where Pete had last dropped Abby off. She might not be the right Chelsea, but I strongly suspected that she was.

I called the salon.

"Hello, could I speak to Chelsea?"

"Speaking."

"I'm looking for Abby. Could you tell me where she is, please?"

"Who?"

"Abby Wakeland."

"I don't know her."

She was lying. It was very unlikely that she would have gone to the same school, in the same year, and yet not know Abby.

"It's important that I get in contact with her," I said. "I'm her mother but this is also a police matter. I'm Detective Sergeant Kate Wakeland. I'll come down and speak with you in person."

There was silence on the line for a moment. When I heard her sigh, I knew she'd made a quick mental calculation and had decided that telling the truth was easier than having me front up at her salon.

"Oh, *Abby*. Sorry, I heard the name wrong. She stayed with me for three weeks or so, but she's gone somewhere else."

"I need to know where."

"I'm not sure."

"I can come down there, if it's easier, and we might be able to piece together where she went."

"She went to Mitch's."

"Okay. Now, who is Mitch?"

"I only know his first name."

"Can you give me an address?"

"You found *me*. You can find him. I've got bridesmaids waiting to have their hair done." The phone went dead.

I stared at my phone, muttering an expletive at it.

Okay. At least she gave me a name. But who the hell was Mitch? I might have to go and visit Chelsea after all. I was certain she wouldn't be impressed with a detective walking in there in front of her bridesmaids. Too bad.

I had a quick look for the name, resigning myself to not being able to find him.

But it turned out to be dead easy. I found a real estate agency named Mitchell Graham Real Estate that was two doors down from the hairdressing salon. When I looked up his social media, I saw a few pictures of him and Chelsea—it seemed that a group of businesspeople from that street met up for drinks after work quite regularly. Many of Mitch's recent photos showed him partying with very young women. He himself looked about forty.

I tried calling the agency, but they told me he was out showing buyers a property. They gave me his mobile number, but when I called, he didn't answer.

I sat back in my chair. Why was Abby staying with a man of that age?

It was when I hopped into the shower that I decided that I needed to take a drive down to Mitch's house.

Pete stuck his head into the bathroom. "Find out anything?"

"Yeah. I found Chelsea. She said Abby's been staying with someone called Mitch. I'm fairly sure that's a real estate agent named Mitchell Graham. I can't get hold of him. But I found his home address."

Pete gave a worried nod. "I don't like the sound of her staying with some strange guy."

"I'm going down there to check it out."

"I'm coming with you." Pete shucked out of his clothes and stepped into the shower.

He brushed my wet hair back from my forehead and held my face between his hands. "We'll figure this out, Kate. Whatever's going on with her, we'll help her through it."

———

Mitchell Graham's house was one of the two-storey mansion-style houses in the newest estate of Tallman's Valley. Pete parked outside, and we walked together up to the front door. No one answered when Pete knocked.

"Abby!" I called.

Still no answer.

"What do we do now?" Pete asked. "Do we just sit in the car and wait?"

"We do *this*," I replied, and began walking around to the side of the house.

Pete followed dubiously. "This is entering private property, right?"

"Sure is." I peered into every window that allowed me a view.

"Abby, are you here?" Pete called, growing bolder.

I shot him a quick grin.

A locked gate blocked our way to the backyard.

"We've gone in this far. Might as well check all the way around." I climbed the fence. Ahead was a neatly clipped lawn and a deep blue swimming pool. A spa trickled water into the pool.

Pete hung back. "She might not even be here. That Chelsea girl could be lying."

45

"She could be. But I think I got the truth out of her. I'll go have a quick look around. Wait here."

"Nope, I'm right beside you."

"Okay. But if you hear a dog growling," I said to Pete, "get ready to race back to the gate."

"Thanks for the warning." Pete peered into the yard, scratching the stubble on his chin. He hadn't taken the time to shave. With his long legs and body, he cleared the gate quicker than I had.

We stole around to the back section of the house. It was all glass bifold doors, giving a wide and clear view inside. A gleaming black and white kitchen stood on a sea of gleaming white tiles.

Pete took a sharp breath. "Hell."

I followed his line of sight.

Someone was lying on the floor. To the far right, near a white leather stool. A thin girl in a long T-shirt, her legs bare and her dark hair pooled on the white tiles.

Abby.

Foamy dribble ran from the side of her mouth. Glazed eyes stared from half-dropped eyelids.

I reached for the nearest of the doors. It was locked tight.

Pete didn't hesitate now.

Grabbing a chair from an outdoor setting, he smashed it into the door. Glass shattered into thousands of tiny cubes.

We ran inside, our shoes crunching on the glass.

Pete lifted Abby's head and torso up from the floor. "Honey, it's us. Mum and Dad."

"I want it... *over....*" she slurred.

I met eyes with Pete. This was deliberate.

"What did you take?" My voice rose to a peak.

She gripped my wrist much tighter than I thought she was capable of in her current condition. "I want it over."

The view of her face hazed through my tears. "We can't let you go. I'm sorry. You're going to live." Pulling myself away, I called for an ambulance.

I sat with Pete in the dim hospital ward, next to our daughter. She slept in her bed, hooked up to a drip.

While Pete and I had been looking for Abby, her life had been slipping away. The doctors told us that in another couple of hours, there would have been no saving her.

What if we didn't decide to try to find her this morning?

I stared at the familiar curve of her cheek bone. Abby's sleep had been restless, punctuated by garbled whispers. She sounded terrified and as if she were unable to escape her terror, even in sleep.

We'd been in contact with Mitchell Graham. He was a divorced father of two. He'd done nothing illegal in offering Abby a place to stay, but still, it made my skin crawl. I'd found out from Chelsea that Abby wasn't the first troubled girl whom Mitch had offered a room to. Mitch seemed to be the kind of upstanding guy who swooped in on fragile young women.

Chelsea had also told us that Abby had been spending up on methamphetamine, alcohol and sleeping tablets. Chelsea had told Abby she had to leave her house because she didn't want drugs there.

Beside me, Pete began sobbing. I leaned my head on his shoulder.

I listened to the sound of the hospital machines beeping, a hollowed-eyed Abby murmuring about nightmare images in her sleep, and my husband's sobs.

How had our lives become... *this?*

8

KATE

Three and a half years after the abductions

Outside the kitchen window, past our yard to the park beyond, the world was still clinging fast to the night. I stood watching while the first rays of sunlight stole onto the playground, lighting it piece by piece, like a stage show. The apricot light this morning was deceptive and seductive, luring you into believing it was spring. But it was mid-winter and bitterly cold out there.

A swing shifted to and fro in the breeze.

For a moment, my mind ran wild, imagining springtime, imagining a small child sitting on that swing. I could almost see her—Ivy—in a little blue dress, with her cherubic little legs and her serene expression.

The image was sweet but not comforting. Because if Ivy was still that small, then she was still just three years old. And she'd have been dead for over three years. A ghost child. Because by rights, she should be six by now.

There was no little girl in the playground. There was just a young man sitting alone on a park bench, looking bored.

Taking the plates from the dishwasher, I stacked them into the cupboard. Pete and I barely needed the dishwasher these days, being that there were just the two of us, but we'd had friends over the night before and we'd had a little dinner party. We didn't have many of those anymore.

Our daughter had moved away to Sydney two-and-a-half years ago. She'd recovered from her suicide attempt and she'd attended counselling. But she kept slipping backwards, using drugs of all kinds and associating with people we'd rather she didn't associate with. Until we lost contact with her. We'd heard from her just twice after that. She didn't want to see us.

There was nothing more we could do for her. Pete and I had received counselling ourselves to help us deal with the pain. These days, we grieved for Abby as much as we grieved for Ivy. Because we'd lost both of them.

And in the last three months, there'd been a new source of grief in my life. My mother had received the worst news possible from her doctor. The treatment she'd been undergoing for her leukaemia had failed. There was nothing more that could be done for her.

The years were growing darker and darker for our family. We were existing, not living.

As I went to pick up another plate, a sharp clatter sounded from another room.

Flinching, I almost dropped the plate.

Was there an open window letting the breeze in? The breeze didn't seem very strong. Perhaps there was a hole in one of the flyscreens, and a bird had gotten inside.

I edged around the kitchen, keeping my back to the cupboards, listening.

Another clatter.

It wasn't the wind or a bird.

Someone was in the house.

It wasn't Pete. He'd gone out to buy some things from the hardware store. He wouldn't be back yet.

I picked up a wooden cutting board—it was all I had at hand. If the intruder had a knife, I might have something to protect myself with.

Keeping close to the wall, I moved to a position where I had a view of the entry.

I caught sight of someone in our oval mirror. A woman. The hood of her top obscured her face. When she turned slightly, I saw that she was carrying a small baby.

Most likely, she'd come in looking for money. I decided to remain calm and ask her what she wanted, rather than ordering her straight out of my house. I replaced the cutting board on the bench and then boldly stepped into the entry. "Hello?"

The woman turned. "Hi, Mum."

It took me moments to adjust to the sight of Abby standing there. She'd filled out in the face and lost the dark under-eye circles. And she had a *baby* with her.

She jiggled the baby on her hip. "This is Jasper. Your grandson."

I struggled for words. *"Grandson?* Oh, Abby…"

"He's four months old."

"Oh, my goodness! Can I hug both of you?" Without waiting for a reply, I ran across and wrapped my arms around the two of them. I kissed both their cheeks. "It's *so* good to see you, Abby. And little Jasper. He's beautiful. Can I hold him?"

"Of course. I brought him to see you."

I cradled his little body against my chest and kissed his downy head. Unlike Abby, he was blond.

"Come into the kitchen," I told her. I carried Jasper through the house, Abby walking beside me. "Do you want something to drink—or eat?"

"No, I can't stay long." She crossed her arms, glancing out the window to the park.

I followed her gaze. The young man that I'd seen earlier was still sitting on the bench.

"Is that… the father of your baby?" I asked. He was too far away for me to pick out any facial features. All I could see was that he was blond.

She nodded hesitantly.

"What's his name? Do I know him?"

"No, you don't know him."

She didn't offer any more information. I didn't want to push. She might run out the door, and I wouldn't see her again for months—or even years. And the thought of that was terrifying. And now, there was a new person in the equation—Jasper. The baby yawned and nestled his face into the crook of my arm. Tears pricked my eyes. It'd been a long time since I'd held a grandchild of mine.

I wanted to know everything about him.

"How did the birth go?" I asked her. "Which hospital?"

"I had him at home," she answered. "He came too quick to get to the hospital. Not like Ivy. She took days."

"Oh no, I had no idea. I hope you weren't alone."

"It was fine. I wasn't alone. It hurt like crazy but it was over before I knew it. Where's Dad?"

"He went out for a little while, but he'll be back soon. I'll give him a call."

"No, don't do that. Don't make a fuss."

"It's not a fuss. He'd want to see you. And he'll be over the moon to meet little Jasper."

"I can't stay." She chewed her lip in the same way she used to do when she was a child. "How's Nanna? I went to see her, first, but she wasn't at home."

I shook my head. "She's not good, Abby. I wanted to let you know, but I don't have your number—or your address. She's gone into the hospice. The one by the lake."

Abby stared back at me in shock. "Why did they put her there? She doesn't belong there."

There was no easy way to explain what was happening with her grand-mother. "I'm afraid your Nanna's doctor said she only has a few months left. I'm sorry."

"Well, then why isn't she *here?*" Abby demanded. "Why aren't you looking after her? You need to get her out of there."

"Abby... of course we wanted her here. She didn't want that. The hospice was her choice." I hesitated. "She'd love it if you went to see her.

And I know it would be very special to her to see the baby. I'm going there this morning. You could come with me."

"I'll go and see her on my own. Anyway, I'd better go. Tell Nanna I have a baby now. I don't want to shock her when I turn up with Jasper."

I eyed her in alarm. I wasn't ready for her to go. Nowhere near ready. "Please... stay. Ask your... boyfriend out there to come in, too."

"I can't. I said I'd only be a minute."

I was unwilling to give Jasper back. It was my first ever cuddle. And I wanted Abby back in our lives.

But he was hers and so I handed him back.

And then she was gone.

9

KATE

The morning turned grey and drizzling as I drove to the Tallman's Valley Hospice.

I was heartbroken for Pete that he'd missed seeing Abby and the baby earlier. I hoped that Abby would make contact with us again soon.

Rain sprinkled my hair and shoulders as soon as I stepped from the car. I walked through the gardens of hedges and roses to the wide lawn that lay between the hospice and the lake. The hospice had been designed to be as pleasant and scenic for its patients as possible.

Bed-bound patients looked out from their windows of the low semi-circular hospital building. All the windows on this side of the facility had a good view of the water and birdlife.

Just a few determined patients dotted the undercover area outside. My mother was one of them.

I hurried across to her. I'd found myself hurrying to her from the day she'd gone into this hospice, two months earlier. My visits were always accompanied with a sense of dread, as if there was no time to waste.

Taking a moment, I rearranged my expression. It was something I'd been making myself do before seeing her, because too often I looked as if I was carrying a heavy weight—almost scowling. I didn't want her to take that memory of me with her.

She smiled as I approached.

I hugged her and then pulled a chair over so that I could sit next to her.

"Are you wrapped up warmly enough?" I asked.

"Like a baby bird in a nest."

"Good. How are you?"

"I'm happy, Kate."

That was her usual response. She no longer gave me a list of ailments. She was merely happy to wake up each day.

"I saw Abby earlier," I told her.

"Oh, I'm so glad. How is she doing? I haven't seen her for so long."

"She went to see you this morning. At your house. But of course, you weren't there. She has a surprise."

"I'm too old for surprises." She gave me half a wink.

I smiled. "It's a baby. Abby's got a little boy. Four months old."

Her eyes filmed with moisture. "Oh, how beautiful. What's his name?"

"It's Jasper."

"Lovely." She wiped her eyes with a tissue she had up her sleeve. "Is she back in the valley now?"

The question hung in the cold morning air.

"I'm not sure, Mum. She didn't stay long. I think she just wanted to show us her new baby. I don't know what to expect."

"Maybe Abby's finding her way back to us," Mum said softly.

"I hope so. I just wish she'd open up to me."

"She will one day. You've always done the best you could, with the kind of job you had."

There it was. *The kind of job I'd had.* My mother had never understood me remaining in detective work after Abby was born. But my mother was from a different era. Women often didn't keep working after children in her day, and they weren't police officers, let alone detectives. I'd been born around the time the contraceptive pill had first come onto the market. I'd never known a time that women didn't have access to it. It wasn't like that when my mother was growing up and when she had me. She'd given up her job and lived on my father's wage. She was born in the twenties and grew up in the depression.

"I've tried hard with Abby," I told her. "But it just wasn't enough. I wasn't able to bring Ivy back to her, either."

"She can't hold that against you."

"I think she does. I know she held it against me that I encouraged her to study for her degree. Because if she hadn't been studying, Ivy wouldn't have been in daycare that day."

"Abby would have made a good lawyer. Always analysing everything. I would have liked to see her stay home with Ivy while she was little, but you did nothing wrong. You were trying to help her."

"It hurts so much, this thing between Abby and me."

I glanced away, trying to hide my tears. I should be here comforting my mother, but instead I was here seeking comfort like a small child. I felt myself dissolving inside. Abby's visit and the discovery of her new baby had brought everything back.

"Lots of things are going to hurt you in life." My mother reached to touch my arm. "Like being stung by a scorpion that's ten times bigger than you are." She breathed deeply. "Some things will hurt more than you ever thought possible. They say that painful things will make you stronger and you'll get past them. But it's not like that. You just have to decide whether to find beauty in the sting. Because being alive means that you will be stung. Over and over again. But if you can feel it, it means you're alive. It means you get another chance."

My mother always was the philosopher. But I didn't want her to say these things to me. Because I struggled to find beauty in the things that were happening to our family. I found no beauty in the fact that I wouldn't have my mother for much longer. But at the same time, I was hanging onto every word. I realised that she was feeding me. Not with a spoon, like she did when I was a baby. But with words.

Moving my chair closer, I laid my head on her shoulder. She patted my hair. I gazed at the dull spots of light and patter of rain on the water.

These mother-daughter moments were coming to an end. There was a time when I'd hear of someone in their nineties who'd passed away and I'd think that they'd had *a good innings*. But now, standing on the edge of it, the reality sharpened and twisted in my chest. It didn't matter how old my mother was, she was never an *age*. She was my mother. She held all the memories of me from when I was very young. There was no other living person who knew all my days as a baby and young child.

She drifted off to sleep.

A nurse came to tell me that Mum should go indoors for a nap now that she was asleep.

Across from us, an elderly man watched the ducks on the lake with a pair of binoculars. He had a sketch pad on his lap, and he drew something with a shaky hand.

"That's Harry Grenville," the nurse told me. "He's our resident artist."

"I've seen him before a few times," I said. "I've tried to say hello but I'm guessing he doesn't like to talk."

"Harry's one of our longer-term residents, from the dementia wing of the hospital," she said. "In the four years that he's been here, he's been very withdrawn and never speaks. He actually used to be an artist, before he developed dementia. Poor Harry."

"He seems to enjoy his binoculars. They look old—are they his?"

She shook her head, tucking the blanket in around Mum's shoulders. "He got them from here. We have lots of retro items in the dementia care unit. Antique dolls, early model cars, anything from their era that they might like to pick up. For the patients who can only remember their child-hood, those things are a comfort."

"What a lovely idea." I watched as Harry viewed the lake through his binoculars.

The nurse smiled sadly. "We had one lady who liked to cuddle a porce-lain baby doll each day. She'd lost her only child when that child was just two. One day, we couldn't find the doll and she cried as if the doll was her real baby. We eventually found the doll—another of the dementia patients had put her under his bed. He'd been trying to protect it. He grew up in London, during the days of the World War Two bombings, and he kept thinking he was right back there."

I pulled my lips in grimly. "It must be so difficult for them when they don't know what's really going on."

"Yep. To think the bombs are coming or to lose a child over and over again. It's distressing for them. But they're not all like that. Harry seems content enough. Oh, his cushion has slipped. I'd better go fix it. I forgot to ask, how is your mother doing today? I've just come on shift."

I stepped across with her as she went to pick up the cushion that had dropped to the ground. "She's doing okay," I told her. "She was in a very philosophical mood."

"I've had some lovely conversations with her," the nurse told me.

I peeked at Harry's sketch. He'd drawn a bear that was standing on two legs and dressed in men's clothing.

"That's a creative drawing, Harry," the nurse said, plumping the cushion before gently placing it behind Harry's head.

Harry made no indication he'd heard her.

"It's getting cooler," the nurse told me. "I'd better get your mum indoors."

I gave Mum a kiss before the nurse wheeled her away.

10

KATE

Pete and I were spending the day weeding our garden, both of us in boots and thick flannel shirts. It was a long overdue task. Our garden was large and unwieldy and every time we got out there to do some work on it, we'd talk about downsizing.

But this was the house that Ivy had lived in and we had so many memories of her tucked away here. We couldn't bear to move on.

It'd been four days since Abby had visited me. She hadn't made contact since. I knew though that she'd been to the hospice to see her grandmother. That was something. I hoped she really *was* finding her way back to us, as my mother had suggested.

A call came through from DS Jace Franco. It was Saturday, and officially, I'd been given the weekend off work. Whatever it was, it had to be important. I met eyes with Pete. He knew what this meant, too.

Wiping dirt from my hands, I took the call.

"Wakeland," Franco said. "Someone called the station about something they saw the night that Harper was murdered. This one checks out."

Previously, no one had seen anything on that night. A witness would be an unexpected blessing.

An image flashed through my mind of the night we'd found her. Harper's parents had been worried and they'd called the police. Harper had told a friend she thought she was being stalked, and the friend had told Harper's parents. Franco and I had traced her phone, and then we'd found her, dead. Deep red marks around her throat. Bruises on her forehead. She'd been murdered less than half an hour earlier.

"I'll be there in fifteen," I told Franco.

After ending the call, I gave Pete a tight smile. "Franco's got something in relation to Harper Rawlings. I have to go."

"Well, that's great. *Go*," Pete told me.

I kissed him on the cheek, lingering for a moment to hug his shoulders. He felt warm and solid even though the day was chilly.

After a quick shower, I threw on a jacket and smart pants, and took a brief moment to do my face and hair. I looked tired, my nose red from the cold temperature.

When I walked into the meeting space, the team that'd been assigned to Harper's case was already assembled. The team used to be much bigger years ago. But financial restraints had whittled us down to a handful. The day-to-day investigation of the case had basically become just Franco and me. Today, there was a face that rarely came to meetings—Detective Inspector Jiro Shintani. Whatever information had come in must be something good.

I prayed that we now had the clue we needed to solve this case— Harper deserved that much. And her parents desperately needed the resolution.

Jiro nodded at me warmly. "How you doing, Wakeland?"

"I'm okay," I lied.

I liked Jiro. In his late fifties, of Japanese descent, he was a sharp, intelligent guy who was a team player rather than a rank chaser.

"Okay, you're all here," he said. "We'll start. So, what we have is a Miss Indira Basak who was shopping in the fresh food market at Close Quarters that night. She works as a computer engineer in CQ, and she'd stopped off to do a bit of late-night shopping before heading home. She happened to look out at the parking bay at one point."

Close Quarters was the main hub of Tallman's Valley. It contained four sections—the information technology and business quarter, the scientific labs quarter, the general department store quarter and the university quarter. The daycare centre was attached to the university.

My lungs tightened with hope. "What did she see?"

"She said she saw a white SUV pull in sharp to the far end of the parking bay," Jiro told me. "Right next to a small car, dark in colour. She saw a man jump out of the SUV and a woman get out of the small car. The man was throwing his arms up in the air. She lost sight of the woman, and the man drove off. That's when Miss Basak stopped watching. She couldn't tell us what kind of SUV it was. She said she's not good with recognising car makes and models, and besides that, years have now passed, and she said her memory is fuzzy."

There wasn't much detail to Indira's story. But the details were right. The location was right. Harper owned a small, navy-coloured car. It'd still been there in the parking bay when her body was found, just metres away from her. Harper had been killed in a small garden area immediately behind the parking bay. We hadn't had any description of a possible vehicle at the crime location before. We hadn't known if the killer had been on foot or had come by car.

Franco glanced at me before turning to Jiro. "Wakeland and I have had success with hypnosis of a witness before. How about we see if Miss Basak will agree to a hypnosis session? She might be able to remember some more details."

"Good call," Jiro said.

I frowned. "Do we know why Miss Basak didn't say anything before now? I mean, it's been almost four years since Harper's murder."

"Apparently she travelled overseas the next morning," Jiro replied. "To India. She went to care for her mother, who'd suddenly fallen ill. Her mother needed ongoing care, and Miss Basak ended up staying there. On her return, when she heard about the murder, she remembered what she saw that night and she gave us a call."

"Makes sense." I exhaled, turning the witness account over in my mind. "Okay, well we need to study all available CCTV footage again. We've got to find all instances of a light-coloured SUV. The night-time lighting can wash out colours. If the stars align, we'll get a licence plate number."

I rubbed my eyes, wishing that the SUV had been an unusual colour— orange or green, perhaps. White and pale-coloured cars were so common. But a lead was a lead, and I was grateful that Indira had come forward.

Franco did a search for the CCTV footage that we'd saved on a computer hard drive. Our small team of six officers sat and watched it all again. We didn't have any footage of the precise location where Harper's car had been parked. But we now had Miss Basak's witness account of a pale-coloured SUV.

While we watched, Franco noted down the times and location of every sighting of pale SUVs that were close to the murder scene before and after the time of the murder. We enlarged the images of the relevant licence plate numbers, but most were too grainy to get enough detail.

It was slow, painstaking work.

Franco and I stayed late while we sent the rest of the team home. Under the LED lights, Franco looked older than his forty-eight years. His dark hair was thick as ever, but he seemed to have acquired many more frown lines over the past couple of years.

"How's things at home, Franco?" I said, munching on a bagel. I'd forgotten to eat earlier.

"Kind of lonely," he admitted. "The cat died yesterday."

"I'm so sorry. Rest in peace, Mugs. She was a good cat."

"The best." He sighed. "Guess they gotta go sometime. She was eleven."

"Yeah. Doesn't make it easier."

"Martina's marrying that jerk she's been dating."

"Oh. How'd you find out?"

"Facebook."

"You're still friends with her on there?"

"Nah." He drummed his fingers on the desk. "I look her up from time to time. Okay, maybe more often than that."

"You have to let her go. I know it's hard, but you have to."

"She should have waited for me. I loved her. I just wasn't sure of that. I didn't know if it was going to work out."

I wished I had some sage advice for him. My mother was better at that kind of thing. Somehow, I'd missed out on the gene for finding the right words.

I shot him a clumsy smile. "Life stings, like a scorpion. It stings all of us. No... that isn't quite right. I mean, if it stings, that means you're alive."

"That's real cheery, Wakeland."

"I said it wrong. But you know what I mean."

"I do. And thank you. We'd better get back to the case. I wanna find that SUV and get the bastard that killed Harper."

"Me too, Franco."

11

KATE

My phone was ringing.

I groaned, trying to wake myself up.

After pulling an all-nighter on the Harper Rawlings case, I wasn't in any mood for an early morning call. It was seven thirty in the morning for heaven's sake. I didn't have to be at work until nine.

It was a message from Superintendent Andrew Bigley. He wanted to see me ASAP. I guessed he wanted an update on the Rawlings case. I didn't have any good news for him though. Franco and I hadn't been able to pinpoint the car belonging to Harper's murderer.

Pete was already up, working out in our downstairs gym. I blew a kiss at him on my way out.

When I walked into Bigley's office, his expression gave nothing away.

"Morning, Kate. Like a coffee?"

"Do I look like I need one?"

"To be honest, yes."

I sighed, sinking into the chair in front of his desk. "Then, okay, I'll have a coffee."

He poured me one and brought it to me, then stood leaning against his desk. "How are things going for you? I've been informed that there's been a breakthrough in the Harper Rawlings case."

"There could be. It's too early to say. We've got a witness who says she saw an SUV at the murder scene that night. We're certainly going to pursue it."

"Good. That's great. I know that case has hit a long series of roadblocks."

His expression became cagey and I realised that whatever he called me in here for, it wasn't just for an update.

"Straight talk, Andrew. Is there an issue?"

Am I going to be taken off the case? Or asked to leave the force altogether? Is this it? The old shuffle out the door? I'm sixty-four years old. Not many homicide detectives hanging on for so long, right?

He remained silent for the next couple of seconds, the time stretching out while my thoughts ran wild.

"Jeffrey Zimmerman had a stroke last night."

"Oh... bad news. Is he okay?"

"The recovery is going to be a rough road, apparently."

"I'm sorry to hear that. Please give him and his family my regards."

He nodded. "I'll do that."

I waited for more. Bigley hadn't called me in simply to tell me about Inspector Zimmerman's stroke. It was sad, but it wasn't something that was urgent for me to know.

"Kate," he said, "this leaves Strikeforce Flying Fox a bit rudderless. Reagan's already leading the day-to-day operations of the team, of course, and Liz Booth's there, but Liz has other cases with the child protection squad. Reagan will be quite a bit on her own with the big picture investigation. There's no one else with her level of experience on the team." He cleared his throat. "If you want it, it's yours."

My throat felt thick, my tongue sticking to the floor of my mouth. I'd wanted this for so long. But over three years had passed. And the investigation had so far gone nowhere. What could I do that hadn't been done? A pot of bitter resentment simmered inside me.

"I need to think about that," was the first response that came out of my mouth.

"Of course," he said. "I understand that this has come out of the blue."

"You've already brought in every available expert," I pointed out. "From here and around the world. I'm not sure what would be expected of me, at this stage."

"I haven't yet brought in Ivy's grandmother."

I was about to blast him for his poorly considered joke. Except that his eyes were serious. "You should have given me this three and a half years ago, you know."

"If I could have, I would have."

"What's changed now? I mean, apart from Zimmerman's stroke? Is there something I don't know?"

"I wouldn't feel right if I didn't throw every resource we have at this. It's been too long. It's time to bend the rules."

"There was never an official rule that I couldn't join the team," I reminded him.

"It just seemed for the best. Maybe I was wrong."

I frowned. "Okay, I think I'm seeing the picture. The third anniversary of the abduction has come and gone. You've come under some kind of pressure from the commissioner, am I right? She wants something to happen. And I'm all you've got. In the absence of any kind of breakthrough, me joining the team is something new."

"It's not that. Yes, there's always pressure, no matter what the case. But the fact is that I've got no one to replace Jeffrey. He's been the public face of the investigation. But Reagan is going to have to step into his role, and—"

"And she's got the public relations manner of a teenage delinquent."

"That's one way of putting it," he conceded. "And Liz Booth isn't much better."

"Is that what the strike force has become? All about feeding messages to the public?"

He exhaled heavily. "You can level criticisms at the team if you want. Or, you can take it on and change the dynamics. Reagan would still be in the lead role, and she's also going to be the acting inspector until we ascertain how long Jeffrey's recovery process will take. But you'd play an anchor role and be the new face of the team."

I swallowed, quickly weighing everything that he'd told me. This could be a bad move for me, personally and professionally. But I couldn't turn it down. This was about Ivy.

"Can I run things the way I want?" I asked him.

He sucked his fleshy lips in. "Of course. Although, that would be something you'd have to discuss with Reagan."

"Sign me up," I told him.

"Great stuff. May your transition onto the team be all smooth sailing."

"Thanks." I stood. "Oh, and Andrew, what's with all the boating terms? The team is *rudderless*, but it needs me as an *anchor*? And you're wishing me *smooth sailing?*"

He shrugged. "People who sail yachts are all like that."

"Noted." I made my way out of his office and into the corridor.

I made a mental note to call Harper's parents personally. They shouldn't have to hear it on the news that I was joining Strikeforce Flying Fox. I wanted to assure them that I wasn't letting Harper go. I'd still be pursuing her case with the same level of commitment as before. They trusted me. I didn't want them to lose that.

And I'd talk to all the parents of the missing nursery school children personally.

The first thing I had to do was to try to find Abby. I wanted to tell her that her mother was taking on finding Ivy and the other four children.

I couldn't guess at how she'd react to that news.

12

KATE

I woke in Pete's arms.

"You were muttering in your sleep," he told me.

I rubbed my forehead. "Too much going on in the old noggin, I think."

"Kate, I can't say I'm not worried. It's a lot for you to take on after all this time has gone past. Maybe too much."

I sighed sleepily. "How could I say no?"

In response, he hugged me closer. "Just... don't expect too much of yourself. You're not in the business of performing miracles."

"I know," I said softly.

"I spoke with Abby last night."

"You did?"

"Yeah. After you were asleep. She called, wanting to meet up for lunch."

"Oh, nice. Did you tell her—?"

"Yeah. I told her about you joining the strike force."

"God. How'd she take it?" Abby hadn't answered my calls yesterday.

"She surprised me. She actually sounded hopeful."

"I don't know whether that's a good thing or not. If things go on as they are with the investigation, with still no breakthroughs, it might end up straining things between Abby and myself even further."

He pressed his lips against my temple. "We've laid out the welcome mat. That's all we can do."

"Did she say much about her boyfriend?"

"Nope. Not a thing. She wouldn't even give me a name. She said she wasn't ready for him to be part of our lives. Do I interpret that as meaning that the little punk has some kind of criminal record?" He made a low exasperated sound from between his teeth.

"I think she knows that if she gives us any small detail about him, we'll be able to find out exactly who he is."

"Yep. All I can say is, he'd better be good to her."

I rolled enough to the left to be able to catch sight of the time.

8:20 a.m.

I sat up. "I'd better run. My first time at a strike force meeting as an actual member of the team."

"Good luck."

———

I walked into the meeting of Strikeforce Flying Fox at 9 a.m. sharp.

It was easy to see that the team had been briefed on my arrival. Conversations halted and gazes veered towards me. There was no need for introductions —they all knew me well. I used to sit in on every meeting. My attendances had become sporadic over the past year. I'd had too many homicide caseloads, and so little was ever happening with Strikeforce Flying Fox that I could quickly catch up. I hadn't attended meetings at all in the past months.

Greeting the team quickly, I went to take a seat. But I was cut off at the pass by Grimshaw.

Striding across to me, she shook my hand with a firm grasp. "Welcome to the team, Detective. If you ask me, this is just a public relations stunt."

I tried not to show how taken aback I was. "Good morning to you, too. How's Zimmerman?"

"Mad as hell. Half his face dropped and his mouth won't work properly, so he can't yell at anyone. He'll need to be hogtied when he finds out what's going on here."

I shrugged. "Oh well, maybe it'll help his recovery. Because he'll be trying his heart out to get back."

That elicited a grin from her.

But Grimshaw wasn't just going to let me slide into place. She obviously still believed I didn't belong here.

I took a seat next to Senior Constable Cameron Vella.

Cameron turned to me with a quizzical glint in his blue eyes. "How're you doing?" he said in his *Los Angelino* accent.

"I'm doing okay."

He nodded in response.

"Okay, people," said Grimshaw. "Following on from our last meeting, we have a few items on the agenda. The priority item is taking a second look at the known paedophile who was visiting his brother at the Tallman's Valley Hospice on the day of the kidnappings. Mr Anthony Pellam was convicted seven years ago of molesting a neighbour's child after enticing her into his house. He served four months in jail."

I already knew about Anthony Pellam. I'd investigated him myself, privately. I'd found nothing that would tie him to the abductions of the children.

Grimshaw fixed her gaze on me while she gave details of his crimes, not giving me any breathing space. She didn't think I should be here, and she wasn't going to hold back.

"The timing is right," Grimshaw continued. "Pellam left the hospital some minutes before the kidnappings. He had a work vehicle large enough to accommodate five small children. The specifics are in the briefing you were given last week."

"Could I be given that briefing?" I asked.

"Look on with Vella's material," she told me. "He can catch you up later."

I listened to her outline of where the investigation was at overall and where it was headed. I couldn't help but feel crushed by the hopelessness of it.

"Wakeland," called Grimshaw, shaking my thoughts loose. "I want you to organise the paedophile arm of the investigations. Collating all the notes. Making sure to dot all the I's and cross all the T's."

My throat felt dusty and suddenly raw. Grimshaw wanted to mire me in paperwork. I couldn't let her sit on my neck. I was here for Ivy and the children. If I had to fight for my right to investigate as a senior detective, I would.

"If it's okay with you and the team," I said, "I need an anchor. A point to gather myself at before I get started."

If sailing terms were good enough for Superintendent Bigley, they were good enough for me.

"What are you thinking, Wakeland?" Grimshaw ground her words down to a sharp point.

I moistened my lips. "Ground zero. I want to start from there."

"That day is long gone," she reminded me flatly. "Besides, you were here for our meetings back then. And if you want to look through the notes, have at it."

"I'd like to interview everyone personally."

She sighed audibly, her eyes bugging. "*That's* what you want to do? Go over old ground?"

"Just to start with. It's how I work."

"Well, I won't stand in your way," she said. "You do you. Just remember that this isn't one of your homicide cold cases. It's been raked over by many professionals from here and overseas." Her tone then softened so abruptly it was jarring rather than comforting. "Wakeland, I know you want your granddaughter back. And I hope that happens. Just, make sure you help the case and not hinder it."

I nodded at her. So, she *was* human somewhere underneath all the gruff. I didn't understand her, and she didn't understand me. I hoped we could meet somewhere in the middle.

For now, I planned to run my own race. And it *was* a race. Just that the race had started over three years ago. And somehow, I needed to find my way back to the starting line.

13

KATE

I sat in my car, parked beside *The Ponds.*

This was where it started. Ground zero.

Slipping my phone from my pocket, I browsed to the video I had of that day—the precious few seconds of video that Kaylee had taken of the children.

There was Ivy in pigtails. Running on the grass.

I've got hold of your little hand, Ivy. I haven't let it go. Not once. I'm running beside you.

Someone had to be there that day. Watching. You went with them because you didn't suspect they were going to take you away. Adults had only ever given you love and care.

But I've still got your hand, Ivy. I'm going to find you.

It was a big promise, and I didn't know if I could keep it. But I had to start the case again, fresh, with all the same hopes that I'd held on the day she went missing. I couldn't let the weight of the past years pull me down.

I knew all the facts of that day off by heart. I also knew that there were often fragments hiding in the nooks between the facts.

Scattered all over the reserve in front of me were invisible parts of a puzzle. Embedded in the soil and in the trees and chilly pools of water.

I left my car and walked down the hill. This was my first interview that I'd conduct on the case, but it wasn't with a person. I was here to ask the landscape for permission to know and understand the hidden aspects of that day. This was how I always began an investigation. It helped me to remember to keep my mind open. I'd seen too much arrogance in the force. Detectives who stuck hard to their first theories about a case. But arrogance could put blinders on your eyes and prevent you from questioning the things you assumed to be true.

I pictured the senior teacher, Justine Farina, rushing along the boardwalk through the rainforest, calling the children. She was the first one to notice the kids missing and the first one to search for them.

I pictured Nola at the top of the hill, talking to the ice-cream van driver. And Kaylee preparing the picnic.

Kaylee hadn't been under suspicion of any kind. She had been filming the kids right at the time five of them had gone missing.

I'd start with Justine. There had been a couple of small discrepancies between the accounts from her and Nola Hobson that had never been resolved. Grimshaw had put it down to the extreme trauma of the day.

I knew from the case notes that she'd moved to England. She'd lost her job on the day of the abduction. I didn't know what she was doing for work now. Unfortunately, it'd have to be a phone conversation.

Taking out my notebook, I looked up Justine's mobile number and then called her.

Her voice turned tight as soon as I identified myself. I predicted that she'd try to get out of talking to me. And I was right. She told me that she was busy. But I'd learned ways of getting people to agree. Especially by letting them know that the conversation was going to happen at some point very soon and so it might as well happen *now*.

"How did you know I was back in town?" Justine said. "Does this mean my every move is being watched?"

She was back in town? I decided not to tell her that I hadn't known that. It might help me win a prompt interview with her.

"Can I come and talk to you?" I asked.

"There's nothing else I can tell you," she answered.

"I've newly been assigned to the case. This is normal procedure. I need to get my bearings."

"They have piles of notes. Detective Grimshaw questioned me at least on five separate occasions."

"It won't take long."

She sighed. "Alright, I suppose so. You have my address."

"Thank you. Now would be good for me. How about you?"

"Okay then."

As I ended the call, I returned to my notebook and looked up the house she used to live in. I wondered when she'd returned here from England.

Justine lived in a very nice townhouse in the new part of Tallman's Valley, with an overgrown hedge and all the shutters closed. The townhouse had an empty look, but I knew that it wasn't.

Justine greeted me at the door before I had the chance to knock. Dressed in a floral skirt and cardigan, she was slimmer than I remembered, with her hair now in a pixie cut. Last time I'd seen her, she'd been a full-figured woman with pink round cheeks.

"How should we do this?" she asked. "Do you want a tea and a chat? Or something more formal?"

"I won't have tea, thank you. But you're welcome to have one, if you wish. And it's just a chat."

She nodded, raising eyebrows that were already perched high on her face, her mouth pursing nervously. "Okay. I'll pass on the tea, too."

She guided me through to a cosy living room that had potted ferns. Save for a skylight, there were no uncovered windows. Photographs of her travels adorned the mantelpiece above the stone fireplace—most of them featuring groups of women in their forties, including Justine.

"How long have you been back?" I asked her.

"Just a couple of months. I haven't told anyone, and I haven't really been out, either. It's nice, being in my own home again."

"Were you working over there in England?"

"For my sister and her husband. They run a travel agency. I grew up in England. I worked as a nanny there when I was younger. I can't do that now. News of what happened at *The Ponds* has pretty much travelled around the world."

I gave her a supportive glance. "So, you made the decision to return to Tallman's Valley?"

She nodded, tugging at the ends of her short hair that were behind her ears. I guessed that the haircut was new. "I couldn't stay away forever," she said. "Well, I could, but my house is here, and I have friends here. It's not fair that I get hounded out of town."

"I wasn't aware that happened to you?"

"I was the most senior childcare worker who was with the children at the time. Of course people are going to blame me. Who else is there to blame?" Her dark eyes raked my face. I knew she must think I blamed her, too.

"It was a terrible time for everyone," I replied. "I know that people look for scapegoats at such times." I kept my voice even, attempting to draw her out by keeping the focus on the distress that she'd spoken of. People liked talking about themselves, even to police. In the past, just by sitting and chatting, I'd found out many unexpected things. Sometimes, people were at the point where they were ready to confess. All they needed was a nudge.

Justine sucked her mouth in, her arms crossed against her body. "People yelled accusations at me in the street, put awful notes in my letterbox, found me on social media. I had no choice but to leave. I don't think I'll ever be forgiven, and I'll have to live with that. I don't have children myself, but I sincerely doubt that any parent can truthfully say that they weren't distracted many times, even just for a few seconds. And that's all it took that day. I swear on my heart, it wasn't longer than a few short seconds."

I let her words rest for a moment. She sounded shaken.

Glancing around the room, I nodded towards the photographs. "Happier times?"

She smiled briefly. "Yes. My friends and I used to go on a couple of holidays per year. Croatia, Majorca, Spain. Places like that. Very good times. A mix of married and single women—mostly single, like me."

"So, you're planning on staying in town now?"

"Yes. Unless things get bad again. I have a friend who owns a patisserie. She said she'll teach me the baking and decorating side of things." A sad smile flittered across her face again. "Look at me. I thought I'd be working in childcare until retirement, but here I am, trying all kinds of different things. Silver lining and all of that."

"I hope you manage to feel settled again."

"Oh, I can't say I didn't dream of taking off and doing something new years ago. Don't get me wrong, I love kids, but looking after a tribe of them every day can get on your nerves. I was too scared to make the leap, I guess. But then I was forced to. Life's funny like that." Her eyes shot wide open in alarm. "Please don't take that the wrong way. It was only the odd occasion that the noise of young children got too much. I would give anything to rewind that day the kids went missing."

I tried to hide the fact that I was watching her expressions intently. She seemed to me to be over-explaining herself. But she might just be anxious. I tried to defuse her before she wound herself up any tighter.

"I understand completely. Kids can drive you crazy at times. I think everyone can understand that."

"I'm glad you get what I was saying. I'm very conscious that you're Ivy's grandmother. You have a personal stake in this."

"Yes, I do. But I assure you I'm here on a completely professional basis."

"Still, investigating this must not be easy for you."

"No." I smiled. "But life is full of hard things. It's not easy for anyone."

Her mouth turned down. "That's the truth."

"Okay, shall we get started?"

"I'd like that. I've got things to do in the afternoon."

"We'll start from the moment that Nola left to talk to the driver of the ice-cream van," I said. "What happened from that point on?"

"Well, Kaylee and I were putting out the picnic baskets and food onto the rugs."

"Did you have a view of the children at that time?"

"Yes. They were just playing happily."

"And then?"

"Kaylee and I finished getting the picnic set up. Three of the kids were involved in a tussle with each other and I broke it up."

"What was Kaylee doing at that point?"

"She was getting the children's cups out of the basket."

"Which way was she facing?"

Justine frowned. "Oh, towards the direction of the lake, I guess. From what I can remember."

"And then what happened?"

"After I broke up the tussle, I looked around at the children. There seemed to be less than there should, and so I told the kids to stop and drop —which is a command that they know. It means to stop immediately and sit on the ground. I did a quick head count. I only counted fourteen. And so I raised the alarm with Kaylee."

I couldn't help but feel an instant chill. She was describing the exact moment that Ivy and the others vanished. Renewed anguish churned inside my chest.

"And then?" I said softly.

"I felt panic, of course, but it wasn't dire at that point. The first thing Kaylee and I did was to look up towards the lake. But they weren't headed that way. I thought they must have just run onto the boardwalk and into the rainforest. I thought I'd find them within a minute. I had Kaylee keep the rest of the children together on the picnic rugs and I dashed off. After a bit, Nola joined me."

"Did you see anything or anyone in the rainforest?"

"No. Nothing and no one."

"Did you hear a car—as in, a car on the road at the other end of the boardwalk?"

"I don't remember hearing one. I wasn't listening for one, either. My thoughts didn't go to abduction then. I was thinking they were hiding."

"Could you tell me how long it'd normally take to set up the picnic?"

She looked confused by my question. "Oh, uh, yes, I can answer that, I think. We used to start getting it ready by eleven and then by ten past eleven we'd have the children ready to eat."

"Did Nola leave before you started setting up, or after?"

"Just before."

"And she didn't return until after you were completely set up—actually, until after you'd started looking for the children?"

"That's right."

"I walked up and down that hill earlier today. It probably took me a couple of minutes. I've seen it in the police notes that you said Nola took far too long. We're talking ten or more minutes."

"Yes, she did. I suppose that amount of minutes is right. It's bizarre, really. I was so traumatised when I couldn't find the kids that I didn't really put any thought into the timeline."

"I know from the notes that Nola denies she took any longer than a few seconds to speak to the driver."

"Well, she's wrong about that. Kaylee says the same as me. Nola took forever, for some reason. She must have started chatting with the driver and lost track of time."

"The driver claims that Nola didn't actually speak to him."

She looked at me astounded. "Really? Well, that's damned strange."

"That was in the media reports."

"I confess to not reading any of them. Too upsetting."

"I can understand that. Later that day, after the police were on the scene, you found Ivy's button on the hill?"

Justine inhaled so sharply that I heard it.

"Yes."

"Did you see her on the hill at any point that day?"

"No. Look, I've gone over this numerous times with the other detectives."

"I'm sorry. I do need to ask these things again. Do you think that Ivy and the other children might have followed Nola up the hill?"

Her gaze darted away. "I think it's the most likely scenario."

At this moment, it seemed as if something inside Justine's mind had unravelled, only I wasn't sure what.

"Is there something you want to tell me, Justine?"

"What? No, there's nothing. Nothing that I haven't already told the police umpteen times.

"Okay, thank you, Justine. I appreciate you having this talk with me."

She seemed surprised when I stood.

The next person on my list was Nola Hobson. I needed to see if she was still refuting Justine's claims. Perhaps I'd imagined that Justine knew more than she was saying. I hoped that talking with Nola might help me figure that out.

14

KATE

I was lucky enough to catch Nola Hobson on a day off from work. She worked two jobs and wasn't an easy person to get hold of.

When I called her, she didn't have the same hesitant note in her voice that Justine had, but she didn't sound overjoyed to hear from me, either. That was natural. No one ever wanted to talk to the police.

I drove to the old, established part of town. Nola's house looked as if it had been built in the forties, with bricks forming tight, perfectly formed curves on either side of the front door.

Nola was still in her pyjamas—a faded pink flannelette set—even though the time was now early afternoon. Her shoulder-length blonde hair had barely been brushed.

"Come in," she told me cheerfully. "Don't mind the mess."

There was a lot of mess not to mind. Luckily, I didn't mind at all. Clothes were strewn across the floor and backs of chairs. A half-eaten pizza was lying on the dining table.

"Sorry," she said, pulling a stack of folded towels off a sofa. "I share this house with another girl, and neither of us are neat freaks. Anyway, have a seat."

"Don't worry about any of that," I told her as I sat myself down. "A bit of mess isn't the worst thing."

I had a view through to the kitchen. Everything looked like the original 1940s build—the kitchen with tiny cupboards and ornate cornices and fireplace.

"How have you been?" I asked her.

"Busy."

"Busy working?"

"Yeah. I work three nights a week at the pizzeria on Main Street. And I work as a private nanny for a family during the weekdays. So, I've got the two jobs and I'm looking for a third—something on the weekends."

"You don't work in daycare anymore?"

"No. I don't think I ever will again. I wasn't fired from the nursery school job, but the director spoke to me very negatively. She made it clear that some of the parents were suspicious of me. It was never going to work, going forward."

"Okay. I'm sorry about all that. So, you're looking for a third job? You don't go out and see your friends on the weekends?"

"I don't really have friends, to be honest. Not even Sophie—the girl I share with. We're not exactly close. I only had a couple of friends at school and they've drifted away."

"That's a shame. No romantic interest, either?"

Her cheeks gained a high colour. "I've started seeing a guy. Bryce. I haven't dated much in the past, so this is all new." Her voice had a shy tinge to it.

"I hope you leave some time to see him."

"He's really busy, too. He works with one of the tech start-ups at Close Quarters. So, he doesn't have a lot of free time, anyway."

I suddenly felt a little maternal for this girl, who sat opposite me in her pyjamas with her hair all messy. But I couldn't afford to feel maternal for her. "Well, I'm glad for you. What's he like?"

"He's really nice. He likes the fact that I'm not a party animal."

"I'm happy for you."

"Thanks."

"Okay, well, we'll get started, shall we?" I said. "I'll let you know that I've just joined Strikeforce Flying Fox. Because of that, I want to connect with the people who were there that day."

"You joined the strike force?"

"I did."

Her blue eyes fixed on me intently. "Go after that kidnapper hard, okay?"

"I plan to."

"Hurts knowing that five of the kids never got to graduate from the nursery school."

"Yes, they'd all be in big school by now," I said wistfully. "Well, I've just had a talk with Justine, so I'm clear on her end of things." I chose not to divulge that Justine had moved back into town. Justine deserved her privacy.

Nola's brow furrowed deeply, and she hugged the cushion to her chest.

"You look a little upset?"

"I haven't spoken to Justine since that day. We had a falling out."

"Yes, I know." I paused. "I'd like to know your side of things. I know you've already told it multiple times, but I'd like the chance to hear it for myself."

She nodded. "Where do I start?"

"You were new to the three-year-old group that week, weren't you? How about you start from there and then tell me about the picnic?"

"Okay. So, I'd been working in the babies' room for the past year. Changing them, doing their bottle feeds, all of that. That was the Brushtail Possums room. Then I was moved to the Flying Fox room. With the three-year-olds. That Wednesday was my first time out on a picnic with them. Justine, Kaylee and I walked the kids down to the reserve. The kids just played while us teachers watched. According to the wilderness program that the school runs, we're to let the kids roll in the grass and collect pinecones, that sort of thing."

"Did you see anyone else at the reserve at any point? Apart from the ice-cream van driver?" I knew that she'd said no to that question to police before, but it never hurt to ask again.

She shook her head. "Honestly—no one. But as you said, I did see an ice-cream van. I went to tell him to get lost. I didn't like how he stopped and watched the children. Looked like a bit of a weirdo."

"What did you say to him?"

"I'm afraid I don't remember."

"I'm guessing you know that the driver doesn't recall you saying anything to him at all."

"Yes, I know. But that's not true. I told him to go."

"Why do you think the driver said that?"

"I have no freaking idea. Either he did something very wrong and he's covering it up, or he's just strange."

"Okay. Well, while you were at the top of the hill, did you call anyone on your phone or do anything other than speak to the driver?"

She cast me an odd look. "Detective Grimshaw asked me that same question. Like, she was trying to make out that I was calling someone to come and kidnap the children. It was horrible."

"Uncomfortable questions are part of the job. But I want you to know I haven't formed that theory at all," I assured her.

"Good. Because it made me feel like absolute shit. I love kids. I would never have done anything to hurt them."

"Of course not. It's just that I saw in the report that you'd taken quite a bit longer than what Justine and Kaylee expected. According to their time-line, you were away for about ten minutes in total."

"No. They were just trying to find a scapegoat. I barely said two sentences to the guy."

"What did you say to him, exactly?"

She stared back at me, pulling her top lip through her teeth. "I told you, I don't quite remember."

"What do you think you said?"

"Just to go away. To leave me alone."

"To leave *you* alone?"

"No, I mean, to leave the kids alone. They were distracted by the music."

"And what reaction did the driver have?"

"He ended up leaving. Took his time about it. I waited until he left."

"So, you think he might have taken ten minutes to leave?"

"No. Justine's confused, or lying. It wasn't that long at all."

"When did you leave to walk up the hill? Before or after the picnic rugs were spread on the ground?"

"At first I thought it was before, but later I realised it was after."

I remembered from Grimshaw's notes that Nola had retracted her first statement.

"Why do you think that both Justine and Kaylee are saying the same thing? They both say you left before they began setting up the picnic."

"You keep asking me to tell you why other people said what they said. I don't know. I can't get inside their heads. Justine even said that none of the kids had been rolling on the hill earlier. And that wasn't true. Of course they were."

"I'm sorry. I'm just trying to make sense of it," I told her, trying to inject warmth into my voice. It had become a tense interview. I sat back, giving her a moment. "That's basically all I wanted to know. Thanks for the catch up."

"I hate remembering that day," she breathed. "But for three years, I've thought about it every day."

Nola hadn't told me anything much different to what she'd told the police previously in reports. But the discrepancy in the stories between Justine and Nola remained. Having spoken to them both in person, I couldn't help but feel that the answer to everything lay within that discrepancy. It was also of interest to me that she'd said she wanted the driver to leave her alone. Was that just a slip of the tongue, or something else? I had to find out.

In my mind, a triangle formed. There was Nola and the ice-cream driver up at the top of the hill, and then Justine and Kaylee down at the picnic area, and then the five missing children at the third point. I just didn't know where that third point was. It was a shifting triangle.

I needed to speak with the driver.

15

KATE

I called the ice-cream van driver, Brent Cole, as soon as I left Nola's house and was back in my car again.

He couldn't see me today, but he could see me tomorrow. He'd seemed puzzled that a detective wanted to interview him again.

I called Franco next.

"Yo, Wakeland."

"Hey, Franco. Have you been able to get our hypnotherapist to see Indira Basak any earlier?"

"Nope. He's still booked up until next week. He said he can't fit her in until then."

"Bother. Okay, thanks. Let me know if anything else happens."

"Will do. I'm taking care of things. You go ahead and make a strong start on the missing kids' case, okay?"

"Thanks. I appreciate it."

After stopping off at the hospice to visit my mother, I headed home.

When I walked in the door of my house and through into the kitchen, I was greeted by the sight of Pete cradling a tiny baby. Abby had come to visit again.

"That brings back memories," I cooed. "Reminds me of you holding baby Ivy. Is Jasper as beautiful as I told you he was?"

Pete beamed, sipping his coffee. "Yep, he's a little beauty."

I kissed both Pete and Jasper. "Ooh, lemme hold him."

Laughing, Pete set down his coffee cup and carefully handed Jasper across to me. "I knew you'd get grabby the minute you saw him."

I cradled Jasper in my arms. "I'm so glad Abby came to see you. Where is she?"

"She went out for a little while. She said she'd be back in ten." He shrugged. "It's been twenty. But, eh, who's counting? Little Jasper here has been my best bud."

Despite the shrug and nonchalant expression on my husband's face, I detected something lying beneath it. "Pete? Has Abby been borrowing money again?"

"Just a little bit. She said she needed some things for the baby."

"And if she comes back empty-handed?"

He hesitated. "What was I going to do? Say no to my own daughter? I haven't seen her for so long."

"I'm just worried. Not that I wasn't worried before. But now she has a young baby to take care of." I snuggled my cheek against Jasper's soft head.

"Kate, I know what you mean. She spent years taking God knows what. And I can't say that it didn't cross my mind that she's spending the money on drugs. But we don't know that she's still taking anything. She looks healthy enough."

I raised my face, exhaling and nodding. "Yes, she looks good. I think it's been too many years of worry and now I can't relax. It's encouraging that she's been coming around to see us. I want to feel happy about that."

"Want me to try and talk to her? See what's going on behind the scenes?"

Opposing thoughts competed for attention in my mind. "I'm scared of pushing her away. It's better that she's coming to see us than not at all. Maybe we should wait and watch for a while."

Someone walked in behind me.

Abby looked from me to Pete curiously. "What are you waiting and watching?"

"Just a case I'm working on," I said quickly. "A murder."

"Oh." She lifted bags onto the kitchen counter. She'd bought two tins of baby milk formula, a baby bottle and some rusk sticks. "What's happening... with, you know, the other case?"

"I've only had two days on the team," I told her. "I'm just getting up to speed."

Her mouth twisted, as if twisting around words she was stopping herself from saying. "Every time I hear from that Grimshaw, it's to say they're doing all they can. I don't hear from her much anymore. I guess they've stopped doing *all they can.*"

"When I attended the meeting yesterday, they were chasing up lots of leads," I told her.

A flicker of anger crossed her face. "Chasing leads. That's all they do. But they never seem to actually find out anything."

"I really wish it were different. I'm certainly going to give this new role all I've got."

Abby's eyes moistened. "Can I have Jasper? I have to go."

"Already?" I said, disappointed. "I just got home."

"I'm sorry. He needs a feed and a sleep. I ran out of formula."

"Okay." I kissed Jasper's cheek. "He's so cute. He reminds me of Ivy."

"He has her mouth and nose," Abby replied, holding her hands out for Jasper. Her expression was flat, as if she wasn't interested in talking.

I handed Jasper over, wishing I could hug her. But she seemed so distant.

She was gone in a flash.

The house suddenly felt emptier.

———

I had an early start the next morning. The sunrise put the mountains in silhouette as I drove down the dark street.

The ice-cream van driver could only see me at six in the morning, unless I wanted to see him on the weekend. I hadn't hesitated to say yes because I wanted to move on this as quickly as possible.

I had to make up for years of not being on the case. Unfortunately, I could no longer call people down to the station to make a statement. That time had gone. I had to work with what I had, which meant working around people's schedules.

Like Nola, Brent Cole lived in one of the old parts of the area. His house, tiny and painted pale blue, stood nestled between tall trees. It reminded me of a baby bird. I knew the property well—I'd driven by many times over the past years, on the lookout for anything unusual—a child's toy carelessly left in the front yard or evidence that he and his wife had left town. I knew that he was forty-three and had a wife and no children. I knew who his immediate family members were and where they lived.

He'd been named as a *person of interest* in the case of the missing children, but there had never been any solid evidence. Driven by desperation, I'd kept a close eye on him.

Brent's wife answered the door and showed me inside. The interior was boxy and cluttered. Despite the cold, there was no heating in use. The woman wore a thick cardigan and old yoga pants that drooped low and made her butt look like it was almost touching the back of her knees. Her cheeks were blotchy, and her nose reddened as if she had a cold. She introduced herself as Sandy. I'd always thought of Sandy as a name for a beach-loving person, but she looked like someone who rarely ventured outdoors.

Brent shuffled out in a singlet top and shorts. He didn't seem bothered by the chill that had swept through the front door. I'd seen him many times, but I'd never spoken to him in person before. He was shorter than me, with a head of dirty-blond waves. His face was creased with wrinkles and rougher skin on one side of his face—typical of those who drove for a living, especially those who drove with the window open.

I introduced myself to him and his wife. "I appreciate you talking to me today, Brent."

He plonked himself heavily on the sofa. "We'd better get straight to it. We don't have much time."

"I'll be quick," I told him, knowing full well that I wouldn't be quick if things got interesting. But I didn't expect anything interesting. Brent Cole had been the one who'd been questioned the most extensively.

Briefly, I explained that I wanted to reacquaint myself with the events of the day that the children went missing and that I'd joined the strike force.

His eyes flicked to his wife and then back to me. "I've told the police everything. Which isn't much."

Sandy rubbed her arms. "I'm going inside. I'm not feeling well."

I nodded and shot her a smile before she left the room. I turned back to Brent. "I'm sorry for the inconvenience."

"It's not all that inconvenient, to be honest. I've got a spare few minutes before I take off for work."

"What are you doing these days? You're not selling ice-cream, right?" I knew this already. I'd been following everything as closely as I could, but I needed a lead in.

"No. No ice-cream. My job got ruined by the investigation. *I* got ruined. I'm driving trucks now."

"I'm sorry that happened. It's been a very difficult investigation, from everything I've heard. Everyone's determined to find the kids."

His entire body seemed to crumple. "They shouldn't have been looking in my direction. I had nothing to do with it. Mate, they were wasting precious time investigating me."

"We have to question everyone. Please don't take it personally."

He raised and lowered his eyebrows in a facial shrug. "How can I not? You tell me. Those detectives actually posed the theory to me that I'd put the kiddies in my van. Zimmerman and Grimshaw, that was their damned names."

I had to play good cop here. Or he might clam up. "That must have been tough."

"You said it."

I took a breath. "Is it okay to get started?"

"Do your worst."

Ignoring that, I asked him about his schedule on the day the kids went missing.

He expelled a stream of air. "I was heading out on a run. During the summer mornings, close to midday, I'd go on a loop around Tallman's Valley. I'd hit the two retirement villages—the old folk liked my ice-creams—and after that I'd hit Close Quarters, at about half-past eleven."

"Was that your schedule every day in summer?"

"It was a new schedule."

"Oh?"

"It was a chance thing. I was driving past Close Quarters one day, and the office workers flagged me down. And before I knew it, a whole load of the techies was lining up for ice-creams. Like little kids. I wouldn't have thought of targeting them. I thought they'd all be into organic sprout salads and things like that. But they seemed to think it was cool to buy old-fashioned ice-cream cones and eat them while sittin' out on the grass. They loved my van. My van looked retro to those hipster kids, you know? They were takin' photos of themselves in front of it and uploadin' it to their social media. So, I added Close Quarters to my rounds. It was good business for me."

I shot him a smile. "Right. And, according to the notes I read, you'd park at the reserve in between the retirement villages and Close Quarters?"

"Yeah. I had some time to fill between each of those runs. I'd park at the reserve and have my lunch—a hotdog and an ice-cream usually."

"How many days a week did you do this?"

"Two days a week. Wednesdays and Fridays."

"Whereabouts at the reserve did you use to wait?"

"Like I told the police, at *The Ponds*. I don't like it near the hospice end. Gives me the cold shudders."

I thought of my mother and the other patients at the hospice. It gave me the *cold shudders*, too.

"And on the day in question," I said, "you observed the nursery kids having their picnic?"

"That's right. I like watching kiddies play. I've got none of my own, but I've got nieces and nephews that I love to bits." His eyes widened. "Oh, hells bells, that came out wrong."

"No, it didn't come out wrong, Mr Cole. I understood you. Look, I'm not here with any preconceived ideas."

"I'm sure my neighbours are gonna think you're here for the wrong reasons. People think I'm a kiddie fiddler. Soon as the kids got snatched, parents wouldn't let their kids near my van. The techies from Close Quarters stopped buying my ice-creams, too. Summer was my best time of year. My business got destroyed. Couldn't recover from that."

"I'm sorry."

"Yeah. But sorry won't fix it. I'm a ruined man."

His eyes welled with tears. I gave him my best sympathetic look. The fallout from these big cases were often severe on the people involved—even if they'd just been unlucky enough to be on the scene at the time. Whether Brent Cole had just been *unlucky*, I wasn't sure of.

"It's been hard on a lot of people," I told him. "The best thing that I can do is to help solve the case."

He raised his eyebrows high. The man had very mobile eyebrows. "Well, good luck with that. It's been years now."

"We never give up on a case. Especially not one like this."

He eyed me with a newly critical gaze. "I know who you are. You're the mother of what's-her-name—one of the kids' parents."

"Abigail Wakeland. Yes."

"I should of twigged when you told me your name. But I didn't. I'm not good at remembering names. Or faces."

"Most people aren't."

"Seems a bit wrong that they've given *you* the case. It's a bit personal and all."

"That's between me and area command."

"Wait, you're the one who marched up to me in the street, two days after the kids got taken. Demanding to know what I'd done with 'em."

I was losing him. I'd been worried he'd remember that encounter. "I'm sorry if I came on too strong."

"Too strong? You wanted to string me up."

"Forgive me. It wasn't directed at you. I was under extreme stress at the time."

"This seems like a bit of a stitch-up now."

"It's not a stitch-up. I give you my word. Can we continue?"

He eyed me suspiciously, his eyebrows on the move again. "Fine."

"Returning to the day the kids went missing," I said, "can you describe what you saw when you were parked at the reserve?"

"The kids were running about. You know, on their stubby little legs."

"Did you notice any of them running away from the others?"

"Nope."

"Did you see anyone apart from the kids and the three childcare workers?"

"Nope."

"Can you describe what happened when Nola Hobson came walking up the hill?"

"I was just sittin' there eatin' my hotdog. She come up the hill, looking all strung out about something. She had a good figure, that one." He cast an eye towards the hallway, in the direction where his wife had gone.

"And then?"

"I probably looked at her a bit too long. She got a bit huffy and just stood there gawking at me. I turned away and stuffed the hotdog in my gob. Switched the radio on, minded my own business, you know. Ate the second hotdog. When I looked back around, damned if she wasn't still standing there gawking at me. I left quick-smart."

"You're saying she was standing there in the time it took you to eat *two* hotdogs?"

"Yup. I eat fast, but still."

"Would you say at least a minute a hotdog?"

He rolled his shoulders inward in a hunched shrug. "I guess."

"Did you tell Inspector Zimmerman and Detective Grimshaw that? About Nola standing there so long?"

"Yes ma'am. But they didn't put much importance on it. Because Blind Freddy could see that they were trying to pin something on me. And what the girl did made me look bad, like she had a reason to glare at me for so long." He shrugged a couple more times, reflexively, like it'd become a nervous tic.

"When you say Nola was gawking at you, are you saying that she looked angry?"

His brow rippled in a deep frown. "Ah, yep. Angry would describe it. But then when I looked back, her eyes seemed to have glazed over. Weird."

"Glazed over? Like she'd kind of zoned out?"

He nodded.

"Hmmm. Thank you. Okay, just a couple more questions. When you drove away, did you see anyone, or any vehicles—as you came around the bend?"

"Nope. And I didn't park the van there anywhere neither. It wasn't me who took those kids. I'm not the bloody pied piper, leading kiddies away with my music."

"I'm not suggesting that you—"

"You don't have to. All the police interest has been on me because I was the only poor idiot in sight. And now you. Mate, I can understand how some people cave in and admit to stuff they didn't do. Zimmerman and Grimshaw kept coming back to me and asking the same things. Non-bloody-stop. Zimmerman actually asked me what I *did* with the kiddies. He asked me if they were dead or alive. Like I would know." He shook his head vehemently, his shoulders jumping. "No word of a lie, if the kiddies had come up to my van, the only thing I would of *done* with them is to give 'em each an ice-cream cone."

Brent Cole suddenly looked ten years older.

He was too visibly upset to continue. Thanking him for his time, I ended the interview.

The world was waking as I drove back towards the hub of Katoomba, traffic beginning to crawl out from side streets onto the main roads.

The interview with Brent Cole had affected me—but in which way I couldn't yet say. On the surface, it was clear that his business had been demolished by the ongoing investigation. But I couldn't allow that to cloud the fact that he was the most obvious suspect. And if he really was the kidnapper, the children had most likely been murdered by him within the first days.

If I had questioned him at the start, I couldn't say that I would have conducted the interview any differently than Zimmerman and Grimshaw had. Sometimes, it took rough questioning to get a suspect to confess.

His statement about Nola was lining up with what Justine had told me. Nola had been distracted.

One thing seemed certain. There was a missing chunk of time in which Nola Hobson had been apparently standing dead still and Brent Cole had been eating his lunch and then drove away, and the other two daycare workers had been together, breaking up fights with the children and looking in the direction of the hill and wondering what was taking Nola so long.

Brent Cole was different in person to what he'd been portrayed as in the media and from what Grimshaw had told the strike force team. I'd had much stronger suspicions about him before than what I had after speaking with him. At the same time, I still couldn't afford to rule him out.

16

KATE

I drove from Brent Cole's house to the reserve. I sat looking at *The Ponds* picnic spot and thinking.

If this were a game, Nola Hobson would be the wildcard. The other players seemed to have definite roles. But any number of things could be true of Nola. There were things that didn't quite add up about Justine and Brent, but it was Nola who raised the most questions in my mind.

I waited until eight in the morning—visiting time at the hospice—and went to see Mum. This time, Pete came with me. He'd been like a son to her and he thought of her like a mother. Seeing her like this was painful for him, too. There had been so much pain and loss in the fabric of our lives these past years.

I then shot over to the station for the nine o'clock meeting of the strike force.

I sat next to Constables Cameron and Ella. I felt my breaths rising hard against my chest wall.

"Jeez, Detective," said Cameron, "you're a caged lion this morning."

I forced a smile. "Just deep in thought."

My smile dropped as I noticed someone new in the room. A well-groomed woman of about thirty, dressed in a pale green skirt and jacket.

She certainly wasn't one of us. She looked far too refined and delicate to be involved in police work.

Ella turned to me, nursing a coffee. "That's Dr Ingrid Byrd. A profiler. She's supposed to be good."

"Haven't heard of her," I said.

"She's English," Ella told me. "Reminds me a bit of Mary Poppins. Like she knows things other people don't. She's a bit scary."

"She can be as scary as a clown in a dark alley if she gives us a clue," I remarked.

"Amen." Cameron grinned.

Grimshaw entered the room. She didn't look happy. "First things first," she said. "Has anyone seen the news this morning?"

I hadn't. I'd been busy all morning.

Grimshaw held up her tablet, with the screen turned to herself. "I'll read it out for you. *News just in. Detective Sergeant Kate Wakeland has been secretly rushed into Strikeforce Flying Fox. Speculation is growing that the police are now looking at the case as a matter of homicide. Fuelling the speculation is the fact that Wakeland is an experienced homicide detective and is also the maternal grandmother of one of the missing children, Ivy Wakeland. People are asking if the nature of the investigation has changed course. The lead detective of the strike force, Detective Sergeant Reagan Grimshaw, declined to comment.*"

Grimshaw gazed around the room. "Damned right I'm not talking with them right now. They can speculate on the bunion on my left foot if they like." Her gaze stopped on me. "How's *ground zero* working out so far?"

"Tabloid nonsense," I responded. "It's normal for homicide detectives to work on missing person cases like this one."

"Yes, but *they* don't know that," she told me. "They weren't supposed to know about you, yet. How'd they find out?"

"I have no idea," I said. "I've been way too busy. No one contacted me for a statement if that's what you're asking."

"Well, *I* was supposed to feed them the statement about you," she said. "But it's already got out. And now they're going at it like a dog on a bone." She scanned the room with a disappointed look on her face as if we were a class of naughty children. "Anyway, I'll deal with that later. I want to introduce you to a criminal profiler who has flown in especially for this case. Doctor Ingrid Byrd. Dr Byrd has extensive experience in missing person and trafficking cases."

Part of me wondered if Grimshaw had negotiated her services as a way of trying to push me lower in the pecking order. There'd been a lot of profilers engaged in the first two years of the investigation, but rarely in the past year as far as I knew.

Dr Byrd smiled at us. Ella was right—she was damned scary. Her smile didn't reach her eyes, which remained sharp and cool. And her smile itself looked a bit predatory. I made a guess that Dr Byrd was one of those profilers who enjoyed the chase—ferreting out the most likely kind of suspects—rather than genuinely being concerned about the fates of the victims.

"This is a highly unusual case," Dr Byrd began. "We have a person, or persons, who brazenly spirited away five children from under the noses of nursery school workers. And they've managed to keep themselves completely hidden from view. I'd assume a well-oiled operation. Perhaps someone paid good money for this kidnapping to happen. It would have to be people with the money to keep it all quiet."

Dr Byrd gazed around the room with a serene expression, as if her words were pearls. "The suspect would certainly have seen the media reports that called them daring and the mastermind of an almost impossible kidnapping. This sort of thing would be seen as high praise to some personality types. Certainly to narcissistic personality types. They would practically be champing at the bit to reveal themselves. And we do see many paedophiles boasting to others about their exploits, including posting photographs and video of their victims. But that *isn't* the case here. This person does not intend to be found out—ever. Which points to a highly sophisticated paedophile ring."

"You're thinking a paedophile ring?" said Grimshaw. "That's where our investigation has been heading. But nothing large or very sophisticated. That doesn't tend to happen in Australia."

"Well," said Dr Byrd, "I think you're on the right track. It's not an easy feat to traffic from Australia, being an island as you are. But that doesn't mean it's impossible. The children could also be trafficked within Australia. My view is that the children were most probably sold for a high price. And they are no longer alive. The person or group who wanted them desired extremely young children. Three-year-olds."

Ella cast a consoling eye my way.

"We're not thinking of anything too sophisticated," Grimshaw told her. "More of a garden-variety ring."

Dr Byrd shook her head. "This has the stamp of something much more than garden-variety."

Grimshaw wasn't looking as pleased as when she'd first introduced the profiler.

DS Liz Booth raised a hand in a casual way. "Why five children at once? We don't hear of this happening, right?"

"Quite," answered Dr Byrd. "Which is what leads me to believe this was extremely well planned. And there is always a first time for every sort of crime. Just because we haven't seen it before doesn't mean it can't happen."

I glanced from Liz to the profiler. "Why do you think the suspect targeted the preschooler picnic? What could have made them believe they'd get away with abducting children—one or more—from under the watch of three daycare workers?"

From this morning, my suspicions had fixed on that missing piece of time when Nola was standing at the top of the hill and the way in which she'd apparently zoned out.

Dr Byrd turned to me, tilting her head slightly and assuming a pleasant expression, like a teacher pretending to give consideration to her student's words. I guessed she had little faith in the skill of detectives to analyse crime scenes. Perhaps my age had something to do with it. She was young, and she looked hungry to prove herself. She probably thought I was stuck in the mud, approaching cases in the same way I'd approached them thirty-odd years ago.

Her lips parted a full second before she spoke. "You're the grandmother of Ivy Wakeland, correct?"

"Yes, I am."

"I'm very sorry for the loss of Ivy."

I wanted to point out that my family hadn't quite lost her *yet*, but that would sound deeply personal, which it was.

"Thank you," I said simply.

"Now, to your question," she said, "we've seen child abductions at supermarkets, parks, playgrounds, streets, hotels, and the child's own home. They've been taken under the watch of their mothers or other carers. Three-year-olds are easier than older children in that they have little ability to recognise stranger danger. They'll go with an adult who offers any sort of incentive—a treat or a puppy, or sometimes even if the adult just tells them to come with them. The reserve from which the five children were abducted had a distinct advantage in that there were no CCTV cameras. There were areas of bright sun and deep shade. The children were fast-moving targets, running between the areas of sun and shade. There were three teachers with a picnic to set out, and small slips of time in which none of them were looking directly at every child."

"So," I said, "you're saying that someone planned to abduct the children with razor-sharp precision, seeing as they only had seconds free at any one time in which to carry out their plan."

"Yes," she said. "Completely brazen. And they had the good fortune of one of the teachers being absent for a time, when she went to speak with the ice-cream van driver."

"You consider that to be a happy accident for the abductor?" I said.

"Yes, of course," came her swift reply.

Cameron cleared his throat. "We were originally thinking that the abductor was someone who knew the daycare routines. Like, a local who knew some of the kids."

The profiler wrinkled her nose as if Cameron's words had a vague unpleasant odour. "Unlikely. I mean to say, they might have studied the routines, and I think they certainly did so. But I'm seeing an outsider being the perpetrator. Someone involved in a large paedophile ring, as I said. As far as I understand, none of the people who have any involvement with the nursery school, nor their friends and family, have been shown to have any such connections—am I correct?"

"That's correct," Grimshaw broke in. "We've had three years to rake over the histories of hundreds of people. But I'm uncertain about a large operation. Our strongest suspects are Mr Brent Cole, the ice-cream van driver, and a Mr Anthony Pellam, who was visiting the hospice at the time."

"What do you think about Brent Cole?" DS Liz Booth asked the profiler, tucking in a shirt that had half-spilled out of her pants. "He was there at the scene, he was an outsider, he had a vehicle large enough to fit five kids, and he had the best incentive he could possibly have—ice-cream."

The profiler pursed her lips. "The question is, if it was him, what did he do with the children? He turned up at his next gig straight after parking at the reserve, right? He would have needed to offload the kids to a secure, locked place or a third party. But CCTV footage of his passage through the streets lined up with his version of events and timeline, yes?"

Grimshaw nodded. "But it wouldn't take long to have off-loaded the kids if he had help. Mere seconds. And a button belonging to one of the missing kids was found on the hill, which means they almost certainly ran up towards his van."

"If he has connections to some big players, he's hiding it incredibly well," said Dr Byrd carefully. "If he's received money, there's no evidence of it, am I correct? He's living in a very modest house, living a very modest life?"

Grimshaw squared her shoulders. "Inspector Zimmerman and I floated the possibility that he was being paid in other ways, such as sexual access to a number of the children that these players have."

"Hmmm," said Dr Byrd. "There's a possibility there. Except that he's perhaps not the type that sophisticated players would place their trust in."

I spoke up. "I was at Brent Cole's house this morning. I interviewed him. I'd be extremely surprised if he ended up having anything to do with this."

Grimshaw and Byrd looked across to me with dubious expressions.

"He's had a lot of time to practice his spiel," said Grimshaw dismissively. "The man was a petty criminal in his teenage years. He's not the innocent he pretends to be. You weren't at the initial interviews and I don't think you've even watched the tapes yet."

I was about to point out that I hadn't been allowed access to the tapes until just days ago, but I chose to remain silent.

The children had become drops in a vast, dark ocean.

If this was the doing of a large operation, then Nola's odd behaviour meant nothing.

But I couldn't let it go.

17

KATE

A call came through to Grimshaw while the strike force meeting was still in full swing. A bushwalker had found possible gravesites near Katoomba Cascades.

Gravesites.

Grimshaw blurted out the news.

The breakfast of scrambled eggs that I'd had between Brent Cole's house and the strike force meeting soured in my stomach.

"Okay, I'll get Booth, Vella and Wakeland to go check it out," Grimshaw told us. "Forensics has already been sent."

Cameron, Liz, and I travelled in the same car to the location—Liz driving. My spine remained chilled all the way. None of us had any idea what to expect.

The spot was easy to get to, and possibly an ideal spot for someone who wanted to bury something. You could drive right up to a parking spot near the top of the cascades. There were a steep set of stone steps down to the bottom of the cascades, but it only took a minute or so. They would have to have chosen a time after the tourists had all disappeared though. Katoomba Cascades was very popular— the falls were small but scenic, with a shallow, natural splash pool at the bottom. A wooden boardwalk led from the falls through a sub-tropical rainforest.

Liz parked, and we raced down past the cascades to the boardwalk. My heart was pumping. In the small chance that what the bushwalker had found were actually the gravesites of the children, I wanted to be there. I especially wanted to be there at the moment that the sites were uncovered. In respect for Ivy.

The spot was off the boardwalk, along a thin dirt track.

My heart fell when I saw the sites for myself. Four, possibly five, suspicious mounds rose from the soil. Moss and small ferns and wild grasses were growing on the mounds.

Three forensic officers were taking careful photographs and collecting soil samples.

"How were these found?" I asked Luke Miller, a member of the forensic services group.

"A bushwalker following an echidna," Luke told me. "Trying to video it, I think. She lost sight of it, tried to find it again. Then she found these."

"How old do you think they are?" My voice had gone hoarse.

"Ah..." Luke looked up between taking shots of the mounds. "Between two and four years. We're not sure."

I nodded silently, my stomach turning.

My back jarred as I heard the first strike of a spade on hard dirt. The digging had begun.

I watched as soil was removed from the first mound.

"I've got bone," one of the forensics group people said.

My hand flew to my mouth, unguarded, my breath hot on the back of my hand.

Everyone stood in anticipation, all conversation stopped still. Every dig in which bone was found was like this. That moment before the reveal. The reveal could change everything in an instant or confirm what we already knew. For me, it was highly personal.

Luke scooped the soil away.

Enough of the skeleton was exposed to see the skull and ribcage.

Not a human skeleton.

I wanted to scream out loud. The tightness released from my chest and I could breathe again.

"A dog, most likely," said Cameron, squinting at the skeleton.

In quick succession, the other gravesites were dug.

Four large dogs. I guessed that the dogs had starved to death, and the owners hadn't wanted the evidence anywhere on their property.

"Get animal welfare on the line," said Luke. "They can take it from here and see if they want to investigate."

———

Liz, Cameron and I headed back to the station. I went straight home for a shower from there. My sense of relief at the dig not uncovering any human skeletons was overcome by a sense of dirt and decay. Any site dig tended to do that to me. I'd seen far too many human remains recovered from shallow graves—or from beneath a panicked pile of leaves and twigs—not to be reminded of those digs. Today had brought no certainty that the children hadn't befallen a fate just like that. And Dr Ingrid Byrd's words still hung heavily in my mind.

Abby turned up at the house while I was showering. I found her downstairs in the kitchen, feeding Jasper a bottle. Pete was out. I loved that Abby was here again, but it wasn't the best time. I felt raw.

"What's going on?" Abby asked. "You look wrecked."

I hesitated. I didn't want to tell her. But today's dig would find its way into the news. Grimshaw would make sure of it. A dig would make it look like the strike force was doing *something*.

"Some dogs were found out in the bush—near Katoomba Cascades. They'd been buried."

"Why would you go out there for *that?*" Her brow crinkled as she realised. "Oh..."

"No one thought it would amount to anything," I said breezily. "What we thought is what we got."

"Poor dogs." She patted Jasper on his back.

"Yes. I hate to think how that happened. Perhaps the owners went off on a long holiday and just didn't bother about the dogs."

Abby surveyed me with her large eyes. "Mum... is there anything you know that you're not telling me? I mean, do the police know things they're not telling the public?"

"Oh, honey, not anything of importance. Seriously, they don't."

"We're never going to find out, are we? Twenty years will go by and Jasper will be grown up, and we still won't know. Like some of those cold cases you used to work on."

"You know too much to lie to you. You're a detective's daughter. It's true, sometimes we never find out. But I'm doing my best to make sure we do. I swear to you, there's nothing I won't do to find her."

Jasper fell asleep with the bottle in his mouth. Abby bent her forehead down to his, tears streaming down her cheeks.

I wished I had some kind of resolution to give her. At the same time, even though the most likely resolution was something very similar to today's dig, my mind turned away from it.

To find gravesites of the children would give a resolution, but it wouldn't give any real peace.

18

KATE

I ate an early dinner with Pete and Abby, while Jasper slept in Ivy's old pop-up cot.

It was nice, a small window into how life could have been if Ivy and the children had never gone missing. Not that things between Abby and I had been perfect, but perhaps they would have smoothed out over the years. For now, I just enjoyed her company.

As soon as dinner was done though, Abby left. Her boyfriend was waiting for her again in the park behind our house. She'd walk through the back garden and out the gate to the park. The young man always stayed at a distance.

I checked my phone. Nola Hobson hadn't answered the text message I'd sent her earlier today. I wanted to talk to her again. According to my notes, she was working tonight at the pizza restaurant. I sat down at my desk to do some quick research on her. Her family background was very fractured.

Grimshaw had only given me a week to complete my own investigations. It wasn't much time. I decided to drive over to the pizza restaurant and chat to Nola.

Dropping a kiss on Pete's forehead, I told him I wouldn't be long. He was sitting in front of the TV, switching channels.

He grimaced. "You have to quit your working day sometime. It can't have been an easy day, with the dig and everything."

I sighed. "It wasn't."

"Stay. Watch a movie with me."

"Nola's a hard girl to catch up with. There's a couple of things I need to ask her."

"Okay. I'll try not to eat all the tiramisu."

"We have tiramisu?"

"I picked it up on my way home. I would have offered some to Abby, but she rushed off." He shrugged. "More for us. Correction. More for me, since I'm going to be alone in the house. You know, with the tiramisu."

"Wait until I get back."

He grinned. "We'll see what happens."

"I hate you."

"You love me."

I shot him a cheesy smile.

―――――

The wind had picked up as I stepped from the car near the pizzeria. I rewrapped my scarf to cover my ears. Gusts of wind followed me inside.

Beyond the signage and front counter, I had a view of about twenty people preparing dough and chopping vegetables.

Nola was rolling dough. She had a younger girl looking on who she seemed to be instructing.

I'd been in here a few times before, but not in recent years. The pizza options had become numerous. Everything from gourmet to gluten-free and keto options. The bases ranged from traditional white flour to coconut, cauliflower and sprouted grain.

A young man of about thirty-five approached me at the counter, his frizzy hair scooped off his face in a top knot. He raised his eyebrows attentively. "Can I help you? We're not actually open to customers for another twenty minutes."

"I'm Detective Sergeant Kate Wakeland. I'd like a word with Nola, if that's possible?"

"Nola? No problem. I'm the manager here. You can take my office, if you like."

"That would be great, thank you."

Opening a flip-up section on the counter, he let me through.

When Nola caught sight of me, I thought I detected a slight look of guilt.

"Nola, the detective would like to talk with you," the young man said. "I told her you two could have my office."

Nola dusted her hands free of flour. "Oh. Of course." She glanced from the girl beside her to the manager. "But the dough...?"

"I'll take over the dough prep and training Leah," he offered.

"Okay." Looking decidedly worried now, Nola walked away with the manager and me. He showed us to the door and then strode away back to the food preparation area.

I closed the door after Nola and I were inside. The office was boxy and cramped, with three chairs placed randomly in front of a desk.

Nola was still wearing her frown as she sat. "I hope the manager doesn't think I'm trouble and fires me."

"He can't fire you because of me speaking to you. If you have any problems with him, talk to me, okay?"

She exhaled. "Do you have more questions for me?"

"Did you get my message?"

"Yes... I did. But I've been busy."

"It's best to answer my messages and let me know when it's a good time to talk. Otherwise we end up with this sort of thing." I gestured loosely at the office interior.

She twisted the ring she wore on her middle finger. "Yes. Sorry."

I softened my voice. "I'd like to show you a clip, and then I want to ask a question. It won't take long."

She frowned again. "What of?"

"It's a re-enactment of the scene from the day the kids went missing. The police had actors from the local theatre put it together. Years ago. I saved it to my tablet yesterday. It was just used for the police, so that they had a visual of what happened. My understanding is that you haven't seen it?"

She shook her head.

"Okay, are you okay to view it?"

"Yes," she said somewhat reluctantly.

Switching on my tablet, I browsed to the relevant clip and then turned the screen around to her.

Tinkling music began to play as an ice-cream van came along the street at *The Ponds*. Small children played on the grass. The driver parked the van. Two nursery school teachers were spreading out picnic rugs. Music blared from the van as a woman walked up the hill. Brent Cole had allowed the use of his van for the re-enactment. The woman stood at the top of the hill, in front of the van.

I kept my eyes on Nola as she watched the footage. Her skin blanched, and her body skewed away. She bent her head, shoulders trembling.

Something about the video had affected her terribly, but I didn't know what. I hadn't expected that reaction.

I stopped the video there. "Nola, what's wrong?"

"Nothing... It just brings it all back, that's all."

She was lying. I had to try to find out what was worrying her.

"Did the scene look correct to you?" I asked.

She nodded without looking up. "Yes, that's exactly what happened." A tremor ran through her voice.

"Yesterday morning, I went to see Brent Cole. He said something a little different to what you told me," I pressed.

"He did?"

"He said that he ate his entire lunch while you were standing there watching him."

She kept her eyes fixed downward. "Why would I do that?"

"I don't know."

"I'm going to play the clip again. But what it doesn't show is the amount of time you spent on the hill. I want you to fill that space of time in for me. Okay?"

I felt terrible as I tapped *play* on the tablet screen. The girl was in distress. But if I let it go now, next time I came back to her she might have steeled herself. There was something she knew but hadn't told anyone.

I barely breathed as the carnival music of the ice-cream van played again.

Nola shook her head, her hands curling into tight fists in her lap. "Turn it off... please. Turn it off."

I glanced at the screen. What part of the re-enactment was disturbing Nola so much? What was she seeing?

When I raised my eyes to her, she was no longer protesting. She was sitting calmly. But her eyes were unfocused and her hands still in fists.

I stopped the clip. "Nola," I called gently. "Nola?"

She didn't respond immediately. She swallowed, blinking, her breaths rapid.

If this had been any other case, would I have pushed Nola so hard? I couldn't answer that. I didn't know. I was so desperate for answers that I wanted to discover what Nola knew, right now. If I'd crossed the line, I'd have to deal with that later.

Nola began twisting her ring to and fro. "Can I go now?"

I kept my voice soft. "I'm not sure that you're in any state to go back out there right now."

"I'll lose my job."

"No, you won't. I'll make sure of that. Nola, can you please tell me what you saw in that clip that made you so upset? Whatever it is, you can tell me."

I couldn't promise though that no action would be taken against her. What had she done?

"It's that music," she said quietly.

"The ice-cream van?" I asked in surprise.

"Yes."

I knew that the music played by the van was *Greensleeves*. When I was a child, that droning tune had been somehow magical, one of the familiar sounds of summer. It had been a signal for us children to drop our scooters and bicycles in the street and charge inside to beg our mothers for money. But it obviously wasn't like that for Nola.

"Nola, do you mind if I record your explanation?"

She shook her head.

"Okay." I switched on the record function on the tablet. "Nola, I have to repeat what I just said. Before you tell me more, I'm asking for your consent to record you. It'll form part of the official police files on the case and could be used in a court of law. Do you understand?"

"Yes," she replied.

"Now, you just told me that you didn't like the tune that the ice-cream van was playing?" I said. "Is that correct?"

"Yes."

"Brent Cole says that you stood still, watching him, while he ate his lunch. Is that correct?"

"No... I don't know. I wasn't watching him."

"What were you watching?"

"Nothing. I just... don't like the tune. I didn't want him there. I wanted him to go." Her voice intensified.

"Why did you want him to go so badly?"

She went quiet for a moment before saying. "It reminds me of a time that I don't want to go back to."

"Can you tell me about that?"

"My childhood."

This had gone somewhere unexpected. I wasn't sure whether to keep pursuing the questions or not. But I'd gone as far as to record the interview. I decided to keep going.

"So, the tune reminded you of your childhood?" I asked.

"Yes."

"Can I ask what it was that made you dislike the Greensleeves tune?"

She kept twisting the ring around and around. "I spent most of my childhood alone, even at school. I didn't have friends. My mum and my stepdad—Russell—worked long hours. I was at home alone every afternoon and even most weekends. I'd hear the ice-cream van go past, but I wasn't allowed outside."

"Sounds rough," I said. "And that's the reason why you have the reaction to the music that you do?"

"There's more," she told me, her voice straining. "Russell lost his job. He'd turned up drunk at work. Both he and mum were heavy drinkers and smokers."

She began trembling again.

"Nola, should I stop here? Maybe we need a counsellor, or—?"

She shook her head. "I think I should tell...."

"Okay."

"That's when the photographs started."

"Photographs?"

"I was made to do nude pictures."

"Oh, Nola...."

She looked at me with eyes framed with wet eyelashes. I wanted to hug her. If my job allowed it and the recorder hadn't been running, I would have.

"I was twelve, the first time I had to do it. It wasn't just... me. I was made to take the photographs with a man I didn't know. While the pictures were being taken... the ice-cream van went past. It stopped outside the house... I could hear children running to it, shouting to each other... having fun."

"That's horrific. Just... horrific. Does anyone else know?"

She shook her head, exhaling an unsteady breath. "You're the first person I've ever told that to."

"I'm so, so sorry that happened to you."

"The pictures got put online." Her left shoulder jerked. "Online, for other people to see. They were sold."

"My God. Look, we can track down the images and have them removed. And have Russell charged with a number of offences."

"Russell?" She stared at me in confusion. "No, it wasn't him. It was my mother. She was worried he'd leave her because there wasn't enough money. Every time she made me do it, Russell was down at the pub. He didn't know anything about it."

"I'm sorry. I jumped in too soon with assumptions," I told her. "Can I ask why you haven't told anyone?"

"Because if I told, then everyone would know about the photos and what I was made to do. I couldn't bear it."

"How long did this go on for?"

"Three years, give or take. I was fifteen when I worked up the courage to leave. I went to live in a share house with other teens, while I finished high school. I've never spoken to my mother since I left. She's an alcoholic who does nothing but drink."

"We can have her charged. I'll support you all the way. I work with a child protection officer, Detective Liz Booth. She can help you."

"There is *nothing* that can help me. It already happened. No one was around to help me back then. No one ever asked if I was okay."

"I'm so sorry about that. But it still matters."

"No, I don't want to."

"Your mother is Adele Hobson right?"

"Yeah, that's her. I see you've been digging into my family history."

"Yes, I did that before I came today. As far as I'm aware, she's been arrested a few times for being drunk and disorderly. Your grandparents have all died and you have no siblings, leaving Adele as the only family you have."

"Great family I have, right?"

I gave her a sad smile. "We can't choose the family we're born into."

I tapped the video recording to *off* and put the tablet on my lap.

"Nola... I know it's been a long time since that period of your life. But I know a couple of really good psychologists, and I think it could be worth it, you know, to talk this out."

"No, I want to leave it behind."

"But *have* you? I don't think so."

"Yes, I'm fine. Everything's good now. I've got the two jobs, and I'm making enough money. And I've got Bryce, my boyfriend. He makes me feel like I'm someone."

Not for the first time, I felt a maternal twinge for this girl. "You *are* someone. With or without a boyfriend."

"Yeah, I guess. But with him, I can see a future, and I could never see that before."

"I'll let this go for now, but I'm going to come back to you. I feel responsible now. I've made you tell me something very personal."

She inhaled a sharp breath. "Nothing's going to happen now, is it, now that I've told you? About the photos?"

"I'll have to tell the strike force about your lapse in concentration when you were on the hill. And I'll have to tell them it was because of the music. But I won't tell them why, okay?"

She nodded.

"It might help the child protection squad if they knew who you were," I added. "If those photos are out there, they've probably seen them. But they wouldn't have been able to discover the identity of the child. You could help close your case. It's up to you though."

"I really don't want to. It's done. It's over. I'd better get back to work."

I stood. "Stay here, I'm going to fetch you a drink. I'll think of an explanation to tell your boss. He seems like a good guy. I think you need a few minutes before you get back to work."

At first, she looked like she was going to protest, but then she nodded.

It was the least I could do.

19

KATE

Driving to the police station, I thought about all that Nola had told me. She must have been standing on the hill that day in a kind of daze, deep in terrible memories of her childhood.

At the station, I copied the interview with Nola onto secure storage. I called Liz Booth first and then Grimshaw.

The three of us held a late meeting at the station. I showed them the recording, and together we agreed on how much information would be made available to the public. I ensured that Nola's confidence about the awful films that had been taken of her wouldn't be betrayed. Nola deserved not to be traumatised further.

Grimshaw called her media contact, and a brief statement went out.

I got home in time to watch half a movie with Pete, eat a bowl of tiramisu, and then fall asleep on the couch.

When morning came, I felt like I'd barely slept, my mind racing and my body heavy. I was still on the couch, with a pillow under my head and a thick blanket tucked around me. And a smear of tiramisu on my chin.

The pillow and blanket were Pete. The tiramisu was me.

I found Pete working out in our gym.

I wolf-whistled. "Looking good."

Grinning, he set down his dumbbells. "Got yourself a good sleep?"

"Yeah," I lied.

"I didn't want to wake you to go upstairs. You seemed to be in a deep sleep."

"Was I snoring?"

"Maybe."

I groaned. "Sexyyyy."

He laughed. "Lori Hinton called earlier."

"Oh?"

"She invited you to a gathering tonight. She said it might be good for everyone to catch up again seeing as you're now on the strike force. And... because of Nola's statement in the news."

A sigh gathered up deeply inside me. "That's in the news already?"

"Yeah."

"Poor Nola."

"Sounds like a difficult conversation you had with her last night."

"It was. I'll tell you soon. I'm just... very wrung out."

"Maybe you should skip the gathering tonight?"

"You're right. They could stampede me for information. On the other hand, I wanted to chat with them all individually. Maybe this might not be so bad. I could knock it out of the way in one night."

"You sure you want to take this on? You've been working a lot of late nights."

"Grimshaw isn't giving me much time to get through all the interviews and catch ups. So, I shouldn't turn this down. Is it at Lori's?"

"She said it was at Penny Foster's. Six sharp."

"Got it."

"I'll miss you at dinner." Pete looked genuinely sad. I'd have to make all this up with him soon.

I smiled. "I'll miss you, too."

"Lori said to tell Abby about tonight."

"I don't think she'll go."

"No, me either."

——————

I spent the morning at the station, working on the Harper Rawlings case, sitting down with Franco and working out a list of questions we wanted the hypnotherapist to ask Indira Basak.

In the afternoon, Franco and I were called to a new homicide case—an elderly woman murdered in her own home. She'd been suffocated from the gas pouring from an unlit stovetop, the doors to the kitchen locked from the outside and the old lady helpless in her wheelchair. It ended up being a murder suicide. Franco and I found her husband dead in the garage. The husband had shot himself.

Franco and I weren't sure if the murder had been some sort of act of mercy or a cold killing. We'd have to piece everything together over the coming weeks, after the reports came in from the autopsies. The couple's adult children would be waiting on us to prepare our report for the coroner. They'd be in shock and wanting answers. I knew two of them—that kind of thing came from living in a small town.

As the sun was setting, I walked into Tallman's Valley Hospice. The sunset had made the lake blush a deep pink.

The dementia ward patient, Harry Grenville, was watching the birds fly over the pink lake with his trusty binoculars.

Mum was outside in her wheelchair. I tried to banish from my mind the sight of the murdered, wheelchair-bound woman I'd seen earlier today. This job brought so many awful images with it. The only way to survive was to set those images aside and try not to dwell on them.

Mum was listening to music with an iPod and earplugs. She handed me one of her ear plugs, and I listened to Neil Diamond's *Sweet Caroline* with her. She was a big fan of Diamond's.

Her smile broadened as I listened.

Suddenly, it got too much. The sight of the setting sun and the sound of some of Mum's favourite music somehow mixed together to produce a sadness that caught my breath. Something within me rebelled against this long goodbye of the past months. I desperately wanted her to *stay*.

Tears pricked my eye and I had to turn my head.

She reached for my hand and squeezed it. She started singing the lyrics of the song in a low voice.

I knew she was silently trying to tell me life was good for her, that it had been good and was still good.

Nodding my head, I began humming and then singing the words along with her, my face tear-stained and voice croaky. I'd normally feel self-conscious singing out loud—I couldn't carry a tune to save my life. But there was no time left to feel self-conscious. No time at all for that.

Soon, we were both belting out the lyrics to *Sweet Caroline* to the ducks and swans on the lake, listening to Diamond's throaty voice.

My mum and Harry were the only patients still left outside. They weren't going to let a good sunset go to waste.

I drove up the long mountain road to Penny Foster's house, through a world that was almost completely dark. Beyond her house, the mountains were encased in a dark twilight and barely discernible. I parked and hiked up her steep driveway.

As Pete and I had predicted, Abby chose not to come to the gathering tonight.

The open curtains gave me a view into a cosy living room, an orange glow emanating from the fireplace. Men and women sat on chairs in a circle, all holding hands. If I didn't know better, I would have thought I was arriving at a seance. But I knew better, and this was no seance.

The group of parents had been gathering once a week for the first year after their children vanished. Abby used to attend the gatherings in the beginning, before she'd sunk too far into depression and cut herself off from everyone. I'd been to a few gatherings myself, but I'd ended up feeling weighed down by a dual burden—I was not only the grandmother of a missing child but a detective. Sometimes the parents would speak negatively of the way the case was being handled by police, and then they'd glance with apologetic expressions in my direction.

After that first year, the group's gatherings had become spaced further and further apart. The disbelief and anguish at the utter dearth of information about what happened to the children had pushed the parents to the brink.

The gatherings were usually held in Penny's or Lori's home because they had no other children. Penny and Lori found it too hard to be around the laughter and play of children when their own homes no longer had those things.

I rapped lightly on Penny's door.

Penny answered, her chalky, drawn face free of makeup and her hair back in a low ponytail. "Kate. Come in. We're all so grateful you could make it tonight."

Inside the open plan space, all faces turned to me. The dining room table was dressed in a formal white cloth, with a variety of cakes and finger food on top.

I spent the next five minutes greeting everyone by name and asking how they and their families were. Even though everyone spoke in a light manner, the tension in the air was palpable. I knew they wanted to know what I'd been doing since joining the strike force, and how I intended approaching the investigation.

It was Lori who started with the questions. When I'd first met her three and a half years earlier, she'd seemed to be the unofficial spokesperson for the group, and that hadn't changed.

"We read about Nola," Lori said. "What does it mean that she was distracted? Could our children have made their way up the hill without her seeing them, after all?"

I took a breath. They wanted answers, but I had none yet. "With this new information, we're currently reworking our scenarios and trying to see if that is a possibility," I told them.

"Why didn't Nola tell us this in the first place?" asked Penny, sounding bewildered.

"I think the news article could have been clearer," I answered. "Nola didn't even realise that she became distracted. The Greensleeves tune has a connection to things from her past. She had a mind slip."

Lori frowned deeply. "I hope you're not protecting her, Kate."

I shook my head. "It's not like that at all. To protect Nola's privacy, I can't tell you what that tune means to her, but it is a genuine issue. It's all on the official police record."

Nick posed his fingers beneath his chin. "So, there *is* a small chance our kids might have run up that hill and into a waiting vehicle. If Mr Cole had already driven away by that point, it could have been a different car. We were relying on Nola's testimony that there'd been no other cars, correct? But now we know she had a mind slip."

"Or," put in Roxanne, glancing at her husband, "it was that bloody Brent Cole who snatched our kids, after all." She gave a determined nod, glancing around at the group for confirmation.

Everyone looked at me expectantly.

"Let's not forget," I said carefully, "that the children would have needed to get past two teachers in order to get up the hill."

Roxanne let out an anxious sigh. "Well, those teachers *were* distracted long enough to allow our children to get abducted."

Lori reached for Roxanne's arm, giving it a squeeze. "I hate to say this, but it sounds to me like the teachers were all trying to save themselves. We don't know how much of anything they told us from that day is actually true."

"Too right." Roxanne drummed her fingers on the table as if she'd just cracked the case. "They would of been trying to save their necks. So, what we've got here is three teachers lying their bloody faces off. And Brent Cole back in the prime spot as the kidnapper."

The floodgates had opened. I'd prepared myself for this, but I hadn't quite been prepared for how intense it would be. I had to admit that in my detective role, I'd known people to tell outrageous lies in order to save their jobs.

Wherever the truth sat, I knew one thing—Nola hadn't been putting on an act when I'd interviewed her last.

"We don't know if this latest information will make any difference to the case," I responded. "All I can tell you is that we're reworking the timelines. And we'll see if that brings us to any new perspectives."

Nick put his arm around his wife, Marcy, who'd begun to cry. "We'd appreciate you keeping us in the loop. You can do that now that you're part of the strike force, right?"

"Yes," I told him. "I can do that, now."

The room went quiet. Most of the parents had wet eyes or looked as if they were just holding it together. The strain was apparent on every face. Over three years had passed, but their desire to have their children back hadn't diminished.

"I promise all of you," I said, "that I'm going to turn over every damned stone I can find. Remember, this is personal to me, too." Tears wet my own eyes. "To that end, I'd like to touch base with each of you. As terrible as it is to think, there might be someone in your wider circles who knows something about our missing kids. I know that you've been through this before, years ago. But I think we need to revisit that. Is everyone okay with some questions?"

To my relief, everyone agreed without hesitation.

Penny showed me to a small second living area at the back of her house. I'd be questioning the parents here.

I started with Nick and Marcy Parrish first. Their circle was very small. They had no family here, and at the time of the abduction, they hadn't yet had time to make any close friends. Still, I took down details of every person they'd worked with or had any kind of contact with.

Lori Hinton came to speak with me next. She perched on the sofa next to me, closer than I found comfortable.

I edged away from her a little, under the pretext of finding a good angle to sit and write down notes. "Your husband's not here tonight?" I asked her.

A bitter look visited her eyes. "We separated. The strain of everything, you know? Although, it's true to say that *I* stayed a lot stronger than *he* did."

"I'm sorry. A separation would be difficult on top of everything else."

"Well, Sean ended up *on top of* another woman. So, there's *that*."

"Oh. That's not good." I kept my reaction understated.

"I tell you, I don't know how he could go thinking of himself and his *you know what* when our daughter is missing. But that's exactly what he did."

I steered the conversation away from Sean, to people that Lori knew who might have known of the nursery school routines, and anything strange that she might have noticed in the past three years.

"I can't think of anything odd," she told me. "But then I'm so busy with work that I might miss some things. My job has long hours and I get sent away on work trips a lot."

"You're a systems analyst for a tech company, right?"

She nodded. "That's right. I evaluate workflow solutions. To help things flow smoothly between the programmers and management, and things like that."

I sat and talked with her for a while longer, trying to ferret out any information about the people she worked with that might be useful. Thanking her for her time, I asked her to send Penny in.

Under the harsher light of this room, Penny's face looked even more pallid. She dabbed at the moisture in her eyes with a tissue.

"How are you?" I asked her.

"I always find the gatherings difficult," she admitted. "But I'm doing the best I can. I haven't been well. I have a stress-induced illness and I'm basically sick all the time."

"I'm sorry to hear that. Are you still working?"

"Yes, I'm lucky enough to have an understanding boss that lets me off on doctors' appointments and things."

"Do you have any support around you? Any family here?"

"Not really. I've got a few who I never see. My husband and I are divorced, as you know. He moved away. I don't have a relationship with my mother. We've never been close. I haven't seen her in forever." Penny gave a sad shrug.

I couldn't help but think of myself and Abby. We hadn't been close for a long time. Would Abby end up like Penny, in her thirties and not having seen her mother *in forever?* The thought made an icicle lodge in my chest.

That really could happen if Abby chose to move away. And I'd never see baby Jasper grow up.

I squeezed my eyes shut and then blinked them open again. *Stay on task*, I reminded myself.

"Okay," I said. "So, your job... Are you still working at the baby goods store at Close Quarters?" I'd seen her in there a few times back when I'd bought Ivy things when she was a baby. Penny had shown me through the bewildering ranges of prams, cots and baby cams.

"Yes. Still there," Penny replied. "My focus is on merchandising, setting up displays and that sort of thing."

"Sounds interesting."

"It used to be. It's just a job for me now. I go in, do what I have to, and come home again."

I spoke with her at length, asking if she'd noticed any odd behaviour from the people she knew. She hadn't but promised to keep me informed if she did.

I moved onto Rhys and Roxanne and Crane next.

The Cranes sat before me. They didn't sit close together like the Parrishes had. I didn't get a sense of easy intimacy between them. Rhys was a thin guy, his beard accentuating the length of his face. Roxanne, in contrast, was solid and well-toned. She wore artificial eyelashes and bright lipstick and was wearing a lot of dark contouring on her face.

"How are you both?" I asked and immediately knew that was the wrong question to lead with.

"We're sick and tired of getting the run around from the cops, that's how we are," answered Rhys. "I've had a gutful. Three years. They haven't found out a thing. Not a damned thing."

Roxanne pressed her lips together hard. "What are the police even doing? Not much, that's what. It's not possible for five kids to just vanish into thin air."

"That's what I'm trying to discover," I told them. I took a quick breath, not leaving enough time for them to air more complaints. "Now, can I ask where each of you were working at the time of the abductions?"

"I was working in a shoe shop then," answered Rhys. "I'm a baker now.

Roxy was a stay-at-home-mum then. She's started up as a gym instructor now."

"Yeah, I'm about to open my own studio," Roxanne told me, with a hint of pride in her voice. "You should come along and do a class sometime." She tilted her head as she appeared to size me up. "We could probably start you on the Tuesday class, for people who are new to aerobics. We'll have one for people your age."

"Sounds... yeah, that's great," I said politely, taking the business card she handed me. I crumbled it as I pushed it into the back pocket of my jeans.

I proceeded to ask the Cranes the same questions about their circles of friends and family that I'd asked Lori, Penny and the Parrishes. Unlike the others, the Cranes had a long list of people they thought were suspicious. It seemed that the pair had deep trust issues when it came to other people. The number of people who had crossed them in some way was extensive.

"Excuse me," I said, "I need to go grab a glass of water. I'll be right back." The couple were starting to give me a headache.

I headed down the hallway that led back to the large living room and kitchen.

A snatch of conversation reached my ears. It was coming from one of the bedrooms—a bathroom most likely, going by the acoustics.

"Yes, she's here tonight", came the voice. *"She's asking lots of questions."*

I stopped still in the hallway, listening. That was Lori's voice. And was she talking about me? *I* was the one asking questions. Who was she talking to? Her ex-husband?

"No, she's not telling us anything new. Not anything more than what's in the media," she said. *"No, I can't meet up with you later. Look, this is all getting a bit heavy-handed."*

I was certain now she was talking about me. I tried to hear more, but her voice was muffled now. Perhaps she realised she'd been speaking a touch too loudly.

As I continued onto the kitchen to fetch myself a glass of water, an uneasy sense crept over me. Lori had seemed upset, almost aggravated.

What was going on with her?

And if it wasn't her ex-husband Sean she'd been having the conversation with, then who was it?

A little niggle started up in my mind.

Penny called everyone for dinner. I'd have to think more about Lori's conversation later—and finish interviewing the Cranes, something I wasn't looking forward to.

20

PENNY FOSTER

Penny browsed the racks of specials at the clothing store at Katoomba. She liked the old, eclectic shops here. So different to the trendy vibe of Tallman's Valley or the chain store offerings of the large department stores in Sydney.

Ordinarily, she bought the upmarket end-of-season clothing and stored them away for the following summer or winter. Her clothing needed to look smart and professional, but it wasn't so important to look fashionable. She worked at a baby store, after all.

She used to buy Max's clothing here as well. No one could say he hadn't been well-dressed, because he had. He'd stood out for having clothing that matched well, unlike a lot of the kids in the area that ran about in old track pants and stretched T-shirts.

Now and then, someone would glance her way. Penny knew that they'd recognised her. Some of those glances turned into sympathetic expressions. But most people turned their heads. Penny hadn't bothered with makeup or doing much with her hair today. She probably scared people.

She pulled her coat in tight, re-tying the soft belt. Looking through a rack of women's clothing on special, she picked out a white cardigan with round, pearl-like buttons. The wool was beautifully soft, and the buttons had a lovely lustre. She liked clothing that was either white or grey. Those colours felt clean and neutral to her. They were colours that would have her go unnoticed in most settings. As much as she liked nice clothing, she disliked standing out.

From the corner of her eye, she noticed a woman who was rustling through the clothing racks with gusto. Roxanne Crane, dressed in her usual gym gear, with her fake winter tan and ponytail extension that resembled a horse's mane.

Penny felt her chest immediately tighten. She didn't feel like talking with anyone today. Especially not Roxanne. Roxanne could be so over-the-top with her washboard abs and rah-rah fitness advice. Penny couldn't stand her.

But how could she escape? She was between the specials rack and the wall, feeling like a trapped rat.

Perhaps she wouldn't be noticed.

Roxanne was snapping up the specials, with piles of clothing already in her trolley. And she was hunting for more—a warrior out looking for animals to spear.

Roxanne seemed to sense she was being watched. As if by instinct, her head swivelled in Penny's direction. "Penny!" She hurried over. "There you are."

"I'm not well," Penny told her, immediately putting up her guard.

"Awww. I know heaps of people have been coming down with the flu. They say there's loads of strains of it about, and—"

"It's not the flu, Roxanne."

She looked confused, as if it couldn't possibly be anything else. Then she blinked. "Oh. Something to do with last night, yeah? That was intense. You could of cut the air with a knife."

"Yes, you could have," Penny agreed. "I don't even know how I got through it."

"We've all been through the absolute wringer. I know exactly how you feel."

Penny's back went rigid and words boiled inside her. But she restrained herself and spoke in a controlled voice. "You can't possibly know exactly how I feel."

"Of course I do. I been through the same as you, you know."

"But you still *have* children. You're still a mother."

Roxanne recoiled as if a large insect had stung her on the neck. "I lost a kid though. You can't take that away from me. I'm the mother of a missing child."

Penny stared at her. "I didn't realise that was a title you wanted to keep."

"Now, that's unfair."

"Unfair? Look at you, with your trolley full of children's clothes and your house filled with your children and husband."

"You don't know anything about my life. All I can say is, life isn't easy for anyone."

"Well, whatever your problems are, I wish I had *those* kinds of problems," Penny snapped. "I really do. I wish I were here buying a child of mine new clothes."

Penny rushed away, leaving Roxanne standing there like a mannequin in a fitness store.

People looked away sharply as she fled down the aisles. They'd overheard the exchange but were pretending not to. *Good.* Perhaps people needed to know how terrible things were for her. There had been endless news stories about the relentless Kate Wakeland and her new position on Strikeforce Flying Fox and all the speculation about her being Ivy's grandmother. Perhaps people needed to remember what this was truly all about.

She headed out into the biting wind. The cold inside her was worse. Her bones were frozen, blood iced, internal organs barely alive.

She'd planned on heading straight home, but she couldn't go back there now. Not to her empty house.

Blundering into a small café down a side street, she ordered a bowl of pumpkin soup and a coffee. The café was known for its winter soups. But too many other shoppers ended up having the same idea, crowding inside.

Every voice and laugh seemed to rise to the ceiling and shatter there, the pieces falling everywhere and the sound magnifying.

Still, she was here now.

She often used to bring Max out for lunch in Katoomba. Taking him out to lunch had been tricky, due to his allergies. Through trial and error, she'd found understanding cafe owners who'd been willing to go the extra mile for her son. They'd make a fuss over him and scowl at her stories of cafe owners who hadn't been so kind. The food had been bland, but at least he got to eat out sometimes, like everyone else did.

Her soup arrived at the table, along with a serve of crusty bread and her coffee. She tasted the soup. It was chalky on her tongue.

Nothing was ever going to be good again. Nothing could be.

It was too hot in here, tiny, invisible jackhammers battering away at her temples until her head felt as if it would explode. Her pulse raced.

How had things gone so wrong?

She needed a way out.

She could crash the car on the way home.

Drive into a truck.

Or run to the train station and jump in front of a train—the station was just a block away from here.

No one could blame her.

She caught sight of a woman in gym clothing hurrying along the side street outside, laden with bags. It was Roxanne again.

As Roxanne reached her car, a man appeared and helped her with her shopping.

Men didn't materialise out of nowhere and help Penny like that. Perhaps if she wore skin-tight clothing they would. She hadn't had a boyfriend in years.

Roxanne turned and thanked the man, kissing him.

Kissing him? That was a bit much, wasn't it? Penny sipped her soup, unable to look away.

The two of them kissed each other deeply and then hugged.

They hadn't just met. And with his ash-blond hair, he was certainly *not* her husband.

Getting into Roxanne's car together, they drove away.

21

KATE

Sweat was sticky hot on my back as I overtook Pete on the mountain path. It was close to twilight, but we'd been putting off a mountain run for too long. We normally did these runs once a week.

Franco and I had spent three days on the Rawlings case—on and off—trying to see if Indira Basak's hypnotherapy session would start a cascade of discoveries that would lead us to the killer. Indira had positively identified the SUV as being a BMW. And we'd found her old neighbour and confirmed the model. My team had trawled the available CCTV footage again, and we'd found two SUVs that might fit the description. But neither of those vehicles were ones in which we could see the licence plate number.

We knew more, but we were still no closer.

For a day, I'd been deep in misery. Caught up in depression over yet another dead end in Harper's murder and the sense of being stuck in concrete with the Flying Fox case.

Was everything I was attempting to do as useless as Grimshaw said it was? She hadn't been impressed with what I'd found out about Nola. It hadn't led to any further discoveries, either.

I'd been doubting my abilities in everything, with the strange sensation of being formless, bodiless.

But this morning, I'd driven down to the hospital to spend time with my mother. Just talking and watching the ducks on the water. Remembering who I was. I'd left there with a new determination. Giving up was not an option.

"Hey!" Pete swiftly caught up with me on the slope.

I gave a breathy chuckle that was caught by the wind. The mountain was throwing everything it had at us—barrelling wind and stones that skittered under our feet. But we were both determined to reach the top.

A few more steps and we were there.

A view of Tallman's Valley opened up below. The view was still sunlit. The peak flattened out into an expanse that ran along a cliff edge.

I laughed again, this time from sheer exhaustion. My knees hurt and I had a dull ache in my lower back. My body was starting to protest more and more at these uphill runs.

"Good to see you like this." Pete ran up beside me, wiping sweat from his brow with his forearm. "You're seeming more like your old self again."

Too out of puff to answer, I smiled and nodded, then bent at the waist, breathing deeply and allowing my heart rate and breathing to slow.

"I like it," he said.

Unlike me, he took only a minute to recover. He stretched and then jumped and caught onto a horizontal tree branch. Then he began a set of chin ups that had been his habit to do ever since we'd been running up this hill decades ago.

I would have joined him, except that I wasn't tall enough to reach the branch without a big jump and besides, I was wrecked. I wasn't nearly as committed as Pete to keep fighting fit. I kept fit enough to chase the average criminal, and that was it. And there was barely any need to chase anyone these days. The kind of detective work I'd been doing didn't lend itself to that.

I contented myself with sitting and taking in the valley view for a bit while Pete completed his set. Pete grunted as he reached the tenth chin up, his steel grey hair in damp skeins across his forehead. I reflected that he was one thing that had remained solid and reliable in my life. While everything else had fallen apart. I was grateful for that. There wasn't much between sanity and a deep dark hole, I'd found.

Pete let his feet drop to the ground. Taking out a small towel from his backpack, he patted his face. "Race you back down?"

I let out a groan. "Are you kidding me?"

He chortled. "Yep. I'm not up for that either. How about a stroll, Mrs Wakeland?" He extended a hand.

"*That* I can do." Taking his hand, I fell into step beside him along the cliff edge.

The wind died suddenly, as if it had forgotten its rage.

"Let me grab a photo," said Pete, slipping his phone out of his pocket.

"Not of me? I'm sweaty as anything."

"You look happier than you have in weeks."

I cringed as he stepped away to a higher point to take the photo. I was seriously sweaty and feeling a bit demolished by the aches that told me I'd have to give up these runs one day soon. But Pete was big on capturing his happy moments, and I could hardly say no.

I was glad I hadn't told him about the turmoil inside my mind today. I planted a smile on my face as he snapped a few pictures with his iPhone. I walked across to a patch of wildflowers, bending to pick one.

Pete drew his face away from the phone. His face was almost in silhouette, but I could see that he was suddenly looking past me, to a spot on the ground.

"Kate, don't move!" he called. His tone was dead serious.

Obeying, I froze. "Why?"

"Snake."

"Where?"

"Doesn't matter. It'll go away if you keep still."

But I couldn't help myself. I angled my head around until I caught sight of it. There it was. Less than four feet away. Reared up and ready to strike —its neck hooked, making its small head look much larger. A fresh sheet of sweat broke out on my back. It was an Eastern Brown. I knew that its venom could kill a human anywhere in between five and twenty minutes.

A primal instinct kicked in, and I wanted to run from the thing. But behind me was a sheer drop of a hundred feet. A deadly drop.

"Kate," said Pete urgently. "Stand your ground. Stay still."

"I'm a second away from running," I said between rigid breaths. I felt as if I were seven years old again. I'd been following my mother along the Blue Lake at the Jenolan Caves. The caves were only an hour's drive from Katoomba, but it'd seemed like an enormous journey at the time. I'd been enraptured by the astonishing milky blue of the limestone lake, not watching where I was going, when a brown snake had reared up in front of me. My mother had been unable to help me, because the snake had been between us both, and within striking distance of me. I was right back there, in that place of terror.

Pete knew that story. He also knew I was stupidly terrified of snakes.

I took a slow, careful step back.

The snake moved forward, rearing higher.

My breath caught tight.

"Hold still," cried Pete. "But if you run, promise me you won't let it chase you to the cliff's edge. *Promise*. If you run, you run to *me*. You'd survive a snake bite. You won't survive a fall off that cliff."

A rush of calculations whipped through my mind. I knew it was a myth that Eastern Browns, or any snake, gave chase to animals who weren't their prey. If you kept still, or backed up slowly, the snake should quickly lose interest. But there was always the odd snake who defended itself more vigorously than the others.

Hold still.

In my pocket, my phone started ringing. I guessed that was Pete, trying to make sure I listened to him.

But I lost my nerve. My legs turned to jelly and stones skittered out from my feet as I backed away again.

In a flash, the snake charged closer.

Hold still. Hold still.

The snake gave me one last look of warning, then slithered away.

Pete came down the incline and hugged me. "You okay?"

"Yeah. I'm okay." I exhaled slowly. "Why do I have to come across so many snakes in the wild?"

"It's only been three. And you were lucky to even come across those."

Lucky. That was such a Pete word. In Pete's mind, you were lucky if something out of the ordinary had happened to you.

My nerves were still tingling from the encounter.

"C'mon, let's head home and grab a coffee," Pete said. "Wait, do you want to check who was calling?"

"I thought that was *you*, to talk me out of trying to make a run for it."

"Nope. Wasn't me."

Taking my phone out, I checked for missed calls. It was the superintendent.

I glanced at Pete. Bigley wouldn't be calling me for anything casual. Pete looked at my phone and I watched his expression grow grim.

"Kate," came Andrew Bigley's deep voice as I returned his call, "we have a situation unfolding with the Flying Fox case."

My breath stopped.

This was not going to be an insignificant situation. I tried to steel myself, steel my backbone.

The gravesites from the other day flashed in my mind. Had more gravesites been found—this time the real ones?

I don't want to see tiny skeletons or graves. Not today. Not any day.

22

LORI HINTON

Half an hour earlier

Lori Hinton parked her SUV in the driveway and hauled her suitcase and carry bags out. Her company had sent her off on a work trip to the Netherlands, but it had been cancelled at the last minute, when she was at Sydney airport ready to board the flight. The business deal that she was being sent to manage had folded.

Jobs that sound glamorous rarely are, she thought ruefully.

She'd been looking forward to the trip. She dreaded walking back into her huge, empty house.

And as of two months ago—she was single. Lori's husband had admitted to his affair, and he'd moved out. Lori had been living in her big house all alone since then. Sean wasn't living with his new girlfriend yet. He was keeping her safely hidden, as if Lori was one of those horror ex-wives who'd take revenge.

Unlocking the door, she stepped inside and slipped off her shoes. She'd wrestle the monster suitcase upstairs later. She glanced around at her perfectly styled furniture, but the scene didn't give her any joy. It almost felt as if the house was conspiring against her, with its utter stillness.

For now, she just wanted her kitchen. The kitchen seemed like the only part of the house that had any life or warmth. She'd grown up in a large family, with everyone centred around the kitchen, her parents always in there together at night, whipping up dinners and desserts.

How was it that she'd ended up so alone?

The cat walked with an uncertain gait towards her. Cinnamon was four years old and something had already gone wrong with her left hip, something that the vet couldn't fix. Lori had never been a cat person, but when Sean had brought Cinnamon home as a kitten, Lori had slowly melted. Sean had found her as a stray in the street where he worked.

She bent to pat and comfort the mewing cat, then padded into the kitchen to put the jug on to boil. From the fridge, she pulled out a selection of crackers, dip, and caramel salted dark chocolate.

But before she could start to unwind, she needed to throw off the business clothes and get into her silk pyjamas. The pyjamas were a new buy—a treat. She'd been on a shopping spree since Sean left. A few times, she'd wondered how much she was going to need to treat herself in order to feel better. Perhaps there'd be no end to it, no way to fill up the void. She'd surround herself with things year by year. Just endless... *things*.

Framed photographs decorated the stairway wall. Lori didn't allow them to capture her attention on the way up the stairs. On a good day, the photos upset her. On a bad day, they had her crying like a baby. Today, she just felt depleted.

A noise came from one of the upstairs rooms.

She stalled. It was a definite noise. Not a *maybe* noise. Something like a drawer opening or a chair moving across a wooden floor.

Someone was up there.

Could it be the pet sitter? No, she wasn't supposed to be here today. Lori had been paying a sitter to come in three times a week to spend time with Cinnamon. But if she'd forgotten and had come today by accident, why would she be upstairs when Cinnamon was downstairs?

Another noise. Something being dragged. The sounds were coming from *her* bedroom—the door was open, but she couldn't see inside from here.

Reaching into her jacket pockets, Lori fumbled for her phone. She remembered then—her phone was in her handbag, downstairs.

A rush of pin-prick nerves travelled down to the centre of her chest. Did they have a knife? They could rush at her and attack her.

A humming sound floated out from the room.

A woman's voice, clear and high-pitched.

Lori stopped. She could tackle a woman, couldn't she? She was fit enough—she'd gone hard on classes at the gym since she discovered Sean's tawdry little affair. Kick-boxing, weights, martial arts. Trying to offload her anger.

But what if the woman were slightly crazed? She could be on drugs and violent. Or just desperate and cornered.

Lori stole up to the landing and across to the doorway of her bedroom.

Wait. What if there's more than one? What if there's a man I'm not hearing?

But she felt committed now to her plan to look and see who was in there.

Her heart jammed as she peered around the door frame, ready to race back down the stairs and out into the street.

A woman was kneeling on the floor, her back to Lori, pulling clothes out from the bottom drawer of the tallboy. She had a long, slender back and well-toned, solid arms and legs. In her casual gym gear, she looked like a suburban mum. Not at all like a common thief. She wore a baseball cap low on her forehead, a long brown ponytail extending from beneath it.

The woman held up a T-shirt, examining it closely before discarding it in a pile that was already heaped with clothing. She took out another shirt, gave it a quick look and then folded it, placing it into a large open suitcase.

That was Sean's suitcase. Those were Sean's clothes.

"What are you doing?" The words jumped out, strange and hard on Lori's tongue.

The woman visibly flinched, whipping around. Her eyes opened up large. She stood, splaying a hand over her heart. "Oh God, I didn't think—"

"Roxanne!" Rapid thoughts tore up Lori's mind. This couldn't be true. It was *Roxanne* that Sean had been seeing all this time? The one he'd been sneaking around with while they were married? It seemed like a sick joke. Like a TV show in which someone would jump out and say, *surprise, you should have seen the look on your face!*

"I'm so sorry," Roxanne cried. "This wasn't meant to happen."

"What? You whoring about with my husband?"

"Please don't say that. I came here with Sean to help him get the rest of his things. But he had to run down to the office. I stayed to finish the packing."

She said it as if the explanation would help her cause.

"Get out," Lori spat.

"I wanted to tell you."

"Does your husband know?"

Roxanne exhaled, her shoulders sinking. "Not yet."

"How could you do this? Sean's a married man. And so is Rhys. You have *children*."

"It wasn't intentional. We didn't mean to hurt anyone."

"And yet you just waltz into my house as if it belongs to you."

"Sean said you were going overseas for work for a couple of weeks."

Lori swore under her breath. "What were you two going to do? Come in here and have sex on my bed?" Lori glanced across at her bed for emphasis, noticing then that the covers were pulled back and the pillows rumpled. "Oh, God...."

"I'll just go," said Roxanne quickly. She took steps towards the door.

Lori made no move away from the door, effectively blocking Roxanne's exit. "Get this straight. This is *my* house. Where I live. Don't you ever think you can walk in here again."

"This was the first time, I swear it on my kids' lives."

"How classy of you. You think you'll be getting your hands on this house, don't you? That's why you got with Sean. You've got those kids of yours jammed in that tiny little house of yours, and you thought this place was just going to waste. I never liked you, but I tolerated you because of what happened to our children. But all those times you came over here for the meetings, you were just biding your time, weren't you? Thought you'd be moving in here one day, didn't you?"

"No. I didn't. Sean and I just... we fell in love." She gave an apologetic shrug.

"*Ugh.* Just go. Take the suitcase with you. You've obviously spent a lot of time carefully folding his stuff. Good luck to you when he starts tossing his dirty clothes on the floor for you to pick up. He's all yours."

Roxanne's expression hardened a fraction. Backtracking, she bent to pack one of Sean's jackets in the bag and then zip it up.

Lori hadn't known what Sean's new girlfriend looked like, but she never would have pictured someone like Roxanne. *What did he see in her?* He'd steadfastly refused to answer any questions about the woman he'd cheated on Lori with. And now Lori knew why.

She watched Roxanne struggle down the stairs with Sean's large suitcase, and then she walked back into the bedroom and watched through the window as Roxanne wheeled the suitcase along the front path.

Sean pulled his car up on the kerb next to Roxanne. Exiting the car, he took the bag and then placed it inside the hatch. He gave her a hug and dropped a kiss on her forehead. Roxanne got into the front passenger seat of Sean's car. Probably crying and wailing about how Lori had spoken to her. The scene was surreal. *Sean and Roxanne together.*

Raising his head, Sean saw Lori at the window.

She stormed away. It was too much. How much more was she going to be expected to bear in this life?

Giving up on her plans to change out of her work gear, she headed back downstairs to the kitchen. She wouldn't be able to relax now. Her house had been violated.

She made herself a coffee rather than the hot chocolate she'd intended. Coffee with milk, no sugar. Bitter.

Sean had been having an affair with a woman who had *children.* Yet, during the past three years, he'd steadfastly refused to have the IVF she'd been desperate for. And he knew exactly how much a baby would have meant to her. Charlotte had been born via IVF. After three-year-old Charlotte had vanished, Lori had felt an overwhelming desire to have another child. Back then, she might have been able to. But she was in her late forties now and her time for babies was over.

Sean's time for babies was over, too. If Roxanne planned to cement the affair with Sean by having a baby with him, she had a shock coming. Sean's sperm had barely been viable five years ago. Hence the IVF. It'd cost them tens of thousands to finally have a baby.

When Lori had discovered Sean had been cheating, she'd thought she hated him as much as it was possible to hate a person. She was wrong. She had more hate left to give.

Taking her coffee, she began pacing, catching sight of herself in the shiny, mirror-like splash back of her kitchen. Her face looked harsh. She *felt* harsh.

What am I becoming? Who am I now?

Nursing her coffee, she sat on the sofa and tucked her legs underneath. Her eyes burned with tears that refused to come. Inside, she was burned dry.

A knock at the door echoed through the empty spaces of the house.

She bristled.

Had one of them come back to grab yet more things? Striding furiously to the front door, she cracked it open.

Sean stood there on the other side.

"Roxy's crying her eyes out." His jaw tensed and he glanced away.

"I'd feel bad too if I got caught in someone else's house," she said.

Cinnamon sidled past Sean's legs.

"Look." Sean sighed, stooping to run a hand along Cinnamon's back. "I thought you were away for a couple of weeks. It's still my house and some of my stuff is still in here. I just thought I'd swing by and grab it."

"You thought you'd swing into my bed with her, too. *My bed*, Sean."

"That wasn't planned."

"I know, I know, *it just happened*. Shut the hell up."

"You won't tell Rhys... will you? About Roxanne and me? She's been going to tell him, but it's been a bad time. His brother died, and she didn't want to make it worse."

"I haven't decided. Just... get out of my face. I don't want to see you. Ever again."

A child wheeled slowly past on her pink and white bicycle. She angled her head around to where Lori and Sean stood. Once she'd gone past, she stopped and rode back again.

Hopping off the bicycle, she propped it up against the letterbox. She glanced shyly up at Lori and Sean, then turned her attention to the cat. "Can I cuddle her?"

"Of course." Lori managed a smile. "Be gentle. She has a bad hip."

The girl frowned as she sat in a cross-legged position and gathered the animal into her lap. She held Cinnamon's face between her small hands, examining her intently. "What happened to her?"

"The vet thinks she has arthritis," Lori told her in a flat voice. She wasn't in the mood for answering questions from a small child.

"Ohhh, poor Cinnamon," the girl said.

"Lori," Sean said under his breath. "She knows the cat's name."

Lori shrugged, not understanding why that was important. She was probably a neighbour's child and had heard Lori calling the cat.

Slowly, the girl raised her head, moving her gaze from the cat to Lori and Sean, her eyes still shy, but now questioning. Her eyes were a clear light brown, her curtain of hair a shiny, thick brunette.

Something about the way she pulled her lips in and the wrinkle of her brow made Lori's stomach clench. If she were to picture the girl that she and Sean had lost three and a half years ago, it would be this child.

Sean's words repeated in Lori's mind: *She knows the cat's name.*

The girl nestled her face into Cinnamon's fur. "I've missed you."

23

KATE

Wind buffeted my face, screaming down from the higher mountain ranges. My heart had already been racing from my encounter with the snake. And now Bigley had news about the children.

"Kate?" Andrew Bigley prompted after my silence.

My fingers trembled as I held the phone. I dreaded knowing what his news would be. I forced words from my throat. "Go ahead, Andrew."

"One of the children has been returned," he said simply.

"*Returned?*" I breathed. Had I heard that correctly?

"She was found," he said, "on a bicycle, riding up to her house."

"Who? Which child?"

"Charlotte Hinton."

My thoughts whirled. "God. Is she okay?"

"As far as her mother can tell, yes."

"I... I can't believe this." A desperate hope rose in my chest. "What about the others? The other kids? Has she been able to tell her mother anything?"

Pete's eyes opened large. He held my arm, moving his face against mine, listening intently to Bigley.

"She's told Lori a little," explained Bigley. "She was brought home in a van. She was driven past her parents' house and shown which one it was, in case she'd forgotten."

My thoughts stretched in different directions. "The children are all alive? They were all in the van?"

"From what Charlotte has said, they were blindfolded and made to stay silent. She's not saying much."

"When did this happen? Just now?"

"Approximately half an hour has passed since Charlotte was returned. Her parents were in shock and didn't call us sooner. Kate, I need you to get down to the station and work out what happens next. We need patrol cars out looking for that van, surveillance of the houses of the remaining parents, and a decision needs to be made on whether we tell the other parents. I'm about to call Reagan."

He ended the call abruptly.

The abductor, whoever they were and for whatever reason, had made a startlingly unexpected move.

Our family could get Ivy back today. The thought sparked a nervous, exhilarated energy through my entire body.

24

KATE

I drove home with Pete from our run on the mountain, both of us stunned by the news.

Along the way, I spoke with Grimshaw, coordinating a network of unmarked police surveillance vehicles.

I had to get this right. Things needed to happen in a certain order, or else things could go terribly, heartbreakingly wrong. And the last thing I wanted was that at some future point, I'd be pulling apart the events of today and realising all the mistakes that I'd had made.

After a rushed shower, I dressed and headed over to Lori Hinton's house.

There were two cars parked outside. And a child-size pink bicycle against the front porch.

I practically raced up the driveway.

Lori's ex-husband Sean opened the door. "Come in, Kate. She's in the living room." His face held an expression of astonishment, as if he'd found an old, winning, million-dollar lottery ticket.

Through the short hallway, I glimpsed Lori Hinton, sitting on her sofa, looking as dazed as her husband. She held a young girl close to her side. The girl certainly resembled every picture and video I'd seen of the three-year-old Charlotte. She had an outward appearance of health. She hadn't been starved.

Constable Ella Valletti was already there, seated in the living room with them.

"Sean," I said, "would I be able to speak with you and Lori in private, just briefly?"

"Of course," he replied and went to fetch his ex-wife.

I gathered them both into the entry, out of earshot of Charlotte.

Lori grabbed me in a quick hug. "Oh, Kate. I can't believe this is happening. Our little girl has come back to us. I'm in shock. I can't stop trembling."

"It's incredible," I replied. "I'm amazed and happy for you."

"Just a miracle," Lori whispered. "She just turned up at our *doorstep*. She was suddenly just *there*."

"It's beyond wonderful." I felt my eyes grow moist. "Did you see who dropped her off at all?"

"No," Lori told me. "Sean and I were... We were having a conversation on the front porch. And then Charlotte came up to us on her bicycle."

"Well, I've currently got police door-knocking your street and neighbourhood to see if anyone saw the van. And we've got police patrolling the area."

"Good," said Sean. "They need to catch this person."

"Also," I continued, "I'd like your permission to ask Charlotte a few questions. At this moment, she's the one who knows more than anyone else. I'll be recording her answers electronically."

A hesitant look clouded Lori's brown eyes. "She doesn't seem to want to answer questions. I don't know what my precious girl has been through. I don't want to push her."

"I won't push her," I assured them both.

"All right then," said Lori, "you can ask her some things and we'll see how it goes."

"Thank you," I replied with a grateful tone. "There's something I need to ask you both first. And it's a little brutal."

Lori's brow furrowed. "I don't know if I'm ready for brutal questions—"

"Are you certain she's your daughter?" I said, cutting in. The question had to be asked and there was no gentle way of saying it.

After a moment of shock, she nodded vigorously. "Oh yes. She's my Charlotte. And she has a mole under her left ear. It's *her*."

"Of course she's ours," Sean told me. "She even knew the name of our cat. The cat was just one year old when Charlotte went missing."

I softened my tone. "Okay. I hope you understand that we needed to get that out of the way. Now, you're telling me that she rode up the street on a bicycle, completely out of the blue?"

"Yes," affirmed Lori.

"I have to ask that no one touches the bicycle now. I'll have police take it down to the station for DNA analysis. Excuse me." I made a quick call to get someone to come and pick up the bike. I turned back to the Hintons with a smile. "Shall we begin the questions?"

Lori took me through to the living room while Sean went to attend to a phone call.

Constable Ella Valletti was sitting next to Charlotte now. After a quick greeting, Ella went to stand by the window.

Lori took her place next to her daughter again. I seated myself on the sofa just opposite Charlotte. I was on edge, desperate to fire a hundred questions at her but knowing I had to hold back and not scare her. She was still just six years old, and Lori was correct that no one yet had any idea what she and the others had been through.

I took a breath, turning the calls off on my phone and turning the video on. I faced Charlotte. "Hi. My name is Kate. I'm so glad that you've come back. How are you?"

"I'm good," came Charlotte's small voice.

"Great. That's great. Is it okay if I ask you some questions?"

She nodded but her eyes were guarded. "Are you the police?"

"Yes, Charlotte. I'm one of the people who've been looking for you."

"I'm Lottie. You should call me Lottie." She had her mother's direct, clear gaze and manner of speaking, despite being away from her for half of her life.

Lori made a disparaging sound under her breath. "It seems that these people who had her were calling her *Lottie* rather than Charlotte."

The girl frowned. "No, it was *Ivy* who called me Lottie."

I stifled a gasp at the mention of Ivy's name.

A single question burned inside me. *Where's Ivy?*

Instead of blurting out that question, I offered to Charlotte to call her *Lottie* if she wanted me to.

Charlotte smiled and nodded.

Lori looked away, as if she were trying to disguise her annoyance.

"Lottie," I said, "We need to know where the other children are. Ivy and Elijah and Max and Olivia. Where was the last place you saw them?"

She bit her lip. "I can't tell you anything, because I was told not to. Because if I do, none of the others can come back."

Swallowing down my frustration, I asked her who said that.

Charlotte's eyes skated from her mother to me. "I can't say it. They told me not to. And I got a new bike as a present, for being a good girl and doing what I'm asked to do."

I reminded myself to keep taking it slow, especially now with Charlotte's revelation about not being allowed to speak.

"That's a wonderful bike," I told her. "I love the colour."

"I chose it," she said proudly. "We all got to choose special gifts to take with us. Because we were all good."

"Okay, you were given gifts? What gifts did the others choose?"

She thought. "Olivia got a doll. Elijah wanted a soccer ball. Hmmm, Max wanted some paints. Oh, and Ivy. She wanted an airplane or a robot. I don't know which one she got."

"Ivy didn't show you what she was given?"

The little girl looked troubled now, and she took a full couple of seconds to reply. "Ivy was sleeping."

"Are you worried about something?" I asked gingerly.

She nodded, bending her head low and bringing her arms across her stomach.

Lori stroked her daughter's cheek. "You don't need to tell anything that upsets you."

Charlotte's breaths grew faster. Terror struck at me. Something was wrong. Something was very, very wrong.

"Charlotte—I mean, *Lottie*," I said urgently. "What do you mean when you say Ivy was sleeping?"

Lori placed the palm of one hand out in a stop gesture, the other hand cradling the side of her daughter's face. "Detective, I think that might be enough. For both of you."

I drew a long breath, nodding. "Thank you, Lottie. You did well."

Ella answered a call. She gestured frantically towards me, her mouth dropping open as she listened to the call.

I followed her as she walked to the entry of the house.

"What is it, Ella?"

She ended the call. "We have a report of another returned child."

I wanted to hear the name *Ivy*. I already knew I wouldn't.

"If the report checks out, it's Elijah Parrish."

25

NICK PARRISH

Nick Parrish snuck a quick cigarette behind a line of trees. His four girls were in the playground, all in his line of sight.

The last thing he wanted was for them to catch him smoking. They'd tell their mother and then she'd give him hell. Actually, all four girls and their mother would round him up and give him hell. They were like that. They tended to form a posse.

The trees were easy to lurk behind at least. The trees were the Australian version of strangler figs—with monstrous branches snaking out in all directions. They were parasites who'd landed on their host tree a long time ago and sucked the life out of it. There'd been a similar kind of strangler figs back on the street he'd grown up on in his native Florida. The trees were one of the things that had made this place seem a bit homely when he'd moved his family to Australia a few years earlier.

He supposed he wasn't meant to be smoking here. The playground was one of the many circular parks in the district that were surrounded by houses. He'd be in easy view of the residents of at least a dozen houses. Anyone watching was probably tut-tutting. *Bite me*, he thought.

His daily cigarettes kept him sane. He'd started smoking again—after a hiatus of ten years—three years ago. After his only son went missing. At first, it'd been a pack a day. This year, he'd wrestled it down to two cigarettes a day. He was damned proud of that. He'd been through more than any parent should ever have to face and he fought multiple small battles with himself every single day.

Disposing of the cigarette butt, he walked to the nearby bench seat and parked himself on it.

He grinned openly as three of his daughters tried to convince their youngest sister to come on the slide with them. Gracie, terrified of slides, shook her head from side to side, giving her sisters what Nick called the *stinkeye pout.*

At only two years of age, Gracie was a stubborn, tiny curmudgeon. She was a lot like him. Once her mind was made up, nothing could change it. Slides were bad news. And that was that. His older three girls, at ages seven, ten and thirteen, had much softer, pliable personalities. More like their mother.

His brown-skinned children stood out among the other kids in the playground. This place was *white.* Although the new facilities and village at Tallman's Valley had brought in professionals from lots of countries, whites still predominated.

Five years ago, he'd been living with Marcy and the kids in Fort Lauderdale, Florida. It'd seemed that half the population was black there. And the rest a mix of white and Hispanic.

He'd known that coming here to Australia would be a big change for him and his family. But in his worst dreams he hadn't expected the incident that would happen just two years after making the move, right before they were due to return home to Florida.

The sun glinted low in the sky, the breeze that swept the dry leaves growing chilly. He wasn't a fan of the winters here. They weren't brutal but they sure weren't Florida winters.

"*Sabrina, Jade, Maya,*" he boomed, cupping his hands around his mouth. "Time to head off. Bring Gracie with you."

Sabrina, his eldest, was now sitting cross-legged on the ground, browsing her phone. He'd told her to leave that thing at home. She was changing too fast. The days of her being excited for a trip to the park were long gone. Month by month, he'd notice some subtle change that was pulling her further and further away from childhood—straightened hair, mascara, glossy lips and an attitude that sometimes left him speechless.

Gracie plonked herself down next to Sabrina, playing with bark chips. Jade and Maya were playing a chasing game with a boy of about five. He had a soccer ball tucked under his arm. He was probably the only kid in the playground who was as dark-skinned as they were. Nick hadn't noticed him before.

The only one of Nick's daughters who obeyed his call was Sabrina. She jumped up, pushing her phone down into the back pocket of her jeans. Nick guessed that was because she hadn't wanted to come to the park in the first place and couldn't wait to go. She stooped to collect Gracie. Gracie made a desperate, last-chance grab for more bark chips.

His other two daughters remained engaged in their game. Time to raise his voice a couple of notches. "*Jade and Maya!* Front and centre."

Sabrina walked across to her father and handed Gracie over.

Nick kissed the toddler on her soft, round cheek. "You have fun, sweetie?"

She shook her head. "Sabby didn't let me put bark on the slide."

"Well, you're not supposed to do that."

"But I want to."

Laughing, Nick gave her a squeeze. "Gracie wants to do everything Gracie wants to do, doesn't she?" He and Marcy were really going to have to put their foot down with her pretty soon. But right now, he didn't have the heart.

A cold feeling passed between his shoulder blades. Everything was moving too fast. The girls, the years, all of it. He and Marcy had been living in a kind of purgatory these past years, but they'd tried to always remember to enjoy each day with their girls. He hugged Gracie a little tighter.

Maya came running in from the playground.

Three down. One to go.

Only his seven-year-old was left. Jade. Normally, she was the easiest child to manage. She must really be caught up in her game. He called her again. This time, she listened. When she came, she had the boy in tow.

"Hey kid," Nick said to the boy. "Playtime's over. We gotta go now. You'd better get on back to the playground."

The boy hugged his soccer ball to his chest, his eyes concealed beneath his cap. "I have to go with you." His voice was deep for a little kid.

Nick gave a short laugh. "Oh, well, my Jade always wants to bring kids home from the playground. But she can't do that. Is one of your parents coming to pick you up?"

The boy shook his head.

Nick glanced beyond the boy to the playground. The kids and parents were fast emptying out. It was late. It'd soon be sunset. There were only two small groups of people left. Which of those families did this kid belong to, if either of them?

"Do you live near here?" Nick asked him.

Dismay entered the boy's voice. "Don't you know me?"

Scratching his ear, Nick eyed Jade. "You know this kid from school, honey?" The boy was slightly shorter than Jade, but he could be any age between five and seven.

"Nope," Jade answered.

"You're supposed to know me," the boy insisted.

"He's... weird," said Sabrina.

"Hey," Nick cautioned his oldest daughter. The last of the stragglers left the park. There was no one except an older couple walking a dog. He turned his head back to the boy. "I'm sorry, kid. We don't know you. So, are you meant to be walking home? It's getting late. I'd give you a lift, but strangers aren't allowed to do that."

The boy didn't reply.

Gracie was grumbling, starting to toss herself about in his arms, as she did when she was tired and hungry. Jade and Maya were poking each other. Sabrina was browsing through her phone again.

Nick wanted to get home, but he couldn't do that until the kid was safe. "Look, I'm gonna call the police. It's okay, my girls and I will stay with you until they get here." He remembered then that his phone was out of charge. He'd have to grab Sabrina's—not an easy task to separate her from her phone.

"No," the boy stated, raising his face. "Not the police. They don't help kids."

The vehemence in the boy's words made Nick stop and really look at him for the first time. The boy was standing practically shoulder-to-shoulder with Jade now that her sister had poked her and made her move. The similarity in features between the two was striking. Nick couldn't stop his gaze from sliding from Jade to the boy, and from the boy to Jade, over and over.

Without warning, the boy turned and bolted across the park. He cut a lonely figure in between the shadows that had deepened in the now-empty playground.

Cogwheels spun inside Nick's head.

"Sabrina," he yelled, even though he was standing close by her. "Watch your sisters." He transferred Gracie to her arms, ignoring the stunned look on her face.

He sped away.

Nick hadn't run in years, and the boy was damned fast.

"Wait up," Nick called between gasping breaths. "Hey! I'm not calling the police. *Promise.*"

Nick's chest hurt. The years of late-night coding, cigarettes, and pota-to'ing in front of the TV had made him soft. But he couldn't let this boy get away.

Because he might never find him again.

Ignoring the awful burn in his thighs, Nick increased his pace, too out of breath now to even call out.

The boy stumbled and fell. He jumped to his feet in a flash, but he'd given Nick just enough time.

That was Nick's chance. Maybe the only one he'd get.

He loped up to the kid and made a grab, knocking both of them to the ground.

The boy was sprawled on his back, looking up at Nick in fear.

Nick spluttered, wheezing in an attempt to regain his breath. "Elijah? *Elijah?*"

The boy nodded, his eyes huge.

"You're *my* Elijah? *My boy?*"

"Yes. I'm your Elijah." The voice was small but definite.

The older couple trotted towards them at a fast clip.

"Get off that kid," the man shouted. "We've called the cops on you."

Tears ran down Nick's face as he raised his head to them. "It's okay. Everything's okay. He's my son."

26

KATE

I stepped out of Lori Hinton's house with Ella, the late afternoon sun glinting hard in my eyes and anxiety stealing through my veins.

"Tell me *exactly* when and how Elijah showed up," I asked Ella.

She nodded. "The reports were somewhat garbled, but that's as expected when reports come in from different sources. The first calls to police came from sets of people who witnessed Nick Parrish chasing down a small boy in Lowan Park and then pinning him to the ground. A couple who'd been walking their dog claimed that Nick said it was okay that he was hurting the boy because it was his son. We don't know if he was actually hurting him or if the boy really is Elijah Parrish or a random child at this point. Police and support workers are on their way."

Ella was right. The first reports that came in about an incident often needed untangling.

"Do we know why Nick was at this park?" I asked.

"Apparently he was there with his daughters."

The phone rang. It was Grimshaw.

"Wakeland," she said, "you didn't answer my calls. Are you aware that a boy fitting the description of Elijah Parrish is currently being escorted to Nepean Hospital?"

"Yes, I am," I replied. "It's not making sense that the abductor knew where Nick was going to be."

"I'm going to take a stab and guess that they've somehow been watching the parents," Grimshaw said. "I want to know if this kid—and the kid who is supposedly Charlotte Hinton—are really them. We don't know that yet and I have to say I'm sceptical. I don't think we should be getting the hopes up of the other parents just yet."

"They'd want to know," I said flatly.

"Look, I don't know what the hell is going on here. This could all be a prank. We could be made fools of."

"Charlotte's parents are certain it's her. She has a mole in the right place."

"Yeah, and moles can be inked on," she answered. "You weren't at a lot of the strike force meetings. We've had hundreds of bogus sightings and weirdos to deal with. One woman was even sure her own biological daughter was one of the missing kids."

"I spoke with Charlotte myself. She's a six-year-old kid. A kid that age can't put on an act that good."

"Fine. All right, then we need to decide how to proceed from here. We have to get this out to the media and see what people might have seen."

I gasped. "That could be disastrous. It's important to wait and watch at this point. The safety of the remaining children is our priority."

"Catching the kidnapper is the priority," she countered. "We don't even know if they still have the remaining three kids. We don't know what they might have done with them over the past years."

"If they're still in town, media reports could have them running away like a rabbit."

Begrudgingly, she agreed to hold off.

"I'm heading over to my house to take over surveillance there," I told Ella. "Ivy grew up in my house. So, I don't know if the kidnapper will choose to return her there or to Abby's house. I'll coordinate things while watching the house. You've worked a full day—you can go home."

"You know what?" Ella said. "If you'll be busy coordinating, you're going to need someone keeping an eye out."

"It would make for a very long day for you."

"I don't mind."

"You're a treasure."

"Let's do this," she said. "I'll drive. You've got better things to do."

I shot her a grateful smile as we drove away.

Abby didn't answer her phone when I called, so I left a text message. Roxanne Crane and Penny Foster didn't answer either. I made a quick call to Pete, to let him know what was happening. He was happy for the Parrish family, but I could hear the anguished disappointment in his voice that Ivy hadn't been brought back... yet.

I gazed at the double row of streetlights that lined the steep hill in front of me.

What is the kidnapper's next move going to be?

We rounded my street. I had Ella park a short distance away from my house, behind a car and beneath the overhanging branches of a tree. We had a good view from here.

The warmth from the car heater seemed to drop a couple of degrees the instant Ella switched off the engine.

I checked with Cameron and DS Liz Booth about what was happening at their ends of things. Cameron had been at the hospital, where Charlotte and Elijah were undergoing tests. Cameron was now on his way back. Booth had organised the unmarked patrol cars. So far, there'd been no unusual activity from any vans in the area. There were a few they were keeping tabs on.

My phone rang. It was Abby.

"Mum? You said you have to talk to me urgently? Is it... Nanna?"

I took a moment to breathe. "No, it's not your nanna. Honey... something has happened. Two of the missing children have been brought back to their parents. Charlotte and Elijah."

"Oh God! They were found?" she cried. "And the others? Where are they? What about Ivy?"

"Abby... Charlotte and Elijah weren't found. The kidnapper—or someone else—brought them back. But we don't know about the other children... yet. We don't know about Ivy."

"The kidnapper brought them back?" Her words tumbled over each other in whispers and cries. "Oh my God. That's amazing. Why don't you sound happy? You should be happy. Is something wrong?"

"It sounds positive, but at the same time, I can't know the mind of the kidnapper. I wish I did."

"But Ivy will be brought back, yes? I mean, if the others got their babies back, then I will, too." Her voice rose to a peak, filled with fear and excitement.

"Honey, I need you to understand that the situation is not under the control of the police. The kidnapper is a criminal and we can't predict what they will do."

"Mum, what should I do?"

"Are you at home?"

"Yes."

"Just... stay there. I'll need your address. So I can send out surveillance units. I'm already watching my house. I'm trying to cover all bases."

Ella and I sat in silence for a time. Pete had more lights on in the house than usual, including the porch light. It was obvious he didn't want the house to be missed in the dark.

Roxanne Crane returned my call. I explained to her what was happening, and she soon spiralled into hysterics. I had to calm her down and ask that she simply remain at home and let us know if she noticed anything unusual.

Everything went quiet again.

My mind was in anguish. I wanted something active to do, not just this sitting and waiting. But this was the way the kidnapper had chosen to do things, and all I could do was wait and hope for the arrival of a little girl I hadn't seen in three and a half years.

"Talk to me, Valletti," I said. "Anything to keep my mind off all of this."

"Uh, what about?"

"I don't know. Why'd you join the police force?"

Ella gave me half a smile. "I guess I just wanted to do some good," she answered. She shrugged. "So far, I've done a good lot of paperwork, but I don't know about actual *good*."

"The paperwork is a killer," I agreed.

"Mountains of it. Some days, I feel like I work in admin."

"Sounds like you haven't had the best introduction to police work."

"No, I don't mean to imply that. Apart from the paperwork, I like it. It's a bit hard on relationships though."

"Oh?"

"Yeah. But I don't want to prattle on about my personal stuff."

"Please do. I mean, unless you want to keep it private."

She sighed. "My boyfriend thinks I've changed a lot this year. I get angry about some cases. The things people do to each other. And he says sometimes when I talk to him, it sounds like I'm barking out orders." She gave a low, sad laugh. "I don't mean to. I don't even notice it."

"It happens," I said. "You notice it more with the young women who come on board than the men. They quickly learn to deepen their voices and speak with authority. We're not used to that from women."

Ella nodded. "To make it worse, my boyfriend is the quiet, artistic type. And while he's not exactly anti-cop, he's not fond of them either. He didn't know I was training for the police force when I met him. I didn't tell him. He was a bit shocked when he found out."

"Well, the fact that he didn't cut and run says something. He's still with you. He must have made peace with it."

"Yeah. He's made his peace. We have fun together. We both bought these—fitness trackers." She showed me the band around her wrist. "We go out on walks and runs on the weekends."

"Good for you. That's what Pete and I have always done."

"I've seen your husband. You both look fit."

"We try. It's getting harder."

We spoke for a while longer and then fell into silence again.

I turned the engine on so we could get a blast of heat. We were no good to anyone if we became frozen with the cold.

My mind railed at the dark, trying to push it back. If we'd had more hours of daylight, so we might have had more chance of finding the abductor. But they'd probably chosen this time of day for a reason. They'd wanted less visibility.

Come on, make your next move.

Ella warmed her hands in the stream of warm air from the car heater. "This is maddening. What are they doing?"

I shook my head. "Making us wait."

Grimshaw called. "I'm going to have to put that call out to the public," she said.

I stifled a gasp. "But we decided not to do that, yet."

"That was two hours ago. This could be someone playing games with us. This softly, softly approach might be a waste of time. We need to go all-out. News coverage. Appeals to the public. Find out who has seen what. And show our police presence."

"What about the rest of the kids?" I managed to say. "We still have good reason to hold out."

"We might not be able to keep a lid on it for much longer. I'm at the hospital. Lori Hinton came marching up to me and demanding that we make this public. She doesn't want the people who took her daughter to get away with it."

"Since when do we take orders from parents?"

"Oh, trust me, I told her to back right down. But Lori is screaming that if we don't put the word out, *she* will. I was forced to put a suppression order out to the press. So, they already know something big is brewing. And then there's the people we've been door-knocking. They don't know exactly what's going on, but some smartacre is bound to guess. And there's also the hospital staff, who know exactly what's happening. We can't keep this quiet much longer. And the thing is, Wakeland, I don't know if we should."

"Just... give it a bit longer. Give the abductor a chance to make another move."

"It's been two hours since Charlotte turned up. We believe that Elijah turned up at a similar time, just that his father didn't know it. Seems that the abductor's run is over and done with. Nothing more to see."

"Just give it one more hour."

"Right. But it's on your head. Just make sure your vision isn't clouded."

She ended the call.

Ella gave me a grim smile. "I want you to know, I'm with you. You're one of the detectives I look up to the most. If you think we should wait, then we should wait."

"Thank you. That means a lot right now."

I leaned my head back on the seat. Minutes ticked past. Ella and I turned the car's heater on and off again. In locations all over town, officers in unmarked police cars were sitting and waiting, just like we were, growing cold and switching the heaters on.

Was this a game the abductor was playing with us? Or something else?

There must be something we were missing.

27

PENNY FOSTER

Penny gazed from her home office window onto the street below. She'd been focusing intently on her computer screen for the past hours, and a headache was hammering her temples.

Detective Grimshaw had contacted her a short while ago to ask if anything unusual had happened today. Grimshaw hadn't given any details. She was gruff as sandpaper, that woman. What was that phone call about? Did she know something?

Worry was a constant tick tocking clock in Penny's mind, but the sound had grown so loud now she could barely hear herself think. Like a grandfather clock in a tiled room, the echoes were bouncing everywhere. She was winding up tighter and tighter, the ticks deafening.

She sighed, rubbing the knuckles of each hand together.

The thoughts that always circled her mind had been ceaseless today. Days ago, she'd been sure she would end her life. But she'd hung on. What was she hanging on for?

Her life was formless, without signposts.

What was she going to do in the future?

She was thirty-seven years old but life had already seemed to pass her by. Her job bored her, and she hadn't accomplished what she'd imagined she would by this age. She'd tried hard with Max's father. She and Duncan had married after just a year of dating, but it'd become obvious within weeks that they were two very different people. Max had been the cutest little boy. But Duncan wasn't interested. He lost interest in her, too. He hadn't cheated on her—Duncan would never do that—but he became like a stranger. Life became all about whose turn it was to do household chores and which bills needed to be paid.

And her only child had been gone from her house for three and a half years.

Life wasn't fair. Some people won the lottery, and they kept winning prizes. Other people, like Penny, kept buying tickets over and over again, hoping for even just a small prize, but it never came.

She closed the file she was working on. Her feet were swollen, and her head felt swollen, too. She might be coming down with yet another cold.

She put on her comfy pyjamas and dressing gown and made herself a tea.

She sat at her personal computer, typing out a post for her online blog. The blog was her own little space on the internet. A place to unspool her thoughts. The messy pieces. The pieces that had come unstuck with the glitter rubbed off and the edges all rough and cracked.

She decided to write in verse.

When I was a child
the sky cushioned me
from the endless dark.
The sky was a pillow
and I its wild-eyed dreamer.
Ever sleeping.
But now I'm free falling.
Hurtling through space.
The sky always was
an illusion.
I have never been
safe.

Lifting her phone, she snapped a photo of herself and posted it with the poem. She looked sad and alone in the picture, but internally she felt a little lighter. She'd released some of the pent-up anxiety.

She glanced out of her window again.

A car that she didn't recognise was now parked out there, just a little way up the street. It was highly unusual to have strange vehicles up this end. The day was still light enough to make out the colour and model of the vehicle. A silver Toyota Corolla. And it was just light enough to see that a man was inside, looking at his phone.

She knew the cars that the neighbours drove, and this wasn't any of them. The car was parked at the kerb of the neighbour's block of land, but she had an uneasy feeling her house was being watched.

She felt raw and exposed, but there was nothing she could do. People were free to sit in their cars and watch you if they wanted.

The phone on her desk rang, making her jump, the rings rattling through every empty corridor and room in the house.

She was almost afraid to answer it.

Who would it be and what did they have to tell her? Would it be Grimshaw again, with an update?

She exhaled a shallow breath and answered.

"Penny? It's Detective Kate Wakeland. I tried to call before. Did you see my message?" Her voice sounded urgent and strained.

"Kate, no, sorry I haven't checked them. Oh, my goodness, what is it? Detective Grimshaw called me earlier, but she didn't tell me what's going on. What is it? Something's happening, isn't it?"

"I have something you need to know. Are you sitting?"

"Oh God..."

"I'll start by saying we don't know anything specific about your Max. But... two of the missing children have been returned."

"What did you just say, Detective?"

"Two of the children are back with their parents. They are Charlotte and Elijah. Now, we don't have firm IDs on these two children yet, but their parents are certain they are their children."

Penny gasped, her voice gone faint. "The children are being *returned?*"

"Yes. I'm afraid we don't know if the abductor intends to return the remaining three kids. All we know so far is that Charlotte was returned to her home and Elijah was dropped off at a playground. We've had no communication with the person who took the kids."

Standing, Penny began to pace the room. "I could get my Max back. Oh my God. What should I do? I don't know what to do. I'll put the porch light on. It's almost night. They wouldn't just shove my Max out somewhere in the dark, would they?"

"You can leave the porch light on. That's a good idea. But Penny... I have to tell you that we just don't know what we're dealing with. We can't say with certainty that any of the remaining children will be returned. We don't know what the situation is. I feel that I should prepare you for any possible circumstance. The abductor kept five children captive for over three years. They are possibly very unstable."

"Unstable? What are you thinking? The children might be hurt?"

"I just don't know. I know this will be a very anxious time for you. All I can advise is that you stay home and remain indoors, away from your windows. At the moment, it's a waiting game. Penny, I need to go. I've got a lot to coordinate right now."

"Of course. Just one thing before you go—wouldn't Charlotte and Elijah be able to say where they've been? I mean, they must know, right?"

"We're hoping that they can. At the moment, they're not in a state to be able to tell us much at all. Please, try your best to stay calm and we will be in contact again tonight."

Penny dropped the phone in the holder, her fingers trembling. Now she knew that it was a police surveillance unit outside.

The dark had already swept through the house.

What would happen by the end of tonight? The *not knowing* made her feel weak.

28

KATE

I stared from my car window out at the night, deep in thought.

At almost the exact time that Lori Hinton had arrived home from a cancelled flight, Charlotte had appeared out of nowhere.

Nick Parrish had been at a park with his four daughters. And Elijah had just turned up there.

So far, it had been assumed that Lori and Nick were being watched, and that was how the kidnapper knew where to find them. But keeping watch on just one person wasn't an easy task, let alone two or more.

Could Lori and Nick have made their locations known online?

I decided to check *Facebook*. I had all the parents of the missing kids on *Facebook*—even Abby, though Abby rarely used it.

Taking out my phone, I hurriedly browsed the internet, looking up their profiles.

I looked at Lori's profile first. There was nothing there. She hadn't posted in weeks. Okay, it was a business flight she'd been going to take, so she might have noted her movements on a business-related site. I checked *LinkedIn*. Yes, there it was: *Arriving at Sydney International Airport*. Then: *Trip cancelled*.

Ella looked on as I browsed.

I tried Nick's *Facebook* profile next. Perhaps he'd posted a picture of the kids at the park. No, no pictures. And no pings. But Nick had four daughters, one of them a teenager. It was pretty certain that she had a phone with the internet connected.

I called Nick.

He answered immediately.

"Nick, it's Kate Wakeland."

"Oh man," he said. "I can't tell you how over the moon we are to have Elijah back. Whatever you did, it worked."

"How's Elijah doing?"

"He's doing okay. We think. We hope."

"I'm incredibly happy for you. Listen, Nick, I need you to tell me something. Detective Grimshaw said that you didn't tell anyone you'd be at the park. Is that right?"

"Yeah. That's right. I have no idea how they found us."

"Did you talk to anyone at all via phone while you were there?"

"Nope. My phone was out of charge."

"Hmmm. Could one of your daughters have given away your location? Via social media?"

"Hang on, I'll find out." He was gone from the phone for about thirty seconds before returning. "Yeah. Sabrina wrote a message on *Instagram* about lame trips to the park with her dad. Nice. Well, that's one lame trip I'll be forever glad of."

"Thanks, Nick. Wait, did she say which park?"

"I'll check," he said. He came back a second later with a *no.*

"Did she post a photo of the park, Nick?"

"Ah, yep. She did."

"Could you send me the snap, please?"

A picture of the playground came through on my phone. It showed more than enough features of the park to be able to figure out which one it was. That pointed to the kidnapper being a local.

"That's great, Nick. Thanks a million. Go enjoy that little boy of yours."

I met Ella's anxious glance as I ended the call. "Well, I think we know how Lori and Nick were found."

Ella shook her head. "That was one of the first things I asked Lori. About if she could have given away her movements on social media. She said no. She must not have counted her business accounts as social media."

Ella and I put our heads together, checking the social media accounts of Penny, Roxanne, Rhys and Abby. But we didn't find anything that would give away their current locations. Abby barely had any online presence at all. She kept herself so private.

"Okay," I said. "Time to call them and find out."

I called Abby while Ella called Penny.

Abby said she hadn't posted anything anywhere. I asked her to post something that gave away her location, just in case.

Penny Foster said she'd been online to post on her blog, and she'd snapped a photo of herself to post along with it. That was enough. The time of the post would be logged, and her photo might show her home in the background.

But if the kidnapper was tracking Penny online, then he or she would know she was at home. Why then hadn't Max turned up?

That left Roxanne and Rhys Crane. I knew they were both waiting at home. The surveillance unit that was watching their house had nothing to report so far.

I called Roxanne, putting the phone on loudspeaker so that Ella could listen in.

"Detective Wakeland?" Roxanne replied, her voice rising sharply. "Do you have news for me? Detective Grimshaw told me that Elijah—"

"Roxanne, I'm sorry, there's no more news," I cut in awkwardly. "I need to know something. Did you have any previous plans for tonight?"

"No, no plans. Like I told Detective Grimshaw."

"Did you go anywhere earlier today?"

"No. I've got the flu. I'm sick as a dog. Barely left my bedroom."

"You were meant to be starting a fitness class, weren't you?"

"Not for a couple of weeks. We were just doing the promotion for it this month. Lena—my business partner—is doing a special promo tonight."

"A special promo? I know you said you were sick, but were you meant to be at the promo at all?"

"No. Lena's doing this one on her own. Good thing, too. Seeing as this flu's knocked me for six."

"Did you talk about the promo on social media at all?"

"Oh yeah. I'm a blabbermouth online and I'm everyone's best friend."

"I didn't see anything about it on your *Facebook* or *Instagram*."

"You should have checked that business card I gave you, Detective. It's got the name of my business on it. Lena and I have a dedicated *Facebook* and *Insta* account set up for it. What's all this about?"

I probably still had her business card mushed in the back pocket of my jeans. "We're just looking at a few different things. Trying to make sure we don't miss anything. Is your promotion at the fitness centre?"

"Nope. At the tech centre at Close Quarters. There's a big tech expo on tonight. We're showing our stuff there because, you know, techies need their fitness and back exercises because they sit on their backsides all day. That's where our classes come in."

I shook my head at Ella. Nothing that Roxanne had told me was sounding promising.

"Were you planning on dropping in at the conference at all?" I asked, seeds of desperation creeping into my voice.

"No. I've been busy with the other side of things. The financials and buying in shipments and all that. We're selling yoga mats and fitness watches. There was meant to be a shipment of fitness watches going with Lena to the tech centre, but it got held up. So, we're missing out on sales. Lena took my watch so she could at least demo it."

Ella's eyebrows shot up. She indicated towards her own fitness band. "These things ping your location," she whispered.

"Roxanne," I said urgently, "does your fitness watch have an online app?"

"Yeah, that's how you track your fitness."

I decided against telling Roxanne any more. She might get her family and friends racing down to the tech centre. And that might just ruin our chances if it spooked the kidnapper.

"Thanks Roxanne. That's all I wanted to know."

"Why all the questions? I don't get it."

"I'm sorry, I can't explain now."

"They're going to bring Olivia back to me, right? I've been waiting and waiting and waiting. I don't know if I can stand this any longer—"

"Roxanne, I'm so sorry, I need to cut this short. I'll be in touch." I took a breath as I ended the call, my heart rate climbing.

29

KATE

Nola dropped a handful of coins into the hot food vendor's hand and took her corncob-on-a-stick. The Tallman's Valley tech conference was crowded and noisy. There were many more men than women—the deep voices loud and noticeable.

A young girl knocked into Nola, clutching a doll. The girl drew back, briefly raising her face to Nola. She had a round, freckled face framed with frizzy blonde waves. She seemed familiar, but Nola couldn't recall where she'd seen her before.

A man walked past with a large box of goods, and Nola lost sight of the girl.

Nola bit into her corncob. What she really craved was popcorn smothered in butter and salt, but there was none of that at the conference centre. The emphasis was on healthy eating, and everyone was supposed to be *woke*. Any snacking had to be done in private—or you faced a drive out to the other suburbs where fast food was still king of the streets. Even the cinema at Close Quarters served a healthy popcorn option.

Anyway, it was better that she held back on the snacks now that she had a boyfriend. She had a reason to look good now, even though she worried that he'd soon realise that she could never look as good as a lot of girls did. Her hips were too wide, her shoulders too small and her features were plain.

Her boyfriend, Bryce Damont, was behind one of the conference stalls, promoting his company's virtual reality software for marketers. She didn't understand the software that he sold, but he made it all sound exciting. There was always something new and incredible happening in technology. Working in the nanny and pizza restaurant jobs that she did, she was a world away from all of that.

Sometimes, she was a little nervous to talk to Bryce about her days. Every day was pretty much the same in her nannying job. At least two of the siblings would spill their drinks. There would be at least ten tussles to break up among the children—fights over crayons or toys. The baby would often spit his milk up or have diarrhoea. It was damned tough facilitating the daily routines and lives of a group of tiny people. For all that, she enjoyed the job.

So far, Bryce had always smiled when she spoke of the children and said that he loved how she loved them. That made her feel warm but with a niggle of concern. Did Bryce want to have children in the future? Maybe he saw her as the motherly type. Her own childhood hadn't been a happy one and she couldn't imagine herself as a mother. The day that five of the nursery school children vanished had magnified that feeling a thousand times. The truth was that she'd planned on not having kids—ever. She didn't have any siblings, so she couldn't become an aunt either. If her future husband had nieces and nephews, of course she'd be happy to be an aunt to them. But it was too early in the relationship to have that kind of talk with Bryce. She just hoped he was on the same page as her.

She walked around, peering at the displays. Virtual reality games, electronic smart devices, sleep-monitoring watches, instant language translators, mixed-reality sunglasses, kitchen processors that could cook entire meals, and a dizzying array of other gadgets.

Human-looking robots on wheeled bases moved slowly around the aisles, offering bite-sized hors d'oeuvres from large trays. The robots stopped still if anyone stepped in front of them and didn't move off again until the path ahead was clear. Another robot collected people's trash and recycling waste. Bryce had said the robots were just a gimmick to impress the families that were coming here tonight.

The voices in the hall seemed to grow louder, clashing together in her head like drums and cymbals.

She was still feeling the effects of that interview she'd had with Detective Wakeland the other night. She hadn't meant to turn herself inside out and spill those terrible secrets. She'd kept that part of her life locked away since she was a young teenager. But now Detective Wakeland knew. She could no longer pretend it didn't happen.

Nola felt renewed disgust in herself. She'd allowed those things to happen to her. Why hadn't she protested and run to the neighbours for help? Why hadn't she told anyone back then?

She wondered if she'd ever be brave enough to tell Bryce. And if she did, how would he react? Would he wrap her in his arms and tell her everything was okay? Or would he look at her with a mixture of pity and revulsion?

For now, she'd keep it to herself. She didn't want to risk losing him.

It was bad enough that it had been reported in the news that she'd blanked out at the top of the hill on the day of the abductions. Bryce had told her not to worry about it. She'd been worried she'd lose her nannying job. She'd explained it to her employer as being due to the heat that day and a bad childhood memory about the ice-cream van. They'd been a little confused at first, but they'd decided to keep her on.

Nola finished her corncob and deposited the corn and wooden stick in a receptacle that one of the janitor robots provided. She carefully wiped her lips with a napkin and swished her mouth out with a gulp of water. The last thing she wanted was to talk to Bryce with a bit of corn in her teeth.

She walked around to the stall where she knew Bryce was working.

His face lit up when he saw her, his grin wide. "Nolahhhh, baby girl. There you are. How'd your day go?"

Returning his smile, Nola shyly avoided the attention of the other men at the stall. "It was a good day. The baby took his first step."

"Awww, cute as pie. Hey, wanna go out for Thai tonight?"

She nodded. "Sounds like a plan."

"Cool. I'm half-starved. The selection of food here leaves a lot to be desired." He winked.

His gaze lifted and he stared at the aisles beyond her, a curious look in his eyes. Nola turned. Three police officers were threading their way through the crowds. They seemed to be searching for something or someone. She recognised one of them. Senior Constable Cameron Vella. He was cute. But it hadn't been under happy circumstances the last time she'd come into contact with him. It'd been the day of the abductions.

Shuddering, she angled herself back to face Bryce. He was her way out of the darkness of her past—all of it. That was a lot to pin on one person. But she lived for his calm, happy personality. When she was with him, her past disappeared.

"I wonder if someone here is selling dodgy goods?" Bryce laughed. "Must be a slow day at the cop shop if they have to send out three of them."

Keeping her thoughts safely tucked away, Nola giggled.

A group of four men stepped across to Bryce's stall and began asking about the software. Bryce immediately switched to speaking in his professional business voice, explaining all the benefits. There wasn't room for Nola there anymore. That was okay. She could busy herself and come back later. The conference would be over in another hour, and she'd be going out with Bryce for dinner. Then they'd go back to her house for a coffee, and he'd sleep there. She lived for the hours she spent snuggled up with him in bed, his body warm against hers. Sometimes she made herself stay awake, just to enjoy that feeling for longer. The mornings always came too soon. He was staying over two or three times a week now. She dreamed of the day she and Bryce were living together. But he'd have to ask her first.

The police officers exited the conference centre. She guessed that Bryce would find out why they'd been here, and he'd tell her later. She suddenly became anxious, wondering what she had to talk about with Bryce over dinner. She needed some hobbies, something to give her conversation points. And she could read up more on current events. Bryce always knew about interesting things happening in the world. But she had so little time in between her two jobs. A wave of depression hit her out of nowhere. She was dull, boring. What did Bryce even see in her?

She decided to run home and change her clothes and spruce up her makeup. She could at least make herself look more appealing. She'd be back in plenty of time for dinner.

Her car was parked around near the nursery school—the closer parking bays had been all full up by the time she'd arrived.

She walked outside and then through the parking areas. Around near the nursery school, the parking bay was deserted, apart from thin drifts of fog. She pulled her cardigan in close around her middle.

She thought she saw a child huddled near the gates of the empty nursery school. Why would a kid be out here on their own? Then she lost sight of the image.

Squinting, she walked closer, trying to find the spot in the darkness where she'd seen the small figure.

There.

A little girl. Crouching in the grass next to the gate. Holding a doll.

She was the child who'd bumped into Nola earlier.

Forgetting the cold and fog now, Nola let her cardigan fly open as she ran across the parking bay.

She knelt in front of the girl. "You must be freezing out here. Come back inside with me and we'll find your parents."

The girl shook her head.

"Did something in there scare you?" Nola asked.

A police car drove past on the road, outside the parking bay. The little girl scrambled back, out of the light.

"Was it the police?" Nola asked. "Were you scared of the police officers in the hall?"

The girl nodded.

"Are your parents in there?"

She shook her head again.

"No parents? Well, you must have come here with *someone*. Take my hand and we'll go back in there."

The girl pointed firmly at the nursery school.

"It's empty. All closed up," Nola told her. "Hey, I bet you've got a little brother or sister who goes to the nursery school, don't you?"

"*I* go there," she said, speaking for the first time.

"You do? You're tall for nursery school."

"I'm three."

"Three?" Nola appraised the girl. She was a long way from being three years old. Perhaps she had a developmental delay.

"What's your name?" Nola asked gently.

"Livvie."

"Do you have a last name, Livvie?"

"I think it is Crane. Like the bird."

Taking her hand, Nola brought her out into the overhead lights.

There had been a little girl that Nola had only spent a couple of days with, at the nursery school, three and a half years ago. She'd had a round face and freckles and her hair had been pale and frizzy. Yes, Nola had only spent a few hours with her, but she'd also seen her age-progressed image on countless news stories.

With a sudden realisation, Nola knew exactly who the girl was.

30

KATE

Cameron called, telling me that he and the other two police officers had not sighted Olivia at the tech centre, nor any little girl on her own.

I had it all wrong. Either the abductor hadn't intended returning Olivia, or they weren't tracking the parents online. I'd needlessly taken three police officers away from their posts.

"It made sense," Ella offered. "We don't have much to go on at the moment, but that was something at least. Not just a stab in the dark."

I exhaled wearily. "Thanks, Ella. Detective Grimshaw won't hold back much longer. This whole thing will be splashed all over the media soon."

There was an incoming call.

It was Nola.

"Hello..." Her voice was hesitant. "Either I'm going half-nuts... or I've just found Olivia Crane."

I gasped. "Where are you?"

"I'm at the Tallman's Valley tech centre."

"I sent police there already. They didn't find her. What's your exact location?"

"Outside, near the nursery school."

"Out there?"

"Yes, she was hiding."

"You both must be cold. Wait inside the tech centre. I'll be there in ten minutes."

I left Ella watching my house while I took my own car. I didn't want to leave my post. But I was desperate to talk to Olivia and gain more information about Ivy and who the abductor of the children was—before Roxanne arrived and potentially refused to allow her child to talk. I'd asked Ella to call Roxanne and tell her the news in five minutes' time.

———

I parked outside the tech centre and hurried inside.

Nola was waiting for me at the entry, a young girl beside her—the girl holding a large doll. The two of them looked like a young mother and daughter, or two sisters. It was difficult to believe that this was Olivia Crane, one of the five children so many people had searched for over the past years. She was tall for age six and easily looked seven or even eight.

I scanned the girl's face. The features seemed right. Eyes that slanted slightly downwards at the outsides. Thin lips. Freckles. Blonde, kinky hair. But she'd still need to be properly ID'ed.

The more I looked, the more I grew certain that Nola was right. This was Olivia.

"Nola, thank goodness you found this little one," I said. "She was hiding out near the nursery school?"

Nola nodded, her eyes huge. "She was actually inside the hall at first. I saw her a couple of times but didn't realise who she was. And then later, when I went out to my car, I noticed a little girl sitting near the gate of the nursery school. She told me she was scared of the police and was hiding from them."

"Oh no," I said. I bent down to the girl. "I'm Kate. I'm sorry you were scared by the police officers. They were trying to find you, to help you."

Olivia's face creased into a scowl. "I can't let them take me away. Polly said I have to find my mother."

She'd just mentioned a name. *Polly.*

I memorised the name.

Olivia sounded a lot more confident and outspoken than Charlotte had. That was good. She might be able to answer some questions.

"I won't let anyone take you away," I assured Olivia. "And you'll be back with your family tonight."

"I can't believe it," breathed Nola. "Olivia. After all this time."

"Nola, can I ask that you don't tell anyone. Not tonight. Until we figure out what's going on?"

"Of course," she replied. "The police obviously knew she'd be here?"

"It was a guess. Wait here. I'm just going to take Olivia over to the seats and ask her a few questions." I didn't want Nola listening in.

Taking Olivia's hand, I guided her over to a line of seats in the foyer.

"Would you like a blanket?" I asked her. I'd brought in a blanket from my car. I'd worried that the little girl might have been outside in the cold for quite a while.

She nodded.

I wrapped the blanket around her. "Does that feel better?"

"Yes."

"It won't be long until your mum and dad and your brother and sister are here, okay?"

"Okay."

"Your brother and sister will look quite a bit different to last time you saw them. They'll be bigger and older. And so are you."

She looked a little confused, so I didn't continue talking about her family.

"I'm so glad to see you," I said. "A lot of people have been hoping to see you again. Did you know that?"

She shook her head, hugging her doll beneath the blanket.

"It sounds like someone named Polly has been looking after you. Is that right?"

She nodded.

"Did Polly have anyone to help her?"

"Bear."

"Bear?"

179

"That's his name."

"So, a man named Bear and a woman named Polly?"

"Yes."

So, there were two people involved in this. Bear's name was obviously fake and Polly's might be, too.

"Do you know where you were living with Polly and Bear?" I asked.

"A long way from here," she responded. "It was a long, long time in the car."

"Who else was in the car with you?"

"I'm not sure. Polly didn't let us see. It was a special game. We had to be good, or we couldn't keep our gifts."

"Did you see Ivy before you got in the car?"

For the first time, she didn't answer my question.

The breath in my lungs felt sharp, cutting. Her sudden silence was telling. I didn't know whether it was right or wrong to keep questioning her about Ivy. She was a little girl who'd be feeling enormous stress right now. And I was the wrong person to be questioning her. I knew that.

Forcing myself to find a calm centre, I slowed my breathing.

"Olivia, can you tell me about Ivy?"

"Ivy called me Livvie. She called everyone names like that. I was Livvie. Charlotte was Lottie. Elijah was Jahjie. And Max was Maxxy."

That hadn't been the information I was looking for. But it rang so true that I had to tell myself not to lose it. It was *so* like Ivy to change people's names. Ever since Ivy had found out her mother's name had been shortened from Abigail to Abby, she'd made it her mission to add an *ee* sound to the end of everyone's name.

"Livvie, where was the last place that you saw Ivy?"

"She was on the ground."

My heart glitched. "On the ground?"

She nodded, her eyes grown distant. "Ivy was under a pile of sticks. I thought she was just hiding, and I got a stick and poked her, but she didn't move. I asked Bear to help get the sticks off her, but he was busy digging in the garden. I asked Polly, too." She took a shaky breath. "Polly said Ivy got sick and got dead, and it couldn't be helped."

A chorus charged through my mind. *Ivy is dead. Ivy is dead. Ivy is dead.*

"What was Bear digging?" The words faded on my tongue.

"I don't know. It was silly because it was time for us to go, but Bear had to stay behind and dig. And we wanted him to come, too." Her forehead creased and her eyes glistened with tears. "Polly said it was a shame about Ivy because we'd all been so good and it was time to go home."

I summoned every ounce of strength I had left. "You've been very brave in answering the questions. You did well."

I drew the blanket up around her shoulders where it had slipped, trying to make her feel secure after her revelations.

A black rage rose inside me.

The fog had thickened outside the plate-glass walls of the entry. I watched a car emerge from the misty haze. Roxanne, Rhys and their two kids rushed out from the car and through the fog.

31

PENNY FOSTER

Fifteen minutes earlier

Penny glanced out the window at the police surveillance vehicle. She could barely see it now through the fog.

Tension knotted and gnarled in her veins.

She needed something. Heading out to the kitchen, she made herself a cup of tea. She stirred the tea loudly, knocking the sides of the cup with the spoon. It was too quiet in the house, far too quiet. The waiting was scraping her nerves raw.

She sat at her desk, opening her laptop again.

Sixty-four people had either replied or reacted to the poem she'd written earlier. People had somehow found their way to her blog when she'd first started it, back when Max was born. He'd been born with allergies, so it was other mothers of allergic babies then. When Max went missing, a new crowd came rushing in. She didn't know whether they really cared, or they were just feeding on her misery.

But they liked her poem, and that was something. People knew about what she was feeling inside.

Browsing to a music site, she listened to some songs she used to love. Anything to take her mind off and fill in the empty spaces of the house.

She returned the teacup to the kitchen. Drifts of fog stole through the yard outside. It was quite creepy. She'd always disliked the fog here. She'd prefer to live in the tropics, where foggy mornings and nights were rare.

A shadow moved in the yard. A figure. Someone was sitting on the swing. Someone small.

With her back rigid, Penny stepped to the back door and swung it open. A boy looked across to her. He wasn't dressed for the chilled air, clad in just a long-sleeved shirt and pants. He was shivering. In his arms, he held a box that was large in size and narrow in depth. Kate had instructed her that Max would be carrying a set of paints.

Her hand reached across her mouth and she stifled a cry.

Max.

32

KATE

My eyes snapped open.

I was in my bed. My bedroom window showed me a rain-soaked day.

I'd just woken, deep in a dream.

In the dream, I'd been in the car with Ella, staking out my house. Ella was sleeping. It was dawn, the sun softly golden. And then she'd just appeared—*Ivy*—sitting on the front step of my house, arms crossed and waiting. She walked down the steps and away from me, down the street. I tried to call her, to follow her, but I couldn't find my voice, nor could I seem to find my way out of the car.

And then I'd woken.

I rubbed my face. The dream had been cruel.

Reality marched in, grey and flat.

By the end of last night, four children had been returned. None of them Ivy.

All the returned children had now said the same things about Ivy.

Ivy was lying on the wet grass. Covered with sticks. Polly was upset and said Ivy had died. Bear was digging in the garden.

My stomach twisted until I wanted to vomit. I sobbed, watching the rain dribble down the window.

The only bright spots of light in all this darkness were the children that had been returned. Charlotte, Elijah, Olivia and then Max.

Max was the last one to return to his family. He'd been sent on a bush track that led behind the houses on Penny's side of the street. He'd been told to go right to the end house, as that was where his mother's house stood. I didn't know about the track and never suspected that the kidnappers would choose to send Max home that way.

It had still been light when Max had been sent on his journey. But he'd gotten lost and afraid, and then he'd fallen asleep all alone beside the track. When he'd woken, he'd found his way in total darkness, to the yard of the house that he hadn't seen since he was three. A remarkable young child. He could easily have gotten lost in the thousands of square kilometres of bushland or blundered over a cliff edge. But he'd made his way home after dark. He was safe.

Max was at the hospital now, with the other children.

Pete wasn't beside me. I checked the clock. 8:42 a.m. Pete would have been up hours ago. I'd gone to bed just after five.

I'd waited for Ivy in my car until dawn.

After I'd spoken to Olivia Crane, I'd returned to watch my house, while keeping in constant contact with the officer who was staking out Abby's house. There had been no activity. No suspicious vehicles. Nothing.

I stepped from the bed into the bracing air and then into the bathroom for a shower. My body and head felt so, so heavy. I washed my face vigorously.

Polly and Bear, whoever you are, I'm coming for you.

I walked down the stairs to the kitchen. Pete was in there, coffee brewing. His eyes were dark and bloodshot.

Silently, he put his arms out. Stepping across, I fell into those arms. His hug was an island, a recharge, a meditation. It had always been those things.

When I'd come home in the early hours, I'd told Pete everything the children had said about Ivy, pouring everything out. Now came the task of telling Abby. Grimshaw had agreed to keep back the details about Ivy from the media until I'd had a chance to speak with my daughter.

"Abby called while you were sleeping," Pete said softly. "I wasn't going to wake you. You needed some rest. She's waiting for me to call to tell her when to come over."

I closed my eyes against a wave of exhaustion. "Call her...."

"Right now?" Pete said with concern. "Are you sure you don't need some time?"

I shook my head. "She deserves to know."

Abby arrived within fifteen minutes. For once, she didn't have Jasper with her. She rushed in.

Her eyes were huge and reddened, her face blotchy. "Mum, please, tell me why? Why were all the kids returned except for Ivy? Where is she? What's going on?"

Inhaling a low, deep breath, I sat her down, and told her everything I knew. By the end, we were both sobbing. Watching the pain my daughter was in was heart wrenching.

I wished I had something better to tell her, even some small thread of hope. But I didn't.

———

The moment I informed Grimshaw that I'd spoken with Abby, she called a press conference. Bigley wanted me to be there. As the detective who'd been the one who was the most intricately involved with the operation last night, he thought I'd be the best positioned to answer many of the questions.

Speaking to the media was the last thing I wanted to do today. Especially now that everyone knew what I knew last night: *Ivy is dead*.

I walked into the station, my nerves on a razor-thin edge. The conference was being held in the media room upstairs at the station. On my way to the lift, I passed by the room where the Flying Fox team was assembled.

"*Good luck!*" they called in unison.

Sympathetic faces turned to me, some with a note of surprise. I guessed that they didn't expect me to show up today. Only around a quarter of the team were in there. I knew that some were out on the job, talking to people and gathering any evidence they could.

Breathing in a deep lung full of air, I continued onto the lift and then rode to the next floor.

Grimshaw nodded at me, sitting behind a desk that was set up with microphones. I took my place beside her at the desk.

She glanced around at the journalists who had gathered in the conference room. "We'll get started, shall we?"

The media cameras were pointed at us and the journalists waited.

"Last night was a good result," Grimshaw began. "Four missing children have been returned to their families. These children have been missing since December 2016. Charlotte Hinton, Elijah Parrish, Olivia Crane and Max Foster. The fifth child, Ivy Wakeland, was not returned. It is with deep sadness that I tell you that the initial reports from the returned children indicate that Ivy is no longer alive. Obviously, this is of deep distress to the strike force team. Our goal in missing person cases is always to return the individual unharmed. This is especially so in cases of children. I want to thank my team for all their hard work and dedication on this high-profile and puzzling case. We have a large number of leads to follow up, and our task is focused on apprehending the people responsible."

"How are the children?" came the first question from the journalists. "When can the public expect to see images of them?"

"The children are currently having breakfast at the hospital," Grimshaw told them. "They are physically well. The head of the psychologist team who has been appointed to the children, Dr Li Zhang, has informed us that the children need rest and to reacquaint themselves with their families. Their welfare is our priority."

A barrage of questions followed.

To me, the voices sounded shrill and like the roars of lions at the same time. I was glad that Grimshaw was taking the brunt of it. I held on, waiting for the end of it.

"Detective Wakeland," said a lanky male journalist. "I saw a report that says you figured out that all the parents were being tracked online. And you figured out that Olivia Crane would be at the Tallman's Valley tech centre, via a fitness watch app, is that correct?"

"The specific knowledge about the fitness watch app was thanks to Constable Ella Valletti," I said.

He nodded.

A question then came at me like an arrow from a female journalist. "Detective Wakeland, is it possible that the abduction of your granddaughter was a kind of revenge plot? A plan to make you pay for putting an offender in jail?"

I gasped silently, feeling as if the wind had been knocked out of me. "That's... pure speculation... and I have no reply to speculation." I followed the rules of replying to journalists who had an agenda. *Do not engage.*

The journalist, an older woman with shrewd eyes and hair in a messy dark bun, fired back with, "But with Ivy dead—most probably murdered—and the other children alive and back with their families, isn't it fair to say that it seems like a deliberate act? You're a senior homicide detective with decades under her belt. You must have put away a lot of crims in your time."

Grimshaw shook her head, holding up a hand. "I'm putting a stop to that line of questioning. The children have only just been returned last night. It's too soon to narrow down theories."

The conference was over quickly. I was thankful that Grimshaw shut it down after fifteen minutes, stating that we had important work to attend to.

I left the conference and went to grab a coffee and sit in an unused office by myself and decompress. I didn't feel like eating. Right now, it seemed as if I'd never want food again. My stomach was churning.

A message came through on my phone. Bigley wanted a meeting with Grimshaw and myself, pronto.

I finished my coffee and headed down to his office.

Grimshaw was already there. I felt distinctly uncomfortable as I walked in, knowing that those two had already been talking.

"How are you, Kate?" Bigley asked.

I sat. "Not good."

He frowned in a commiserative way. "It's a horrific outcome for your family. How did your daughter take the news?"

"I'm worried for her," I replied. "This is incredibly cruel."

"Yes, it is. Astonishingly so. I've, ah, just seen the press conference. Streamed via closed circuit. Thank you for braving that. Those were some difficult questions that reporter levelled at you."

I nodded. "That's their job. To speculate and make a story out of nothing."

He crinkled his heavily hooded eyes in a kind of wincing gesture. "It might not be entirely nothing."

"What do you mean?" I asked him.

"This is not an easy thing to say. But it does seem odd that you joined the strike force... and then suddenly, the children are returned."

"You think there's a connection, too?"

He exhaled. "The situation we have on our hands is that four of the children have been returned. While one of them has not. And the one that hasn't been returned is your granddaughter. And from what we understand, all five were alive and well up until yesterday."

I glanced at Grimshaw. She was staying silent, but I guessed she'd known exactly what Bigley had planned to tell me.

"What are you saying, Andrew?" I said sharply. "Plain words."

"In plain words, it could be that Ivy was abducted due to a grievance that the abductor had with you. And then killed for the same reason."

I was stunned into silence. He was basically saying the same thing the reporter had. Was everyone thinking the same thing?

"Kate..." He sighed. "You know as well as I do that many threats are made against detectives. It's possible that the two abductors decided to act instead of threaten."

"That's a big leap to make, Andrew. A very big leap."

"Yes, but it can't be ruled out. This case has been extraordinary in all measures."

"If it were true," I said, my voice straining, "then why wouldn't they just take Ivy? Why five children? And for so long?"

"I can't answer that," he said. "But it could be someone who is prepared

189

to play the long game. Someone who planned for this moment in which they'd release four of the children, except for one. Ivy."

"Who would do such a thing?"

"Perhaps someone who got out of jail three and a half years ago," he replied. "Or perhaps relatives of a person who is currently in jail."

I'd dealt with lots of people in my job who hated me with a fury. They believed that their spouse or family member who I'd arrested for murder was innocent, and they still believed it, years or decades after the person was convicted and put in jail.

My head suddenly felt hollow, dizzy.

I looked from Bigley to Grimshaw. "Do you think the same?" I asked Grimshaw.

"Yes," she said bluntly. "It's a possibility. Doesn't mean it's true. But it is true that you've put a lot of people behind bars over your career. And the developments yesterday proved that something very unusual is going on. It seems to me that these unusual circumstances could have impeded our investigation over the years. Because it's a very difficult task to find a person who is out for revenge. They're not going to have the same trail to follow as other criminals—such as paedophiles or extortionists."

I sank back in the chair. Of course Grimshaw was going to go along with what Bigley was saying. It let her off the hook for a strike force that had achieved nothing and an investigation that had gone nowhere.

I was the scapegoat.

But could there be a shred of truth in it? A reel of faces spun through my mind, the faces of criminals I'd arrested for murder.

"Kate," said Bigley, cutting through my thoughts. "Due to these developments, I think it best that you take a few days off from Strikeforce Flying Fox."

"What?"

"You'll still be part of the team," he explained. "But you won't join the meetings. I hope you understand, this is to protect you."

"You only just put me onto the team," I argued. "Just days ago."

"Everything changed yesterday," he told me. "You're dealing with the probable death of a grandchild. The media attention is already extreme and it's going to be unrelenting. I don't think it's wise to put you under that kind of pressure."

"Because you think I'm going to crack?" I said.

He studied me for a moment. "Kate, I'm trying to help you... not hurt you. You're a boat in turbulent seas right now."

I wanted to walk out, but I didn't have the emotional energy for that. My soul felt punctured.

"I have a request," I said.

"Of course," said Andrew.

"I want to be able to speak with the returned children. As soon as they're ready to talk. If I'm still a part of the team, then I should be able to do that."

Grimshaw nodded. "That's fine. I'll let you know when and where. I'd rather take you along than Booth. Booth is very good, but she's been in the child abuse squad for years, going hard after paedophiles. Her skill set is in dealing with those kinds of people. I've heard that her squad doesn't tend to send her out to talk with children. She has a bit of an abrupt manner."

"Okay, I'll wait for that call," I said. I bit back tears. I was not going to cry in front of these two.

33

KATE

Bigley was correct about one thing. The intensity of the media attention. Dealing with the media attention was something I'd been used to for decades—every serious crime attracted the focus of crime reporters. But the return of the children had whipped up a ferocious level of interest.

I stayed away from the news coverage. I didn't want to see pictures of Ivy with the word *dead* attached to them. And I didn't want to know any more about me being the reason for Ivy's abduction. Privately though, I searched through old homicide cases of mine, thinking deeply about who could be possibly be responsible for this.

Police had sent out requests that reporters stay well clear of my house and Abby's house, due to the fact that the kidnappers had been in the process of returning their abductees. But it was clear to everyone that Ivy was not going to be returned.

When I woke, there were rogue reporters camped outside our house.

Pete was at the window in his undershorts, looking out and scowling. "This isn't right."

"No, it isn't," I said, joining him at the window. "They just don't care. This is our family and we've just had the worst possible thing happen."

"I'll go down and grab the hose and spray them all in a minute," he said. "In this weather, they'll freeze."

"Pete..." I said. "I have to say something. And it's terrible."

He turned to me.

I swallowed. "I've been thinking. If it's true, about the vengeance plot, then... then if the kidnappers do return Ivy... it might be her body."

Gently, he brought my head against his shoulder. I could feel the tremble in his arm and body.

"We'll make sure that someone is always here around the clock," he said.

"I think that's best. We just don't know what they're planning."

———

It rained hard for the next day, the kind of torrential rain that seems as if it will never end until the water has risen over all our heads.

I spent the day at home, researching deeply into my case files of Brent Cole's cousin, Dale. He'd killed another man in a knife fight. At the time, it had seemed like someone else was responsible for the killing until I'd uncovered a vital piece of evidence that implicated Dale.

Could he have held a hate for me so strong that he'd retaliated with the kidnapping plot, all these years later? I stayed up way into the small hours of the night, turning it over and over in my mind.

The next day, the news came through to police that the four returned children were cleared for an interview.

The hospital had finished their tests. The children had been positively ID'd, and they'd had their initial physical and psychological examinations. All four were well-rested, having had lots of sleeps and counselling.

The psychologist in charge of the children's welfare indicated that they were ready for a light level of questioning.

Right now, that was the best news I could hope for. The four children were the key to the identity of the abductors. My desire to find Bear and Polly burned inside my chest with a furious intensity.

I drove to the station and met Grimshaw at a back exit. We drove to the hospital together. A police compositor named Lucas Salisbury was going to meet us there, to help with the interview.

At the hospital, Grimshaw and I met with a psychologist in an office near the children's ward. Her name was Dr Li Zhang and she was smartly dressed in a white blouse and skirt.

"Before you begin," Dr Zhang said, "I want to tell you that there is something causing me great concern."

I braced myself. Because whatever these four children had undergone, Ivy was likely to have undergone, too.

"But I'll get to that in a minute," Dr Zhang continued. "Overall, the children are remarkably well-balanced, everything considered. We've been assisting them through their reintroduction to their families. They don't remember them well, which is upsetting for everyone. Everything is strange and new to the children. The adjustment period is going to take some time."

"Charlotte wanted to be called Lottie last time I spoke to her," I said. "And Olivia said all of them had nicknames. Should we be mindful of that?"

"No special names," said Dr Zhang. "Charlotte's mother insisted that her daughter answer to *Charlotte*. And she told all the parents to ensure their children were called their right names. She can be quite... forceful."

"Lori Hinton—forceful? I don't believe it," Grimshaw quipped.

The psychologist shrugged helplessly.

"Is it possible to speak with each child alone?" asked Grimshaw.

A niggling frown indented Dr Zhang's forehead. "They can be seen without their parents, but if it's any kind of intensive interview—longer than two or three questions—I recommend that the children are all interviewed together."

"That might cause issues for us," said Grimshaw. "Because if we have a group together, they might start agreeing with each other rather than drawing from their own experience. It's called eyewitness distortion, and I'm going to take a stab in the dark and guess that young kids would be even more prone to that than adults."

Dr Zhang shook her head. "It's less than twenty-four hours since they were returned. They're fragile. And I'm afraid they're showing distress when they're separated and in the company of strangers. We must remember they've been isolated from the world for over three years." She drew her small, rosebud lips in. "Also, it seems they've been taught to fear the police. So that's an added reason to keep them together. They might feel safer."

"Shame," said Grimshaw. "Were there any physical signs of abuse—sexual or otherwise?"

"None that could be detected," Dr Zhang answered. "No signs of sexual abuse. And no bruises, apart from small scrapes on the knees and shins that you'd normally expect young children to have. The X-rays from last night didn't show any old broken bones. Of course, there might be things they're not ready to tell us yet. As I said, it's been less than a day."

I was relieved to hear that much. I'd give anything to know that Ivy hadn't suffered in the years since she'd been gone.

"You said there was an area causing you concern?" I asked Dr Zhang.

"I'm afraid so," she said. "The thing is that the children don't know how old they are. It's like it's been one long year since the time they went missing."

I gasped. "So, they think they're still... *three?*"

Dr Zhang nodded in confirmation. "Yes. They know they've gotten bigger and they know they're not so little anymore. But their perceptions are very skewed. None of them have any idea that they're six years old."

Grimshaw scowled. "That's bizarre."

"Yes, it is," agreed Dr Zhang. "It's going to make the adjustment period harder for them."

I sighed, my breath tense. "I'm guessing it's going to be difficult to interview them, everything considered."

"Yes," she said. "I've done my best to prepare them. I've told them that the police who are coming to talk to them today are good people who want to help them. Their parents are waiting in another room. If the children should become distressed, I'll bring the parents in." She paused. "Well, I'll show you through."

Grimshaw and I met up with the police compositor, and we followed

195

the psychologist to an airy space with brightly coloured walls, toys and plush floor cushions. I guessed that it was normally a playroom for the child patients at the hospital. There were also chairs, a desk and a projector screen.

Four young children sat cross-legged on cushions.

Seeing them filled me with a mix of delight and sorrow. I tried to imagine Ivy sitting beside them, but I couldn't. Ivy, in my mind, was still a tiny child of three.

The children resembled their age-progression images, but they were also very different. The age-progression drawings had been based on a number of guesses, such as if a child's nose or mouth or chin was going to develop to look more like their mother's or father's. And it was just an educated guess how much thicker or darker their hair might grow. Adult teeth were another thing that greatly changed a child's appearance. When they were three, the children all had their milk teeth. Now, they all had their adult teeth growing in.

"Elijah, Max, Olivia and Charlotte," said Dr Zhang, "I know that one or more of you have already met these two ladies, but for those of you who haven't, this is Reagan and Kate. And this man is Lucas. He'll be drawing some pictures for you."

"Good morning, Reagan. Good morning, Kate. Good morning Lucas. We'll have a great day together," they said in unison.

Their chant surprised me. It was the exact same chant that the kids at the nursery school were taught when Ivy used to go there. They said it each morning when greeting the teachers.

"Okay," Dr Zhang said to the children. "Reagan and Kate would like to ask you a few questions. Nothing too hard." She smiled, showing even teeth. "I'm going to be staying. I'll just be right here."

Dr Zhang took a seat at the back of the room. Grimshaw and I each took a seat at the front. The seats were child sized. Grimshaw sat awkwardly, perching on the edge. I was out of practice with sitting in such tiny chairs myself. It'd been a long time since I'd sat and played tea parties with Ivy.

Lucas went to sit on the only adult-sized chair and placed his computer on the nearby desk. He fiddled about getting set up, connecting his computer wirelessly to the device that would send pictures to the projector screen.

In the meantime, I asked the children some light questions about how their day had been so far. Grimshaw seemed relieved that I'd taken the lead with the children. This scenario seemed way out of her comfort zone.

Lucas indicated silently that he was ready to begin.

"Kids," I said, "if you could take a look at the screen over there on the wall, Lucas is going to play a game with you."

The children looked across the room to the screen with interest. The screen showed a picture of the shoe from the nursery rhyme, *There was an Old Woman Who Lived in a Shoe.*

Lucas grinned at the children. "I know that you kids lived somewhere together just before you came here," he told them. "And I have to guess what it looked like. This is my first guess. A big shoe!"

That produced a laugh from the children. They shook their heads. It was a good start.

Next, Lucas brought up a picture of an igloo, a tent, a pumpkin and then a range of houses.

Lucas kept guessing wrong. When he guessed they'd lived in a single storey farmhouse style home, the children didn't seem certain whether he'd guessed right or not.

Immediately, Lucas began showing pictures of different farmhouses. The children agreed that one of them was more or less correct.

A chill sped through me. Was this the kind of house the children had been kept at over the past years? Lucas's method was certainly efficient. He'd narrowed down the style of house within minutes.

Lucas began altering the picture of the house, adding bits and taking bits away as the children instructed him. He added a chimney and the children nodded. Elijah said there was a big tree out the front. Lucas added the tree, then went through the same process of cycling through different trees. The right tree ended up being a Moreton Bay Fig.

Next, Lucas began painting in details of the surrounds. First, he drew houses either side. The children shook their heads. He took the other houses away and drew in more land. The children kept nodding as he drew in a broader and broader landscape, until the house was small on a wide space of land.

"Like this?" Lucas asked them.

The children nodded.

Grimshaw and I exchanged glances. The children had been kept on a large property.

He continued as far as he could, drawing in details. A ladder against the tree. A round window in the front door. Flowers either side of a porch.

Lucas looked across at when he was done. I understood that he wanted instruction on how to proceed from there.

"Kids," I said. "We'd like to know who lived at that house."

The children reeled off the names. Charlotte, Ivy, Elijah, Max, Olivia, Polly, Bear.

"Who can tell me what Polly looks like?" I asked.

"She looks like Doris Day," Olivia told me.

Lucas shot me a quizzical look.

"You mean, Doris Day from the movies?" I said to Olivia. The children must have been watching some very old films.

She nodded. *"With Six You Get Eggroll.* That was one of our favourites."

Lucas took the cue and began showing pictures of blonde women aged anywhere from thirty to sixty. The children settled on a picture of a smiling woman of about forty. Lucas got to work on her features, making her nose and eyes different shapes and asking the children if he was *warmer* or *colder.*

The process soon fell apart as the children found it difficult to pinpoint her features.

Grimshaw then asked the children if they could tell us what Bear looked like. The children were a lot more definite about his features than they'd been about Polly's. Again, Lucas cycled through pictures of men, trying younger and older men.

Bear ended up looking about thirty-five, with an open, genial expression.

"You've done so well," I told the children. "Just a few more questions. Is that okay?"

They nodded, but they were starting to grow a little restless, looking about and touching the nearby toys. I'd have to be quick.

"Hmmm, I'm thinking about... pets, now," I said. "Did you have any pets?"

Elijah put up his hand. "We have dogs."

"Wonderful!" I smiled. "I love dogs. My family used to have a cocker spaniel. It used to stand on its own ears sometimes." I pulled a humorous face.

The kids giggled.

"What kind of dogs did you have?" I prompted.

"They're big. Real big," said Elijah.

"Were they always big?" I asked. "Or did you get them when they were small, like puppies?"

"They fit into a basket at first," said Olivia, extending her hands out about thirty centimetres. "But then they got bigger and ate the basket."

I laughed. "When did you get them?"

The children seemed stumped with that question. I knew some things were going to be hard for them to remember. They were just tiny children when they were abducted.

Charlotte knitted her eyebrows together. "They were always there. They were the first things I saw the first time I walked into the house."

Of all the children, Charlotte seemed to have the best memory recall. She'd remembered her parents' faces and the cat that she'd had at age three —Cinnamon.

"What colour are the dogs?" I asked.

"White," Olivia piped up.

Lucas took the cue and cycled through pictures of large white dogs. The kids couldn't decide between a white German shepherd and a very pale golden retriever.

"That looks just like Elsa," said Olivia when Lucas showed a photo of a golden retriever running in a field. The retriever was cream-coloured.

The other children nodded.

"Any other pets?" I asked.

"We had chickens," Olivia told me. "They didn't let me catch them and hug them. Polly sent us to get the eggs every morning. We all had two eggs every morning. Polly, too."

"Chickens!" I exclaimed. "Lovely. Chickens are fun."

"Are we going to go back there?" said Max, speaking for the first time. "I miss Snowdrop and Elsa and the chickens." Tears wet his cheeks.

"Are Snowdrop and Elsa the dogs' names?" I asked.

He nodded.

Elijah locked his arms around his knees and began rocking.

"Elijah," called Dr Zhang, "are you okay?"

His brow crinkled and a look of confusion entered his dark eyes. "I have a new sister. Gracie."

"You've been away for a while," Dr Zhang told him carefully. "While you were away, your parents had a baby."

"She's this much." Elijah held up two fingers. "And I'm this much." He held up three fingers. "But I'm big. I'm big like Jade. I'm not little."

I knew that Jade was Elijah's seven-year-old sister.

Charlotte bit her lip. "We got big. Because we ran a lot and climbed the tree. That made us big and strong."

Max nodded at Charlotte, content with that explanation.

Elijah fixed his gaze on me. "Jade said she was in big school. In Year Two. Am I supposed to be in big school, too?"

I wasn't sure what to answer.

Olivia began humming, playing with her fingers. "Don't ask them. Polly and Bear said the police are not our friends."

"You're all correct about how big you've gotten," the psychologist told them. "You're all so much bigger and stronger." She glanced across at Grimshaw and me. "I'm going to ask the parents to come in. Maybe just a couple more questions, but that's all."

"Thank you," I said. I'd been worried she was going to end the session right there and then. With the interview about to wind down, I had to ask the questions that we most needed the answers to. Perhaps it was best that the parents be here, because the following set of questions might well prove to be the most challenging for the children.

Taking out her phone, Dr Zhang made a call.

The parents of the four children were quick making their way to the room. I imagined they'd been sitting in the other room worried and wondering about what their children were telling us. None of the children's siblings were present.

The parents assembled at the back of the room, smiling at their children but their eyes anxious. Lori Hinton seemed to cast a distasteful glance at Roxanne Crane as she passed by her. Sean Hinton kept his head down and stood beside Lori, but not close to her. Rhys wasn't there. Nick and Marcy Parrish were holding hands. Penny Foster had her lips pressed firmly together, looking as if any minute she might dissolve into tears.

"Reagan, Kate and Lucas have been asking the children some very interesting questions," Dr Zhang told the parents. "And Lucas has drawn some fantastic pictures. There are just a few questions to go."

I briefly smiled in acknowledgment at the group of parents and then nodded at Dr Zhang.

"Okay," I said to the children. "We're going to try to play a remembering game. Can anyone remember a day at a place called *Tall Ponds*?"

Taking the cue, Lucas put up a picture of *The Ponds* on the screen.

"You had a picnic there," I told the kids.

Next, Lucas put up a photo of the picnic rugs and food. We omitted any pictures of the children when they were aged three. The psychologist hadn't been certain if the children were ready to see them.

The children shook their heads.

"There was an ice-cream van at the picnic one day," I said.

Lucas showed a picture of Brent Cole's van. And then a picture of Brent himself.

None of the children showed any recognition at all.

The children had vague memories of their families and the nursery school, but it seemed that for the most part, their memories began at the house that they were taken to. I had no chance of discovering anything about the day they were taken. And there was no point in asking them any more questions about it.

I had some difficult questions on my list. I thought I might as well get them out of the way.

Charlotte yawned. The other children followed suit.

I made an exaggerated yawn. "Well, I'm thinking about sleeping, now. Because I'm a little tired." I yawned again for effect. "Can you tell me where you slept when you lived with Polly and Bear?"

"Me and Olivia and Ivy slept in a big bed," Charlotte told me. "And Elijah and Max slept in a little bed."

I inhaled slowly before asking my next question. "Did anyone else sleep in the beds with you?"

A few of the parents covered their mouths with their hands, visibly upset by the question.

But the four children shook their heads firmly.

"Never?" I said. "Did any of you ever sleep with Bear or Polly in *their* bed?"

The children giggled, seeming to find that funny.

"No," Charlotte informed me. "We never did that."

"Okay. Got it," I said, relieved. "What kinds of things did Bear and Polly do with you?"

It was a loaded question, but the children wouldn't guess that. It was my way of slowly unfolding the facts, without leading them. I didn't want to put thoughts and ideas in their heads.

"Bear played games with us. Lots of games," Elijah volunteered.

"What kinds of games?" Grimshaw asked.

"Hide and seek!" Olivia piped up, still looking down at her hands.

"Great," I said. "What happened when Bear found you?"

"If we got found," Olivia said. "then we had to help Bear find the others."

"What other games did Bear play with you?" I said.

"*What's the time, Mr Wolf?*" answered Charlotte. "And charades. And dance competitions."

The games all sounded like normal childhood activities.

Those were my hard questions out of the way.

The burning question that remained was why the children were kidnapped and kept. Who were Polly and Bear and what was in it for them?

"Kids, do any of you know the name of the road that you lived on?" asked Grimshaw.

None of the children did.

"How about the suburb?" Grimshaw was beginning to sound a bit desperate.

The children didn't know that, either. They were disengaging, picking up toys and playing with them.

Dr Zhang gave me a wind-up signal.

"Children," I said. "This is the last question. Did anyone other than Polly and Bear ever come to the house?"

Charlotte and Olivia shook their heads, yawning. Max shrugged.

Elijah then did a curious thing—he turned and eyed Lori Hinton.

Lori's mouth dropped open and she frowned at him. Elijah swivelled back around.

"Elijah?" I pressed. "Did you see someone other than Polly and Bear at the house?"

For a moment, he didn't answer. He focused his gaze down on the toy train he was holding. Then he gave a shake of his head without looking up.

34

KATE

Grimshaw drove the car as we headed back to the station. She was one of the most impatient drivers I'd ever been in a car with, jerking us about as she constantly overtook other vehicles on the highway.

"At least we extracted a few tidbits of information from the kiddies," Grimshaw said. "We know generally what these people look like and how old they are. And we know the kids were kept on a big property. That's more than we knew yesterday."

"Yeah, the kids were great. But—this is odd—did you notice Elijah turn to look at Lori when I asked if anyone else had ever been to the house?"

"Yup." She wrinkled her nose dismissively. "But I don't think we can read anything into it. The kids were bored out of their skulls and trying to get away from us at that point."

"Yes, they were getting bored, but it was still odd. Maybe I should check it out."

She sighed heavily as she made a sharp turn around a bend. "Go for it. While I get on with the investigation."

"You know, you could try to dislike me just a little bit less."

"I don't dislike you, Wakeland. I'm just frustrated with your methods. You seem to go over ground that doesn't need going over."

"So, our methods are different. That doesn't have to be a bad thing. Why don't we just say that you paint in broad strokes and I paint in cross-hatch."

"What?"

"I did an art course once with my daughter. I learned there are lots of ways to complete a painting."

"Cute. Let me ask you something. In all of your homicide cases, what percentage of offenders ended up being the person most likely?"

"Most."

"Right. Broad strokes. Gets the job done quick."

"Can't argue. But what do you do when there's no perpetrator in plain sight?"

"You follow a process. You make a solid plan. Most of the time, you're going to find your target. Unfortunately, with this case, there wasn't much to make a plan with. So, we had to default to being informed by other cases of missing children. We made plans based on what we knew, rather than what we didn't. When you do that, you know you've done your job."

"I understand. But sometimes you have to make plans on the fly."

She shrugged, making another tight turn. "Going by instinct can only get you so far."

An image of Harper Rawlings flashed in my mind. Everyone knew my team hadn't yet found her killer. Was Grimshaw alluding to that?

When I glanced back at her, her expression was giving nothing away.

"I still think it's worth following up," I insisted.

"To follow up on a kid who was looking aimlessly around a room because he was bored? Knock yourself out. Just remember, these people had your granddaughter for three and a half years. And we're on the edge of finding out who they are. Look, I'm not personally invested like you are, but believe me, I'm just as invested professionally. I want to find them."

"I'm invested in all possible ways."

The way she overtook a truck left me breathless. "I know you are," she said. "I'm sorry about Ivy. I know you need to know what they've done with her. But my focus is on finding the abductors. At this point, I don't know whether it's impeding the investigation just having you on the team."

"Because you think the whole thing is an act of vengeance against me," I said flatly.

"You can't say it doesn't fit," she answered.

"I don't know what fits where," I said. "Until I do, I intend looking in all possible corners."

"Wakeland, your granddaughter was killed on the day the kids were returned. What more do you need? The abductors sent out a message, loud and clear."

My throat constricted. "I'm not listening to them."

"Broad strokes," she said. "Who was there on the day of the abductions? Brent Cole. Whose cousin was once arrested for rape and murder? Brent Cole's. Who grew up with said cousin? Brent Cole."

I turned to her in astonishment. "That's where the investigation has gone to in my absence? Back to Cole?"

"Yes, it has. And why shouldn't it? We know the kids went up the hill. Ivy's button was found there. And Cole was at the top of the hill."

"How did he manage to get rid of all DNA evidence out of his van, then? There was no DNA of any of the children found in there. He was stopped just half an hour after the children went missing."

"He might have been well-prepared. He could have lined the van in plastic and then tossed the plastic out after he off-loaded the kids. Look, we didn't have a solid motive for him before. But now we do. He either wanted to get back at you or his cousin arranged for him to get paid. And you interviewed him just before the kids were brought back. Think about that."

Brent Cole had been the first person I'd considered over the past couple of days. But whichever way I'd looked at it, I couldn't make it fit. Not totally. I hadn't sensed any animosity towards me when I'd interviewed him. And as far as I was aware, Brent hadn't even gone to visit his cousin in prison.

"But if it wasn't Cole?" I said.

"Whichever way you look at it, he's involved," she snapped. "He might have just been the bait to get the kids up the hill. There might have been a second vehicle waiting for the kids. And I can't say I'm not suspicious about

Nola again now. Maybe she was having an affair with Cole and she thought she'd help him out."

"You've seen my interview with Nola," I said bluntly.

"She could be putting on the performance of her life for all I know."

"Do you really believe that?"

"What I know is that we have to stop looking at whether we think people are telling the truth and look at the evidence. We have to look at the scene that day for what it was and stop looking for alternate theories."

"How does the vengeance plot fit into this? How did they manage to take Ivy? If a group of children did run up the hill, there was no guarantee Ivy would be among them."

Her mouth twisted. "We know that Justine and Kaylee were both distracted and busy at the time. Who's to say that Nola didn't either take Ivy by the hand or whisper to her to come with her? And then a few of the other children followed?"

Her theory hit me like a brick wall. It was simple and plausible.

Although I couldn't picture Nola doing that, I was now filled with doubts.

Grimshaw and I spent the rest of the long trip back to the station in silence.

———

I called Nick and Marcy Parrish as soon as I returned home. They agreed that I could talk to Elijah tomorrow. Dr Zhang had told the parents the children could go home by then. Both Nick and Marcy had noticed Elijah looking around at Lori and had been confused by it.

The next day, at ten in the morning, I drove to Nick Parrish's house.

"Come through," Nick told me after he greeted me at the door. "They're all in the living room."

I hadn't been to the Parrish house before. The interior of the house looked much larger than it had from the outside—one of the modern homes in the new area. The living room was a space at the end of a lengthy hallway and a series of rooms. The fireplace was putting out a lot of heat. I tugged my scarf loose from around my neck.

A boy sat cross-legged in a bean bag, watching a movie while surrounded by four girls. I guessed he was a celebrity in his house. A long-lost brother. The middle two girls would barely remember him. The youngest would never have even met him.

"Elijah," called Nick. "Kate would like to see you, just for a couple of minutes. Girls, could you go upstairs for a little while?"

The boy looked reluctant to give up his movie. But unlike most children, he immediately nodded. The girls took longer to make a move. I made a quick guess that there had been strict discipline in the house where Elijah had been the past three years.

I sat opposite Nick, Marcy and Elijah.

Photographs of the four girls adorned the mantlepiece, walls and side tables. There were photographs of Elijah too, but the photographs stopped when he was just a toddler. There was no *first day of kindergarten* photograph of him, no soccer or sporting team pictures. It told a sad story of a missing child.

"You seem to be settling in well back at home, Elijah," I began.

Nick gave a wincing smile. "The girls won't give him any space. They get jealous if we hug him too long."

I grinned at Nick and then spoke to Elijah again. "I want to thank you so much for all your answers to our questions the other day. They were very helpful."

"Okay," Elijah said in a small voice.

"There was one of your answers I wasn't sure about," I continued. "I asked if you'd seen anyone else ever come to Polly and Bear's house. And when I asked the question, I saw you look at someone in the room, and I just wondered—"

"She came there," he said quickly.

I drew a breath. "Who?"

"Charlotte's mother."

Nick and Marcy stared at each other.

Pinwheels formed in my stomach. "Did she come inside the house?"

"No," Elijah told me. "She stayed outside and talked to Polly."

"What did they talk about?"

"I was inside. I didn't hear them."

"Oh, okay. So, you were inside. looking through a window?"

"Uh huh. We were told to go to the playroom. But I had a sore tummy. So I went to my room."

"Oh dear, I'm sorry you had a sore belly."

"It was my fault. Polly said the apples on the tree weren't ripe, but I had one anyway."

"Ah, yep, unripe apples will hurt your tummy. Are you absolutely sure it was Charlotte's mummy that you saw?"

He nodded. "I went to tell Charlotte, but when we came outside, she was gone."

"Did you see her any other time?"

"No," came his answer.

"Do you know how long ago you saw her? Days? Weeks? Months? Or years?"

He frowned. "I don't know. Not days or weeks. A long time ago."

I smiled warmly. "Thanks, Elijah. You can go back to your movie now."

I stayed seated for a minute, watching the flames in the fireplace.

Elijah would have seen Lori at the nursery school lots of times. Both Charlotte and Elijah were attending three days a week. Which would explain how he knew her and why he was certain it was her.

But he was just a child and children could be wrong about things like this—adults, too.

The Parrishes walked me to the front door. I asked them not to say anything to anyone while I looked into it.

I walked down the path to my car in mental turmoil.

Should I just confront Lori with this and see what she has to say?

If I did that, that stopped any other option dead. There wasn't much point to putting her under surveillance if I'd already confronted her.

I decided to follow her. If she'd been keeping secrets about the missing children all this time, I was going to find out what those secrets were. Every single one of them.

35

LORI HINTON

Lori hummed as she took a pair of tiny pink sandals out of her daughter's bedroom cupboard and replaced them with a pair of white boots with sequins on the heels. The sandals were toddler-sized while the boots were sized for a six-year-old.

Life had reset itself. Charlotte was back now. And Lori had begun the task of replacing everything in Charlotte's room.

She spun around, surveying the room critically. The bed was all wrong. It was far too babyish for Charlotte now. It had been a cot once, and the cot had been converted to a small bed once Charlotte had turned two. There were little dancing bunnies in tutus on the headboard. Charlotte used to love rabbits. And ballet.

Did Charlotte even like bunnies and ballet anymore?

Lori barely knew her own daughter. She'd have to find out everything about her and become the most important person in her life again. She used to be the sun in Charlotte's sky. She'd loved her daddy, but it was always Lori that she missed the most.

Sean had moved back into the house. For now. Lori had told Sean that Dr Zhang recommended that he do that. It was a small lie, but she felt that the universe would forgive her. It would be confusing and traumatic for Charlotte if her parents were apart.

Lori couldn't help but feel a small pinch of pleasure at Sean being in the house again. It was nice seeing his tall frame walking through the house, like before. And Roxanne would be driven half-crazy wondering if Sean would decide that he didn't want to leave, after all.

He was downstairs in the office right now, getting a project done. Charlotte was with him, drawing pictures. Lori had been horrified when Sean had said he needed to *get back to the salt mines*, in those exact words. As if his job was more important than his newly returned daughter. The only way Lori had found him working acceptable was if Charlotte could be there alongside him. So she'd set Charlotte up with paper and coloured pencils.

She wanted to run out and get Charlotte everything she needed—all at once. She hadn't been able to buy her daughter a single thing in three years and now she just wanted to buy her the world. Lori didn't want to leave her, but perhaps if she were busy with Sean, she could slip out without Charlotte even realising. She could be back within the hour.

Making her way downstairs, she glimpsed Sean in the kitchen. Two glasses of freshly squeezed orange juice sat on the bench. *Good.* He was doing something for Charlotte. He barely used to do anything for her—always too busy working or relaxing. He had earphones in, nodding his head along to whatever music he was listening to. He was focused on his mobile phone, tapping out a message. Probably talking with a work colleague.

Lori moved up behind him. She ached to slide her arms around him and rest her face against his back. Like in the old days.

When he turned slightly, she caught a look at his phone screen.

Sean: *Missing you like crazy*

Roxy: *Not as much as I'm missing you*

Sean: *Babe, we need to rent a hotel room for a couple of hours*

Roxy: *omggg yes, dying for just a taste of you*

Sean: *I'll make it happ—*

Lori didn't mean to cry out loud. But the sound fled from deep in her throat.

He startled, whirling around. "Lori. What the hell are you doing sneaking up on me?"

"I came down to make our daughter a snack."

He pushed the phone into his pocket. "Well, she's fine. I asked if she wanted something to eat but she just wanted a juice."

"Can't you stop yourself from thinking about sex with that woman for just one day? Especially when you're meant to be spending time with Charlotte? And *working*, I might add."

He blew his cheeks up and exhaled. "I'm sorry. I didn't stop to think."

"No, you didn't. It's inappropriate, Sean. And pretty damned shitty."

"I'll... leave the house."

She blinked. "What?"

"I'll rent something small again and then have Charlotte over to stay with me."

"No, that's not happening. I'm not allowing Charlotte out of my sight."

"Well, I can't stay—"

"Why not?" she demanded. "Because you can't bear not to be bonking *her* for a few days?" Lori couldn't bear to say her name. Not anymore. Her name had become something that tasted rotten on Lori's tongue.

"Look, Charlotte's going to hear us," Sean said.

"Oh, you're finally thinking of our daughter, are you? What do you think it would do to her if you moved out right now? What would I tell her? Oh, it's lovely that you've come back to us, but Daddy is moving out."

He shook his head. "I don't know what to say. I'll take her the juice, and we'll talk about this later."

"Fine."

Sean took the two drinks and left the kitchen.

Things weren't *fine* at all.

Charlotte was back but everything else was upside-down and wrong. Lori could never have guessed that one day her own husband would be in their house texting—or *sexting*—another woman.

A cloud of anger whirled inside her chest. Roxanne was simply awful.

She should be focusing on Olivia, but instead she was sending messages to someone else's husband. Yes, Sean was still Lori's *husband*. They weren't divorced yet. And Rhys was still clueless that Roxanne was cheating on him. Lori was desperate to tell him, but she wasn't sure what would happen if she did. If everything were out in the open, Sean and Roxanne might move in together.

The shrill rings of the home phone echoed through the house.

She jogged out of the kitchen and through to the living room. She'd set her mobile calls up to divert to the fixed-line home phone if not answered. She'd have to change that, now that Sean was here. Else he'd be answering her personal calls.

She snatched up the phone from the holder.

"Hi Lori," came a familiar male voice.

Lori's heart dropped. "I can't talk right now."

"Why not?" he said.

She glanced behind her, looking for Sean or Charlotte. She headed upstairs before speaking again. "Because there's nothing left to say. I gave you the last payment. And we agreed that was the last of it."

"But it's not over. Not yet."

"It *is* for me."

"Don't forget that I made things happen. Don't forget that."

"Look... I really have to go."

"Fine. But you'll see me tonight. At eight."

"No, I won't. I can't. I've got dinner planned with Sean and Charlotte."

"After she's in bed then. Ten sharp."

Lori jammed her eyes shut as the line went dead.

Somehow, she had to fix things.

36

KATE

Rain drenched the streets, bucketing against the windows of every house and racing along the gutters. The bones in my knees were aching. I told myself it wasn't arthritis, but the signs were there. Rain and cold seemed to make the pain worse.

The abductors had made no further moves over the past two days. I was still no closer to finding them or Ivy. I knew that Grimshaw had called Brent Cole down to the station to question him over her new theories. My investigation of his cousin Dale had turned up nothing significant yet. He'd had a troubled existence in jail, being involved in a multitude of fights and assaults. He'd also had a troubled childhood. I remembered I'd felt sorry for the way his early life had gone at the time I'd arrested him. Was he really capable of coldly directing a kidnap plot from his jail cell?

I'd had Senior Constable Cameron Vella keep a watch on Lori during the daytime, and I'd watched her during the nights. But nothing of note had happened. Grimshaw wasn't happy about me wasting manpower, but she couldn't do much about it—except report me to Bigley. Which she might do.

I'd hidden a tracker on Lori's car two days ago. I watched her every movement. She hadn't gone anywhere much so far.

My phone made an alert sound.

It was 9:50 p.m. and Lori was leaving her house. It was late. Lori had already been to the shops for groceries early in the morning. Was this another dash to the shops? Or something else?

I kissed Pete and headed out the door. The rain had grown heavy. I checked the tracker display on my phone as I jumped into my car and headed in the same direction as Lori.

Lori was driving down towards the SkyWay parking area. The Scenic Skyway was a cable car that ran hundreds of metres above the ground, taking in views of the Blue Mountains and The Three Sisters.

The tourist attraction wasn't running. It never ran at night as far as I knew. Nothing to see in the pitch dark of night. The parking area was almost empty.

Damn. It was going to be difficult to keep tracking Lori out in this lonely area without raising suspicion. I had to hang back and stay hidden.

What was she even doing here?

She pulled up alongside the only other vehicle.

A man exited his car and stepped into Lori's.

Okay, that was definitely *something*.

Was she having a secret relationship with this guy? Lori didn't need to sneak around, did she? She was getting a divorce. Maybe the guy was married.

Rain slashed across my view.

Damn.

I needed a clear view of the guy's licence plate number.

Taking out a camcorder, I set the option to night vision and filmed the scene before me.

I could see a fuzzy image of Lori inside the car with the man. They weren't hugging. Or kissing. They just appeared to be talking. Lori was throwing up her hands quite a bit. Were they having an argument, perhaps? A lovers' tiff?

Whatever this was, it was compelling enough to make Lori leave her house—and her newfound daughter—in the driving rain and at a late hour. All to come to an empty carpark to talk to some man.

The man climbed out of her car and back into his own. The whole exchange had happened over barely ten minutes.

Playing tag, I dropped following Lori and began following the man as he drove past.

I lost sight of him after four blocks. The guy must have known he was being followed because he'd hidden himself well. Who the hell was he?

Between the dark night and slashing rain, I didn't have much hope of finding him. I headed home. I hoped that I'd taken some clear-enough footage of his licence plate number. Because if I did, he wouldn't be able to hide for long.

I caught sight of myself in the entry mirror as I walked inside my house. I barely recognised myself with the hollow eyes and damp hair stuck to my head.

Pete had fallen asleep on the sofa.

He roused as I walked into the living room. "You okay?"

"Yeah. I was just following up on something."

"You can't run yourself ragged like this."

I ran a hand through my hair, ruffling it. "I'm looking pretty ragged, right?"

"I didn't mean it like that. Anyway, take a look at me. I'm not looking so hot, myself."

As he said that, I noticed just how weary he looked. He had the same dark circles under his eyes that I did. I'd been so caught up that I'd barely noticed the changes in him. This was affecting him as much as it was affecting me.

He smiled. "Okay, quit staring at me, will ya? Go get yourself a hot shower."

"Will do."

When I reached the top of the stairs, I decided to swap the shower for a bath. I was achy.

I filled the bath and then sank myself into the soothing water.

A couple of ice-cold drips of water landed on my face. The damned skylight had run a leak again. When we bought the house decades ago, I'd thought it wonderful to be able to see the sky above the bath. Now, the skylight was nothing but trouble.

Rain pelted against the skylight glass, bringing another set of drips down onto my face. At the same time, the pain in my knees subsided beneath the warm water. I could hear my mother saying, *yes you can have everything you want, but not all at the same time.*

Letting my eyelids drift downward, I let the past few days drift through me. Like a river streaming through reeds. This was an exercise I often did. Grimshaw wouldn't approve. I'd let the water run freely in my mind and try to observe what passed around the reeds and what got caught fast. I needed to focus on the things that got caught in the reeds and find out why they were catching.

A knocking sound boomed from downstairs, making me sit bolt upright. The knock was loud and determined. The kind of knock I made on people's doors when I meant business.

What if it was that guy I'd followed tonight? What if, in turn, he'd followed *me* home?

Making a huge splash, I stepped from the bath. I dried myself, then threw on my pyjamas and robe. I ran out to the stair landing.

Pete had opened the door. A slim, bedraggled girl holding a baby stood in the entry. Abby.

Pete, Abby and the baby stared up at me in unison.

"Abby!" I called. "Goodness, get up here and we'll get you and Jasper into some dry clothes." We still had some old baby clothes of Ivy's.

"Jasper's dry," Abby told me. "His coat's waterproof. And so's mine."

"Okay. Well, get over to the fireplace." I hurried downstairs.

Pete took Jasper, and then Abby wriggled out of her jacket and hung it on one of the hooks near the door.

Abby stepped across to the fire and sat, looking morose. Pete carried Jasper over.

"Are you okay?" I asked her.

"Logan and I had a fight. Things got... heated."

Logan—that was the first time Abby had ever spoken his name.

Pete scowled. "Did he hurt you or Jasper?"

"No, we're not hurt," she said. "Everything's okay. I just needed to get out of there for a while. Let it all calm down."

"Good choice, honey," said Pete. "When things get rough, you get *out*." He kissed Jasper's forehead.

"You stay here as long as you need to," I told Abby.

"Just for tonight. That's all," she replied.

"Why not stay for a few days?" I suggested. "Give yourself a chance to get a better perspective."

"A better perspective of what?"

I shrugged. "I don't know. Of what whatever went wrong."

"There's nothing wrong with Logan and me."

"Abby, there's a bruise on your forehead."

Pete studied his daughter's face. "Hell. I'm going to kill the little piece of—"

"Dad. No. I must have done that to myself. I got angry, and I was throwing things around, and—"

"Things got thrown around?" I queried. "That's gone quite a few steps further than a verbal fight."

"Can we just... leave it?" Abby stared at the flames.

I tried to hold back, but I couldn't. I was raw and overtired. "Abby, you've been going through hell the past week. This is a time when you really need people you can rely on. I don't know what happened, but Logan needs to be understanding."

"It's not his fault. It was just a dumb argument."

"He could have cut you a little slack." I couldn't help but leap to her defence. She was my daughter. This wasn't a police inquiry.

She fell silent for a few moments. When she turned to me, her expression was different. "Is it true... what they're saying?"

"What's that?" I asked. But I already knew.

"About you," she said. "Is it true that someone took Ivy to spite you?"

Pete stepped straight in before I'd had time to form a reply. "No. There's no evidence to say this is connected to your mother. They're grasping at straws. Five kids were kidnapped, not just our little Ivy."

Her eyes grew bright with tears. "They always intended returning the children. But not Ivy. They never intended returning her."

"We don't know that," Pete said.

"The same committee that organised the vigil wants to organise a special day for Ivy." Abby wiped at her eyes. "Like, a remembrance day. I don't want that. I don't want to remember her. I wanted her back."

"It's far too soon," I agreed. "We don't know anything. We just don't know."

She eyed me through her tears. "People have been laying flowers for Ivy. They've been bringing them to *The Ponds*."

"Oh, God," I gasped. "I didn't know. I'll do what I can to stop that."

Jasper began to fuss and cry.

"Did you bring some bottles of formula for him?" I asked.

She shook her head. "I've got nothing. I didn't stop to think. I was so angry. I just stormed out."

"I'll go pick up whatever you need," said Pete.

I stood. "I'll go."

"No, love," said Pete. "What if Logan comes back? Things might get a bit uneasy."

"I can handle myself. It might be better me than you. You might want to flatten Logan on sight. Besides, I know what a baby needs."

I headed back upstairs to change out of my pyjamas. I chose the kind of clothing that Abby had always said were a dead giveaway that I was a detective. Smart trousers paired with a heavy-duty jacket. If Logan happened to be there, and gave me any trouble, I'd be psychologically ready for him.

37

KATE

The downpour had eased somewhat. I jumped in my car and headed onto the road. But there was still enough drizzle for the oncoming headlights to spread in fractured starburst patterns. Dappled reflections of streetlights shone at me from puddles on the side of the road.

I'd lost my fatigue and was wide awake, now.

A large part of me hoped that Logan would be there at the house, even though Abby was sure he wouldn't be. I was desperate to know who my daughter was with. Back when Abby was in her late teens, she'd dated all kinds of bad boy and petty criminal types. I never knew who she was trying to hurt more—me or herself. Was Logan going to be another one like that? Even if he wasn't the petty criminal type, it sounded as if the two of them together were a volatile mix.

Abby's house was only a couple of blocks away from Nola Hobson. I'd driven past this street the day I spoke to Nola, never knowing my own daughter lived on it. The house looked like a thousand others in these neighbourhoods. A modest single storey dwelling that had been built many decades ago and was showing its age.

Parking in the driveway, I checked my surroundings. If Logan had returned, he might become enraged that Abby had sent one of her parents here. I wasn't in the mood for being jumped by a crazed young man.

I wriggled the key in the lock until I managed to get the door to open. The lights had been left on, saving me from fumbling around for the light switch.

I walked in on a scene that showed a lot more mayhem than what Abby had described. Chairs were upturned. Things seemed to have been swept from cupboards and benches in a rage. I was horrified for Jasper. A little baby didn't deserve to be in the middle of this.

Taking out my phone, I snapped photographs around the rooms. It was force of habit. If it turned out that Abby needed these images in the future, I'd have them. Nothing could substitute for a photo or video. Even I would remember the scene wrong, given enough time.

Picking my way around the mess, I began collecting everything Jasper might need. I found Abby and Logan's bedroom. Everything was neat and orderly. The fight hadn't started or ended in there. A passport was lying on top of a set of drawers. I flicked it open. I caught a glimpse of a good-looking young man and his name: *Logan Norwood*. So, this was Abby's boyfriend.

The second room that I tried to enter was locked. The third bedroom was Jasper's. It was as old and worn as the rest of the house, but it was spotless. Abby had put colourful toys and books up on shelves, and posters on the wall.

I took a few things from Jasper's room and then headed back to the living room. I stooped to collect a toy train from a corner of the room—one of those chunky plastic toys with a zillion gadgets for babies to poke at and spin. A small round object lay beneath it.

A ring.

I inhaled a short breath. Was that an *engagement* ring? The ring looked expensive. But it could be costume jewellery? Bending down, I took a closer look. It looked real, made of white gold, with a large sapphire and a diamond either side.

I'd seen the ring before—Abby must have worn it over to our house at least once. If it was an engagement ring, did that mean the relationship had just ended? After all, Abby had thrown the ring on the floor. I snapped a picture and left it where it was.

Packing up the baby things into the bag I'd brought along, I took a minute to run through the checklist in my head, to see if I'd forgotten anything. The rain started up again outside, and I decided to make a run for it before it got heavy.

Back at home, I walked into a scene of Pete sitting in his armchair with his eyes half-closed, murmuring a song to the baby he was cradling. Abby was curled up on the sofa nearby, also asleep. The fire was the only thing in the room with life and movement.

The scene reminded me of the days when Ivy was a baby.

Not able to help myself, I snapped a picture of the three of them with my phone. No matter what happened in the future, I wanted to remember moments like this. I had to cling to the good things.

———

Rain was still pattering on the roof at eight in the morning. I'd slept in longer than I'd intended. Jasper had become unsettled in the hours between three and five in the morning. Pete and I had taken turns to feed and rock him back to sleep, to allow Abby to get some rest.

Rising, I went to check on Jasper. He was fast asleep in Ivy's old portable cot. Abby slept in her single bed, skeins of hair tangled across her cheek. With her face completely relaxed, she looked like a teenager. She had her hands together and beneath her chin, almost as if in a gesture of prayer. Her fingers bore only one ring—a plain band with a tiny diamond that she'd been wearing since she was fourteen. A boyfriend had given it to her. It was too small for her now, so she wore it on her pinky finger.

I recalled the ring I'd found in her house. It was a lot fancier. If Logan had bought her that ring, he must have paid a lot for it.

An image of the sapphire and diamonds formed clearly in my mind.

I froze.

I *had* seen that ring before. But not on Abby's hand. It had been on someone else's hand.

With rigid steps, I exited the room and blundered back into my own bedroom.

Pete woke as I was hurrying to change out of my pyjamas.

He sat, rubbing weary eyes. "Kate? What's going on?"

Walking up to the bed, I hugged him. "I've got some things to check out. Pete, until I know more, under no circumstance is Abby to see Logan or go back to the house."

"You ran a check on him last night, didn't you? What did you find out?"

"I didn't run a check. I found something, and I didn't twig to what it was until just now. But I need to be a hundred percent sure before I accuse anyone of anything. Pete, just trust me. I need to go figure this out and talk to some people."

"Okay. I'll make sure Abby stays here. After the night we all had, I bet those two will be zonked for quite a while." He sounded casual but a dark, worried look had moved into his eyes.

———

Jefferson Blade Mechanics had just opened for business. The first cars of the day for repair or service were up on hoists. The smells of grease and oil wafted thickly through the dark, cavernous workshop.

Logan was under a hoist, adjusting a wheel. I couldn't see his face clearly. But I could see enough to match him with his passport photograph.

I approached him. "Logan Norwood?"

He stilled, then twisted his head back over a shoulder. "That's me."

Logan was very handsome in person. Dark eyes beneath a sweep of blond hair. And a smooth grin and voice to match.

Oh, you're a charmer. I can see why Abby fell for you. But who are you, really?

"I'm DS Kate Wakeland from Katoomba area command. Do you have a minute?"

"Yeah. No problem at all." He smiled again, grabbing a rag and wiping his hands.

If he thought that his looks and smile would hold any sway with me, he had another thing coming.

His eyebrows shot up. "Wait, did you say *Wakeland?* You're Abby's mum, aren't you? Yeah, I remember you from the TV."

"I'm not here as Abby's mother. I'm here in an official capacity."

His expression changed. "Right. So, Abby told you what happened last night. And you're here to lay charges." He shook his head, exhaling. "I didn't think she'd do that to me."

"That's a separate issue. I'm not here about that."

"Okay. You've got my attention."

I brought up the picture of the ring on my phone and turned it around to him. "What can you tell me about this?"

I watched him carefully as he frowned and inspected the image.

The last time I had seen a ring like that had been on Harper Rawlings's hand, in a photograph of her. Her sobbing parents had told me that six pieces of jewellery were missing from their daughter's body. A necklace, a ring, and two sets of earrings. Whoever murdered Harper had taken the jewellery—either to sell or as a souvenir. The necklace and earrings had been custom-made, a graduation present from Harper's parents. The ring had belonged to Harper's grandmother—it was store-bought, but it was old and there were not many of that style around.

The fact that a ring exactly like Harper's had turned up was extremely suspicious.

Before coming to the mechanics to see Logan, I'd secretly returned to Abby's house to take the ring. Then I'd gone down to the station to look up the photographs that I had of Harper when she was alive. The ring was an exact match.

I had to fight the urge to haul Logan down to the station and question him there. But if I did that, he could refuse to talk. And then I might get nowhere. I needed to take things one step at a time.

Logan flicked his gaze from my phone screen to me. "I gave it to Abby."

"Where did you get it from?"

"This is personal, isn't it? You said this wasn't about me and your daughter. But it is. You're worried I've asked your little girl to marry me."

"I promise you, this is nothing to do with Abby. Please just answer the question."

"As if. What is this? You're using your position with the police to come here and heavy me. This isn't legal."

"Mr Norwood, I repeat, this isn't personal. You can answer my questions here or answer them down at the station." I was threatening him with the very thing I didn't want, hoping he'd change his mind.

He shrugged. "I bought it from a friend."

"Can I have the friend's name, please?"

"His name is Ricky."

"Ricky who?"

"No idea. I just know him as Ricky."

"Where does he work?"

"He doesn't work."

"Okay, where does he live?"

"At the same place I do."

"I didn't see anyone when I went there last night."

"You went to my house? And just broke in?"

"Abby gave me the key. She needed some things for Jasper."

He shot me an odd look. "That was when you saw the ring, isn't it? I remember now. Abby threw it at me."

"Yes. That's when I saw it."

"And you saw all the mess, too."

"Yep."

He blew out an agitated breath, running a hand through his hair. "You're going to try and make sure I don't see Abby and Jasper again, aren't you? Well, Jasper's *my* son. You can't do that. And Abby... well, up until now I would have said that me and Abby were pretty tight. We had an argument, but it'll blow over. It always does."

"That happens often?"

"Abby gets into... moods. She throws things around. She doesn't mean anything bad."

"You're trying to tell me *Abby* did all that?"

"Yeah."

He sounded so sincere. I didn't trust him as far as I could throw him.

"Right," I said. "Back to the reason that I'm here. So, I can find that Ricky person at your house? Why wasn't he there last night?"

"He went away. He does that. Just disappears. As long as he pays rent, I don't care."

"Where'd he go?"

"He never tells me. I don't ask." He frowned at me. "Hey, is the ring stolen property? Is that what this is about?"

"I'm not at liberty to say. Do you want to talk me through how you came to buy it from him?"

His expression became even more guarded. "It's personal."

"It's in your best interest to tell me."

He sighed with an air of defeat. "Okay, so... you'll hate hearing this, but I wanted to ask Abby to get engaged. Before I did that, I mentioned it to Ricky. And he told me he happened to have a few rings. They belonged to his grandmother and he got them when she died."

"You believed that?"

He shrugged. "Why wouldn't I?"

"And, you bought one of them?"

"Yeah. I had a look through what he had and I liked the blue one. Abby's favourite colour is blue. I paid him a hundred and fifty bucks for it."

Abby's favourite colour is blue? So many things I don't know about my own daughter.

"Well, I'll have to check your story out with Ricky," I said. "When I find him."

"He was at the house this morning before I left."

"Great. Thank you."

"Do you have to let Abby know? Like, do you have to tell her that I bought the ring from Ricky?"

He was either terminally genuine or a talented liar. And if he was a talented liar, then he was also a cold-blooded killer. For now, I'd let him believe that I was pursuing stolen property.

"Thanks, Logan. I'll let you know if I have more questions."

I turned to leave.

"Detective Wakeland?" he called from behind me.

I faced him.

He had a faint grin on his face, his eyebrows hooked upwards in an ironic expression. "Nice to finally meet Abby's mother. It was a pleasure."

38

KATE

I headed into the station, checking my watch. I needed to talk with Ricky—the guy with the suspicious ring collection. If Logan was lying, then I had to protect Abby and the baby. Who knew what Logan was capable of? Harper had been callously hit with a blunt instrument and then strangled to death. The person who'd done that to her was a monster.

I also needed to follow up on the mysterious man that Lori had made contact with last night. I hadn't had a chance to check the pictures I'd taken. Taking a minute to sit down, I examined the images on my police camcorder. Even though the images were in night vision, the heavy rain had partly obscured the licence plate number, as I'd feared. I sent through the footage and photographs to Constable Ella Valletti, asking if she could follow up. I couldn't send the images to Grimshaw. She'd assign a priority so low it wouldn't get attended to.

My pulse was running at a million miles per hour as I walked up to Franco's desk at the homicide unit.

Franco was at his desk. He frowned at me. "Didn't think you'd be in for a while."

"I've found a ring that is exactly like Harper's." I showed him the picture on my phone.

He peered closely at it. "Hell. Where?"

"At a local house. I'll explain on the way."

"I'm driving," he said. "You're a bit shaky, Wakeland."

I looked down at my hands. The phone that I held *was* trembling a little, but I wouldn't admit that to Franco. The sleepless night and my busy mind were getting to me.

"Sure, drive if you want to," I said casually.

We headed down onto the street to Franco's car and then drove out onto the road.

"You okay?" he asked me. "You've looked better."

"Thanks," I said dryly. "I was up all night with my daughter's baby."

"That'll do it to you."

"Too right. Babies are little terrorists."

"I've got a new girlfriend. Daniella."

"Oh yeah? Is she nice?"

"I don't know about *nice*, but she's organised."

"What does that even mean?"

"She does that Kondo type of thing where she only keeps what she needs."

"Not looking good for *you* then, is it?"

"Ouch." He grinned. "The woman is so organised that there's nothing in her wardrobe that she doesn't wear. I swear there's not one old bit of clothing anywhere."

"What about your stuff? Is it safe from her clutches?"

"She's making noises about my collection of Kiss T-shirts."

I snorted, knowing that Franco had a few old Gene Simmons T-shirts with holes and paint splatters. God only knew how long he'd had them for.

Inhaling slowly and deeply, I began to relax. Franco had that effect on me. Whenever the job got tense, I could rely on him to show me that life still went on.

We entered the street that my daughter, Logan, and Ricky—apparently—lived on. I told Franco which house it was and he parked outside.

When I knocked on the door, no answer came.

"Hey," Franco called. "Police."

Still nothing.

We made our way around to the back of the house.

The backyard consisted of a featureless patch of straggly lawn and an old shed. A stumpy, tattooed man and a rake-thin woman sat together on plastic chairs, smoking. Both were possibly still in their twenties, but their facial skin looked a little patchy, as if they'd weathered the effects of drug addiction for years. Probably methamphetamine. Whether the addiction was past or present, I couldn't tell.

"Ricky?" I queried.

The man put his hand up. "Yo."

"We're Detective Sergeants Kate Wakeland and Jace Franco," I told him, walking across the lawn. "I've just spoken with your housemate, Logan Norwood. Would you mind answering a couple of questions?"

It was easier warming people up by mentioning someone that they knew. They didn't know what the other person had told the police. Accordingly, they were generally more open to telling the truth.

He spoke a very uncertain, "Okay".

His companion pulled herself unsteadily to her feet, her eyes a little unfocused. I guessed she was drunk as well as on drugs.

"I better go, Ricky," she said. "Gotta get home to the kids. Hope they haven't started a house fire." She cackled to herself at her joke, then coughed.

"Yeah, you go," Ricky said. "You're a good mother, Trissie."

Trissie shuffled away on sandaled feet that looked blue with cold. I hoped her children weren't too young to be left alone. But due to her age, I suspected they were.

"What can I do for you two fine people?" said Ricky. "Pull up a seat, get comfy."

"We're okay, mate," Franco told him.

"Yeah, right, suit yourself." Ricky shrugged.

I showed Ricky the photo of the ring. "Can you tell me about this?"

"Oh..." He seemed to struggle to remember. "I found that one."

"Found it where?" Franco asked.

"On the street, mate." Ricky nodded. "Just pure luck."

"You must *find* a lot of rings," I said. "Logan said you had a collection."

"Nah. I'm not *that* lucky. Most of them were from my granny. She died. She had a lot of rings and stuff."

I showed him pictures of Harper Rawlings's earrings and necklace. "Do you happen to have these, too?"

"Nope. Don't think so."

Franco glanced at me before turning back to Ricky. "How about you show us your jewellery collection?"

Ricky looked unsettled. "All right, all right, I'll show ya. What's the big deal about this ring?"

"I'm afraid we can't tell you that at the moment, sir," I said.

We followed Ricky inside. He unlocked the door to his room. Now I knew whose room it was behind the locked door I'd tried to open last night.

The room was filled with junk, much of it in cardboard boxes and shoe-boxes. He was certainly a collector of bits and bobs, which could fit with him having found the ring.

Had the killer stolen the ring from his victim and then decided it was too dangerous to keep, and he'd thrown it from his car window? I didn't especially trust Ricky, but was he a murderer? Murderers were sometimes people just like Ricky. They looked harmless, and they mostly were—but a sudden burst of anger or severe bout of mental illness had driven them to commit a terrible act. Harper's murder had been particularly cold. Ricky didn't seem like the type. And would he have ever owned the expensive kind of SUV that the murderer had almost certainly been driving the night that Harper died?

Picking up a letter from a box, I noted Ricky's full name. Richard Brian Pickett.

Ricky brought out a wooden box with a sliding lid. It looked like a kid's box of treasures, containing some pieces of costume jewellery, a few old lighters, a small pinecone and a tangle of necklaces. I picked through the necklaces. I found nothing that looked like Harper's.

Ricky sighed through his teeth, making a whistling sound. "She was a nice lady, my granny. The only person who ever thought of me, you know? But she's gone now. Smoker's lungs."

"I'm sorry to hear that," I told him. "She left you some nice things."

His expression brightened. "She did, ay? She wanted me to have this stuff. Poor granny."

Franco was already looking restless. He'd be itching to demand answers from Ricky. I shot him a look that said, *wait*.

I picked up a brooch and rotated it between my thumb and forefinger, pretending to admire it. "Ricky, can you tell me exactly where you found the ring? I'd really appreciate knowing that."

He scratched his head with both hands as if he were in some vaudeville movie. "Nope, not coming to me. Sorry, me memory's gone on that one."

Franco jumped in. "How long ago?"

Ricky shook his head. "Mate, I couldn't tell ya. Too long ago."

"Years?" I asked. "Or months?"

"Maybe," he said. "Yeah, years."

Franco, muttering darkly under his breath, left the room and went looking around the house.

I crossed my arms. "Ricky, have you ever owned an SUV?"

He pulled his mouth down in an exaggerated expression. "I thought this was about jewellery an' stuff."

"So, did you own one?" I pressed.

"I might have."

"What kind?"

"I had a Jeep Wrangler that came off the factory line the year I was born. 1990. How about that? Good car, too."

"Any others?"

"Nah."

"Ever owned or driven a BMW X5?"

"In my dreams, yeah."

"Okay, well, that's all. We'll be in contact if we have any more questions." I glanced around the room. "And clean up. This is a fire hazard."

I hated the thought that this man lived in the same house with my daughter and grandson. He was a dodgy character and his room was a powder keg of cardboard boxes and wooden things and paper. The only positive was that I hadn't sighted any drug paraphernalia in his room, nor had I smelled anything of that nature.

I walked out of the house with Franco.

Franco bit his thumb, which was something he tended to do when he was thinking. "Either he's Harper's killer, or he's lying about how long he's had the ring."

"Yeah," I agreed. "No way would he hang onto something worth money for even five minutes unless he had a very good reason to."

"So," he said. "do we think he's keeping her necklace somewhere in his birds nest of a room? Squirrelled away somewhere?"

"Maybe. But we've probably tipped him off now. If we come back with a search warrant, he'd have gotten rid of it."

"What if he's just covering up for someone? Like Logan."

"I did get the feeling he was covering his tracks." I rubbed my forehead. "We should try for a warrant."

"I'll get that organised. You've got your hands full."

I threw him a look of appreciation as we got into the car.

The phone rang. It was Ella.

"I found him," she said.

"You did?"

"Yeah. It wasn't easy. He's a tricky one. I'm going to bet he's got infrared lights attached to his licence plate. Because it shouldn't have been as obscured as it was when you used your night vision to take the footage. But you got one lucky shot. And I found him. His name is Kyle Wheeler. He's a private investigator. Looks like Lori Hinton's been keeping tabs on someone."

"You did an amazing job, Ella—thank you. Hmmm, interesting. I wonder what she's using a P.I for?"

"Her husband, maybe?" Ella suggested. "They're getting a divorce, aren't they? Maybe she needs some extra dirt."

I gave a short laugh. "Yes, maybe."

But there was still that odd conversation of Lori's I'd overheard. *You're not off the hook yet, Lori. I'll be getting back to you.*

39

KATE

Franco and I headed back to the station to write up a file on our encounter with Ricky. And figure out if we had enough evidence to get a warrant.

With nothing else to follow up as far as Harper's case went, and with Bigley's directive to stay away from Strikeforce Flying Fox for a few days, I left the station. I planned on having a late breakfast and then sitting down and poring over every second of CCTV video that the police had been able to obtain from when each child had been returned. I'd requested that Grimshaw send it all through to me. After that, I'd be conducting some research on the private investigator that Lori had been seeing.

Reporters were waiting for me outside the station. All of them desperate for information about the Flying Fox case. Microphones thrust at me. Cameras pointed my way.

I got no *grieving grandmother* allowance from the press. They yelled out questions about whether police had figured out who had been trying to plot their vengeance against me. They knew that Brent Cole had been interviewed by Grimshaw, and they were out for blood. The news had been filled with speculation over whether Brent and his cousin Dale were behind the kidnappings.

I answered none of their questions. A few of the reporters followed me all the way home, filming me as I exited my car and walked into the house.

Inside, Abby was peering out at them from between the blinds, Jasper asleep in her arms. "Why won't they just leave us alone?"

"Some of them are just vultures," I replied. "That's why."

"Good word for them." Abby scowled. "Vultures. They prey on the dead. And people who are just barely hanging on. They just don't care."

"Try to ignore them. They'll go away, eventually."

Pete walked upstairs from the basement, dabbing at his face with a towel. He'd been down there working out.

"Are there reporters out there again?" he said, wrinkling his forehead. "If they're not gone within ten minutes, I'm going to go out there and tell them to get lost."

"They'll probably stick that on the news, Dad," Abby said.

"Let them," Pete growled.

Abby eyed me with an expression that'd grown suspicious. "Are they following you for a reason? Has something new happened?"

"No, honey, there's nothing new," I told her.

Her expression didn't change. "Where'd you go earlier? You're not supposed to be with the task force team right now, are you?"

"I was just taking care of some other things."

Her lips drew into a straight line. "I talked to Logan."

"Oh?" I replied as innocently as I could manage.

"He said you just raided his house, looking for stolen jewellery."

I sighed, crossing the room to sit on the sofa. Ricky must have called Logan and told him that I'd been around there at their house this morning. "Abby, it wasn't a raid. Detective Franco and I just went to talk with Ricky, that's all. Look, I need to talk with you. Come and sit."

She remained standing, folding her arms. "Why are you even interested in stolen goods? You were just trying to find some dirt on Logan, weren't you? That's not fair. That's exactly why I didn't want you to know who he was. I bet you looked him up and found out that he went to juvie for a while when he was a kid."

I couldn't deny that. After finding the ring, I had run Logan's name through the system. I'd discovered that he'd gone to a juvenile detention centre when he was fifteen. For stealing a bike from a bicycle store. But I hadn't been idly looking for dirt on him.

"It's not like you think," I said. I glanced from her to Pete. "You might as well both hear what I have to say."

"Sure." Frowning deeply, Pete came to sit beside me.

I took a breath. "You both know about the ring. I saw it on the floor of your house, Abby. The next day, I remembered where I'd seen one just like it before. I've... I've had to send the ring away for DNA testing."

Abby gasped. "Why?"

"Because I've been looking for a ring just like that one for years now. A young woman from one of my homicide cases was wearing a ring like that one the night she died. The ring was taken from her body shortly after she was killed."

Pete stared at me in shock.

Abby's eyelashes grew wet. "I didn't know..." She sniffled. "But Logan didn't do anything wrong."

I nodded. "He isn't under suspicion. He gave me information as to where he obtained the ring and I'm looking into it further. I'm not saying it's certain it's the same ring. But there is a very good chance that it is."

"Is this to do with the case that I think it is? Harper?" asked Pete.

"Yes," I answered.

"I knew the ring was second hand," Abby told me, wiping her eyes. "Logan knows I love old stuff like that. But it wasn't custom-made or anything, right? So, there are probably hundreds of them out there."

"Yep," I agreed. "There are others. But it was a limited run. It was an expensive ring, sold only in one store in Sydney, a long time ago. So, I hope you understand why it had to be sent away for testing." I stopped for a moment, biting down on my lip. I knew this was really hard for Abby on top of everything else she was going through. "Abby, I'll let you know that we're trying to get a warrant to search the house. It's best if you don't go back there for a while."

"Why do you need to search the house?"

"It was a set of jewellery that went missing from Harper's body. A ring, necklace, earrings," I said.

"But why do you think you'd find them at our place?" Abby demanded.

I exchanged a tense glance with Pete. She obviously didn't know Logan had bought the ring from Ricky. It was best not to tell her any more.

"It's just procedure," I told her.

She began pacing, jiggling Jasper as if trying to get to sleep, except that he was already asleep. "What if Logan decides that I'm too much trouble, and he walks away from me? I was a total wreck when I met him. I don't know what he saw in me. I need him. I can't deal with everything on my own."

Pete went to her. "Settle down. You're worrying about things that haven't happened. Give Jasper to me and I'll go put him in his cot."

She handed Jasper to her father, but she didn't stop pacing. Without Jasper in her arms, she started flexing and shaking her hands. "I don't know what to do. I can't lose Logan, too."

I stood. "Abby, please just give it a few more days. If the police search goes ahead, it'll just be more worry for you.

Pete placed the baby gently in the cot.

Voices echoed out in the street. Pete marched over to the window and peered through the blinds. "You're kidding me. There's a reporter trying to interview our neighbour. That's it. I'm gonna make them move off." He stormed out of the house.

"I'm going to have a sleep," Abby told me. "Let me know if the baby wakes."

I stood alone in the now-quiet living room, my appetite for breakfast completely gone.

———

At midday, I stopped my research to make a big pot of soup. I chopped and diced the vegetables with gusto, channelling my pain and frustration.

After lunch, I asked Abby to bring the baby and come with me to see her grandmother, but she declined, saying she'd go see Grandma in the morning. Before I left, I heard Abby sobbing in her bedroom. It broke my heart all over again.

As I left the house, I was glad to see the reporters gone. Pete must have had the right words for them—he was anything but subtle when he was angry.

My shoulders sagged with exhaustion and defeat as I drove along the road that hugged the reserve. The air streaming through my car window had a gentle warmth that belied the winter season. After days of rain, the sunshine was welcome. I needed any small measure of light and hope I could find.

I pictured Ivy in the reserve, running and playing. In my mind, she was always there. Always playing. I still could barely accept the stark reality of the past week.

Renewed grief welled inside me.

I spotted the pile of flowers at *The Ponds* that Abby had told me about, the flowers being in remembrance of Ivy. I reminded myself to call someone about that and have it stopped.

I continued driving until the lake glittered in my wet eyes, almost blinding me, then I steered the car between the clipped hedges of the Tallman's Valley Hospice. Many of the residents were outside this afternoon, propped up on deck-style wooden chairs or wheelchairs.

Threading my way through the patients, I greeted the ones who were awake. I headed for my mother, the white-haired lady with the porcelain quality to her skin. Her eyes were closed, but she appeared to be lightly resting rather than sleeping.

I kissed her forehead and hugged her. "Hi, Mum."

Her eyelids fluttered, and she blinked a few times before focusing on me. Gently, I removed the pair of glasses from her hands and placed them on her face.

"Kate. Oh... Kate. Any news?"

I sat beside her. "No news. We haven't been able to find Ivy yet."

I'd asked the hospice not to tell mum what had been reported in the news about Ivy. Mum didn't watch TV and never saw the news for herself. There was no point in her knowing. It was far kinder for her to slip from the earth believing that Ivy would be coming home to her family.

Her thin lips pressed together in an expression of sadness. "I know you'll be trying your heart out."

"I am. I'm giving it my best. My best just isn't good enough."

She took my hand, and I laid my head against her shoulder. "Yes, it is. *It is.*"

I hadn't realised I was about to cry until I did.

There was no one who understood me as she did. Not even Pete. My mother had raised the girl who'd grown into the young woman with a burning ambition to enter the police force. She'd been terrified of me joining the force, but she'd taught me what to believe in.

I let the tears flow freely. Tears for Ivy, tears for Abby, tears for the children who'd been returned. And tears for Harper.

Mum stroked my head. "You've been caught up in a whirlwind."

"I don't understand what happened. Why people do the things that they do."

We sat in silence for a few moments, watching the ducks and black swans glide on the lake. An elderly man wandered down to the lake's edge and waded in as far as his knees. A hospital care worker rushed after him and guided him away. I knew that the man was one of the patients with Alzheimer's disease. Some facilities kept such patients indoors all day, where they were easier to care for, but this hospice had the policy of allowing the dementia patients to spend most of their days outdoors. They were in their last weeks or months of the disease, and the hospice allowed those who could safely be outdoors to be outdoors.

Harry Grenville sat in his wheelchair sketching the ducks, his silvery hair blowing in the breeze and exposing the age spots on his scalp. I knew that he was one of the handful of dementia patients who'd somehow kept on living way past the time they'd been expected to live. The thought of Harry being here for years, happily sketching away, gave me a small measure of comfort.

Keep bucking the trend, Harry.

Wiping my eyes, I moved back. "You're looking lovely," I told Mum.

I never said that she looked well, because she wasn't well and it sometimes irritated her when people said that. But it was true that she looked lovely. Her white hair was still thick and had a shine. Her skin still had a luminous quality. Mine didn't and never had. Mine was closer to being ruddy. Abby's skin was more like Mum's. For all that, Mum did look increasingly fragile and somehow diminished. The more I tried not to see those things, the more apparent they were.

She smiled. "I drew a picture of the ducks yesterday. Me and Harry Grenville over there. I thought I'd give it a go." She indicated towards Harry. "Harry draws better than me. You should see what he does sometime. You'll be very impressed."

"I'll do that. But where is *your* drawing?" I didn't want to tell her how much I'd like to have it. Any personal keepsakes were precious.

"Oh, I gave it away. Doreen had family come to see her, and her great-grandchild got bored. He was quite spirited, trying to wheel his poor old great-grandmother around in her wheelchair. So, I gave him my picture to colour in, and a nurse gave him some pencils. That kept the little tike busy for a while."

I grinned, imagining it. "That was nice of you."

"My good friend died yesterday. Beryl Southmore."

I eyed her with alarm, taken aback. My mother had a way of slipping in some rather large news items into conversation without any warning. And she was tending to do it more and more often with every year. Perhaps, with life growing short, you didn't bother as much with small talk and got straight to the facts.

"Oh no. I'm so sorry, Mum." I reached to hold her hand.

"She was ninety-six, Kate. At that age, you know what's coming up. The very best thing you can hope for is to leave the earth quickly. And she did. It was a good death. We don't talk about good deaths. But we should. Beryl lived a happy life on the farm with Les and the kids."

I smiled at her. "You're right. A good life is something to celebrate."

She smiled back, but then a frown flittered across her forehead. "Why hasn't Abigail come?"

"She's not doing so well right now."

"Of course she's not. Poor girl. I'd love to see the baby again, but I understand."

"She's having a hard time dealing with life right now. She still won't open up to me though. I just can't manage to build a bridge with her."

Mum sighed. "That's such a shame."

My eyes moistened again. "Our relationship has been so difficult. I must have made some big mistakes when I was raising her."

I steeled myself for my mother's response. Unlike me, she'd been a stay-at-home parent. She'd been there when I came home from school, with a battery of scones in the oven, at the ready to hear about my day. That kind of thing hadn't been possible in my line of work. I'd been to every school play and sporting game of Abby's that I could manage. But I couldn't be in all places at all times. Abby and I used to have fun when she was a young child. I'd felt as if we had a special connection. But ever since she'd hit age fourteen or so, things had rapidly gone downhill. I'd hoped like crazy that once she moved into her adult years, things would turn around. Especially so when Ivy was born. But nothing got better.

"You mustn't blame yourself, Kate," said my mother. "Sometimes, children strike a path that's far away from the one that you put them on." She smiled widely. "Like you."

I laughed, feeling a little lighter. "I'd have been a nurse if you'd had your way." Mum had been a nurse before she married Dad.

"Yes. But you had your heart set on going into the police force. Oh, how Thomas and I worried. But here you are, all these years later. Your father was always proud of you, you know. You've done a lot of good, Kate."

I squeezed her hand gratefully.

Across from us, Harry Grenville lowered his binoculars and began sketching a duck in flight. He seemed totally lost in his own world.

"Do you want anything, Mum?" I asked her. "A drink? Another blanket?"

She shook her head. "No, I don't need a thing." She studied my face. "How are you?"

"Exhausted. Trying every avenue I can think of to find the people who took the children."

"How are the others—the little ones who came back? And have they said anything more about who did this dreadful thing?"

"They're doing okay, considering. They've told us some things. We've got two names. Polly and Bear, if you can believe it. Of course, we don't know their real names. We know what kind of house they were kept at and that there was a lot of land to run around on. They chased chickens around the yard for fun. They all had two eggs for breakfast every morning, including Polly. Apparently, Bear was at work most of the time and only ate dinner with the children."

"Sounds a lot like my childhood," my mother mused. "What strange people though to take someone else's children and raise them like that."

I nodded. "Extremely strange."

"They must have had quite a few chickens to lay all those eggs."

"Sounds like it."

Mum stroked her cheek with her index finger, looking deep in thought. "Two eggs for each child per day, plus Polly, you say? That's a dozen eggs. And at least a dozen chickens, probably more. Because every hen doesn't lay an egg every day, especially as they get older. It used to be my job to collect the eggs before school. I'd sell the excess in a stall outside our front gate, right after school."

I grinned at her memory. "The kids seemed fond of the chickens. They had a couple of pet dogs, too. Golden retrievers, we think. We're not sure. We showed them a few different pictures, but they couldn't decide."

"What colour were the dogs?"

"Oh, very pale. I guess like those golden retrievers that are a creamy white?"

She clicked her tongue. "Oh, none of you are farm folk, that's for sure. If they were keeping chickens on a large property, then the dogs might well be sheep dogs. You know, to keep the chickens safe from the foxes and stray dogs. Eagles too."

"Hmmm, like an Old English Sheepdog? I don't think those dogs would match with what the kids described."

"No, I don't mean them. Heavens, what was the breed? Beryl Southmore used to have them. I can't ask her now that's she's died though." She sighed heavily. "I'm going to miss her."

"She was a lovely lady," I said.

"Maremma."

"Sorry? What?"

"The name of the dog breed. It's *Maremma*. They look a little like golden retrievers, but different. They're white, for one thing. And they're not a common dog. People don't buy them as pets usually, because they're a working dog. They'd get bored silly if they didn't have a job to do. But they're beautiful dogs. Lovely soft fur and nice natures."

"Maybe you're right. The dogs might have been Maremmas."

I sat and talked with Mum for a few minutes longer, until she nodded off to sleep again.

At the back of my mind, I kept thinking of the dog breed she'd told me about. I was certain that the children hadn't been shown an image of a Maremma. Charlotte had said the dogs were white. Even the lightest golden retriever wasn't white.

If the dogs did turn out to be Maremmas, then the dogs were probably bought from a breeder. Mum had said they weren't common dogs, and so the list of possible breeders might be quite small. And the breeders might keep records of who buys their animals.

Gently, I kissed Mum and hugged her. "I have to go," I whispered, "but I'll be back as soon as I can."

40

KATE

I drove back home, mentally planning out what I'd be working on tonight and tomorrow. If the children's pet dogs were actually Maremmas, and if I could find the breeder who'd sold those dogs, then I might find my way to the abductors.

It sounded too simple. Far too simple. But it was also true that even the best executed plans had oversights.

Walking into my kitchen, I put the jug on to boil, then called Grimshaw to talk about the possibility of the children's pets being Maremmas.

"Slim chance, Wakeland," she responded. "They identified the dogs as goldens."

"They didn't really identify them," I told her. "One of them said those were the dogs and the other three agreed."

"So?"

"So... *memory distortion*. Their memories might be distorted by the one kid who thought the dogs looked like goldens. I'm thinking of printing off a photo of a Maremma and going to check it out with each of the kids."

"And what's to say you won't get yet more distortion? We've got a mile

244

of leads here to burrow through. And we've had calls coming in from every-where after the news reports."

"If the kids are still confused after I show them the picture, I'll call it quits."

"Wakeland..." She sighed. "What are you trying so hard to prove? That you like going your own way on a case?"

"That's not it."

"Well, it sure seems that way. First, you wanted to re-interview every-one. Then you wanted to put one of the parents under surveillance. All of that went nowhere. Now you want to investigate the exact breed of dog kept at the property. I can't keep up. Don't take this the wrong way, but I might need to have a word with Bigley."

"If it comes to that, let *me* do the explaining."

"Explain all you like. The thing is, I need someone who can lead a solid investigation. You're spending not only your own time on your side projects, but you're using up the time of certain members of the strike force. Seems that you've convinced Vella and Valletti to join you on your exploits. Which puts me in a quandary."

"What you call *side projects* is the way I investigate."

She inhaled and exhaled so hard I had the mental image of her nostrils flaring. "Right. But things have changed pretty dramatically since I okayed that. Four of the kids have been returned. We're running a different race, now. It's no longer a cold case. It's red hot. And we've got to strike while the iron is hot."

"That's not—"

"You're going through a rough time," she cut in. "You're in mourning. I understand. The thing is, if the kidnappings really were directed at you, then the integrity of the strike force is being affected by you staying on it."

I took a breath, my stomach churning. I needed to remain calm with her. Yelling and cursing would get me nowhere. I'd never seen Grimshaw let loose, and I suspected she would find any such show of emotion to be more evidence that I was losing the plot. "But we have no proof it was directed at me."

"We have an absence of any other solid motivation for the crime. The most likely answer to a question is usually the right one."

"If we backtrack just a few short days, you'd have to admit that the case was running in the wrong direction with Ingrid Byrd and her theories."

There was complete silence on the line for a moment.

"You're using your own car. We need all ours," she said finally.

The conversation was done.

I was left shaken. If I lost my place on the team, I couldn't investigate in the same way that I was now. I wouldn't be privy to anything and I couldn't interview who I wanted. One of my lines of investigation had to pay off fast. Not only to keep my place on the strike force, but to grab hold of the kidnappers before they slipped away from us. Because the thought of never bringing those people to justice was unbearable.

The problem was that there was only one of me, and Grimshaw was refusing to give me anyone to help out. I could go sit down with Bigley and tell him what I needed, but that would take precious time. And besides, I couldn't be certain whether he'd end up agreeing with Grimshaw or me.

I ran my hands through my hair, ruffling it in agitation. I had to decide on how I was going to proceed. Grimshaw was right—the things I'd been following up on might all lead to a heaping pile of nothing. But I never left things unexamined, not the things that stuck in my mind.

I poured myself a coffee and then sat myself down on one of my kitchen stools. Opening up my laptop, I switched it on and then began researching Maremmas.

As my mother had said, the dogs were bought for guarding livestock. They were fiercely protective of their charges—those charges usually being chickens and sheep. They were independent thinkers, making decisions on the fly about when to act on a perceived threat and when to keep watching. They weren't aggressive but would take action when needed. They were even known for taking down wolves in Russia.

I sat back, thinking. Was it feasible that the dogs had been used not only to watch over chickens but to keep watch over a group of three-year-old children, keeping them within the boundaries of the property?

Yes, that might have seemed feasible to the kidnappers.

With anxiety gathering in my chest, I made a decision to go against Grimshaw. I couldn't do this alone.

I called Ella and asked her if she'd be able to print out the pictures of Maremmas that I was about to send her and then take the pictures to each of the three children. She'd be late to the strike force meeting. Ella said yes without question.

That was one weight off my back.

I returned to viewing the collection of CCTV footage of the returns of the children. I'd been carefully analysing every moment of the various films ever since I'd obtained them days ago. The kidnappers always seemed to know how to stay out of the line of sight of the cameras. None of the films showed the point in which the kidnappers put the child out of the car.

After half an hour, I called Ella, anxious to know if she'd been able to see any of the children yet.

"Detective," she answered, "I'm at Elijah's house. He told me that…"

She said more, but I couldn't catch it over the background noise. Music and voices boomed loud in my ear. Even Ella's voice was shouty.

"Ella, could you repeat what you just said?"

"Sorry, Elijah's family are all here. I mean, *all* of them. They flew over from America to see him. It's a big family celebration. It's been going on for two days, apparently. They won't let me leave. They're trying to feed me a big stack of pancakes!"

I smiled. Ella sounded a bit overwhelmed.

The background noise lessened, and I guessed she'd walked away from the hub.

"I'll try again," she said, still with a raised voice. "Charlotte and Max's mothers said they were still sleeping, and they didn't want to wake them. I'll go back later, after the strike force meeting. But I've been to Olivia house, and now, of course, I'm at Elijah's. Both kids were both positive the Maremmas were the dogs."

My breath caught. "They were certain?"

"No hesitation at all," she told me.

"Never mind about the other children," I said. "That's enough to go on. Thanks, Ella. I appreciate this so much."

A surge of energy built inside me. This was a lead. A real lead.

I looked up breeders in the Blue Mountains area. I found four registered breeders, and a couple more that seemed to be backyard operators.

I tried calling the registered breeders first. I was able to get in contact with three of them. All three breeders kept records and had been breeding for longer than three years.

I asked for the records of owners from the period of time that the children had been taken. I ended up with a list of seven people and their addresses. I looked up each of the seven people and ran police checks on them. None of the houses of the Maremma puppy buyers matched the description the children had given. That didn't rule those people out, but it wasn't a start either.

I'd already wasted over an hour on this. Time was running away from me. I called the two backyard breeders that I'd found. Neither of them kept records. Both claimed that the litter they currently had for sale was the first litter their dog had ever been pregnant with. One woman sounded especially nervous at my questions about the puppies. I wasn't sure why. Backyard breeders weren't illegal. I browsed online for the regulations for dog breeding while I was speaking to her and I thought I had my answer. Puppies were required to be microchipped before selling. Whoever this person was, I suspected she was skipping that step.

41

KATE

Calling the backyard breeders back, I lied to each one of them, saying I'd been given good information they'd been in operation for longer than a year. They both crumbled and admitted to being in operation for at least five years.

I decided I needed to go pay each of them a visit.

Pete had been out on a morning run. I needed to wait for him. We'd been making sure someone was at home around the clock, just in case the kidnapper made a move. For the past few days, Pete been taking runs up in the mountains, pushing himself to extremes. I worried for him.

My phone tinkled. It was Cameron.

Snatching it up, I answered, hoping there'd been a breakthrough at the strike force. "Hey, Cam. What have you got?"

"Nothing. Grimshaw has me pinned down with busywork. You got anything? Ella said you've got something on the boil. About breeders of the pet dogs the kids had."

"Grimshaw needs you. You'd best stay on whatever task she's set for you."

"She's got me on a door-knocking spree for the next two hours. If people had seen something, they be calling us."

"Not always. Some people need a prod."

"Maybe. You didn't miss anything at the meeting earlier. Grimshaw's plans seem to be all focused on seeing who saw a van in the areas where the kids were dropped off. Trouble is, hundreds of people saw things, and their stories all conflict with each other. I don't think anyone saw anything of note. The abductors were just a bit too clever for that."

"Frustrating."

"You said it."

I *could* use Cameron today. A second pair of eyes was always useful when going out on things like this. He might spot something at someone's property that I missed. On the other hand, Grimshaw wouldn't tolerate Cameron joining me. I was certain she'd try to make it look as if I was going off the deep end.

"I'm just going to be following you, Detective," he said. "Could be pretty annoying. So, you might as well let me go with you."

"I'm about to head over to Blackheath and Megalong Valley," I told him. "But I warn you, I'm scratching. I've got nothing solid."

"Be there in fifteen," he said.

Pete walked in the door, his face red and sweat on his brow.

"You okay?" I said with concern.

He nodded, grabbing a cold drink from the fridge.

By the time Cameron arrived, Pete was outside, furiously digging in the garden. I knew it was his way of dealing with everything.

Cameron whistled when he saw the car we were driving today. Mine was a high performance sports car that Pete had bought me for my birthday five years ago.

"I'll drive," Cameron said.

"Not a chance, Vella," I told him.

"Some of the highway cops have these," he said wistfully.

"Tell you what, if we find out something *good* today, I'll let you drive it home."

"Serious?"

"No." Chuckling, I got into the driver's seat. My car's enhanced engine growl came through the stereo speakers.

Cameron's expression changed to pure bliss. "The things I'd do to have that sound in *my* car."

I shrugged. "It's fake."

His expression didn't change. "It's the dream that counts."

I laughed, pulling onto the road and heading for the highway. I was glad that Cameron was coming along today. As well as helping to spot any irregularities, he'd be a distraction from the spin of thoughts in my head.

We drove over to Blackheath first. It was the nearest suburb of the two. The breeders looked disturbed at my unexpected visit—an older couple of about my age. They had a large yard, and the dogs looked well-cared for. Despite having told me over the phone that they never took down details of puppy buyers, when I asked in person, they ended up showing me a list of buyers, all dated. The list was better than I'd hoped for. There were a few people who'd bought two sibling puppies at the one time, between three and four years ago. I'd be checking up on them afterwards.

Cameron and I jumped back into the car and kept driving, turning off from Blackheath onto Megalong Road. This road was a long, narrow snake, twisting endlessly around mountains. Deep rainforests lined each side of the road, the sun barely penetrating.

"So, how's life treating you, Cam?" I said.

He shrugged. "Can't complain. I like my job. I've got a good bunch of friends I meet up with on the weekends. What else is there?"

I knew that Cameron's family had moved out here when he was just fourteen. His parents had moved back to California when Cameron was twenty, but he'd decided to stay and join the local police force.

"Sounds okay to me. Most people hate their jobs." I steered around a bend. "Do you get away much? See the rest of Australia?"

"I've been on some surfing trips around the coast, yeah. But I don't go away that much. Need someone to go away with."

"Got your eye on anyone?"

"Well, yeah. I did. But then she got a boyfriend. He's an artist, apparently. Guess I'm not her type." He shrugged again.

I frowned, chewing on my bottom lip. "Ella?"

He let out a good-natured curse. "Good sleuthing, Detective. How'd you work that one out?"

"Like a broken clock, I'm right at least twice a day."

"Thanks for the dad joke."

"You're welcome. I'm sorry things didn't work out. With Ella, I mean."

"It's okay. There are other girls." But he sounded uncertain of that.

The land widened out into grassy fields, flat-topped mountains rising on one side. Megalong Valley consisted of huge acreages, some of them worth millions. It had everything from modern, expensive homesteads to historic homes built in the 1800s to some ramshackle homes that were built in the 1970s or later.

We turned onto Peach Tree Road, crossing Pulpit Creek, then onto a dirt road called Churchyard Circle. We passed a small church. I guessed the road had been named after it. But the church was long abandoned, with trees growing through the middle of the crumbling sandstone and a group of cows the only parishioners.

I drove along the bumpy road, wishing I was in a police vehicle rather than my own. We passed two farmhouse style houses on large properties, then the house I was looking for. It was a two-storey weatherboard building, painted white. Someone had once attempted to put down pavers in the yard immediately in front of the house, but tree roots had upended most of them.

A woman came out of the house as we parked—her relaxed stride growing rigid as she neared my car. I guessed she'd been expecting puppy buyers. But instead she'd gotten two cops. Cameron was in police uniform, and he was unmistakable as a member of the police force.

She looked about thirty-five and was as scruffy as her house. Everything about her had that couldn't-be-bothered look. Her hair looked knotted and her long, cream-coloured cardigan sported some stains.

"Her name's Tiff Lantry," I told Cameron quietly. "Like the last couple, she lied at first about how long she's been breeding the Maremmas."

"Hope she looks after the dogs better than herself," he muttered.

Cameron and I exited the car and went to meet her. I introduced Cameron and myself.

"You're the one who called me earlier," she said with a confused look in her eyes.

"Yes, that's right," I said breezily, as if it were the most natural thing in the world for a detective to follow up on a dog breeder. "Can we see your dog breeding setup?"

"Not much to see. I don't have any pups for sale right now."

"You were advertising pups for sale."

"I sold them."

"All? There were four pups in your ad."

"They sold this morning. I'd been waiting on a couple of people to make up their minds. And they came and got them."

"Two each?"

"What?"

"The pups," I said. "You said there were two people who came this morning and now all the pups are sold. Did they take two pups each?"

"Oh. Yeah. They did."

She was obviously lying yet again.

"We're not here about whatever practices you use when selling your puppies," I assured her. "We're interested in some of the people you've sold them to."

"I thought it was damned odd—two detectives coming out here about the dogs." She flicked an eye over Cameron.

I noticed Cameron straightening his back, looking just a little pleased. Tiff didn't seem to know the difference between a detective and a constable. Perhaps that was in her favour. She might not have had much contact with the police before.

Tiff looked distinctly more relaxed now. "So, this is about one of my customers?"

"Yes," I said. "You told me on the phone that you've only got one Maremma female that you breed?"

She nodded. "Just one."

"We need a list of who you sold your Maremmas to about four to three and half years ago," I said.

"Hmm, well, that's a long time ago," she told me. "I'm afraid that's too far back."

"Your Maremma female would only have one litter a year, right?" I asked.

"Sometimes two," she said. "I only have one Maremma female. Pearl. But I've had other breeding dogs. So, that's a lot to keep track of."

"How long have you been breeding Pearl for?"

"I breed my males and females up to about age seven or eight, then I retire them. The girls are too old to keep having pups and the boys' sperm is degraded. The litters start getting too small, and there can be genetic issues with the pups due to the older males' sperm. I pride myself on producing quality pups." Tiff had a confident tone in her voice now, as if she were in her comfort zone.

Cameron angled his head as he gazed around the front of the property. "What happens to the mum and dad dogs? You keep them?"

She shook her head. "I have to sell them. I can't keep them all, even though I'd like to. I make sure they go to good homes."

"Okay. Mind if we see the dog pens?" Cameron asked her.

"Sure." She led us around the back of the house. There were four dog pens, all empty. And a large chicken pen, full of chickens. Tiff opened up every door, then stood back to allow us to have a good look.

Was I wrong about her? Unless she'd hidden some pups, there were none here.

"That's a lot of chickens," I commented.

"They're Isa browns. Good layers. About 300 eggs a year. I sell the eggs at a market stall every second Sunday. Sometimes, I bring my friend's rooster here, and then I have baby chicks to sell."

"What about the mother dog—where is she?" I said.

Tiff closed the pen doors. "Pearl took it hard when her puppies all left this morning, so she's at a friend's house. My friend has some cattle dogs, so Pearl will have some company."

She had a ready explanation for everything.

I smiled. "I see. Well, we'll leave you to it. Can you please put together a list of buyers for us—only for the Maremma and only within the time frame that I indicated? I'll call you tomorrow. You can give me the list over the phone or email it." I handed her my card.

Cameron and I saw ourselves back to my car.

"I don't trust her," said Cameron.

"Oh, yeah?" I said. "That's how I was thinking, but these days I'm not sure if I'm losing perspective. Anyway, I think it's just because she's cutting some corners in her business. All I can do is hope she remembers who she's been selling to."

I sat in the driver's seat of my car again, a sense of defeat washing over me.

I started the engine. Cameron didn't have the same reaction to the engine sound this time. He had his face screwed up tight.

"Wait," he said. "I thought I could hear dogs."

"You could?"

"I think so. But not over that racket."

"Oh, so it's a racket now?"

Cameron nodded, grinning. "No."

Tiff had followed us out to the front of the roadside and was standing there watching.

"What if I drive up the road a bit?" I suggested.

I eased the car over the uneven dirt road and headed further along Churchyard Circle. Finding a flat, grassy spot, I pulled over and switched off the engine.

"Hear it now?" Cameron asked me.

I closed my eyes, listening. "Nup."

"You can't? It's faint. But I can hear barking."

"Nope, can't hear it." I didn't want to admit to Cameron that my hearing wasn't what it used to be. "Are we still on Tiff's property, do you think?"

"I think so," he said. "I haven't seen a fence."

I decided to keep driving down the road. I could hear the faint yelps and yaps of the dogs now. Cameron shot a triumphant glance at me.

Shielding his eyes from the sun, Cameron craned his head to gain a better view. "Okay, we just passed a fence. That's probably the boundary."

"So, the dogs we're hearing belong to the neighbours. I guess we head back."

"Unless," said Cameron, "our good friend Tiff is paying her neighbour to keep her little dog breeding operation happening down here, away from the pesky neighbours."

Cameron had a highly suspicious mind. I liked that.

I kept driving. This property was much larger than Tiff's. A line of pine trees kept the house secluded.

I caught glimpses of the house through gaps in the trees that were only a few inches wide. You wouldn't notice the house at all unless you were specifically trying to peer beyond the trees. The house was single storey. Older style. Tall, narrow windows. A gnarled tree to the right of the house with low, outstretched branches.

I jerked the car to a stop before I even realised I'd hit the brakes.

"Surely not..." I stared through a gap.

"What?"

"That house. I'm sure I'm imagining it, but the kids described a house a lot like that one."

"Can't see much of it from here, to be honest."

"I saw bits and pieces as I drove past."

He looked sceptical. "You weren't expecting to find the house here, right? Unless I missed something?"

"No, not at all." I chewed on my lip, contemplating the tiny vertical snippet of the house that I had a view of. I drove a little further. There was a chimney, on the left. Just like a million chimneys on the left-hand side of an old house.

I looked across at Cameron. "I'm going to check it out."

He lifted his eyebrows in surprise. "Okay, let's do it."

I parked, and we walked up to the front gate.

The gate was securely padlocked. The gate, like the fencing, was wooden with wire strung through it.

With no other way in, I began climbing the fence.

"I think you've snagged yourself, Detective," said Cameron.

"Mind yourself," I snapped good-naturedly.

It was a short walk from there to the pines that fronted the house. We stepped along the dirt pathway and through the pines. The dogs were much louder now. I scanned the property left and right, touching my fingers to my gun holster. If a large dog—or dogs—suddenly rushed at us with bared teeth, I'd have to fire some warning shots.

Turning my head, I looked directly in front.

The house was in full view.

It wasn't exactly like the picture the police compositor had drawn. But it was similar enough to send a rush of needle-like pricks straight down my back.

42

KATE

My gaze shot everywhere as I took in the features of the house.

Climbing tree. Right-hand side. A ladder tied to the branches.
Single-storey house. Farmhouse style. Nondescript in colour.
Steps in the middle. Flowers either side.
Wooden shutters.
Chimney to the left.
Front door with a round glass insert.

Was this the house? Could it really be it?

The shutters were closed on all the windows, except for one. The room beyond the unshuttered window was dark. If this was the house, then Elijah's story checked out. A child could easily stand in one of those rooms and not be seen by someone out here. He'd thought he'd seen a woman that looked like Lori out where I was now.

On legs of jelly, I attempted to sprint the rest of the way.

My pounding on the front door left an echo. "Police! Open up!"

I heard nothing inside. No voices, no sound. Just the distant barks of the dogs.

Spinning around, I ran back down the steps, almost knocking into Cameron. "I don't think anyone's home."

I went to look inside the room with the open shutters. There was nothing in there but a bed and a freestanding wardrobe. The bed had no mattress.

"Let's go check out the back," called Cameron.

I nodded, my lungs growing tight.

Cameron cupped his hands around his mouth as we rushed around to the back of the house. "Hello? Anyone here?"

Still no answer.

Someone had lived here recently. Extensive vegetable patches were growing all kinds of things. Corn, pumpkins, tomatoes and more vegetables that I couldn't see from here. There were fruit trees, too. Avocado, lemon and others.

An apple tree caught my attention. Elijah had said he got a sore tummy from eating unripe apples from a tree. The apples were ripe, now.

A hollow place opened wide in my chest. If this was the house—and my gut told me it was—then Ivy could be buried here. The horrific scene that the other children had described flashed in my mind. Standing here in the yard, the scene took on a terrible, macabre reality.

Ivy lying unresponsive on the wet grass, covered in sticks. The man called Bear digging in the dirt.

I scanned the property, looking for fresh mounds of soil. But the ground had been dug everywhere for the gardens.

Far to the right and back of the property, I could see the dog pens.

Cameron knocked hard on the back door. "Police. Open the door." He turned to me. "Okay, if anyone's in there, they've had fair warning. What comes next?"

I exhaled. "We break in."

"Can we do that?"

"Section 9. Emergency. We have reason to believe there may be a child or children inside and in danger."

He looked at me askance.

"If these people abducted five children, then they might well have abducted more," I explained.

The words dried on my tongue. That wasn't my real reason. My real reason was that I wasn't willing to wait a moment longer. The house was right here in front of us. Ivy might be lying under the ground here. And her abductors were almost certainly fleeing.

"Okay, we're doing this," Cameron responded. Striding up to the back door, he kicked it twice. "Damned thick door." He looked inside the window. "They've got some heavy locks on it, too."

"Don't break your foot." Picking up a rock, I tossed it at the kitchen window. "Done."

The shatter of the glass set the dogs off barking again. I half-expected a siren to go off, but none did.

We knocked out the remaining glass and climbed inside. A large farm-house-style kitchen surrounded us.

A heavy stink of bleach saturated the air.

"Phwoar." Cameron clapped a hand over his nose and mouth.

"Let's go," I said.

Cameron and I took opposite sides of the house to search. My side led into a hallway, off which there were a few bedrooms and a bathroom.

I ran from room to room, looking for something—*anything*—that would act as proof that the kids had been kept here. But the rooms had been stripped of everything except for the furniture. The bed bases were the old type made with springs, the springs sagging and a little rusted. Dust had settled on the worn floorboards. The rooms were otherwise clean. Each room held the overpowering stench of bleach.

What had the kids said about the interior of the house? I tried to remember.

They'd described a big kitchen, but they'd disagreed on the colour of it. They'd told us about the patterns on their bed coverings, but that was all gone now.

The beds—what had Charlotte said? She'd said she slept in a large bed with Ivy and Olivia. Polly and Bear had slept in a large bed, too. And the two boys had slept in one single bed.

I hurried back to check all the bedrooms again.

Two of the rooms had queen-sized beds and one of them had a single bed. One of the queen-sized beds sagged in the middle, as if a couple had slept in the middle of the bed every night. Was this where Polly and Bear had slept? The configuration of beds was exactly as Charlotte had described.

It still wasn't proof though. Lots of households would have that same configuration of beds.

I checked the bathroom next. It was lined in cracked, pink tiles and floral wallpaper, with a freestanding basin that had discoloured around the drain. The mirror had been removed—a square of lighter coloured wallpaper showing where it had been.

Bleach was an indicator that the owners might have tried to get rid of any DNA. By the smell of it, the bleach used was not chlorine-based but oxygen-based. Which told me that the people who'd cleaned the house might know a thing or two about bleach and how to destroy DNA evidence.

So far, it was all circumstantial. I needed strong evidence. If we found nothing in the house, then it could come down to a forensics investigation team digging the ground outside and looking for clues and a possible body. That could take weeks.

I grabbed the basin, steadying myself. I'd grown light-headed. I wasn't breathing right. The bleach seemed to have sucked the oxygen out of the entire house. It wasn't just the bleach—it was the overpowering sense of loss and regret. If I'd found the house just days ago, Ivy would be safe and alive.

"Detective," Cameron called.

I rushed to the living room.

"Look up," he said.

I followed the direction of his gaze. Up high, a bracket had been nailed above a door.

"There are a few of those around the house," he said. "They might have held cameras."

"Cameras?" I breathed. "What were they doing with so many cameras?"

"I don't know. Maybe I can find a screwdriver somewhere and take one of them with us, then check it out at a camera store."

"No, leave them in place for forensics." I snapped a picture of the bracket using my phone. "Did you find anything else?"

He shook his head. "They've gone through the place like army ants, eating anything that's not nailed down."

"Okay, let's swap sides of the house and see if we missed anything."

I began looking around the living room while Cameron disappeared down the hallway. This end of the house held two living rooms, a small sunroom and the kitchen. Cam was right. It had all been picked clean.

Heading back outside, we circled around the vegetable patches and a large shed. The shed door was locked. Cameron aimed a kick at the door, and it gave way without protest.

The floor of the shed was floorboards that looked a lot newer than anything else on the property. The floor was scuffed with marks that ran in a large circle. The air held the same smell of bleach that the house did.

I studied the floor. "The only thing I can think would have made those marks is kids on tricycles and scooters. On a wet day, when they couldn't run about outside, this space would have been perfect."

"Did they tell you about riding bikes in a big shed when you questioned them?" Cameron asked.

"Nope. But we didn't ask, either. With kids, you don't always know what the right questions are."

We walked down to the dog pen.

There were three adult Maremmas, one of which was guarding tiny Maremma pups.

Tiff Lantry, I've got questions for you. Oh, so many questions.

43

KATE

Tiff Lantry was about to leave as Cameron and I zipped back to her house in the car. She'd been speedy in showering and changing her clothes.

Guilt was fairly evenly plastered all over her face as we walked up to her. She wasn't even attempting to hide it now.

"You're back again?" Tiff crossed her arms protectively, her gaze skating between us, looking increasingly more worried.

"How far does your property extend?" I asked her.

She pointed to the right. "As far as the first fence line, that way."

"So, the house on that other side of that fence doesn't belong to you?"

Now she looked cagey. "Not to me, no."

"You looked uncertain of that," I said bluntly.

"It belongs to my parents. But Dad got sick, and they moved to Sydney to be near his specialists."

"How often do they come back to the house?"

"They don't. Not for the past five years or so, anyway. I drive down to Sydney to see them."

Cameron gestured in the direction of the farmhouse. "What's the deal with the dogs in the enclosures over there, then? Who's looking after them?"

She puffed up her cheeks. "Me."

"So, you *do* have more dogs that you're selling?" said Cameron.

"Yes," she admitted.

Cameron scowled. "They need water."

"Look..." Tiff's shoulders rolled inward. "I keep the dog over there because the neighbours complain. Even though my closest neighbour is quite a distance away, they can't stand the barking. Maremmas bark a lot. It's how the breed is."

"And the vegetable patches?" I said impatiently. "You grow vegetables all the way down there rather than on your own property?"

"My parents started the gardens, so I just continued them," she told us.

I'd handed her that one. I was feeding her questions that she could easily find answers for. Tiff might be good at thinking on her feet.

Cameron's phone rang, and he excused himself, stepping a short distance away.

"What have you been using the house for?" I asked Tiff.

She shook her head. "I don't use it for anything."

"When was the last time you went inside?" I said.

"Years," she answered quickly.

"Has anyone else been in the house recently?"

"No. No one."

"Are you sure of that?"

"Yes. Very sure."

That had been the make-or-break set of questions. She couldn't quick-step her way out now.

I levelled my gaze at her. "Someone has just been in that house. They've cleaned every inch of it. With a cleaning solution. Can you tell me about that?"

Tiff was a deer in headlights now. "You went *inside?*"

"Yep, we did." I didn't explain.

Her expression crumbled.

I took my chance before Tiff had time to invent something. "I need you to tell me the real story. This is very important."

"I rented the house out for a little while."

"Okay. Now we're getting somewhere. Who'd you rent it to?"

"It wasn't for long. I just needed some extra money. Dog breeding doesn't bring in enough, that's for sure. Neither does my job at the super-market. And five years ago, my husband got sick and stopped working. And then there's all the trips back and forth to Sydney to see my parents—"

I held up a hand to stop her. "I'm really very sorry about all of that. But I don't need to know your reasons why you rented the house. I'll take a guess that you were getting the rent money cash-in-hand?"

She bent her head, staring downward. "Of course, I'm going to declare the income when I do my tax. And I'm planning on giving my parents their half. But I just needed to clear my own debts first."

Did she honestly not get what this was about? It wasn't about her renting the house out illegally or her dog breeding business.

"Tiff, I'm going to make myself very clear. What I want to know is— who was in the house? What were their names?"

"The woman's name is Polly. I don't know his."

I crushed my eyes closed for a minute, composing myself. The chance of the house being the right one was now a hundred percent. The name Polly had been suppressed from the media accounts of the returned chil-dren. Grimshaw had considered that the name was false and wasn't helpful for the public to know.

Snapping my eyes open, I let air enter my lungs. "Describe Polly."

"About my age. A little on the large side."

"And the man?"

"I only saw him sitting in the car. I don't know. Brown hair. Maybe a similar age."

"Who else lived at the house?"

"They had a few foster kids."

"Describe the children, please?"

She shook her head. "I never saw them, except in the distance a few times. I work during the day."

"You never saw the kids? But you saw Polly quite a bit?"

"No. She paid by the month, leaving the money in my letterbox. Like clockwork."

"What about when you went to tend to the puppies for your business?"

"I didn't run it, not while Polly was there. I stopped breeding dogs for the past three odd years, because I had the rent money coming in."

"But there are pups there now."

"Yeah. I've got a lot of bills right now. It's winter and there's going to be lots of heating costs. So, I decided to breed Pearl again. The pups are just four days old."

"Why are you selling pups that young?"

She sighed. "I'm not. People like to come and have a look at the mother and newborn pups. Helps me to get them sold ahead of time, so that I get a down payment from the buyer."

"Hmmm. Okay. How did you meet Polly and Bear?"

"Polly came looking for Maremma pups to buy. That's when I met her. She bought two female pups. While she was here, she asked if I knew anyone with a house to rent, cash-in-hand." Tiff licked her lips nervously. "And well, my parents' house was just sitting there...."

"Right. And the two girl dogs that Polly bought are the ones in the pen right now? Plus your dog?"

"Yes. There's my Pearl. And Elsa and Snowdrop. The kids named the other dogs."

"Okay," I said. "Tiff, there is going to be police everywhere within the hour. I'm going to need you to stay here and answer questions."

"Am I in trouble?"

"That depends on whether or not what you just told me is true."

Leaving Tiff to consider that, I walked across to Cameron.

He placed a hand over the phone. "It's Detective Grimshaw. Wanting an update on where I am and what I'm doing."

I took the phone from him. "Grimshaw," I spoke into the phone. "Cameron and I have just found the house. We'd better get forensics mobilised."

Dead silence fell between us. Then I heard her lightly clucking her tongue. "What house are we talking about?"

"The house where the kids were kept. It's on Churchyard Circle, Megalong Valley."

Another silence. Then, "How did you manage that? Former address of a felon you put in jail?"

"Nope. Next door to a Maremma dog breeder."

I could almost hear her mind ticking over. "You'd better be damned sure before I put the call out."

"I couldn't be more certain," I told her.

44

KATE

The Forensic Services Group had arrived and were currently spreading all over the house and land. It was time for me to leave and allow them the time and space to do their job.

I was a bundle of nerves and sorrow and rage.

The place where the children had been kept was no longer a mystery. I might have just walked over the ground where my granddaughter was buried.

Tiff Lantry was refusing to answer any more questions. She'd gotten spooked when the mass of police had descended, and she'd decided she needed a lawyer. The only thing she would agree to was a session with the police sketch artist, Lucas Salisbury. She was being taken down to the station right now, to give Lucas descriptions of Polly and Bear.

I needed to go and talk to Lori Hinton. Now. Perhaps her mysterious male companion could be explained, but Elijah had seen her at that house, and there was still that odd phone conversation of hers. It was time to confront her.

I headed home for a shower to wash off the stench of bleach and get changed.

After the shower, I went to find Pete. Following the sound of hammer blows, I found him down the back of the yard, fixing the fence.

When he turned to me, I realised his eyes were wet and his cheeks tear-stained.

"I used to make sure this fence and gate were in good repair," he stammered. "So that little Ivy didn't get out. I've been wanting to fix this for a while now... so...." His shoulders trembled in a silent sob.

"Oh, Pete." I slipped my arms around him.

He enclosed me in a hug, nestling his face against my neck. "On the day the kids came back, for a few wonderful hours, I thought she was coming back, too."

"I know...."

"I wish I could have traded places with her. Me for her."

"I'd do the same." Putting my head against his, I let moments pass us by. I'd come looking for Pete for his hug and his reassurance. It ended up that he'd needed those things as much as I did.

"Pete... I found the house today."

Raising his head, he moved back to face me. "You don't mean...?"

I nodded.

"How?" His expression was incredulous.

I explained about Mum's suggestion in relation to the Maremmas and then about Tiff Lantry.

"They're digging up the grounds now?" he asked in a hushed voice when I'd finished.

"Yes. It was the eeriest feeling, being there." Taking out my phone, I showed him some of the photos I'd snapped.

He shook his head, studying the pictures. "Let's hope the kidnappers left behind evidence all over the place," he muttered darkly.

"I hope there's something they've overlooked. Trouble is, they took every effort to wipe the place clean as a whistle. The whole interior has been bleached."

"Hell."

I kissed him. "Pete, I've got to go. There's someone I need to interview."

We hugged again... until I felt strong enough to keep going.

Lori was at home. Sean had taken Charlotte over to his mother's house so that she could spend time with family. Since Charlotte had come home from the hospital, Lori had apparently not allowed her to step foot outside. Until today.

Lori met me at her front door. She was dressed in her signature pastel colours palette, her brown hair in a tight knot at her nape.

"Come through. Can I get you a drink, Kate? A tea or coffee? Something cold?"

I walked inside, half-regretting ever telling the parents of the missing kids that they could call me *Kate* rather than *Detective*. Because now, there wasn't as much professional distance as I would like.

"No thank you," I replied. "I'm fine."

Lori headed for the living room, but I asked if we could instead talk in her formal dining room. I could write up my notes easier at a table, I told her. What I didn't tell Lori was that I'd rather the more formal setting. The living room seemed more like a place to sit and have a casual chat, and this was not going to be a chat.

I sat myself at the table. Lori positioned herself on a chair near me and clasped her hands together. "Has something happened? Something new?"

"There are lots of things happening at the moment. But this involves you."

"Me?"

"Lori, this is a difficult question. I'm just going to say it straight out. You met with someone a few nights ago. A man. At the parking area for the cable car."

Her eyes grew large and worried. "Am I being *watched?*"

"Yes," I said bluntly.

"Oh my God. Why?"

"You deserve to know that. Really. But first, I'd very much like to know who that man was."

"Well, I'm not having an affair, if that's what you're thinking." She gave a short laugh and then cleared her throat. "He's a private investigator."

I squared my shoulders into the back of the chair. She'd immediately told the truth. I pretended as if I didn't know. "An investigator? Can I ask you his name?"

"Kyle. Kyle Wheeler."

"Thanks. What did you engage him for?"

"It was back when Sean and I were still together. Sean seemed to be sneaking around, and I suspected he was seeing someone. And so, I engaged the services of an investigator. And, of course, he found out that Sean was cheating. For an additional fee, he said he'd find out all about the woman Sean was seeing. I wanted to, but Kyle had become quite forceful and I felt too uncomfortable with him, so I didn't go ahead. Of course, I know *now* just who Sean was seeing all that time. Roxanne Crane."

"Roxanne?" I hadn't guessed that. It explained why I'd seen Lori giving Roxanne dirty looks.

"Yes, *her*."

"I'm sorry."

"The whole thing is just revolting."

"It was months ago that Sean moved out, correct? I mean, I understand that he's back in the house now. But he initially moved out at least two months ago?"

"Yes, that's right."

"Can I ask why you're still meeting up with the investigator?"

"He told me he could find the children. That he could find Charlotte."

"Right. Okay, so, you re-engaged his services?"

"Yes."

"But, the night that you were seen with the investigator was *after* Charlotte was returned. What was the reason for that?"

Her chest sank in. "He thinks there might still be some danger from the kidnappers. These people are crazy. They could decide to snatch the children back again so that they couldn't give away any vital clues. And this time, they'd kill them."

My eyebrows tensed. "And, what does he propose to do about that?"

"Find the kidnappers."

"Don't you think that job is better left to the police?"

"Yes, of course. But I'm terrified that Charlotte is still vulnerable, you know? She was missing for three and a half long years. I can't let anything happen to her again. I'm sure you understand."

"Yes, I do. It's very understandable that you're feeling like that. But my concern would be that he's preying on those feelings. How does he propose to find the kidnappers?"

"He says he has his methods."

"Have you been paying him large sums of money?"

Exhaling, she glanced down at the table. "Yes."

"It seems that there was some sort of argument between him and yourself on the night in question?"

She stared at me aghast. "The police really *have* been watching me closely."

"So, there *was* an argument?"

"Yes, there was. I felt that he was asking for too much money and being too demanding."

"That alone should tell you that he's not very professional? Whose idea was it to meet up so late that night—and in an isolated spot?"

"His."

"So, he's putting you under a lot of pressure."

Nodding, she pressed her lips into a thin line. "But the way he puts it, he's just passionate about his work and he really wants to get a result." She sighed, frowning. "He even said that it was his investigation that prodded the kidnappers into releasing the children. He was getting too close and lighting a fire under them—that's what he said."

"Hmmm, interesting. Sounds like a real shyster."

"Perhaps he is. I'm starting to see him in a very different light. Anyway, I told him no. I'm not paying him any more money."

"Can I ask if you had a phone conversation with him the night of the gathering at Penny's house?"

"Yes..." She stared at me. "My phone's being tapped, too?"

"You were telling him about me asking questions at the gathering? Why was that?" I said, ignoring her last comment.

"Because he asked. He was insistent on knowing everything the police knew."

That had just solved the mystery of Lori's phone conversation.

I remembered something. "Lori, did you happen to inform Mr Wheeler when I was put onto the Strikeforce Flying Fox team, a week ago?"

She nodded faintly.

"Okay, now I know how that piece of information got out to the media so fast. I think Mr Wheeler was selling information to a journalist or two."

"Oh no."

"Looks like he was trying to get money any way he could."

She threaded her fingers together, twisting them. "Is he the reason I was being followed by the police?"

I shook my head. "I'm going to level with you. There's no easy way to say it, so I'm just going to say it. One of the children believes that they saw you on the property where they were being held."

Her mouthed dropped, top lip quivering. "Excuse me?"

I repeated what I'd just said.

She shook her head a few times before answering. "What on earth? What are you trying to say? That I *knew* where the children were?"

"We haven't formed any opinion," I told her.

"This is... unbelievable," she said indignantly. "How could you possibly..." She took a breath. "You must have run into a brick wall with this investigation to be coming after the parents of the missing children."

"I'll tell you something. We haven't hit a brick wall. We've actually made a very large discovery. I can't tell you what it is yet."

"Which child was it? It can't be Charlotte, so that leaves the other three. I'm going to guess it was Olivia. More like, either her mother and Sean put it into her head that she'd seen me there. Make me look like a batshit crazy woman who'd steal five children. The two of them probably want to take Charlotte away from me." Her voice was rising to a croaky shriek.

"I'm afraid I can't say who it was."

Her eyes bugged and her words all started to run together. "Oh, wait. *Wait.* I remember something. Elijah looked at me strangely on the day you

273

and Reagan were questioning the children. You asked if anyone else had ever been to the property, and he turned to stare at me. I was very confused. I thought he must have believed I knew the answer to that question. I had no clue he actually thought that he'd seen me there."

"Lori, please, slow down. I can't tell you which child it was, and it doesn't matter. If you look at it from our perspective, you'll understand why we had to follow up on it. Just... breathe."

"Well, if it's at all true that the child saw someone, then it was just someone who looks somewhat like me."

"That's possible. But listen carefully to what I'm about to say. It wasn't said that you saw the children. It was said that *they* saw *you*. You—or someone who looks like you—were seen by the child from a window. Do you understand me?"

She nodded rigidly.

"So," I continued, "if we look at it from that perspective, it could have happened that you visited the property totally unawares. Now, have you, within the past three and a half years, been to any large properties in the Blue Mountains area, for any reason?"

"Sometimes. I've picked up flowers for girlfriends' weddings a few times. Most of them are on their second or third marriage, and they don't want to go to the expense of formal flower arrangements. Hmmm, and I've gone to buy farm-fresh eggs and tomatoes—things like that."

"Have you gone to buy any pets? Such as puppies?"

"No. I've got our cat, Cinnamon. She doesn't like dogs."

"Okay. Have you been to visit someone at a large property, but got lost and turned up at the wrong house?"

"No." She frowned. "Just, I went to buy chickens about a year ago, for an elderly neighbour who wanted some Isa Brown chickens. I found some for a good price out at, oh, where was it? Maybe Blackheath? Or Little Hartley? Or maybe Megalong Valley? I have a terrible memory for places. And I did get lost that day. I was talking on the phone and missed the house I was looking for."

"Can you describe the house you turned up at? And which street it was?"

"Not really." She turned away, appearing to think. "No idea which street. All I remember is that the house was behind a bunch of pine trees. I had a brief conversation with the woman who lived there, and she told me they didn't have chickens and to go next door. She was a bit rude, actually."

Lori met my gaze, shock registering on her face. "Dear God, don't tell me I actually walked onto the property where the children were being kept?"

45

KATE

The morning after Cameron and I discovered the house at Megalong Valley, nothing of note had yet been found at the property.

Lori Hinton's story about her elderly neighbour and the Isa Brown hens seemed to check out. It also made sense that she didn't have a clear memory of the property where the children had been kept. She'd visited farms on many occasions and her memories of them had largely blurred together. I called her into the station early this morning for further questioning by myself and Grimshaw to see if we could glean more details about Polly.

After the questioning was done, I went to grab a quick breakfast of bagels and coffee.

Grimshaw called and wanted me at today's strike force meeting. I had to hold myself back from pointing out that I achieved more by not being at her meetings. But there were lots of things to discuss and investigate now. A team of police was better than one person.

The strike force members clapped and cheered as I entered the room.

I grinned at their enthusiasm. "Hey, it was a team effort." I gestured at Cameron and Ella.

"It was all you, Detective," said Cameron, "I was just glad to be along for the ride."

"Nope," I insisted. "It was you who heard the dogs. Or we wouldn't have even headed any further down that road. And Ella…" I glanced over at the beaming Constable Valletti. "Ella did the legwork with the kids to find out if their pet dogs really were Maremmas."

Grimshaw's gaze skated between the three of us, her mouth set in a grim line. It was clear she wasn't amused we'd joined forces behind her back. But there was nothing she could say about it. We'd just found the house, which was the first and only major discovery since the children had gone missing.

"Okay," Grimshaw said, "if we're done with the mutual appreciation society shizz, let's get on with business, shall we? I'll get Detective Wakeland to explain how everything happened yesterday."

I stood at the front of the room, telling the story of how the day unfolded, leaving nothing out except my emotional response when I realised what property it was. I answered some questions and then Grimshaw took over again.

"We're keeping a lid on the finding of the house," Grimshaw told the team. "The last thing forensics need there are sightseers. Now, you've all seen the photos we have so far of the house and grounds. I've spoken with forensics this morning and they've made a discovery. Apparently, there were cameras in every room. Everything from tiny, hidden cameras to large cameras capable of rotating in multiple directions. The cameras are gone, now, but there are holes drilled everywhere."

My stomach turned. Cameron had suggested that the brackets high on the walls could be for cameras when we were there. And now it had been confirmed.

Grimshaw sat on a swivel stool, crossing her arms. "So, what we have so far is a remote house on a large property, filled with cameras. What does that tell us about the people who had the kids?"

Liz Booth winced. "Were the cameras in the bedrooms and bathrooms, too?"

"There is only one bathroom," answered Grimshaw, "and they didn't find evidence of cameras having been there. Doesn't mean there wasn't. A mirror had been removed from the bathroom wall. The mirror was found in a shed. There were cameras in the bedrooms, except for one, and we assume that's the room that the mysterious Polly and Bear slept in."

"Ugh," Booth said, shaking her head. "Could someone other than Polly and Bear have been watching the kids through the cameras? Like, some sort of sick business where they sell streaming video of young children?"

"That's a distinct possibility," said Grimshaw. "But what kind of videos are we talking about? So far, our questioning of the children hasn't uncovered any hint of nude films or photography."

"The films could have been made when they were much younger," stated Booth, "and they've since forgotten—or been made to forget."

Grimshaw nodded. "But why then did the people keep the children so long? Why keep them and feed them and clothe them? Doesn't seem like a good way to run a business, because the profits would be eaten up, right?"

I stared at Grimshaw with growing surprise. She was brainstorming with the team. That wasn't her usual method of operation at all. Usually, information came in and then she set out tasks for everyone to complete. We exchanged glances, and it seemed that she understood that I'd noticed her change in style, but I could never be sure with her.

I realised something then. Part of the reason Grimshaw would have wanted me not attending meetings over the past days would have been so that she could lead the team in a discussion about me—about the kidnapper vengeance theory, specifically. Maybe the brainstorm session was for my benefit, to show that she wasn't stuck on the one theory anymore—even though she most probably was.

I stayed quiet, not engaging in the discussion. I couldn't bring myself to speculate on the gritty details.

Booth screwed up her face, seeming deep in thought. "Could keeping the kids for years be some kind of experiment? Maybe someone else was directing the whole thing. This other person maybe wanted a group of children kept isolated and prevented from even knowing they were growing older."

"That sounds nutty," said Cameron. "Who would do that?"

Booth shrugged. "Don't know. Someone interested in raising kids totally natural? Like, on farm-fresh produce and fresh air and no school or electronic devices."

"Seems far-fetched," said Grimshaw.

Booth shrugged again, fixing her ponytail. "I remember reading about triplet boys who were adopted out to three different families and the families weren't told the boys had triplet siblings. It was an experiment to see how differently the boys might grow up. Nature or nurture."

Cameron made an exaggerated blink. "Hell. That's sick."

"But in the case of the nursery school children," said Ella. "Why abduct children at age three? They've already had their vaccines and exposure to modern day life."

"Maybe it was too hard to take babies?" suggested Booth.

"True," said Grimshaw. "There would be an enormous level of difficulty in stealing five babies."

"It fits, right?" said Booth. "The experiment was at an end, so they gave the kids back. Except... something went wrong at the end."

"There is one more thing that forensics found so far," Grimshaw told us. "Some of the brackets were for TV screens. There were screens mounted in every room."

"Maybe they used the screens as a babysitter for the kids?" Ella suggested. "Like, the kids were watching movies and kids' cartoons?"

"I'd agree that's likely," said Booth. "I know you're not meant to, so don't hate on me, but I used to set my kiddies up in front of the TV before their daily nap. Gave me a break."

Grimshaw wrote a list on the whiteboard.

Motivations:

1.Experiment—children raised in a natural environment

2.Business—selling videos of children to a third party

3.Retaliation—against Detective Wakeland for putting a murderer in jail

"There we have it," Grimshaw stated. "Three theories. An experiment or a business or retaliation. One of them has to fit." She levelled her gaze at me, unblinking. "What do you think, Detective?"

She'd put me on the spot, perhaps as a way for her to keep her dominant position in the strike force. But she wasn't going to make me falter. "I'm sorry," I said, "none of the theories so far are clicking into place for me. None of them appear to fit with the length of time the kids were kept. I consider that there was some other factor behind the kidnappings."

She crossed her arms. "Well, okay, what are your thoughts, then?"

"I don't know. I'm still figuring that out."

I was saved then as the police sketch artist, Lucas Salisbury entered, a large foolscap folder under his arm.

Lucas placed a portrait drawing of an older woman up on the six screens at the side of the room.

"This is Polly," he said. "According to Tiff Lantry. Tiff was good at remembering facial details—better than most people. Let's hope her memory is accurate." He then put up the composition of Polly that the children had helped him draw. "As you can see, it's a pretty good match for what the kids told me, just more detailed." He put up one more drawing of a woman's face. "Now, this is a drawing of Polly I did just this morning. This is Lori Hinton's memory of Polly. Tiff and Lori's versions of Polly match up pretty well."

"Good stuff, Lucas," said Grimshaw. "We'll get those two new drawings out to the media. Shame Tiff didn't get a good look at the man. Mostly what we've got for him are just some kids' drawings."

Lucas gave a nod. "I wanted to have a chat about that. There's something a bit odd there."

"Oh?" said Grimshaw.

I leaned forward, listening intently.

Shuffling through his folder, Lucas produced a pile of paper. "These are the kids' drawings of Bear and Polly. I retrieved the last of these yesterday, from the psychologist who'd been treating the kids—Dr Zhang." He began putting up drawings of Polly that the children had drawn.

"Now," Lucas explained, "this set of pictures of Polly are what I'd expect from a group of six-year-olds. The drawings are a little inconsistent, but that's fine. Kids tend to draw from the perspective of what a particular person means to them or what their personality is like. Someone who's angry might get big black eyebrows, for instance. Also, a lot comes down to artistic talent, to be honest. So, you might get a head the size of a grape and legs like hot-air balloons, that kind of thing. Polly has been drawn all kinds of different ways."

Lucas lifted out another set of drawings. Half of the six screens filled with children's pictures of a man. "Here we've got the kids' sketches of the man they call Bear. What you'll notice is that they're a lot more consistent."

He was right. While the pictures of Bear contained a lot less detail than the pictures of Polly, they tended to all show a triangular face, a wide, smiling mouth, bear ears and very open eyes.

"Are they the drawings of all four children?" I asked.

"Yep," Lucas replied. "Their names are on the back. Dr Zhang thought it was unusual, and I do, too. I don't know what to make of it. The kids might have been schooled on how to draw the man. Maybe he was the one with the most to lose if he were discovered as the abductor. Or, he wore a mask every time the kids saw him—and although that sounds like a long shot, it seems likely to me. I'll tell you why. It's because his features are too consistent. Perhaps it's a mask that has a man's face and bear's ears. I was lucky enough to get another example of this from Tiff Lantry. Even though she only caught a glimpse of him, she saw enough for me to be able to get something down on paper."

He put up one final picture. It was drawn with an expert hand and gave a pretty clear image of Bear's face.

"Again," said Lucas, "The fact that Tiff remembered such a distinct, even set of features from a glance of just a few seconds makes me think it's a mask."

Words formed in my throat but didn't make it out.

I'd seen that face before, hadn't I?

Where?

46

KATE

"I have to go," I told Grimshaw, packing up my things.

She stared at me in annoyance. "But we're only just getting started."

"I know." I shoved my notebook and pens into my briefcase.

"Well, you can't go back to the house, if that's where you're headed. Let the forensic team do their thing." To Grimshaw's credit, her tone softened somewhat. "You'll be called the moment they find... *anything*."

"No, that's not where I'm going."

Her expression divided itself between suspicion and interest. "What have you got?"

"I'm not sure, to be honest. I need to go check something out."

"Take an officer with you. Valletti, go with Wakeland."

Ella raised her eyebrows at me questioningly. Grimshaw had gone from not wanting to allow me to take any officers with me to trying to push an officer onto me. I suspected that she only wanted Ella with me so that she could quiz her later on what I was up to.

I shook my head. "I need to do this alone."

"Right," said Grimshaw in a vaguely disappointed tone. "Go."

Grimshaw's control over my movements was just a formality now. We both knew it.

I hurried out to my car. It was still covered in dust from the dirt road I'd travelled down yesterday. *Dirt that Ivy might have once stepped on.*

As I drove away, a tension headache fired up in my right temple.

Where I was going, I didn't want another officer with me. It was a place that was intensely personal.

———

The light dappled gently on the lake outside the Tallman's Valley Hospice today, the sky overcast. The patients were out on the lawn, as usual, wrapped up in coats and blankets and knitted hats.

Mum wasn't among them.

My heart glitched. I told myself not to panic. Rational me knew that the hospital would call me the moment that my mother had reached a critical stage, or if she had suddenly died during the night. Either of those two things were coming soon, but I still wasn't ready for them.

But I found her in her room, in bed and sleeping.

Pulling the blanket up, I kissed her lightly on her cheek and brushed the hair back from her forehead.

"She seemed especially tired at breakfast today," a voice said from behind me.

I turned to the nurse who'd entered the room.

"Was she okay?" I asked the nurse.

She frowned. "I'm not sure. She didn't eat her toast and eggs. She might have picked up a tummy bug."

"Could she have flu?" I put a hand on her forehead. "No, she doesn't feel hot. Maybe a bit cold and clammy, actually."

"Sometimes older people don't get a fever when they have flu. I'll keep a close eye on her."

"Thank you." I smiled briefly. "Would the hospice please call me if she isn't feeling well when she wakes?"

"Certainly. I'll put that in her notes."

"I'd appreciate that." I paused, knowing my next request was going to seem odd. "Is it possible that I could see Harry? Harry Grenville? He's a patient here."

"I'm afraid not. He's not well. I think there's something going around. But he can't tell us when he's ill, poor thing. He collapsed and was taken to emergency at the hospital last night."

"Oh no, that's not good."

She sighed. "No. Poor old Harry."

"I've seen him busily drawing, every time I've visited Mum. He seems to love the birds on the lake."

"Oh yes, he does. Harry loves to sketch them. He's our resident artist."

"Would it be possible for me to see his sketches? I've never quite had the chance."

"I don't see why not," she said, but her smile was tinged with a vague question. *Why are you interested in his pictures?*

I kissed Mum again before I followed the nurse out and down the hall-way, then through a set of locked double doors and into the dementia care wing.

Harry's room had the blind up, with a view to the reserve. His bed was neatly made. A set of pencils and a pair of binoculars sat on a shelf. I hoped he would make it back here.

The nurse opened a cupboard and lifted out a pile of drawings. Taking them, I began spreading them out on Harry's bed. There were lots of sketches of ducks and swans on the lake or in the grasses at the lake's edge. Some of them were of the resident cat, Maple.

There it was. A picture of a bear in men's clothing and standing on two legs. Or at least, a white, grinning man with a black nose and bear ears. My blood chilled.

I kept sifting through the pictures. There were repeated drawings of the bear-man.

I turned back to the nurse. "Do you happen to know why he drew the bear? All of his other pictures are of real animals." There were no bears in Australia, and certainly no bears that wore clothing.

"Perhaps it's real to him," she said softly.

I smiled. "Perhaps. But it's odd. Do you know when he first started drawing these ones?"

Was I grasping at straws? This was a long stretch. A very, very long stretch.

I picked up the pair of binoculars from the shelf. "Do you mind if I—?" Not finishing my sentence, I took the binoculars over to the window. Harry's window faced *The Ponds*, where the children had picnicked. The binoculars were old but must have been expensive in their day, because I could see clearly across the grounds to the picnic area.

Did you see something out there that day, Harry? Someone wearing a mask and hiding behind those trees? Or did the ice-cream van driver don a mask that day?

Carefully, I angled the binoculars to look up at the top of the hill. I would have been able to see the ice-cream van, if I'd been looking that way with these binoculars on the day of the picnic. But could I have seen faces with any clarity?

I attempted to focus in on the faces of two people who were walking across the reserve. I kept losing them and then refocusing. Finally, they stopped still. Yes, I could see them both. They were a young couple, the man with a toddler on his hip.

The child held a toy rabbit. She laid the plush rabbit down on the growing heap of flowers and soft toys on the reserve.

My teeth clenched, and I moved the binoculars away from my eyes. I wished people would stop bringing flowers and toys to *Tall Ponds*. It was too soon. Far too soon.

My gaze fell back on the drawings on the bed.

I wished I could ask Harry questions about them. But even if he were here, that wouldn't be possible.

"Harry's eyesight," I said to the nurse, holding up the binoculars, "is it good enough to be able to see much though these?"

"Yes," replied the nurse. "I've seen him draw birds from long distances away. And I know they were there, because I looked through his binoculars myself. You know, trying to enter his world a little so that he doesn't feel lonely. It's just his short-range eyesight that's failing. Like all of us." She laughed.

"Would you happen to know how long he's been using the binoculars?"

Her smile faltered. "I could find out. Is there... a reason that you want to know these things? The questions seem quite... specific."

I turned to her. "Yes. Sorry. I'm afraid I can't say right now, but it might be important."

She gasped. "Is this about the case? The missing kids?"

I nodded. "Do you mind if I take some photos of these?" I gestured at the drawings on the bed.

"Yes, go right ahead."

As I framed a drawing up in my phone's camera, my breath caught.

Harry always drew his subjects right where they were. Whether they were on the lake, on the grass, in the sky or in a tree. He'd drawn the bear in a location at the bottom of the hill, at the start of the boardwalk that led through the rainforest.

If that was where Harry had seen his bear, then it was very unlikely to have been Brent Cole who took the children. There simply wouldn't have been enough time.

47

KATE

We had no leads on the mysterious Polly. But now I had a clue about Bear.

A bear in the woods. Wearing a mask. Concealing himself.

I walked from Harry Grenville's room and out of the hospice.

Tapping on the internet browser on my phone, I looked up masks. The masks I found on first try were all wrong. Hairy, scary grizzly bear masks. I typed in *Teddy Bear's Picnic masks*. An array of furry teddy bear heads appeared on my screen. They weren't right either. I added latex to my search query. That brought up another assortment of masks.

Something occurred to me then. There had been head bands with bear ears lying discarded on the ground the day of the abductions. If the kidnapper had known that the children would be wearing the bear ears every picnic for that term, he could have come prepared and have been wearing his own.

I began looking up male face masks. But I found nothing that matched well with Bear's face.

If I was going to bring this to the strike force, I needed something solid. At the moment, it wasn't solid. I hadn't found a good match for the mask. And to begin with, Harry had a form of dementia in which he spoke to no one and no one knew what he was thinking. His drawings were not evidence.

Perhaps I was all wrong about this.

Franco called. "You ready for Dr Suderman?"

I glanced at the time on my phone, shaken from my thoughts about bears and masks. The appointment with Indira Basak and the hypnotherapist was this afternoon.

"Be there in twenty," I told Franco.

———

I walked with Franco into the slick, expensively furnished hypnotherapy offices. It was late in the day, and they were empty.

Dr Blake Suderman had helped us out on quite a few occasions before. I suspected that the way he helped mostly was by removing the biases from people's minds that clouded their perceptions of an event—as much as possible anyway.

"I should get me some head therapy while I'm here." Franco side-eyed me.

"About time," I replied. "The doctor can psych you out of slurping your coffee."

"I don't care about that." He grinned. "I just need some therapy to learn how to play it cool around Daniella. I keep blowing it. You've got to keep your cool around women. It's what they want."

"Really?"

"Yeah, really. I keep reverting. I pretend I've got important things on and I can't see her. Next thing I know, I'm running puppy dog rings around her ankles."

"You're a sad case, Franco."

"Tell me about it."

"Why don't you just quit pretending but keep your boundaries?"

"You don't know what her hair smells like. It's like... berries. Makes me completely fall apart."

"That's just shampoo."

"It's damned good shampoo."

"Someone should bottle that," I said dryly.

Suderman came out to see us and shake our hands.

"You didn't bring the lady with you?" Suderman asked.

"Indira's coming here separately. She told us she's running a bit late," I told him. "She has a large family, apparently, and she has a ton of things on all the time."

I handed him a piece of paper with the questions Franco and I had prepared for Indira Basak days earlier—questions about what she'd seen in the parking bay the night that Harper Rawlings had been murdered.

Just as I did that, a woman who I guessed was Indira came bustling in behind us, laden with shopping bags and a cake box. Her long black hair was half-falling out of its ponytail. Franco and I hadn't met her yet.

"Sorry!" she cried. "I've got my brother's engagement party to organise for tonight. Ugh. Everything gets put on me. I don't mind, really. Except when I do." She set her things down on two empty chairs and then turned to shake our hands. "I'm Indira."

Dr Suderman showed us into his consulting room. There was a high-backed, comfortable office chair that was obviously Suderman's, two plush armchairs and two fairly hard-looking leather chairs.

I gestured at Indira towards the plush armchair and then took the other one. Before Franco could get to it.

Franco and I moved our seats behind Indira's and got our notebooks ready. Suderman didn't allow us to record his sessions electronically, but he did tape them himself and would have records if we missed something.

Dr Suderman crossed his legs and adjusted his glasses, looking like a grandfather who'd once been a professor. "One thing I can guarantee, Indira, is that you'll leave here feeling relaxed. And considering how busy you've been, it sounds like that's a very good thing."

She laughed. "Oh, yes. Without a doubt."

He led her through a set of exercises. I knew to tune out, because even his voice tended to lull me.

"Indira," Dr Suderman said, "you were shopping that night. What were you buying?"

She breathed easily, taking her time. "I was buying groceries for myself, my sister and her husband. I was living with them at the time. I was a student."

"And you happened to look out into the parking area?" he asked.

"Yes."

"Describe the whole scene for me. No one thing is more important than another. Every small thing is of equal importance."

Indira's eyes closed. "I see cash registers. A few people. It's cold. They're wearing scarfs... jackets. The wall is plate glass. It's night and it's dark out. I can see the whole parking bay. Most of it. From where I'm standing, I can see a girl get out of her car. And a young man get out of his. They're having an argument, arms in the air. I'm worried for her. But I'm paying for my groceries. I lose sight of the girl. The man gets back into his car. It's an SUV. Large. He backs out. The girl's car stays where it is."

"Good." The hypnotherapist raised his hands to his face as if he were about to play a flute, but he paused them beneath his chin. "I want you to keep looking at the SUV. What do you see?"

Her forehead wriggled in an animated frown. "It looks expensive."

"Why does it look expensive?" Suderman asked.

"The shape," she answered. "Looks pretty similar to a neighbour's SUV, except his is dark blue. And I know his cost a lot. He likes to brag."

Suderman nodded. "Why does it look similar, Indira?"

"Hmmm. It has the curved roof. And, oh, I remember, it had a distinctive grille on the front. Sort of like butterfly wings."

"You saw the car from the front?" Suderman asked.

"Yes, I'd forgotten. He backed away and drove in one direction. Then he came back again, and I saw his headlights on the girl's car, and again, I didn't see her. I guess I thought she'd gotten into his car. Window tinting is very dark, you know. And it was at night. He stopped and got out for a few seconds. Then got back in and kept driving."

"Can you tell me what car your neighbour drives?" he said.

"I'm not good with cars. And he moved away, so...."

"That's alright, Indira." He asked her a few more questions from our list and then the session was done. He brought her out slowly, and as he'd promised, she did seem far more relaxed than when she'd run into the office.

We sat for a few minutes having a coffee and a chat. Indira had done us a big favour in coming down here today for the hypnotherapy session. Franco and I wanted to ensure she felt good about it.

We headed back to the station and began the task of collating the additional information. It still wasn't much, but it was something.

We knew two things we didn't know before. The style of SUV. And that the SUV hadn't exited to the left of the scene—he'd exited to the right. That would help narrow things down.

Franco browsed the internet on his computer, looking up SUVs that were current four to six years ago. "Curved roof... grille that reminded her of butterfly wings... 2016. Maybe the BMW X5?"

I looked over his shoulder. "Not much like butterfly wings—the grille."

"Try squinting."

I chewed on my lip as I studied the picture of the SUV. "It *is* in two equal parts, like wings. And the car has the right roof line. Let's try sending a pic through to Indira. We'll see what she says."

Franco nodded, catching my eye. "Wakeland, just don't get too hopeful. I know that look."

My back sagged a little. "This case has moved so slowly. That guy has been out there this whole time. *Free*. He doesn't deserve to be."

"Yeah, I know," he said. "But we're moving in the right direction. Step by step. We're going to get him."

48

KATE

Grimshaw especially requested that I attend the strike force meeting this morning. She said they had some vital things they needed to discuss.

"Good," said Grimshaw as I walked in. "Everyone's here. We have a very different meeting on our hands today."

I eyed her with a measure of dismay. She had an odd, playful look on her face. Playful looks didn't sit well on her. I could have sworn her nose was twitching. I was certain she was about to wheel out another expert who would waste our time. A profiler or someone like that. Not that many profilers weren't good. It was just that the last few she'd chosen hadn't been helpful.

But she startled me by reaching into her pocket and pulling out a kids' party blower. She blew on it. "We've all been invited to the children's combined birthday party this morning. They're having a special celebration for all the birthdays they missed. The parents wanted us there, as a thank you for all the countless hours we've put into this case."

I was surprised by two things: the meeting being a party, and two, Grimshaw having a sense of humour, even though it was dry as crackers.

Everyone cheered.

Closing my eyes, I smiled wearily. It was a nice moment in the middle of all the darkness of the past week.

We piled into cars and headed over to The Party Rooms at Close Quarters. Ivy had had her first birthday party there. The Party Rooms were a series of spaces that could be decorated in all sorts of different ways.

We walked into a disco, complete with party lights, music, and a disco ball.

The parents of the returned children were all there. Lori and Roxanne were standing a good distance away from each other. Sean was by himself, looking uncomfortable, as if he couldn't wait for the party to be over. Rhys was chatting to Nick and Marcy Parrish. Penny stood behind Max, her arms protectively around his shoulders.

Four large cakes sat on the table, each with a different design and each bearing the name of a child. Elijah, Max, Olivia and Charlotte. And each cake held candles in the numbers of four, five and six.

I would have given anything in the world for there to be a fifth cake, with Ivy's name on it.

The children's psychologist, Dr Zhang, walked up to greet me.

"How are you, Detective?"

"Surviving."

She gave me a look of empathy. "I've heard bits and pieces on the news. I feel deeply for you and your family."

"Thank you. I appreciate it. This is nice—the party. Looks like it's actually quite a number of parties."

Dr Zhang nodded. "My team and I considered that the children were going to need help in transitioning to the understanding that they are now six years old. They turned four and five and six during the time they lived with Polly and Bear. We thought it best that they transition together, with all the families present, so that they have the benefit of social confirmation. If everyone they know thinks it's true, this will help them believe it as well."

I smiled. "That's a great idea. I imagine it will help the parents, as well."

"Very much so," the psychologist agreed. "Each little step helps them to accept the years with their child that they lost." She hesitated. "Your daughter was invited along today, but she declined. I thought she might say no."

"To be honest, I think I might have declined, too, had I known what Detective Grimshaw was asking me to come to today."

"The parents really wanted you to be here," she said gently.

She left then, to go and speak with Penny.

Already, I felt grief large and heavy in my chest. It was in these moments between the rush and knife-edge events of the past days that I found the loss of Ivy unbearable. I tried to picture her on the dance floor, whirling around with the other children. I wondered, for the thousandth time, what she would have looked like now. What would she have sounded like? Had she still covered her mouth when she giggled?

Ella headed over to me. "Are you okay? Would you like me to get you a drink?" She shoved a plate of food at me—crackers, cheese, guacamole and olives. "Here, eat."

"I must look like I'm about to keel over," I joked.

"You just look a little... lost," Ella said.

"That's a good description for how I feel."

"Of course." Ella nodded.

I glanced down at the plate of food. "That looks like a feast," I said. "Thank you." I didn't have the heart to tell her I wasn't hungry.

"I wish I could snack on that kind of thing." She groaned. "I've got ten kilos to shift."

Ella was quite a bit shorter than me, with rounded hips and a nipped-in waist.

"You're beautiful as you are," I told her. "I'm sure your beau is smitten."

She grinned. "I'm the one who's smitten."

I was reminded of the day I found out that Cameron liked Ella in a romantic way. I was sad for Cameron because Ella was obviously entranced by her boyfriend.

Ella and I watched as Charlotte Hinton marched up to Cameron and tapped him on the arm. Ella stifled a giggle as Cameron began an awkward waltz with the little girl. Charlotte didn't seem to notice how ungainly her dance partner was.

Elijah came and bowed to Ella and then waltzed her away. It seemed that the children had been taught to dance during their time with Bear and Polly. I caught sight of Cameron grinning at Ella, and I knew then that he'd sent Elijah over to her.

A couple of feet away from me, Max sat alone on a chair, playing Jacks. He tossed the plastic jacks up with his right hand and then caught four of them on the back of the same hand.

Grimshaw approached him. "Knucklebones, eh?"

"Huh?" Max raised his face to her.

"They used to play this game with real knucklebones," she told him. "Sheep knucklebones."

"Ewww." Max seemed a mix of horrified and intrigued.

Grimshaw winced uneasily, looking as if she wished she hadn't started the conversation. "It's a very old game. Ancient Greece. They didn't have fancy toys back then."

"Oh."

"Play you a game," Grimshaw said, sitting beside him.

That surprised me. I wouldn't have blinked an eye if someone had told me that Grimshaw had never played a game with a kid. Ever. Not even back when she was a kid herself.

Max nodded.

I looked on as they played for a few minutes.

Grimshaw actually had great balance and reflexes. I remembered then that she had a stellar record with gunmanship. I mused that she conducted her police work in much the same way as she did everything—in a direct line from A to B. But her gun skills consisted of target shooting in a controlled environment. As far as I knew, she'd barely had call to use a gun out in the field.

Nick Parrish announced that it was time for the cakes to be cut.

Everyone assembled around the table.

"We've gathered together to celebrate the birthdays of four very special little people," Nick said. "Charlotte, Max, Olivia and Elijah. We're beyond grateful that they are back with their families. And we want to thank the police for their dedication during these years, including their great work over the past week. We never anticipated the day coming when our children would be back with us. We hoped—but it was a very, very distant hope." He paused. "Let's thank Strikeforce Flying Fox!"

Cheers went up around the room.

I couldn't help but notice that it'd been someone other than Lori to make the speech. She was very subdued, seeming content to take a backseat for once.

The children walked out of the room then, and I wondered what was happening.

"We have a fifth cake," Nick announced.

The four children came in with another cake. This cake was sky blue and decorated with pink airplanes. The name Ivy was written in white icing. Ivy had loved airplanes when she was little. And I'd been told by the children that she'd chosen an airplane as her *special gift* from Bear and Polly.

Tears sprung to my eyes.

"The children also wanted to celebrate Ivy's birthdays," Nick said.

I was asked to blow out her candles, along with the children as they blew out the candles on their own cakes.

I did as they requested, but I barely managed to get through it. My breath kept catching as I tried to hold myself back from breaking into a sob. I was glad now that I was here, to do this for Ivy.

The *Happy Birthday* song was sung to each child, including Ivy.

Overcome, I needed to find a place to sit.

Someone handed me a plate with two slices of cake. Both of them Ivy's —chocolate sponge cake beneath the blue icing.

Grimshaw had taken off early from the cake-cutting celebration, too, and was sitting alone on a chair.

I carried the plate over to Grimshaw. "Here. You look like you could use some cake."

She raised her face to me. "I don't eat it."

"Well, we've got something in common, then." I smiled.

She didn't smile back. "Sit." She nodded at the seat next to her.

A wave of exhaustion hit me as I seated myself. I felt as if I were weighed down with an anvil.

Grimshaw twisted her mouth to one side, looking around at me. There was obviously something on her mind. What was she about to offload? Was she going to apologise for the way she'd behaved towards me over the past week? I didn't think she had it in her.

"Don't get excited," she said, "but I had a thought that's a bit offbeat."

"Oh?"

"Max said something that I couldn't quite piece together. So, I asked him a couple more questions. But it's still not making sense."

"Shoot."

"I was telling him I used to play Jacks with my brother, using small river stones. He told me they played Jacks with Bear sometimes...."

My ears pricked at the mention of *Bear*.

"And then I told him that my brother and I invented slightly different rules," Grimshaw continued, "in which we flipped the stones from one player to the other. And then Max said they did the same."

"Right. Got it," I replied, trying to force my foggy mind to focus.

A deep pucker appeared between her eyes. "And I made an offhand remark. I said to Max, 'Well, I bet you kids were better at it than Bear'. And I won myself the strangest look from him. You would have sworn I'd sprouted a beanstalk on my nose."

"Maybe Bear was a crack shot at playing Jacks," I said lightly, hiding my disappointment. I'd hoped for something substantial.

"Hold on," Grimshaw told me. "There's more. I asked Max if Bear hadn't liked the change of rules. You know, maybe he was a stickler. Nothing wrong with that. Then Max told me that the kids couldn't throw anything to Bear, nor could he catch anything they threw. I said, *ever?* And he said, *not ever.*"

I sat back in my chair, thinking. "Maybe Bear has some kind of disability? But that doesn't fit with him chasing the kids from room to room or playing skipping games and all the rest of it."

"Precisely. And here's the kicker. Max then said that Bear is everywhere and nowhere."

Grimshaw had my full attention now.

"He said *what?*"

"Weird, huh?"

"What on earth did he mean by that?"

"I don't know. Maybe it's a game he played with them. Maybe it's something else. When I asked him, he said it was just something Bear used to say."

"*Everywhere and nowhere,*" I pondered. A dozen thoughts shot through my mind, but nothing was sticking. Was Bear even real? He had to be, right? He interacted with the kids. They had conversations with him. And Tiff Lantry had seen him in person. "Could it mean that Bear positioned himself as some kind of god to the kids?"

Grimshaw's eyes widened, as if an idea had come to her. "Think simpler, Wakeland. I mean, if Bear was streaming himself to the screens in the rooms, then he really *was* everywhere, right? And at the same time, he was nowhere."

I stared at her. "Damn."

"Right?"

I nodded, exhaling. "He wasn't there. Not in person."

"Yet he's the one who appears to have had the most impact on the kids," she said. "As far as I'm aware, they talk about Bear about five times as much as Polly. But... they never told us that Bear was on a screen."

"Maybe he became so real they just stopped seeing the screen," I mused. "Like, he was really there."

"That makes a lot of sense," she said.

I gazed over at the party, thinking. How should we approach this?

The kids had now finished their cake and were running around in circles on the dance floor, laughing. Except for Max. Penny had felt unwell, and Max's allergies had a flare-up, and she'd decided to take him home. And except for Olivia, who stood near her mother, looking upset. Roxanne and Rhys Crane appeared to be having an argument with each other—the kind of argument people have when they are looking straight ahead but talking angrily at each other out of the sides of their mouths. I guessed Rhys either suspected or knew that Roxanne was having an affair. I felt sorry for

Olivia—and for Charlotte—that all of this had exploded right before they were returned to their parents.

I watched Olivia walk away from her parents and across to the party tables to take another slice of cake. She sat glumly on a seat near us, eating her cake.

"Do you happen to have a pen and notepaper?" I asked Grimshaw.

"Of course," she said, taking out a small notebook from her pocket with a pen clipped to it.

I knew she would. She was organised like that.

Taking out my phone, I looked up the picture of Bear that the police compositor had drawn. Resting the notebook on my knee, I did my best to copy it. Then I drew a rectangle around him.

Taking the notebook, I went to sit next to Olivia. "Enjoying the cake?" I asked.

She nodded. "It's pink. Pink cake tastes good."

"Sure does. Are you okay?"

"Yes. My mother and father are having an argument." She said the words *mother* and *father* as though they were new words to her.

"I'm sorry about that. People get cranky sometimes."

"Not Polly or Bear. They never were."

No, they're just cold-blooded killers, I thought privately.

"Olivia, would you mind if I showed you a picture?" I put my drawing in front of her.

"Oh. That's Bear," she said.

"Yes. I drew him on a TV screen."

She frowned deeply then, tracing the outline of the rectangle with her index finger.

Raising her face to me, she looked puzzled. "He was on a TV screen...." she said slowly, as if she were on the edge of realising something for the first time.

"Most of the time?" I asked her. I showed her Lucas Salisbury's drawing of Bear on my phone. "Like this? On a screen?"

She nodded but then squeezed her eyes shut, as if the question was too hard. "He was... everywhere... and nowhere."

"Thank you," I told her, closing the notebook. "I loved your cake. So pretty."

She nodded, smiling, seeming relieved not to have to think about the strange case of Bear on a TV screen.

Charlotte ran over to pull her onto the dance floor. I took Olivia's plate from her and went to have a quick word with Dr Zhang. I explained what had just occurred with Olivia and asked if she could talk with her a little later and check if she were okay.

I then went back to sit with Grimshaw.

"It seems to check out," I told her. "From Olivia's reaction, I'd say that yes, Bear was streaming himself live on screen in that house."

"So, we need to see a camera and video expert and see if we can find out how he managed to do it," she said. "I already sent some officers over to the camera superstore a couple of days back. Apparently, there was a robbery three and a half years back."

"There was?"

"Yep. That could be our guy. But police never found out who did the crime."

"Hmmm. Interesting." I handed her the notebook and pen. "Should we go check it out?"

She sighed. "I've got a meeting with Bigley in twenty minutes. He wants a full briefing. I've already put him off twice. I can't get out of it."

"Well, I'll make a start and tell you what I find out."

"You okay to do that?"

I nodded, standing. "I'm already on my way."

49

KATE

I headed from the party rooms to the camera superstore. I didn't have to drive. The camera store was also at Close Quarters.

The store was vast but neatly ordered, all white walls and floors, with plexiglass stands displaying all types of camera and video equipment.

I walked in and asked for someone who could help me with my enquiries. A store assistant named Blair Ableman was sent to speak with me. He looked younger than Abby. Maybe even still in his teens. I hoped he knew his stuff.

I explained a hypothetical situation that matched with what the forensic team had told me so far about the camera setup at the house.

He tilted his head. "We had some police in here the other day asking about cameras. Something big must be going down."

"We do have some things we urgently need to find out," I told him.

"Well, I told them all I could," he said, shrugging. "That kind of camera setup is pretty costly. Big dollars."

"What if a person wanted to put themselves on a screen in someone else's house? Could they do that, I mean, from their own house? Even if it was far away?"

"How far away are we talking?"

"Hmmm, about half an hour's drive away. Wait, no, about ten minutes, as the crow flies."

"In real time?"

"What's that?"

"I mean, like, a live stream?"

"Yes. A live stream."

"Yeah. You can do that. In the suburbs around here that have good wifi connections, no problems. You can live stream anything you want all around the world. But it depends on your connection and their connection. Because there can be lag or glitches or it just doesn't work at all. The signal's the same with either a cheap or an expensive setup, so no problems there. You just need USB 3.0 ports to plug your cameras into—those are the faster ports for streaming. You'd also need your computer to be equipped with an encoder. Hmmm, and you'd also need a good processor to handle the speeds. And then there are the screens and the cameras that can automatically swivel around to follow you. That's where all the expense comes in."

Okay, the kid knew his stuff. Maybe I couldn't exactly follow it, but I trusted that he was well-versed in cameras and streaming.

"Great, thank you. I heard that there was a robbery here years ago?"

"Yeah. That was before my time working in the store."

I knew it would be, I thought privately, *because you still would have been in school.*

"Is it at all possible that I could see the footage?" I said. "I'm sure that I could dig it up back at police HQ, but it would be quicker if you have a copy of it here."

He eyed me in surprise. "The last lot of police didn't ask to see it—the ones that came in the other day. I know the manager would like you to see it. He's still cranky about it. He's my dad."

He showed me into the back offices and switched on a desktop computer. He quickly found the relevant files and began playing the first one.

"This first footage was taken with the thermal imaging camera, outside the back of the store. It was after Dad had locked up for the night. It was misty and drizzling outside. The normal cameras can't see well in those conditions. That's where the thermal imaging cameras come in."

I watched a figure stride across an empty parking area.

"Is that the thief?" I asked.

Blair nodded, scowling. "Yeah. Dirty dog. He comes up warmer than the surrounding area because the camera picks up heat. Exposed areas of skin show up warmer than areas that are under clothing."

I leaned closer, studying the person. I couldn't see their facial features clearly. "Why is their face showing up as cooler than the body, then?"

Blair's smooth, freckled forehead creased. "Hmmm, he must have had cold skin. Maybe he reacts to cool temps badly. I don't know."

I kept watching as the man walked into the store through a back door, managing to tap in a code and deactivate an alarm.

"Okay, have to switch to another file now," Blair informed me.

The new file was in full, natural colour and fairly clear. Unlike the fuzzy footage I too often saw. The man strode in and around the store, collecting items and placing them into his large backpack. He was fast and efficient, keeping a smile on his face the entire time, as if he were pleased with himself.

"Okay, one more file," Blair told me.

The last file showed the man walking out of the building again, in a thermal imaging display.

There were other figures that showed up on the footage as well.

"Who are they?" I asked.

"They all are or were employees of companies here at Close Quarters—as far as I know, none of them attracted the interest of police."

"Do you have their names?"

"Dad probably does. But he's not here right now."

"Okay. Thank you. You've been incredibly helpful."

"Glad to be of service." Blair looked genuinely pleased. He was a nice kid.

The sun was low in the sky as I drove to Megalong Valley and down to Churchyard Circle.

The forensic teams were still there, but they were packing up for the night. Caravans had been brought on site so that security guards could stay overnight and keep watch. The quiet, empty house was quiet and empty no longer.

I walked up to a forensics specialist that I'd spoken to on many occasions. David Benning. I liked him. He didn't pull any punches. No softly-softly with him.

"What's been happening here, David?"

He ran a hand over his smooth, bald head. "Lots of samples. Five kids' socks, a hair ribbon, a few small toys. We're not disturbing too much of the soil yet. We've got cadaver dogs organised for tomorrow morning."

"Thanks, David."

I scanned the wide property, trying to imagine Ivy here. If we couldn't have her back, I'd give the world to have videos of her. Just to see her. To know what she was like during the past years. But in spite of all the cameras they'd had here, it didn't sound as if they'd taken videos of the children—or if they had, the footage had all been destroyed.

It was dark by the time I arrived back at Tallman's Valley.

I walked inside my front door wanting to throw myself down and curl up in a ball. The day had been long and emotionally draining.

Pete was in the kitchen, juggling Jasper on his hip while making him up a bottle. The look on his face had me instantly on edge.

"Is Abby upstairs?" I asked with hesitancy, tickling Jasper under the chin.

Pete sighed, shaking his head.

"Pete? Something's wrong, isn't it?"

"She sent me a text message a few minutes ago," he said in a flat voice. "She... asked if we could mind Jasper for the night."

Worry raced through my chest, making my breath catch.

"A whole night? *Without Jasper?*"

"I couldn't call her back. Her phone's been off since she sent that text."

"I don't like this, Pete. I'm betting she's gone back to Logan. He's violent. I saw what he did to their house. And then there's the whole thing about the ring. I have a gut feeling it's Harper's. I'm not saying Logan had anything to do with it, but is he covering up for the guy who did do it? I just don't know."

Pete crushed his eyes shut. "Can we... do something? Could the police pick him up for domestic violence? You've got the evidence—the photos you took."

"I've got the photos, but no witness statements. I know Abby won't give a statement to police. And if no one else saw him do it, we're stuck." I paused. "I'm going to go find her and bring her back here. No ifs or buts. And before you say what I know you're going to say—it's easier if it's me that goes. If I have to get information out of people, I've got ways of doing that."

Exhaling hard, Pete nodded. "Let me know the second you find her."

In response, I hugged Pete and Jasper.

Pete stroked the back of my head. "I hope she changes her mind on her own and just comes back here."

"Me, too." Just for a moment, I let my body rest against his arm and shoulder.

50

KATE

I pulled up sharp outside the house that Abby and Logan shared with Ricky. There were no lights on. Cursing, I hurried from the car and knocked on the door. No answer came. I was about to leave when I heard a scuffing noise inside.

Okay, you're in there. Don't make me wait too long. I knocked again. Twice.

A sleepy-looking Ricky finally came to the door, dressed only in a towel around his waist.

In the living room behind him, a woman sat on the sofa, covering herself up with a blanket, the soft light of a TV set flickering on her face. She was the same woman who'd been with him in the backyard the other day—Trissie. It wasn't hard to tell that the two of them had been there naked on the sofa when I knocked. I wondered if her kids were home alone again.

The distinct odour of pot drifted out from the living room, along with a faint scent of beer.

"I kind of have company right now. Not a good time," said Ricky.

"Lucky I don't want to talk to you, then," I told him. "I just need to know where Logan is."

"Logan, eh? Yeah, well, the problem is that he doesn't leave me a note every time he leaves the house."

"Save the sarcasm. Where do you think he might be?"

"Ask your daughter."

Ricky was different from how he'd been the other day. I couldn't tell if he was more drunk or less drunk, but he certainly wasn't as accommodating.

"I'm unable to contact Abby right now," I said.

He made a throaty, dismissive sound. "This ain't official police business, is it now? You're worried about your little girl being with the big bad Logan. She left him and then she went straight back. Like a fish who keeps jumping back on the hook."

"So, Logan is with my daughter?" I said, ignoring the rest.

"He might be."

"This is important. If you want me to leave so that you can get on with your night, then you're going to have to give me some pretty good clues as to where they could be."

"That's police extortion."

"You don't have a clue what extortion is, do you?"

"Nah. But it sounds good. Like a TV cop show."

"This isn't a TV cop show. Maybe we can talk about your collection of stolen jewellery instead?"

"It's not—"

"I wasn't born yesterday. You're lucky I'm a homicide cop. I'm not interested in your stolen trinkets. But our theft and robbery squad might be."

He sighed, rubbing his head. "Logan took some lanterns and rope and stuff. He takes that kind of thing when he's going to the cabin."

"What cabin?"

"His brother has a cabin. I been there once."

"Exactly where is this cabin?"

"The Avenues. Don't remember where."

"The Avenues? Which one?" The Avenues were to the east of town—a series of long, narrow dirt roads in the middle of vast bushland, where there were barely any houses. There were at least ten avenues, and then numerous offshoot roads leading from them. Finding Abby there would be like finding a needle in a haystack. And it was already dark.

"Hell, lady, I said I don't remember. It had a creek at the back of it, that's all I can think of."

Pulling out my phone, I searched for the Avenues, and then looked at where the creek lines intersected with the properties. I was in luck. There were two creeks—Yosemite and Govetts. But Govetts didn't intersect with any of the Avenue roads. Yosemite intersected on eighth and eleventh avenues.

I showed him the map. "Okay. Two possibilities. Eighth and eleventh. Which one?"

"Eleventh, I guess. It was a long way off the main road."

"Right. Anything else you remember about the property? Something to mark the front of the block?"

"Nah. It's just all trees, mate. Nothing but gum trees everywhere."

I started to get the feeling that Ricky could be sending me off on a wild goose chase. Just to get rid of me. I didn't have any time to waste.

"Wait, yeah. There's a bird nailed onto a tree. A magpie."

I felt sick. "A real magpie?"

"Nah. Just a painted one."

I had to take the chance that Ricky was telling the truth about the cabin. I'd run out of threats and I had nothing else to push him with.

"Would Logan have any guns with him? Pistol or rifle?" I asked.

"Don't know. Don't think so," said Ricky.

Trissie left the lounge, dragging the blanket with her. "Logan's got a rifle in the shed out back."

Ricky half-turned and cast an exasperated glance in her direction. "Mate, you didn't have to tell her that."

She shrugged. "I don't like guns."

"So, Logan does have a gun," I said to Ricky pointedly.

Ricky faced me again. "I forgot about it. It's his brother's. His brother's gone overseas, so Logan's been keepin' it here. It's under lock and key. I dunno if he took it or not."

"Go check," I told Ricky.

"What? It's freaking cold out there," he protested.

"So, go throw some gear on," I said.

He scowled. "Jeez. I'm going to make a complaint about this."

I shoved my hands in my pockets, which were starting to freeze at the fingertips. "Thirty seconds."

Ricky disappeared inside. The woman gathered up her blankets and trudged back to the lounge. Picking up a beer from the floor, she began drinking.

Ricky re-emerged from the hallway, with pants on and a hoodie.

I followed him out to the back of the house.

At the other end of the yard, a weathered shed stood under a solar light that had been nailed onto its roof.

"There's no light inside the shed," he told me, pulling out a torch from his pocket. "You stay here. I'll go look and see if the gun is still there, and then I'll come back and tell you."

"I came out here to look for myself."

"There are nails on the floor and old saws and stuff. You might get hurt."

"Thanks for worrying about my safety," I said dryly. "Okay. So, there is something in the shed that you don't want me to see."

"Nah, mate, it's nothing like that. I'll just clear some stuff out of the way and then you can come in."

Ricky broke into a jog, making it quickly across the ground. He pulled the door open and vanished inside. The door swung shut behind him.

Something wasn't right here.

There came a scraping sound, like a window being opened. A dark figure shot out from behind the shed and along the fence line. Was he carrying something? I could barely see in the darkness. I lost sight of him behind a tree. Then came a large thud and the sound of something smashing.

I sprinted after him. I caught hold of his legs just as he had almost made it over the fence.

Breathing hard, he stopped still. "I was just returning something to my neighbour. That's all."

"What were you returning?"

"Just some tools. Jeez. Get off me."

Letting go, I climbed up beside him, on the lower beam of the wooden fence.

I grabbed his torch and shone it over the ground of the next-door-neighbour. Ricky had thrown some kind of small hydroponic setup down there. Tiny plastic pots lay on the ground with soil spilling from them. Seedlings.

I flicked the torch's beam in Ricky's direction. "So, you had a little pot plantation happening in the shed?"

"Those aren't mine. They belong to my neighbour. What? They're pot? He didn't tell me that."

"I'm not interested. I'm not the drug squad. Now that you've got your shed cleared of drugs, can we go see if Logan has taken the gun?"

He hung his head, like a small kid who'd been caught with his hand in the cookie jar.

I kept alongside him as we walked back to the shed.

He pressed a battery-operated light on.

"We have light," I commented.

"Yeah." He didn't even try to come up with an explanation for that.

There were five or so roughly made shelves, packed with things— mostly junk. A tall steel cabinet had been fixed to the wall.

Ricky tried to pull the door of the cabinet open. "Nup. Locked."

I tried the handle myself.

"You're so trusting," Ricky remarked in a hurt tone.

"What else would Logan take if he'd gone to the cabin?"

"How would I know? Sleeping bags maybe." He looked around the shelves. "Yep, they're gone. I'd head off to the cabin now if I were you."

I poked around for a little longer. "What's this?" I pointed to a soft, cylindrical bag.

"Just one of Logan's old tents," Ricky told me. "Got a big hole in it. Found that out the hard way last time I borrowed it to go camping."

Something about the strain in his voice had me on alert.

I pulled the bag from the shelf.

"They don't need a tent," Ricky said quickly, reaching to take it. "They went to a cabin."

Stepping back, I kept a firm hold of the bag. I stuck my hand in and pulled the tent out. Something hard and rectangular was wrapped up in the material of the tent. I unwrapped it.

It was a plain wooden box.

"More jewellery, Ricky?" I raised my eyebrows.

"Nah mate," he said, shaking his head. "I never seen that before."

I pried it open.

The box contained nothing except for a necklace and two sets of earrings. I went to pick up the necklace then snatched my hand back. Switching on my torch, I trained the beam on the jewellery. The necklace and one of the sets of earrings looked antique, with single black pearls inlaid.

His eyes opened wide. "That's not mine."

"Stay there," I instructed him.

Stepping outside the shed, I made a call. "Franco," I said, "I just found Harper's missing jewellery."

51

ABBY WAKELAND

An hour earlier

The lights of Close Quarters were squiggly through the rain. It was getting a bit airless inside the parked car. Abby, sitting with a box of pizza in her lap, rolled down the car window a little. The smell of the pizza was turning her stomach.

"You'll let the rain in," Logan told her. She wasn't sure if he was disappointed in her or just nervous about what they were about to do. Her nerves were jumping in her veins at the thought of their plans for tonight.

"Are you finished with the pizza?" she asked.

"Yeah."

"Good. Because I'm throwing it."

"I'll do it." Pulling his hoodie over his head, he sprinted down the street to dispose of the pizza box.

Droplets of water sprayed everywhere as he returned to the car.

He turned to her with intense eyes, his jaw and neck muscles drawing tight. "You ready?"

"No." She inhaled a breath that felt as if it reached all the way to the pit of her stomach. "Yes."

"Okay, then let's go."

Logan drove away, cruising slowly past two blocks of houses.

Abby looked for the house numbers in the dark light.

"92," she said. "That's it."

He kept driving, around the corner, parking next to a wide swathe of vacant land. The rain had sputtered to a stop.

They exited the car and ran across the long, soaked grass. It was going to be easy to climb the back fence of the house, because there was a stack of discarded wooden crates on the ground. Standing a crate on one end, Logan stepped on top and then vaulted the fence. Abby made the next climb, Logan helping her over.

She glanced up at the house next door. It was as tall and expensive-looking as this one. *Do they have CCTV cameras? They probably do.*

Relax, she told herself. Even if they did, they'd hardly have them pointing at their neighbour's yard. Anyway, any night-time footage would be grainy as anything. And their faces were fairly well concealed beneath their hoods.

They made their way to a plain, unlocked door at the side of the house. It led into a large laundry. Abby kept her eyes on Logan as they removed their shoes and hoodies. She needed to see him, to reassure herself that he was here beside her every step of the way.

The stairs made tiny noises as they stole up them.

Through the open door of a bedroom, Abby spied a small child, curled up in bed like a question mark, the blanket hanging off him.

"You said no one would be here," she whispered to Logan.

In response, he shook his head.

What did that even mean? Did he or did he not know that the family who lived here would be back from their trip away?

Down the hallway, she heard the muffled sound of a TV set. The kid's parents must be in bed watching TV together. It made sense to do that on a cold night. If they'd been downstairs, the couple would have seen Abby and Logan breaking in.

Her fingers clenched tightly together, like knots at the end of a rope. They were here now. They needed to keep going.

Logan indicated towards a room that looked like a study.

She could scarcely breathe as they searched the room. Behind a glass cabinet was what they'd come for. Tens of thousands of dollars' worth of equipment. All luxury speakers and 4K short-throw laser projectors. Neatly packed away in carry cases. The residents of the house owned a tech store at Close Quarters.

Logan found the key in a drawer and unlocked the cabinet.

Abby packed as many items as she could fit in her backpack, her heart galloping. Logan crammed his own backpack.

They headed straight back down to the laundry. Abby pulled on her cold, wet hoodie again, then fitted the backpack over her shoulders. She pushed her feet into her shoes.

Alongside Logan, she stole across the lawn to the back fence.

She shivered, waiting for Logan to climb it. Then she handed the backpacks over to him, before climbing the fence herself.

She almost slipped. Her fingers were locking up with the cold. The world seemed savage tonight. She couldn't wait to be home again, with Logan, wrapped up together in bed, catching a late movie. Right now, she appreciated those simple moments in a way that she never had before.

Logan handed her a bag. She strapped it to her back.

"Remember," he warned her, "whatever happens, do not stop. We need to get to the car and get out of here."

"Yeah." She stuttered the word out, her teeth chattering.

So far, they'd been lucky. No one in the house had seen or heard them. But that didn't mean a neighbour hadn't spotted them from a window.

Together with Logan, she raced across the vacant land and up the dark street to the car.

Wordlessly, Abby jumped into the front passenger seat. She exhaled a cloud of white air.

They'd done it. She didn't know whether to feel exhilarated or terrified.

She wanted to speed away, but Logan eased the car onto the road with painstaking care and then drove slowly. He kept the speed at a crawl until they were at a good distance.

"You okay?" His voice had a harsh edge.

"I don't know."

"What do you mean you don't know? You gotta stay strong, Abby. If you crumble, it's all over. And then we're going to jail. Do you want that?"

She shook her head.

He pulled the hood back from his head. "Anyway, better call him."

"Yeah." She took her phone out from the console of the car.

"Hello, have you got it?" came the voice.

"Yes. We just need a couple of days," she told the man on the phone.

"You don't have a couple of days, remember?" the man said.

Abby blinked back tears. "We're doing all we can."

"Do better," the man responded.

She stared at Logan as the call ended.

"Don't worry," Logan told her. "We've got it covered."

"Hey, you missed the turnoff. My parents' house is back that way, remember?"

Logan had a grim look on his face she'd never seen before. "Change of plan. We're going to stay at my brother's cabin tonight."

"What? *No.* I have to get back to Jasper."

"He'll be okay for one night. Your parents looked after him for you the other night while you slept. Isn't that what you told me?"

"Yes, but I was *there.*"

"Do you trust them to look after him?"

"He's never been away from me."

"You survived childhood unscathed, right? That means your parents are capable of taking care of a kid."

"Yes, but I... I need him with me."

Ivy had vanished at a time when she was separated from Abby. And now, Abby was never going to get her back. The thought of Jasper being apart from her was unbearable.

"Abby, you're not going back there tonight. We're going to the cabin."

"You don't trust me," she accused. "You think if I go home to them, then I'll cave in and tell them what's going on."

When he didn't answer, she forced out a long breath between her teeth.

"Just because my mother is a detective," she pressed. "That's why. You think she'll get the truth out of me."

"She's pretty fierce," he admitted. "She'd get blood out of a stone. And think about the other side of it. We've got a lot of expensive items sitting in our bags. We need somewhere to put that until we can offload it. You can't take it to your parents' house, and we can't take it back to ours. Too risky."

"I didn't think about that."

"Well, I did."

She thought fast. "What if I pick up Jasper and then head back to our house? You could take the gear to the cabin."

"I'm not leaving you and Jasper alone at that house. Not with Ricky and some of the types he brings around. And I can't leave the gear at the cabin unattended. We're not the only ones who know about it being there." He let his tone go soft. "Abby, send your dad a text message. *Now*. Before we get to where we're going. Tell him you needed a night away to get your head straight. Then we're going to turn our phones off and leave them at our house."

"Why?"

"So that your detective mother can't come looking for you. Or me."

Reluctantly, she typed out a message for her father on her phone: *How is Jasper?*

She waited for two minutes before a message came back from Dad: *All good. Just had a bottle and he's sleeping like a baby ;)*

She inhaled sharply before texting again: *Dad, I really need some time away. Please look after Jasper for me tonight? I'll be back first thing tomorrow. Give Jasper a kiss for me. xx Abby.*

She switched her phone off.

Logan kept driving through town, to where the roads became pot-holed and the houses small and modest.

As he drove near their house, Abby peered out of the window in shock. "That's my mother's car. Right there."

Logan swore. "What's she doing here again?"

"I don't know. That's not right. She's been targeting you from the night we had the argument. She's crazy." Logan didn't even know what Abby knew. Mum had been trying to pin a girl's murder onto Logan. But Abby knew Logan and Mum didn't. Logan wasn't capable of doing anything like that.

"I can handle it—and her," he said. "But you've got enough to worry about. Anyway, no one came back to search the house. That proves they've got nothing." Leaning across, he kissed her.

"I was going to run in and grab some blankets," she said. "But I can't now. It's going to be cold at the cabin, isn't it?"

"Yeah. But it's okay. I grabbed us some sleeping bags earlier, plus some big jackets. And some food."

She shot him an appreciative glance.

"We've gotta get rid of the phones somewhere," he said. "Hold tight. I thought of somewhere."

As he drove away, she chewed the inside of her cheek, desperately wanting this night to be over.

Ten minutes later, he'd disposed of the phones. He drove into Katoomba and then headed north, past Katoomba cemetery.

She turned her head away from the graves, not wanting to see them. A streetlight outlined Logan's profile. She'd never seen him look so determined.

"Where's the cabin?" she asked. "There's nothing up this way."

"It's not far."

It seemed to Abby that there was suddenly nothing but bushland in all directions.

Logan seemed to know where he was going, driving down one dirt road after the other.

He turned off onto a narrow road, so narrow that the car barely fitted between the two trees on either side. "The cabin's just up here."

After a minute, the car's headlights picked out the shape of a small cabin made of wood. A car was parked nearby.

Abby grabbed Logan's arm. "Someone's here."

Logan nodded. "Yeah, they're staying with us tonight."

"What? Who?"

"A guy I know and a girl you know."

"Who's the girl?"

"Nola. I don't know her last name. She said she went to school with you."

"Nola Hobson?" She turned to Logan in a panic. "What on earth is *she* doing here?

"She's my mate's girlfriend. Bryce. Bryce and I planned to do a spot of fishing this weekend. So, it worked out. Gives us an alibi, just in case. Nola and Bryce can testify that we were here all night."

"This is *crazy*. What if they find out we've got stolen stuff in the car?"

"They won't. They're not going to check our backpacks."

"I don't... I don't want to hang out with Nola. She was one of the daycare workers looking after Ivy on the day she went missing. I don't blame her, exactly, but she's not someone I'd choose to stay the night with."

"Ah, hell. I'm sorry. I didn't realise."

"Why haven't I met Bryce before?"

"He's a friend from way back. You and I have only been back in town for a short while. I haven't had a chance to catch up with him."

The sound of their car tyres on gravel echoed. Logan parked the car behind Bryce's and gazed at her quietly. "Just one night? That okay?"

Biting down on her lip, she nodded.

52

PENNY FOSTER

Penny loaded her groceries into her shopping trolley, looking out through the store window at the dark parking bay.

It was a drizzly night out. But she didn't care. Soon, her little family would be away from this cold place with all its misery. They'd be off to a place where they could live in the sunshine and put all this behind them.

She'd had to leave Max at a trusted neighbour's house. She was out of food and there was nothing for dinner or breakfast. There was no time to get an online food delivery this time of night.

She caught sight of a couple sitting in a car together, outside. They were off in a small pocket of the parking area, but she could see them from where she was standing, right down the end of the store. And she knew who they were.

Roxanne Crane and Sean Hinton. Smooching.

Now she knew who the man was who she'd seen with Roxanne the other day. Sean.

She wondered how often they sneaked away to smooch. And to do other things. Both of them were still living with their spouses, as if everything were normal. Their behaviour was completely disgusting. They had their children back, but here they were, more interested in each other than their long-lost offspring.

She finished loading in her groceries and paid for them. The rain had started to come in harder, slashing diagonally across the beams of illumination coming from the overhead spotlights.

Before the rain had a chance to come down any heavier than it already was, she headed out.

She had the sudden uneasy feeling that someone was watching her.

Someone stood in the shadows, looking on. She was sure of it.

Was it just someone who recognised her from the recent media articles about the missing children? Well, if they were curious about how the parents were doing, then they should take a look at what was happening in the car over there. A shot of Sean and Roxanne would give them gossip for days.

Unsettled, she forgot where she even parked the car.

She'd just have to make a run for it and figure it out.

Putting a spare plastic grocery bag over her head, she headed out into the downpour.

The mysterious person seemed to follow her. A man.

A thread of worry tugged at her. What if it wasn't just some curious onlooker? What if he were someone more sinister?

She reached her car and opened it up.

The man stopped hiding himself and stepped out. He wore a rain jacket and hood.

"Let me help you." Without gaining her consent, he picked up all four of her grocery bags and loaded them in. He shut the hatch and then pushed the trolley away.

Terrified, she told him thank you and jumped into the driver's seat of her car. As she went to close the door, he stopped her.

Using his arms and body, he stopped the rain from getting in.

"I need to go," she told him. "Please go away."

"Penny, I just want to talk to you."

"How do you know my name?"

"I've been wanting to talk to you for a while. Look, why don't you let me into the car for a minute? All I ask is a minute of your time."

"You want me to let a total stranger into my car? You've got a nerve."

He sighed, shrugging. "I know you'll want to hear what I have to say."

53

NOLA HOBSON

Nola gave a grin that felt awkward as Abby and Logan entered the cabin.

She'd been here for just an hour, enough time for her and Bryce to get the fire started. The cabin was cramped, with a tiny living room and make-shift kitchen, and two bedrooms that were barely big enough for the beds they held.

Bryce had mentioned camping and fishing this weekend with an old friend, but he hadn't mentioned anything about Abby Wakeland until about five minutes before she arrived. Abby hadn't liked her when they were both in school, and Nola was certain that Abby liked her even less now. Nola had told Bryce about the fact she'd been there at the reserve the day Ivy Wakeland had vanished, but Bryce had calmed her right down, telling her that you couldn't live your life apologising.

Besides all that, Nola had been shocked that Abby would come and stay at the cabin at all, considering all that had been happening, with reports of Ivy having been killed by the kidnappers.

Abby turned her head in Nola's direction. She'd always had an air of something tragic and gothic about her, with her small chin and large eyes and flow of dark hair. But the effect was somehow amplified tonight, with her hair being damp and her expression haunted.

"Hi." Abby gave a small wave, but she didn't return Nola's smile.

Logan greeted both her and Bryce with a back-slapping hug. Logan was so good looking that he made Nola nervous. She hoped no one would notice, especially Bryce.

"Okay, ladies and gentlemen," said Bryce. "We've got food, we've got good company, and we've got beer. What else do we need?"

"You got it." Logan pulled out a seat for Abby and then one for himself. "We should do this more often."

Bryce was the only one in the room to make an affirmative grunt. He handed Logan and Abby a beer each. "You two look like drowned rats."

"Yeah, just a bit," said Logan.

Bryce grinned widely. "The fire will dry you out."

Abby seemed lost in her own world.

Logan slugged the beer. "I'll go out and grab our stuff."

"I'll help you, mate." Bryce pushed his chair back. "You can help me cart some of my stuff in, too."

Abby looked a little dismayed at Logan leaving the cabin, but she remained silent.

Nola twisted the ring on her finger. "How have you been, Abby? I've been following the news... and I'm so sorry..." Her voice faded.

"Thanks," Abby responded.

Nola struggled to think of another thing to say. "Do you and Logan go away fishing much?"

She shrugged. "Can't do much with a baby in tow."

"Oh, right. Stupid question." She'd almost forgotten Abby even had a baby. The first time she'd learned that Abby even had a new baby was in a photograph on a news site.

"Jasper's with my parents tonight. It's the first time I've been away from him." Her voice had a stiff quality.

"Well, I'm sure he'll enjoy some time with his doting grandparents."

"My dad's been spending lots of time with him. Mum's been too busy. With the case... and everything."

Nola hoped Abby didn't notice her wincing. Detective Wakeland had interviewed her twice in the past week. And then again when she'd found Olivia.

Silence pushed between them again.

Nola hoped that tomorrow, when they were fishing, Abby would start to open up. Maybe she and Abby could even become real friends. If Bryce and Logan were good buddies, then it made sense if she and Abby got along with each other. She allowed herself to imagine a future in which she married Bryce and Abby married Logan. In the near future, the four of them could at least double date.

She had to make sure she didn't say any more dumb things to Abby, and then maybe Abby would start to warm to her.

Despite the awkwardness, she felt a tiny bubble of excitement that she was actually doing something on her weekend. At the pizza restaurant, when the others asked what she'd done on the weekend, she could say, '*Oh, my boyfriend and I went away with another couple. It was fun.*' That was the kind of thing other people said, but never herself. Before she'd met Bryce, she'd hated being asked the *weekend* question.

Her daydreams dissolved as she realised that Abby was staring straight at her.

"It must have been strange to find Olivia Crane after all these years." Abby's voice had a hard edge to it.

Nola nodded, swallowing. "Yes. Sure was. It took me a while to even realise it was her."

Abruptly, Abby rose from her chair. "I'm going to go see if the boys need a hand." She left the cabin without another word.

Nola inhaled a deep, sighing breath. The short conversation had been nothing but tense. She wondered if she and Bryce could leave early tomorrow. There was never going to be a friendship with Abby. She'd been stupid to even think it.

With fumbling hands, she boiled some water in the kettle over the fire, and then made herself a cup of tea.

The door swung open, letting in a burst of cold air.

Bryce and Logan stomped in one after the other, laden with gear.

Logan dumped his stuff in one of the bedrooms, then swung around with a frown on his face, looking back at Nola. "Where's Abby?"

"She went out to help you," Nola told him, feeling guilty now, as if she shouldn't have let Abby go out there on her own.

Bryce eyed Logan with a frown. "I didn't see her out there. We'd better go find her before she gets herself lost."

54

KATE

"Ricky Pickett," I said, "you're under arrest."

The dim light of the shed fell over his face, which was screwed up in shock.

"It's an offence to resist," I told him. "Turn around, please, with your hands behind your back."

He did as I asked, and I took the handcuffs from my utility vest and clipped them onto his wrists. "You have the right to remain silent. Anything you say can be used against you in a court of law."

Ricky spun around. "You're arresting me for the hydroponic pot? You said you didn't care about it. You're a dirty liar, lady."

"It's not the pot, Ricky. It's this jewellery." I gestured towards the small wooden box sitting on the shelf. "It belongs to a young woman who was murdered. The ring you sold to Logan makes up the rest of the missing jewellery."

His jaw went slack. "Who was murdered?"

"Her name was Harper Rawlings."

"Don't even know her."

"All of the jewellery missing from her body has been found at this house."

"You got that box out of a tent bag belonging to Logan. Why are you arresting me?"

"I don't know who put this in the bag. What I do know is that both you and Logan are claiming that he sourced the ring from you."

Ricky shrunk back against the shelving, leaning heavily against it. "Okay, I have seen that box before. That's where I got the ring that I sold to Logan."

"So, you put the box in the tent bag?"

He nodded, sighing. "But don't go getting ideas. I found the box hidden in the wall. Look." He nodded the side of his head towards a section of wall in between two low shelves. "If you look there, you'll see a bit has been sawed out of the wood. The box was jammed in there."

"Move away," I instructed Ricky. I didn't trust him.

I waited until he shifted and then I bent to peer between the shelves. There was indeed a rectangular shape cut out of the thick wooden beam, just large enough for the box. There was a thin piece of wood that fitted back into the hole, like a lid. Someone had gone to a lot of trouble to conceal the box.

"Did you cut this hole?" I asked Ricky.

"Mate," he said, "why would I tell you about it if I done it? Wasn't me. Must have been the people who lived here before us."

"So, you're saying you found the box of jewellery, took out the ring, and then put the box in Logan's tent bag? Why would you do that?"

"Trissie came up to the shed last time I was lookin' at the jewellery. I didn't want her to see it. Because then she'd want it. She's got grabby hands, that one. So, I shoved it in the tent bag. Logan never uses the tent. He says he'll fix it one day, but he never will."

"What did you intend doing with the jewellery?"

"Selling it. But I don't know how much it's worth. I couldn't find anything like it online."

"Okay, just... come back into the house."

I walked Ricky inside. Was he telling the truth? Was he an innocent who'd just gotten lucky and found a box of jewellery? It'd been almost four years since Harper's murder. It could have easily been a prior resident who concealed the wooden box in the shed. I shivered. And it could have just as easily been Logan.

I needed to find Abby *now*.

We stepped inside the house. Trissie appeared to have gotten tired of waiting, because she'd gone.

The lights of three police vehicles flashed outside. I waited for the group of detectives to come inside—all members of my homicide team, including Franco. Walking away from Ricky, I gave Franco a quick rundown of the events of the past half-hour.

"Ricky could be covering up for Logan," Franco commented.

"That's what worries me," I said, exhaling a taut breath, trying to calm the nerves that raced up and down my body.

"Someone is lying through their damned teeth," said Franco. "It comes down to who hid the box in the shed. Ricky or Logan."

"We also need to run a check on the past tenants of this house," I told Franco.

"I already got that done," he replied. "Ricky's been renting the house for about five years. Logan's brother is a friend of Ricky's, and Logan has lived at the house on and off."

"Hell. So, it does come down to just those two."

"Yeah," said Franco. "Pretty suspicious, right? We'd better haul our friend Ricky down to the station. And get forensics in. You're keeping them busy lately, Wakeland."

"I can't go down to the station, now," I told him. "I need to go bring Logan in. My daughter's with him."

"No, you don't," he said, his tone firming. "I can see beneath the surface with you. You're bouncing off the walls right now. Your daughter has gone off to stay at a cabin with a guy we don't trust. Let me and Lavers handle it. We'll go find Logan."

"No." I shook my head. "I'm going. No two ways about it."

I turned to Ricky, taking a few steps closer. "You'd better not be trying to fool me about where Logan might be. If you know for certain, you should tell us."

"I already said as much as I'm gonna say," Ricky said. "You said I didn't have to talk, so I'm not gonna. Lady, you don't slap handcuffs on people who you want information from. It's not nice."

———

Franco and I headed away in my car. He knew better than to argue with me. I had to make sure that Abby was safe. She was in love, and she was blind to my deep concerns about Logan.

I drove while Franco called the station to run a trace on Abby's phone.

He looked up. "They're at the Katoomba train station."

"God. We'd better hurry. They must be about to catch a train. Damned Ricky. I wonder if he knew that?"

Browsing on his phone, Franco looked up what time the trains were running. "I think we're okay. We've got fifteen minutes to get over there. We can make that."

Still, I wanted to put my sirens on and get there in record time. But if I did that, Logan and Abby might be alerted.

We drove across the railway bridge. Katoomba station sat below. I craned to see if anyone was standing on the platform. The station was only small—a little country station with the original old weatherboard buildings of yesterday. But I saw no one. Anyone there was probably taking cover from the drizzle.

My heartbeat slowed. Abby had to be here somewhere. I could get hold of her, keep her safe. As for Logan, we'd be hauling him off to the police station for questioning.

I pulled up in the commuter car park, and we went running through the rain to the platform. There was an older couple sitting huddled together. And a solo man in a long jacket and boots. There was no one else.

"Check the toilets." I gestured to Franco towards the toilet blocks.

He checked the gentlemen's toilet block while I checked the ladies'.

We met up again, shaking our heads. They weren't here—anywhere.

"Wait," said Franco. "The tracker is still saying they're here... somewhere back near the car park."

We raced back again. Franco pointed ahead. There was a tiny section of trees and bushes to the left. What on earth would Abby be doing in there?

He ran ahead of me.

He returned a few seconds later, holding up a plastic bag. He tore it open. Inside the bag was a watertight plastic click lock box containing two mobile phones.

55

ABBY WAKELAND

Abby felt her eyes sting with tears. She was glad it was so damned dark outside the cabin. She didn't want anyone to see her right now.

She wished Logan had brought her anywhere but here. Nola Hobson was too much of a reminder of what she'd lost. Nola had let Ivy slip through her fingers. And then she'd found Olivia and had been praised as a hero. As if that made up for everything.

It was salt in a wound that had been bleeding for three and a half long years.

The other families had their children returned to them. Abby had nothing. Nothing but a picnic ground heaped with rotting flowers and toys that Ivy would never see. And Abby was denied even holding a funeral for her daughter. No resolution, no end point. No chance to hold her daughter's still body one last time and tell her that she loved her and that she'd never stopped loving her.

She'd told Nola she was going out to help the guys. But instead, she walked in the opposite direction, down a bush track. Rain-soaked leaves hung low from branches, brushing past her face. The rain made sloshing sounds deep in the bushland.

Someone was walking after her.

She whirled around. "Logan?"

Bryce walked out into her torchlight.

"Oh, Bryce. It's you."

"Logan and I came looking for you. Thought I'd come this way because I dropped my wallet out here earlier. Two birds with the one stone." He shrugged. "Did you happen to see it?"

"No. What colour is it?"

"Brown. Leather. Not helpful I know. Going to be hard to see."

He stepped up beside her. She'd just been co-opted into helping him search.

She kept her face away from him, shining her torch around the ground, hoping he'd go away. "Might be better to search tomorrow, when it's light."

"Yeah. Except an animal might decide to take off with it."

"I don't think the koalas have a big interest in your credit cards, Bryce. Unless there's a gum leaves dispensing teller in the woods."

"You're funny." He poked at the ground with a stick, moving leaf litter aside. "So, you and Nola used to be friends at school, huh?"

"Not really. We didn't hang out with each other."

"Oh. I thought you might be able to help me out. Nola has been a bit... strange, and I can't figure it out."

"Strange how?"

"I think she had a rough childhood. She spaces out and stuff like that."

"Yeah. Well, she should never have been a nursery school teacher. She wasn't safe to look after kids. She zoned out one day, and five kids got past her. Anyway, that's in the past. No point talking about it."

"I read that in the news. About the kids getting past her. I haven't talked about it with her though. She gets real weird if I mention any of it. Like, angry. And other times, she really makes me wonder who she really is."

"What do you mean?"

He sighed. "I don't know. I just... don't know. One night... in bed, she made a mistake and called me *Brent* instead of Bryce."

"Oh my God."

"Yeah."

She trembled, almost fainting. Brent Cole was the ice-cream van driver. Could Nola have had a romantic connection with him? The thought was sickening, horrifying.

Bryce caught her in his arms. "Hey, you okay?" His arms came around her. "I'm sorry... I shouldn't have off-loaded like that."

She squeezed her eyes shut against his chest, her mind racing. As soon as she and Logan got home, she'd have to talk with Mum about Nola. No, she'd talk with Detective Grimshaw. Mum seemed to talk about Nola in sympathetic tones these days. She probably wouldn't believe anything bad about her.

Bryce kissed her, his cold lips tasting of beer and woodsmoke.

She shrunk back.

"Sorry," Bryce said, "I misread the situation."

She sighed, feeling clumsy and embarrassed. He must have thought she was making a move by practically falling into his arms. "We'd better get out of the rain. Getting heavier."

"You okay?" he asked gently.

"Yeah, I'm okay."

Logan came running from the opposite direction. "Abby! I went looking for you up the other way. Where'd you go?"

"Just for a walk."

"In the rain?"

"Yeah. I needed air."

Logan glanced at Bryce, then hooked an eyebrow high as he looked back at Abby. He shook his head then, as if whatever he'd just been thinking was stupid. "Let's get you inside."

Nola gave an uncertain smile as Abby and Logan stepped through the door. "Where's Bryce?"

Bryce walked in behind them, beaming. "Right here. What's cooking good looking?"

Nola's half-smile spread into a wide grin. "Food."

Bounding over to Nola, Bryce put his arms around her. "Smells good."

They ate a quick dinner of nachos and then sat playing cards.

Abby wasn't in the mood for it, but at the same time, it helped keep her mind off things.

Nola looked over and gave her a shy smile. Abby managed a quick return smile. Nola kept doing that. It was a little weird, almost as if she were a lost puppy trying to find someone to take it home. She'd been a weird girl back when they were at school. Really quiet and never engaging with anyone. And she was still weird. Had she really been having an affair with Brent Cole? Or had it just been a slip of the tongue?

Bryce and Nola went to add some more wood to the fire. The flames were growing low, allowing a noticeable chill to enter the air.

Abby ducked her head against Logan's shoulder. "I just want this night done," she whispered close to his ear.

Logan stroked her head. "I know. Won't be long. But everything's going okay, so don't worry."

She nodded, trying to let herself be soothed by his voice.

56

ABBY WAKELAND

The fire was close to its last gasp. The temperature in the cabin was dropping fast.

Logan rose from the table. "Better go grab some wood from the shed."

Bryce rubbed his face tiredly. "I'll come help you, mate."

"Sure?" Logan shrugged. "You look knackered."

"Yeah, long day at work. But I need to stretch my legs."

Abby watched them leave, wishing one of them had stayed. She didn't want to be alone with Nola.

"We should do this again." Nola toyed with the ring on her finger.

"Yeah," Abby lied.

"I hope the rain stops by the morning. Bit hard to go fishing in the rain." Nola kept playing with her ring. Twist... twist... twist.

Abby was reminded of the ring Logan had bought for her, wondering if she'd ever get it back. Her mother was coming after Logan hard. It wasn't fair. Was Mum trying to make sure she lost both Logan and Ivy? She ached to hold Jasper. Her arms felt strangely empty without him, as if he were still as much a part of her as when she was pregnant with him.

"I'd like it if it rains all night long though," Abby replied. "Helps me sleep. Hope you don't mind, but I'm kind of tired. I might go read my book."

"Oh, sure." Nola gave a smile that looked disappointed.

Abby rose from her chair and went inside to the room she was to share with Logan tonight. She closed the door. She'd told a fib about having a book with her. She just couldn't bear to spend another minute alone with Nola.

Curling into the foetal position on the bed, she gathered the sleeping bag tight around her. Tonight, she'd become a criminal. She'd done something she could go to jail for. She wanted escape from everything, especially herself. She felt herself drifting and fought it for a while, before she gave in and slept.

She woke with a start, in the middle of a terrible dream about Ivy. She'd had hundreds of such dreams.

The cabin air was so cold her nose felt frozen.

She couldn't hear Logan or Bryce or Nola.

Were they all asleep? Why wasn't Logan in bed with her?

Wrapping the sleeping bag around herself, she got up from the bed and stuck her head out the door.

No one was in the living room. The door to the other bedroom was open. Abby tiptoed across the living room. The other bedroom was empty.

She had the sudden horrible sensation that everyone had gone, and they'd taken the cars and she was stuck here alone. She acutely felt the loss of her phone. If she still had hers and Logan had his then she could call him and find out what was happening. She checked the old analogue clock on the wall. It had been half an hour since the boys had left the cabin to get firewood.

She waited for five minutes. Then ten.

There was no good reason for the three of them to be out there for so long.

Returning to the bedroom, she dressed herself in a jacket that Logan had packed for her. She shoved a penlight in the pocket. Bringing the hood of her jacket over her head, she headed out. The jacket had been a good choice of Logan's—it was lined with a thick, fake fur that made her feel instantly cosy.

Everything was quiet and still outside, apart from the lightest sprinkle of rain.

The only light outside was the lantern that Logan had hung on a tree branch earlier. It had illuminated the cars and the surrounding area. Now, only one car sat beneath the lantern. Where had they taken the other car? And why had they left her alone?

What if a stranger had hurt Logan and Bryce and had taken their car? And then Nola had gone outside, and the stranger had hurt her, too? Every story Abby had ever heard about whackjobs killing random people for fun seemed like they could be real life now.

But that was stupid. She wasn't a kid and she didn't need to be afraid of the dark. The three of them would be back soon.

She walked across to the shed where the wood was kept. That was where Logan and Bryce were supposed to have gone. She shone the penlight over the stack of wood inside.

No one was here.

57

ABBY WAKELAND

Worry burrowed into Abby's stomach. Logan and Bryce had gone to get firewood, and they hadn't returned to the cabin. And she'd woken from a short nap to find Nola gone, too.

She began walking along the dirt track that she'd driven in on with Logan, heading towards the road. Misting rain was still falling, trees rustling in a low breeze. A eucalyptus scent from the wet gum leaves wafted around her.

She thought she heard something—a twig cracking underfoot. She stopped dead still, listening, breaths pulling tight in her chest.

Someone grabbed her arm.

She spun around.

Nola stood in front of her in the darkness. "Abby, I don't know where the boys went."

"I thought you must be with them." Abby swore out loud. "They could have at least brought some firewood back and told us they were taking a drive somewhere."

Nola gave a breathy, fearful sigh. "I don't know what's going on. I heard shouts out in the woods."

Abby crossed her arms. "Maybe Logan and Bryce got separated from each other and got lost? But what were they even doing in the forest? This makes no sense."

"No, it doesn't."

"Let's take Bryce's car and see if we can find them." The last thing she wanted to do was to get into a car with Nola. What if Nola really *had* been having an affair with the ice-cream van driver? If that was true, what did it mean? Bryce seemed pretty certain she'd called him Brent by mistake.

But it seemed wrong to leave Nola on her own. She looked half-scared to death.

"I don't know about that." Nola shook her head. "Bryce is pretty particular about his own stuff."

"Well, they should have thought of that before taking off for so long. Just tell Bryce it was all my idea. Okay? Wait here and I'll go back and grab the keys."

Not waiting for a reply, Abby jogged back to the cabin.

Inside, the cabin was even colder and emptier than before.

Snatching up Bryce's keys, she turned to head back outside.

Where was Nola? She must be a slow runner if she hadn't made it to Bryce's car yet. Abby decided to go and start it up and get it warm.

This night had been one she couldn't wait to put behind her.

She'd almost reached the car when arms slid around her neck, yanking her towards the trees. This time, it wasn't Nola.

58

KATE

I drove onto Eleventh Avenue. The dirt road and surrounds were pitch dark.

"Okay, I think this is the spot where we turn off," Franco told me, studying the GPS.

I turned the car onto a narrow dirt path, between two trees that were barely wide enough to fit through.

"Someone's running up there." Franco jabbed a finger to the left.

The headlights picked out the shape of a young man with a lanky frame. His arms were behind his back, tied.

I drove up alongside him, our car tyres bouncing and skidding on the loose stones.

The man spun around. It was Logan.

Franco and I jumped out.

"Stop! Police!" called Franco.

I rushed around the car and over to Logan, breathing hard. "What happened, Logan?"

He had a cut across his cheek, dark blood dribbling down to his jaw and neck. "Someone hit me from behind, tied me up. You've got to help. The girls—"

"Is Abby here?" I cut in.

He nodded, gasping, a thin stream of blood running into the side of his mouth. "Abby and Nola. I don't know where Bryce is. Untie me. I'll take you to them."

I'd had no idea Nola was here, too. "Where are they?" I cried urgently.

"The cabin, last I saw them," Logan told me.

"Who hit you?" Franco asked.

Logan shook his head. "I don't know. Someone else is here. We have to go!"

Franco side-eyed me. Could we really trust Logan's story?

Franco grabbed his arm, wrestling him across to the side of the road. "Mate, I'm going to have to handcuff you to this tree over here while Detective Wakeland and I go check this out."

"What the hell?" Logan exploded. "No, I can't let you do that."

Logan swung his head and shoulders back, straight into Franco's nose, making Franco lose his grip. He charged into the forest.

I pulled out my gun. "Stop! I'll shoot!"

Franco held his bloodied nose, groaning at the pain. "Let him go, Wakeland. Come on!"

We raced back to the car and continued along the road. My heart thudded in my throat.

59

ABBY WAKELAND

Terror struck at her, cold and sharp like the swing of an ice pick. Her mind blanking and limbs immobile.

Large, strong arms wrapped around her torso and shoulders. Dragging her into the forest.

The man had come out of nowhere. A stranger.

Where were Logan and Bryce? Had this man hurt them?

Adrenaline surged. She kicked and arched her back.

A fierce scream shrieked from her throat. His fingernails scraped her face as he repositioned his hand over her mouth, making her silent again. His hand was grimy, smelling of beer and cold sweat.

She'd been dragged beyond the line of trees now. Only a faint light reached in.

He shoved her to the ground. With sickening speed, he was on top of her. A predator.

His hold over her mouth loosened only enough for her to breathe.

Abby gasped for air. "Who are you? What do you want?"

"I want *you*."

She cried out.

It was Bryce's voice.

He pressed a knee into her belly. "It's you and me. Right now. Tonight."

"Why are you doing this?" She could barely wheeze the words out with his knee pushing her stomach up into her lungs. It was like every nightmare she'd ever had in which she wanted to scream but only a whisper would leave her lips.

She struggled against the knee that was driving into her ribs.

He was stronger.

"*Get off.* Logan's on his way. I called him two minutes ago."

"Oh yeah. Funny that. Logan told me you don't have your phones tonight."

"Logan will kill you for this."

"He won't... because you won't tell him. Because if you tell him, I'm going to tell the police what you and Logan did tonight."

"I don't know—"

"Oh, you don't know what I'm talking about? Little Miss Innocent. I know you do. Why do you think Logan asked me here tonight?"

She struggled again. "It was just a trip away. A fishing trip."

"Do you think I'm here for a *fishing trip*? No, little girl. Logan told me he needed quick money, and I told him exactly how and where he could get it."

"Then why didn't you steal the stuff yourself?"

"Because I'm not that stupid, that's why. I'm not going to make myself a suspect. But I know where to sell the stuff discreetly. That's why Logan and I went for a drive. We drove up the road a bit and he showed me the haul. I'm going to start planning where to sell it."

Her thoughts spun. Logan said he'd asked Bryce and Nola to the cabin tonight so they could give the police alibis if things went wrong. Logan lied.

"What do you get out of it?" she spat at him.

"A cut. But don't worry, you'll get most of it. I know you really, really need the money." He strung out each word, seeming to revel in the control he had over her.

"Where's Logan?" she breathed. "Did you hurt him?"

"He's tied up. When he wakes, he's going to think a stranger did that to him. Why don't you just be nice to me and make sure I keep my mouth shut about the crime you committed tonight? Because *you* might escape jail, but Logan wouldn't."

A mix of fear and fury flashed in her brain. He grinned as she flailed, seeming to enjoy the fight. With one hand, he pushed the side of her face down into the wet dirt. Scents of rain and rotting leaf matter rose from the disturbed ground. She tasted mud in her mouth.

He tugged at the zipper of her jacket. It snagged. He ripped at it, tearing the fabric.

A choked, guttural sound emitted from her throat. "You lied, didn't you, about Nola? She didn't mistake your name for Brent's. You made that up."

"Yeah." He laughed. "It worked though. You were in my arms within a second. You just shouldn't have pulled away from me. If you'd been nice from the start, we wouldn't be here right now."

"What did you do to Nola?" Abby cried desperately. "Where is she?"

"She's in the cabin. Like a good girl."

"No, she isn't. What did you do to her?"

He pushed himself up with his arms, furrowing his brow. "You're trying to psych me out. I followed you two when you were walking back to the cabin. Then I heard the cabin door, and I knew you and Nola went in there. But when I looked, only *you* came out."

"No. *I* ran to the cabin by myself. Nola's still out here."

"What?" He turned his head to look around.

A figure emerged from the bushes.

Nola. With a thick branch in her hands.

With an enraged yell, she swung the branch into the side of his head. The branch made a dull cracking sound.

And she hit him again and again and again.

60

KATE

A lantern illuminated two parked vehicles. I made out the outline of a cabin that sat a short distance away.

A scream tore through the forest, making my back go rigid.

A woman's scream, high-pitched and clear.

I jammed the brakes and parked. Franco and I sprinted towards the sound.

A scream rang out again, much lower and more guttural this time. We wouldn't have heard it had we not been so close now.

"Over there." Franco flashed his torch beam over the line of trees to the left of us.

Guns drawn, we headed in.

A figure lay on his stomach on the ground, his forehead bruised, bleeding. He looked as if he'd been crawling and then passed out.

Had Logan done this? Or the stranger that Logan claimed was loose in the forest?

Franco crouched down to the man, checking his pulse. "He's alive." Grabbing his radio, he called for an ambulance.

We ventured further in, stepping into a small clearing.

I flashed the beam of my torch over two figures. Abby and Nola. Both kneeling.

The side of Abby's face was coated in mud, leaves strung through her hair, her eyes huge in the torchlight. "Mum?"

I rushed to her. "My God. What happened here?"

Franco shone his torch over Nola. Her hair fell around a face set with a numb expression. She was rocking to and fro while sitting on her heels, her arms around her stomach. A stumpy branch lay beside her.

"The scream we heard," I said, "was that you, Nola?"

Nola met my gaze with dull eyes.

"She's in shock," Franco said to me quietly.

He was right—Nola was locked up in her own world at this moment.

I scraped dirt away from Abby's face. "What happened?"

Abby looked away, her eyes distant. "Nola went crazy. She just came out of nowhere. She hit Bryce. Again and again."

"God," I breathed, seeing red marks under the mud. "And what happened to *you?* Your clothes are torn. And you're scratched."

"I was scared and tried to run away," Abby answered. "I got snagged on a tree. But I'm okay...."

Sirens wailed in the distance. Backup was almost here.

61

KATE

Bryce Damont was swiftly taken to the local hospital, where he was now in intensive care, apparently in a coma from the blows that Nola had delivered.

Police also escorted Abby to the hospital. She had scratches on her forehead and ripped clothing. She claimed to have run into a tree, but she needed to be examined by a doctor and have medical photos taken. I was suspicious of her story. Pete came down to the hospital with Jasper to stay by her side.

Nola wasn't speaking to anyone and had been taken to a psychiatric ward for evaluation.

The last person to be accounted for was Logan Norwood. Franco and I, together with the backup team, found him lost in the dense bushland. Without any source of light, with his hands tied behind his back, he'd become disorientated.

We found something else, too. A haul of stolen goods in Logan's car. Two bags stuffed full of tech gear. No robbery had been reported yet, but it was safe to assume that within a day or two, the missing goods would be noticed.

I was terrified at the discovery. Abby had been with Logan all night. Did she know about the robbery?

We didn't locate anyone else in the forest. No strangers. A team of police was still there, looking. A helicopter had been brought in to search via thermal imaging.

Logan was given treatment for his injuries and then brought down to the police station for questioning. His injuries amounted to a large bump on the back of his head and a cut on his cheek. The bump on the head correlated with his story about being hit from behind. But had he given that injury to himself? It would be difficult to do, but not impossible.

I sat in the police interview room with Franco, waiting for Logan to be brought in. Logan had to be cleared by a doctor before he could attend the interview. If he were later considered to have had an impaired capacity of any kind, that could affect the validity of the interview.

Nerves charged through me. I felt as if I were running a number of different races, on a number of different tracks, all at once.

Franco eyed me with trepidation. "Are you cool to go ahead with this?"

"Yeah. I'm ready for it."

"We're playing it the usual way?"

I nodded.

Franco generally played the laid-back cop who was concerned about the welfare of the suspect, while I kept the pressure on, screwing down each nail on the lid, until they had no way out except to confess.

If Logan was like most murder suspects, he'd refuse to talk, and he'd get himself a lawyer. If he did that, it would be a matter of painstaking work to figure out what really happened tonight and who put the jewellery box into the shed. I wanted a result *now*. I wanted to be able to tell Harper's parents who the person was who'd so callously murdered her. They'd waited long enough.

The door finally cracked open.

An officer brought Logan into the room.

Scratches crisscrossed his face, as if he'd been racing through the bush-land and he'd been scraped by tree branches. That must have been after he got away from Franco and me. The cut on his cheek had been bandaged.

"How's Abby?" he asked me. "The police wouldn't tell me anything. They wouldn't even let me talk to her."

"She's recovering," I replied.

"What about Jasper?"

"He's fine. He's with his grandfather and Abby. I'll remind you this is a formal police interview. I won't be answering any more questions about Abby or Jasper."

"Got it." Logan inhaled deeply.

Franco began by asking Logan his name and birthdate and then asking him if he wanted to exercise his right to remain silent.

Norwood looked directly at me. "I don't want a lawyer. I want to talk. Go ahead and record me."

I tried not to show my shock at him agreeing to speak with us.

"All right. Conversation is being taped," Franco told him. He leaned back in his chair. "You look pretty scratched up, mate. That must have hurt."

"I was trying to get back to the girls. My face got shredded by a branch." Logan crossed his arms under his ribcage.

"Describe what happened," said Franco. "Set the scene for us. We know that you, Bryce, Abby and Nola were at the cabin. Abby told us that you'd all had dinner. You played a few friendly rounds of cards. That right?"

"Yeah. Exactly right."

"Then you went to get more firewood?" Franco raised his thick eyebrows.

Logan nodded. "With Bryce. Yeah. But first, we decided to go for a short drive, to the top of the driveway, out near the road. Bryce had lost his wallet earlier, and he'd gotten out of the car at that spot—so we went to see if it was there. Soon as we got out of the car, Bryce heard something—voices, he said. We went to check it out. Bryce went ahead of me. He called out to me like he was in trouble. I ran in to help him. Couldn't find him. Then I got hit from behind." Logan reached around to a spot on the back of his head. "Right here. I was unconscious for a while. I don't know how long.

When I came to, my arms were tied together with duct tape and my feet were, too."

"How did you get the tape off your feet?" I asked.

"It wasn't easy. I just kept kicking until it loosened. But I couldn't get the tape off from my wrists, and I had no time to lose. I had to get back to Abby."

I pushed a large piece of paper across the table at Logan. "This is an aerial print of the cabin and the property. Could you please mark where you were when you say you were tied up with tape? And where you first entered the forest, looking for noises? And also, where you were when you were hit on the back of the head?"

"You come prepared," Logan remarked.

"Always," I said.

He marked one location and then creased his forehead. "That's about where Bryce and I went into the forest. We went in that direction. I can't tell you exactly where I was when I got king hit."

"That's all right, mate," said Franco. "You might remember later."

I faced Logan, pointing to the map. "So, we'll find the duct tape that you got off your ankles in this general location?"

"Oh, right," Logan said, his jaw muscles rippling. "You think I made it all up? You think I tied myself up and put a lump on my own head?"

I ignored that. "What were you planning on doing after you got back to the cabin?"

"To get the girls in my car and get out of there."

"You planned to leave Bryce behind?" I asked.

He hunched his shoulders. "What else could I do? I didn't know where he was. And the girls were in danger. I was going to send the police there once we got away."

"Why didn't you call the police as soon as you freed yourself from the ties?" I kept a direct gaze on him.

"My hands were tied." His eyes evaded mine.

"Where there's a will, there's a way," I said. "And we didn't find a phone on you when you were searched. What happened to your phone?"

"I didn't have it," he mumbled.

"Is there a reason why you didn't have it?" I widened my eyes to make a point.

"I left it somewhere. Not sure where."

"You really don't remember where you left it?" I said. "We actually found it. In the same place Abby's phone was."

His eyes immediately jammed shut. "Shit. Okay. So, you found the phones." His eyelids drifted open, but he didn't look at me. "We just wanted a peaceful night away. No phones. Abby needed a good rest."

"You left the phones in a plastic bag at Katoomba train station, hooked onto a tree branch," I said. "Correct?"

"Correct, yeah," he affirmed in a begrudging tone.

"I have some more surprises," I told him.

I hauled two backpacks of tech equipment onto the table. Both backpacks were in clear plastic bags.

Logan had an immediate reaction, his jaw trembling and his fingers clenching into fists. He looked younger than his age in that moment, almost like a teenager.

One thing was certain. Logan Norwood was unable to keep a cool demeanour. He was going to flatten like a house of cards.

I'm building up to the big question, Logan. Did you kill Harper? But I have to take this step by step. Before I squash you.

I took a moment to compose myself, to keep my anger off the boil.

Franco seemed to take the cue. Sliding disposable gloves on, he opened one of the bags, showing Logan the contents. "After you were taken away from the property, we found these two bags in your car. Are they yours?"

Logan didn't answer for a while. Then he released a stream of air from between his teeth. "Yes."

"And the stuff inside?" said Franco. "The sound equipment, the TV projectors—did you put them in there?"

"Yep," Logan answered.

"Okay." Franco sat back in his chair, pulling his gloves off. "Would you like to tell us where that came from?"

"I took it. From a house," Logan admitted.

"Which house?" Franco frowned and inclined his head as if trying to understand a puzzling story. That was Franco's way. He interviewed suspects like they were telling a fascinating story and he was interested in every last detail. No matter what kind of horror story they were telling. He did the same thing with the rapist murderers we'd interviewed, too, getting them to tell the awful details of their crimes—details that I barely had the stomach for.

Logan gave him the address of the house, and Franco wrote it down.

"What did you intend doing with the stuff, mate?" Franco asked him.

"I was gonna sell it," he said.

"Who were you going to sell it to?" Franco hooked his eyebrows.

"Don't know," Logan muttered.

"Doesn't sound like much of a plan." I shook my head, sighing. "I find it hard to believe that you stole these very specific kinds of items without already knowing who you'd be selling them to."

"Well... I didn't," he responded.

"How did you know that you'd find those goods in that particular house?" I asked him. "You must have known what you'd find there?"

"I'd seen the guy at Close Quarters," Logan told me. "He's got a whole tech store full of that stuff. Wasn't hard to figure out he'd have some good gear at his house."

"So, when did you take the gear?" Franco asked Logan.

"Tonight," Logan answered in a low voice. "Just before I went to pick up Abby to go to the cabin."

"Okay," said Franco. "Can you give us the addresses, or approximate addresses, of other houses you've stolen goods from?"

Logan bent his head, studying the red marks on his wrists that had been left behind by the duct tape. "That was the first and only one."

"We'll be getting a search warrant for your house," Franco told him. "So, it's really better if you tell us now what we might find there."

"You won't find anything else," Logan said.

In response, I brought another box onto the table, which was also in a clear plastic bag.

Logan raised his head, glancing at the jewellery box. "What's that?"

"It's something we found, at your house," I told him.

"Never seen it before," he said. "Must be Ricky's."

I slid photographs across the table. The photographs were of the jewellery from inside the box—the necklace and two sets of earrings. I watched Logan's face carefully. "What can you tell me about these items?"

"Nothing," Logan said without hesitation.

"Did you steal them?" I asked him.

"No."

"Did you take them from someone?" I said.

"That's the same question." He eyed me with a deeply puzzled expression. "The answer is still no."

"They were in the shed at the back of your house. The box was hidden in the wall." I pushed across another picture, of the hole that'd been cut into the wooden beam.

"I don't know who did that," Logan said.

I exchanged a long glance with Franco.

Logan watched the glance, his voice stretching to a nervous pitch. "What's going on?"

I pushed across another photo. It was a photo of Harper, wearing the jewellery. "Can you tell me who that is?"

He studied the picture. "She looks familiar."

"Where do you know her from?" I said.

"I don't know her. I've just seen her face before."

"Her name is Harper Rawlings," I said, keeping my tone as level as I could manage. "She's twenty in that picture. She didn't get to be any older than that. She was murdered, in the parking bay outside Close Quarters. Hit with a blunt object and then strangled."

"Hell. I might have seen her face in the news, then."

"Where were you living four years ago?" I asked.

"In the city."

I followed up with, "What were you doing in the city and why did you come back here?"

"I left the Blue Mountains when I was eighteen and went to live in Newtown, in the city. I was a musician for years. I met Abby a bit over a year ago. Decided to move back to the mountains after Jasper was born. So,

I'm a mechanic now. It's my brother's shop—he's gone overseas for a while."

"How often did you come back to town during those years?" I said.

"Every few months," he responded. "To see my parents or my brother. About three times, I moved back to town, but it never lasted long. Too restless, I guess."

He went silent for a moment. Then his gaze moved between the photograph of Harper and the wooden box and the photograph of the jewellery. He jerked his head up. "You're not trying to say it was *me* who did that to her?"

"Her jewellery is in your shed," I stated. "Ricky says he found it there."

He stared at me with an incredulous expression. "I *bought* the ring from Ricky. Why would I buy a ring that I'd stolen from a dead girl?"

I shrugged. "Maybe you wanted Abby to have it. But you needed an alibi in case you were found out. So, you made sure that Ricky found it. Then you told him you needed a ring. And then Ricky thinks it's his lucky day and sells it to you."

"That's insane," Logan responded, his mouth dropping open. "You've had it in for me ever since you found out I was with your daughter."

"Not in the least," I stated firmly. "I've been working on the case of Harper Rawlings ever since the night she was murdered. And now, we've found her missing jewellery. The thing is... we know two things. You're a thief. And the stolen jewellery was in a box in *your* backyard shed."

62

KATE

Harsh shadows fell across the faces of Franco and Logan in the police interview room. Even Logan, aged in his mid-twenties, was looking drained and pale under this lighting.

It was time to go in hard and strong. I prepared myself mentally to put Logan Norwood through a gruelling, unrelenting set of questions about Harper's murder.

Logan had admitted to the theft of the tech gear without any resistance. But he was strongly resisting admitting to any involvement in the murder.

Logan asked for a drink and Franco fetched him one.

Something Logan had said earlier slid into my mind. He'd said that he'd robbed the house before picking up Abby. And he'd said he'd picked her up from their house. But that wasn't true, because I was at their house at that time, trying to get information out of Ricky about where Abby and Logan were.

My throat went dry. Abby must have accompanied Logan on the robbery.

I could almost hear a ticking sound inside my mind. This interview was counting down to events that were unexpected, that could impact Abby in a very negative way. If Abby had gone with Logan on the robbery, then she was guilty of the same offences as him, as far as the stolen goods went.

Why did the two of them do it? For drug money?

There was a time that Abby had been a substance abuser, but I'd thought those times were long gone. But I didn't know for sure, and Abby was always so secretive.

I pictured her as she was when I found her tonight, sitting on the cold, damp ground, with leaves in her hair and dirt on her face.

"Detective?" Franco prompted me. "Are we ready to continue?"

I rubbed my face with my palms. "Give me a moment."

The scene in the woods sharpened in my mind. I pictured Abby and Nola and Bryce, seeing a triangle form between them. A connection.

Nola with the large stick beside her, unable or unwilling to speak. Abby, with her wide, open eyes and the dirt on her face. Bryce, lying a short distance away from the girls, his head bruised and bleeding.

I snapped my head around to Franco. "I need to make a call."

Franco met my gaze with a perplexed look. "Sure. Go ahead."

Rising, I pushed my chair back and then left the room.

A few people from our team were still outside. Avoiding them, I went quickly into an office and made the call.

"Kate?" came Pete's anxious voice. "How are things going? Are you done for the night?"

"No, I've hit a snag. I need to talk to Abby. Are you at home now?"

"Yeah, we got home from the hospital fifteen minutes ago. Jasper's unsettled, so I've been walking with him. I'll get Abby for you."

Abby's voice was small and uncertain when she came to the phone. "Hello, Mum?"

"Abby," I said. "I need you to answer some questions for me, and it's really important that you tell me the truth. You had mud on your face and your clothing was torn. Did someone attack you?"

"No... I told you. My jacket got ripped on a branch, and then I fell on the ground, straight on my face. Clumsy."

I didn't have time for her denials. "Was it Bryce?"

"No. I fell."

"You would have put your hands out before falling on your face, Abby. Yet you barely had any mud on your hands. Someone pushed your face down into the ground. So, the question is, who did that to you? The teams of police searching the area haven't found anyone else. And it was unlikely to be Logan, because he was up the other end of the property at that time. And then we have Nola, sitting there with a big stick beside her. And Bryce, with his head bleeding."

"Mum... please. Leave it alone. This isn't one of your police cases. It was just a night away for me and some friends. Everyone will be okay. Nola just snapped, that's all. Maybe she has a mental problem. She always was weird, right? I just want to forget it."

"I'm going to put it to you that it was Bryce who attacked you, and then Nola hit him with the stick. That explains the condition that Bryce was in. And also explains why Nola was in shock. She'd just found her boyfriend attacking you and then she hit him. And it also explains the two different screams we heard. The first one was you. The second one was Nola."

Abby began crying before I'd finished. "You don't understand... please... just leave it alone. Leave *me* alone. If you care about me at all. If you ever cared about Ivy...."

"Of course I care," I snapped. "Listen to me. I've been in the interview room with your boyfriend for the past hour. He's already admitted to serious break and enter and stealing offences, and there is more to come. Much more. It's important that you—"

She gasped, her breaths trembling from her sobs. "Police found the bags?"

"Yes. They did. You were there, right? When the goods were being stolen?"

"Did Logan say that?"

I didn't answer.

"Yes... I was there," she admitted.

"You silly girl." It was an automatic response and one that I instantly regretted. But I was too fatigued to be subtle.

"You don't understand."

"What don't I understand?"

"We did it for Ivy."

Silence hung between us on the phone line. Within that silence, I struggled for an answer.

"Abby... talk to me. What are you saying?"

"We were given an offer from an expert who told us he could do what the police couldn't. Bring Ivy's body back to me...."

I inhaled a rapid breath. "Oh... Oh, God. Who?"

Then I knew. I knew without any doubt. The private investigator that Lori Hinton had used. It had to be him.

"Mr Kyle Wheeler," I said in a dead tone.

"Logan told you that, too?" she said in a shocked, hushed tone.

"Honey... why? Why did you believe that guy? Wheeler preys on vulnerable people when they're at their lowest point. I'm going to nail him to the wall for this."

"But he said—"

"That's the only thing he's good at. Talking. Convincing people to give him their money."

I heard a fresh round of sobs. "I just wanted her back, Mum. So that I can bury her properly. It just feels like... she's a ghost, you know? I have nothing of her. I can't explain the emptiness I feel...."

"I'm so sorry, honey. For you, for Ivy... for what this Wheeler guy did to you."

"I was just... desperate."

"Abby, I need you to tell me where Logan fits into this."

"Logan was just trying to help me," she said in a tearful voice.

"Help you with what, exactly? To get money for Mr Wheeler?"

"Yes. The investigator wanted ten thousand dollars. And I just... didn't have ten thousand dollars. I knew you and Dad wouldn't give it to me. I had an idea of how I could get it, and that's the night Logan and I had our big fight. Because he wouldn't let me do it."

"What wouldn't Logan let you do?" I held my breath.

"I thought I could... work for a while. Don't judge me, but I thought I could do web cam work. I have a friend who does that. She said I could have a few of her hours." She breathed in and out heavily. "Logan said no. I completely lost it and got angry, and I started throwing things. Logan left the house, telling me he was going to find another way of getting the money. He... ended up coming up with the robbery idea...."

I took a long breath, absorbing everything she'd told me, tears moistening my eyes. "Honey, you should have told me."

"You wouldn't have given me the money," she said rigidly.

She was right. I wouldn't have. I could see that it was an impossible situation for her. But that man, Wheeler, would have just taken the money and run away with it.

I couldn't focus on Wheeler right now. I'd deal with him later. I had to return to what happened right before Franco and I turned up at the cabin tonight.

"Abby," I said gently. "Thank you for explaining. It helps me a lot to understand how things fell into place and why. I also need to know what really happened tonight. I need to know about Bryce."

For a moment, I was certain she was going to end the call. All I could hear from her end of the phone line was sobbing.

But then she began speaking again. "Okay... this is how it happened...."

63

KATE

Things happened in a rush after Abby told me everything.

Late that night, Franco and I conducted a search of Logan Norwood's house. First, we'd looked up the history of vehicles that he and Bryce Damont had owned in the past. Bryce had owned a BMW SUV in 2016. Bryce had also known Ricky for years and had been around to the house that Ricky lived at on occasion. That was enough evidence for us to gain a search warrant for Damont's apartment, too.

We found nothing at the house that Logan and Ricky lived at.

But we were stunned by what we found at Bryce's apartment.

Bryce Damont had never even been on my radar before. Neither Franco nor I had even known his name before tonight. But we knew it now.

Bryce had photos of himself with Harper Rawlings. They'd dated briefly, it seemed, roughly six months before she was killed. While that didn't prove that he'd killed her, another item he had at his house did. He'd snapped a photo on his phone of her, straight after he'd killed her, uploading it onto a private site online. We might never have found the photograph had Bryce not been viewing it just before he'd gone to the cabin last night. It horrified me to know he'd been looking at that image just before going to stay the night at a cabin with Abby and Nola.

Franco and I guessed that Bryce had returned to take the photo a minute after he left the scene of Harper's murder. That explained why Indira Basak had seen his car coming back. Bryce had forgotten his trophy photo.

As well as being a killer, Bryce was into morbid keepsakes. It seemed he'd wanted to keep items from her murder, to gloat over and gain some kind of sick satisfaction.

It chilled me that Abby resembled Harper. Both with luminous skin and long dark hair. Bryce had obviously wanted Abby, but he'd known that Logan stood in his way.

It was Bryce who'd hidden the box of jewellery at Logan's house. He'd been too afraid to keep it at his own place. Bryce had no idea that Ricky had managed to find it. And he also didn't know that Abby had begun wearing the ring.

Bryce had recovered quickly from the coma, waking within hours. The coma had been a blessing—preventing him from returning home and destroying evidence.

We weren't certain of the reason why Bryce chose to take the life of Harper that night. We guessed that she'd stopped wanting to date him and he'd stewed on that for months. For the moment, we had no way of finding out, because Bryce had secured himself a lawyer and was refusing to say a single thing to us. That would all have to come out in court. Harper's parents knew nothing about all of this. It wasn't something I could or should tell them over the phone.

I drove over to their house the next day, feeling battle fatigued.

Harper's mother was out the front, doing a bit of gardening and getting rid of the flowers that had died in the chill of winter. She looked up in surprise and then anxious anticipation as I approached.

"Donna," I said gently. "I have news. Is Gerald home, too?"

"He's just taken our little dog for a walk," she said, rising and dusting off her hands. "He'll be back any minute." Her eyes were already wet.

Her voice grew hoarse. "Have you found out... who it was?"

I nodded.

She began sobbing, her shoulders hitching. I held her as her knees buckled. We hugged silently as she cried, while we waited for her husband to return.

The investigation was over, as far as finding out the identity of Harper's killer. But it would never be over for Harper's parents. They would carry the weight of what Bryce Damont had done for the rest of their lives.

64

KATE

I drove from the Rawlings's house to *Tall Ponds*. It was a place I kept finding myself returning to. It was almost night.

I haven't let go of your little hand, Ivy. In life or in death.

It was vile that Kyle Wheeler had tried to profit from the parents of the missing children. The man had no morals. He'd driven my daughter to the point of stealing to give him the money he'd demanded.

As yet, there hadn't been time to get Abby down to the station to make an official statement about Wheeler. Once I had the statement, I'd be turning him over to the fraud squad.

I sat watching the trees rustle in the wind that had whipped up. The toys and mounds of rotting flowers had been removed. The council had finally put up a sign requesting that no more items of remembrance be left on the grounds.

My back tensed at a new thought.

Wheeler had been the one who stood to profit from the abductions. Could he have been behind the abductions in the first place?

He was around the right age, with an angular face and brown hair. He could match the description that Tiff Lantry and the children had given.

And he would have good knowledge of police procedures and surveillance cameras and how to hide.

My mind spun.

But why would he have left it so long to start targeting the parents for money? Three and a half long years. He would have spent a lot of his savings just paying for many of the things the children needed, plus having to pay rent to Tiff. Why would he do it?

Had he tried to contact any of the other parents? If he had, who would he choose? Penny. He'd choose Penny. She was on her own and she suffered from anxiety. She'd be his perfect client.

Starting my car's engine, I drove away, heading for the mountain road that led to Penny's home.

There was no point trying to find her at the baby good store. None of the parents had been back to work since their children had come home. Apart, perhaps, from Sean Hinton, according to Lori.

Penny's car was in the driveway.

I parked and walked up the path, the thick mist dampening my face and hair. Through the window, I spotted boxes stacked up in the living room. I noticed Max then, peering out of the window at me.

I smiled and waved.

He waved back, then ducked.

Penny opened the door. "Kate. I'm glad you came by. I wanted to see you."

"You did?"

"Yes. I haven't had the chance to thank you personally. I know we had the party day and everything, but it's not the same."

"I'm just happy that you have your little boy back."

She closed her eyes for a moment, her mouth set in a sad smile. Her pale, drained face of the past had brightened. It was the first time I'd seen her with colour in her cheeks. "Oh, it's wonderful. But I just wish things could have happened a little differently."

"Me too."

"Oh, of course you do." A pitying look visited her eyes. "There should have been five children come back, not four." She paused. "I do want to thank you personally for all you've done. You told us you weren't going to stop until you found the children, and that's exactly what you did."

I gave a small, taut smile of appreciation, then glanced around. "You're packing up house?"

She nodded. "I've got my Max back. He's my family. I don't need the house. I always wanted to live somewhere warmer. And Max's always been a water baby." She shrugged happily. "So, off we go on an adventure. A new chapter of our lives."

"I'm happy for you."

"Thank you, Kate."

"Where are you going? I'll have to get an address."

"Cairns. I can buy for a good price there and then arrange for this one to be sold. Nice and warm there. We're not the only ones leaving town. The Parrishes will be heading back to Florida soon. I've promised Max that we'll go visit them. He and Elijah are great friends." She frowned. "Sorry, I'm running off at the mouth. Forgive me, I'm just excited about a new life for Max and me. Did you stop by for a reason?"

I watched Max run a toy car back and forwards over a large box. He turned his head from me whenever I looked his way.

"Yes," I said. "I have something to ask you. There's a man. A private investigator. He's been in contact with two of the parents of the missing kids. He's been very forceful in asking for money in return for his services. He claims to be able to find out things that the police can't."

She was nodding before I finished my sentence. "Oh, my goodness. Yes. Someone approached me in the parking bay outside Close Quarters. It was night and I'd just gotten my groceries. He insisted upon getting into my car so we could talk in peace, or some damned thing. He seemed very shady. I got rid of him, quick. But still, I found his card in my shopping bags."

She headed out to the kitchen and then returned with a business card. The card was definitely one of Wheeler's.

"Okay, well, I'm glad for you that you're starting somewhere new. Make sure you give me your new address. So that I can contact you if I need to. Enjoy the sun in Cairns."

She folded her arms, looking wistful. "You know... for the first month after he went missing, I woke up every morning hoping to see him in his bed. Just tucked up and sleeping peacefully. Hoping that the kidnapper had just snuck into my house in the middle of the night with him and put him back where he belongs. Well, the dream did happen. And I can still barely believe it."

When I left, both mother and son were gazing from their front window, Max running a finger over the condensation that had gathered on the glass.

Max wasn't missing any more, but he and Penny would soon be missing from our town. The abduction of the five children had changed the lives of all the children's families. For all of the parents, it had completely changed the course of their lives.

I now knew for certain that Wheeler had contacted three of the parents. The ones who were on their own and most vulnerable.

Making a call to Grimshaw, I mentally prepared myself. She'd most probably dismiss the idea. I didn't have a solid reason for why Wheeler, if he were the abductor, would have kept the kids for years before beginning to pursue the parents.

She shocked me by saying that she'd call him in for a police interview tomorrow.

65

KATE

"Wheeler's agreed to talk with us," Grimshaw told me when I walked into the station.

"Great news," I breathed.

"That might change once he gets into the interview room and he starts hollering for a lawyer," she said. "But right now, he's willing. I say strike while the iron's hot."

I nodded tensely. "Can't argue with that. Let's go for it."

She raised her eyebrows at me. "Hold your horses. You can sit in, but not speak. Let me conduct the interview with Mr Wheeler."

My defences switched into overdrive. "What? No. It was my actions that uncovered him."

"I'll do a better interview," she said coolly.

"Really? I intend tearing that guy open until every last thing he's been doing spills from his guts onto the floor."

"That's exactly why you're not doing it. He's savvier than the regular. He's a P.I. He could try to get a rise out of you. And if you put one foot wrong on the recording, his defence will use it in court to claim you had a vendetta against him—because of what he did to Abby. They'll make it look personal."

I felt my shoulders sink, in spite of myself. She was right. And I hated that she was right.

"Go for the jugular," I said.

Her lips flicked upward. "Oh, I intend to. In the politest possible way."

———

Wheeler didn't front at the station until the early afternoon.

He wore a blue business shirt that had a few open buttons at the neckline. A casual jacket and carefully tousled hair completed his look. Wheeler seemed to consider himself hot stuff.

Grimshaw got his consent to record the session, and then she began.

"Can I have your name, please?" she said.

"Kyle Wheeler."

"Date of birth?"

"20th July 1981."

"Okay. Could you explain your connection to Lori Hinton?"

"I was engaged by her as a personal investigator."

"For what services?" she asked.

"Lori thought her husband was doing the dirty on her. So, she contacted me to find out if that was the case," he answered.

"Right. And after that, Lori used your services to find her missing daughter, Charlotte?"

"Yup."

"In this instance, did she contact you or did you contact her?"

"It was a mutual thing."

"Who made first contact in terms of services to do with Charlotte?"

"Possibly me. I'm unsure."

"Right. And Lori paid you a weekly retainer?"

"Yes."

"And once Charlotte was found, you wanted to keep this arrangement going, is that right?"

"I thought I could help."

"Did Lori want to continue with your services at this point?"

"Yes."

"I have a statement here from Lori that says she wanted to stop the payments, but you coerced her to keep them going. Lori stated that you said, '*If you don't keep up the money, then you lose my protection. And I have a bad feeling your daughter's going to get snatched back by the kidnapper. And this time, he'll kill her.*' Is that correct?"

For a moment, he appeared anxious but then a veil of calm came over his face. "Those weren't my words."

"Lori says that's word-for-word what you said," Grimshaw told him.

"Well, she's been through a lot of traumas. She's probably getting a bit hysterical."

"Did you say anything with the same meaning?"

He shrugged. "Well, I really thought that could happen. About them snatching the kids back and killing them. I mean, they whacked the other kid."

"You mean, Ivy Wakeland?" Grimshaw said.

"Yup." He briefly glanced in my direction and then flicked his gaze away again, running a hand through his hair.

He'd spoken about Ivy so dismissively I wanted to jump down his throat and eviscerate him. He'd used Ivy's death as a tool to strike terror into Lori. But I'd agreed to keep my mouth shut.

"Okay," Grimshaw continued, studying Wheeler's face carefully, "that brings us to Ivy's mother, Abby Wakeland. Abby stated that you contacted her two days after the missing children were returned, correct?"

"Yeah. I guess."

"And you told Abby that she'd never get her child back to bury her, because the police had bungled everything. And that you could set things right. Can you confirm that?"

"Doesn't a mother want her dead kid back so she can bury her?" He flexed his shoulder blades, leaning back in the chair and adjusting his confident pose. In that moment, I understood why Kyle Wheeler had agreed to this interview rather than remaining silent and getting a lawyer. He was someone who possessed an extreme measure of cocky self-assurance. He didn't even seem to recognise the fact that Grimshaw was steadily building the case against him.

"That's not what I asked," Grimshaw asserted. "I asked if you told Abby that you could succeed in returning Ivy's body to her?"

"The thing is," he drawled, "you gotta admit that things didn't go well with the police investigation. I mean, three and a half years and the kids didn't get found. And then the police get the kids handed back on a silver platter. Except for Ivy. She's dead and buried and the kidnappers aren't going to let you know where she is, because they're terrified they've left their DNA on her. So, I was just trying to help Abby out."

I wanted to reach across the table and throttle him until his face turned purple and his neck went limp. I realised I was breathing a little too rapidly when Grimshaw shot me a warning glance.

The glance was subtle, but Wheeler seemed to catch it. His mouth pulled up on one side in a kind of veiled smirk.

"Mr Wheeler," Grimshaw said, doubling down on her terse tone. "How do you know that the kidnappers were worried about leaving their DNA on Ivy?"

His mouth dropped a little before he clamped it shut again. "I was just assuming."

"Hmmm. Is it true that you told Abby that if the police hadn't put your mother, Detective Wakeland, onto the strike force team, then Ivy would still be alive?"

Wheeler turned to face me, speaking to me directly. "It wasn't just *me* saying that. It was being said in the news. Someone wanted vengeance. And they got it." His tone had switched, going from mere self-assured shyster to someone who believed he was now in control of the interview.

"The difference is," countered Grimshaw, "that you said it directly to Abby Wakeland, while pushing her to pay you money. A *lot* of money."

The muscles in his face seemed to pinch. "All investigators charge for their services. Without being paid, they can't operate."

Grimshaw went silent for a moment, keeping her eyes directly on him. At first, I thought he'd stumped her. But then I understood that this was a technique of hers. I'd never seen her interview anyone before. I hoped she had something damned good up her sleeve.

His bold, chest-out posture folded a little as he waited.

Grimshaw sucked her mouth in, frowning deeply. "Okay. I'm going to put it to you that you were attempting to extort money from vulnerable people any which way you could get it. Your contract with Lori Hinton was coming to an end. You were upset about that. She was about to cut off a source of revenue. You kept demanding she see you, harassing her until she agreed. So, she meets with you in an empty carpark at night, where you again attempt to pressure her. Lori is in her forties, with a good measure of confidence in herself. You don't succeed. You then target Abby Wakeland, a young, vulnerable mother, at a time of enormous grief and trauma. She's just been told her little girl is dead, most probably murdered. You tell her that her mother is standing in the way of her getting her dead child back. She doesn't have any money. You pressure her into getting the money any which way she can. You tell her she's got three days, or she's got no hope of getting Ivy's body brought back. She's desperate to give her a proper burial. At the same time, you attempt to do a similar thing to Penny Foster, the mother of one of the returned children. You give Penny the same spiel you gave to Lori Hinton. You rush out at Penny at night, in the rain, in the parking bay outside CQ. She's a single mother with severe anxiety issues. You prevent her from being able to close her car door before she hears what you had to say. What you did is to choose three vulnerable targets and pursue them."

He bent his head, his breaths heavy. "It's my job. I have to find work."

"By preying on vulnerable people?" Grimshaw pressed.

"It's not intentional. It's a sales technique." Both his body and demeanour seemed to have been crushed.

"So, you admit that you used pressure and forceful tactics to try to get these women to agree to pay you money for your services?"

"No, I wouldn't go so far as to say that," he insisted. "You've got me all wrong."

By the cold glint in Grimshaw's eyes, I could see she wasn't finished. I

371

understood then what the ice-cream van driver had been talking about when he explained how harsh his interview with her had been.

Grimshaw folded her arms. "When I said the word *services*, I used it lightly. Because I cannot for the life of me see what services you actually provided. Do you actually have any information about the kidnappers? Because the police would really like to know."

"I don't have to tell the police about my investigations," he muttered.

"Well, Mr Wheeler," she countered, "it's a pretty big result that you were promising those mothers. One could conclude that you had knowledge of where the kids were." She paused for a moment. "Did you know where the children were being kept?"

"I was getting close."

"You were? In what way?"

"As I said, I'm under no obligation to give the police my information."

"Mr Wheeler, did you kidnap the children?" she said.

His head jerked up, eyes wild and wide open. "What the hell? *No.*"

"It could line up that you kidnapped the children with the intention of extorting money from the parents." She raised her eyebrows at him.

"Wouldn't getting ransoms from the parents have been easier?" he said from between clenched teeth. "Like... three and a half years ago?"

Grimshaw shrugged. "Maybe ransoms proved too difficult."

"What would I do with five ankle-biters for years? I have a job."

"We have good information that one of the abductors had a day job," she told him.

She had fast replies now for everything he said. The second that he spoke, she had a firm rebuttal.

His movements became jittery, and he looked as if he'd really like to escape from the room. "Are you two trying to pin this on me? You're making me the scapegoat because *she*"—he pointed at me—"is Abby Wakeland's mother. This is a big set up. I walked straight into the trap, didn't I?"

Grimshaw had been dead right about me not participating in the interview. Because Wheeler had taken things to the place that she said he might take them. He was losing ground and now he was attempting to play the victim, at my expense.

I broke my silence. "I'm only here to observe. I'm not conducting the interview." I kept my voice calm in spite of the storm wailing inside my mind.

"There's no set up," Grimshaw told him. "I'm just trying to ascertain the facts."

He exhaled a long, tense breath that almost sounded defeated. "I've got a night job, too," he said.

"Oh?" Grimshaw lifted her eyebrows high.

"I'm a bit of a gambler," Wheeler said.

Grimshaw leaned forward, almost conspiratorially, lowering her voice at the same time. "How much of a gambler are we talking?"

"I hit the poker machines just about every night."

She inclined her head, her voice still softer. "If that's true, then there are people who'd know your face. The bar staff and the other workers at wherever it is that you gamble."

"Yeah. Yeah, they know me," he mumbled.

"So," she said. "You're telling me you have a gambling addiction?"

"Yes."

"And do I assume you're deep in debt? Can't pay your bills?" Grimshaw was playing nice, concerned cop now.

He nodded. "It's hard."

"And so, to help clear your debts, you used forceful language and manipulative tactics to try to get money from Lori Hinton, Abby Wakeland and Penny Foster?" she asked. She kept her tone in the nice cop register.

Dropping his head back, he stared up at the ceiling, exhaling hard.

"I'm not proud of it," he said.

"So, that's a yes?" she asked.

"Yes," he replied.

Grimshaw exchanged glances with me then fixed her gaze on Wheeler. "Mr Kyle Wheeler, you're under arrest for extortion. There may be further charges on subjects not discussed in this interview. Do you understand?"

He simply nodded.

I squeezed my tired eyes shut. Kyle Wheeler wasn't our guy.

66

KATE

Two hours after the interview with Kyle Wheeler, Grimshaw and I found that Kyle was the chronic gambler he claimed to be. Club staff confirmed with us that Wheeler fronted up to the slot machines every night, from six to ten at night.

Wheeler was a dead end.

I headed off to my own desk to think.

I had one thing left.

The mask.

But to make something out of that would be like squeezing blood out of a stone. I half-smiled in a rueful way, remembering Abby telling me that Logan had said that about me once. That I looked like I could get blood out of a stone.

With no way forward on the mask idea, I considered something. Perhaps there were things about masks that I couldn't begin to research because I just didn't know enough about them.

On the night I'd been trying to figure out how the abductors knew where the parents would be, I hadn't known anything about fitness watch apps. I didn't know what I didn't know.

It was a shot in the dark, but if I could find someone more knowledge-able about masks than me, I might find a small speck of light.

Grimshaw was at her desk as I strode past, deep in thought.

"Where are you off to?" she said with a curious note in her voice.

"I'm not sure yet," I answered.

I drove to Close Quarters and parked outside the foyer. I stepped out into the freezing temperature. Two degrees Celsius this afternoon. A thin mist hung in the air.

The vast, marble-like foyer welcomed me in—or at least, it felt that way. With the piped, serene music and muted background noise. A lot of care had been taken with the acoustics here. Everything smelled so new, as if they were pumping in air direct from the mountain tops. But CQ was already a decade old.

I walked up to the information desk—named the quarter deck, which was an enormous semi-circular structure on a raised platform.

Three men and two women were busily working at the desk, directing visitors to where they wanted to go.

I stepped up to the nearest of them, a woman of about thirty, dressed in a practised smile and a perfectly fitted jacket.

"Hello, I'm Detective Kate Wakeland. I need a bit of help with something."

"Certainly," she said, her accent distinctly American. New York city, I thought.

"Okay," I said. "I know there are a couple of large party stores here. What I'm looking for is something more upmarket than your usual party or Halloween masks. I'm looking for something that is ultra-realistic. And more than that, I'm after some very specific kinds of information. Would the party stores be my best bet... or?"

"Hmmm." She tapped a manicured finger to her chin. Then browsed on the computer in front of her. "This is outside the box, but there's a supply store for theatrical and movie productions in the technology quarter. They don't advertise, as they're not open to the public. Sanjay would be your best contact. I could contact him if you wish?"

"That... sounds wonderful."

"Just a moment." She made a call. "Good timing. Sanjay was about to head out. He said he'll stay a bit longer to chat with you. You'll find *Aeschylus Theatrical Supplies* on the third floor. Head to the right after exiting the elevator."

"Thank you."

I strode away, glancing upwards at the three mezzanine levels of the tech quarter. Hundreds of businesses and start-ups were being run here, but I had little idea of what the majority of them even were.

I ascended to the third floor and located the theatrical supplies business. It had no glass display walls or windows. Just a door. I knocked but no one answered. Opening the door for myself, I stepped inside.

I'd expected to see a room crammed with movie props, but what greeted me instead was a large space that was mostly empty. There were mannequins wearing body suits that looked like something in between wetsuits and uniforms from a sci-fi movie. The room also held a vast array of face masks on dummy heads. The long walls were painted in a lurid green.

A man walked out from an interior room. "Detective Wakeland? I'm Sanjay. Pleased to meet you." He was tall and good looking, his skin deeply olive and his accent a mix of Indian and Australian.

I shook his hand. "Latex masks have come a long way."

"Oh, those aren't latex," he told me. "They're silicon. And top notch, super realistic."

"They're certainly realistic. Scarily so."

He looked pleased with my comment. "A couple of our models have fooled people out in the field. We're improving our techniques all the time."

"I see." I gestured around the room. "What are all the suits on display?"

"Those? A mix of animatronics, virtual reality gear and some very expensive motion capture suits."

"Okay. Amazing. You have a lot of space in here. I didn't realise it would be so big from the outside."

He spread his arms wide. "We demonstrate all our models here at *Aeschylus*—lots of free space to run about. The walls are the green screens. A film maker uses those to put different backgrounds on a scene."

"I've heard of green screens. Those walls are certainly bright."

"They're just for demo purposes for the animatronics. The motion capture suits don't need green screens obviously."

"Obviously," I repeated, though not having a clue why. "And the name *Aeschylus*—is that the owner here?"

He laughed. "No, I'm the owner. *Aeschylus* is an ancient Greek playwright. He's called the father of tragedy."

I smiled. "I don't know my ancient Greek playwrights very well, do I? Okay, now, the masks... can you walk me through what they are and what they're used for? And if they're comfortable to wear for hours? Things like that?"

"Of course." As he walked towards the tables of masks, I followed him. "Our masks are made with a special system," he told me. "They're soft and flexible, and they allow heat to disperse. They won't discolour or lose elasticity, even over years of use. With other, older technology, you might be required to wear a thick cream on your face. With ours, you do not. Ours are designed to fit closely with the skin and muscles of your face, allowing the silicon to move with your facial expressions."

"Interesting. They actually move as your face does?"

"Yes. Even the mouth is designed to fit over your own lips, so that you get mouth movement when you talk."

"How realistic is it?"

"Well, not so realistic if you try to smile big and show your teeth. But they're pretty good. Would you like a demonstration?"

"Yes, I very much would."

"Watch." He picked up a mask of an elderly man with a skin tone that matched his, and he slipped it over his head. Looking in a mirror, he wriggled it into position.

"What do you think?" he said.

I gasped. "That is crazy good. You've just aged fifty years. And your lips are moving."

"Yes. The mask is designed to cup the lips snugly. And notice that the eye cut outs fit smoothly around the eyes. You can apply makeup and also match your natural skin tone with foundation, if you wish. Of course, it's best if the mask suits your skin tone from the start."

"Amazing. So real."

The mask didn't allow for the full range of expressions and the lip movement didn't quite follow along with all the usual movements during speech. He couldn't quite make the mask smile, but his lips and the forehead moved upward when he raised his eyebrows.

But it was very, very good. Quite scarily so.

Gently, he pulled the mask off. "You have to be careful you don't pull the material too hard." Putting the mask down, he ran a hand through his ink-black hair.

"Thanks so much for the demo, Sanjay. Do you sell any of these retail?"

"No. Few people want to spend upwards of a thousand dollars for a Halloween face mask. That can be a steep price for even an indie film maker, depending on their budget. We do sometimes sell off the masks that weren't quite up to scratch."

"How do you sell them off?"

"Usually we just put the word out in amateur theatre groups and indie film maker circles. They get sold pretty quickly, as we sell them at a large discount."

"What about people who work at the tech quarter? Would they know about the sales?"

"On the rare occasion, yes. We have pranksters here who get a kick out of masks, especially the horror ones. Goes with the territory. Lots of geeks." He laughed again.

"What if," I said, "someone wanted a custom mask? Could you make one?"

He nodded. "That's most of what we do. For film producers. Depending on what is wanted, it can get very costly."

"Would you mind taking a look at this picture and telling me if you've made a custom mask that looks anything like it?"

I showed him the composite that Lucas had drawn of Bear.

Sanjay thumbed his chin. "I don't think so."

I felt my shoulders rise in a silent, disappointed sigh. "Would you have anything like it? Or have you had anything like it in the past? I'm talking about three to four years back."

"Whoa, that's a long way back." He studied my face for a second, his dark eyebrows knitting. "I'm guessing this is about a crime that was committed, using a mask."

"Perhaps. We're uncertain."

He looked at the image again. "It does remind me of something. This was years ago. Maybe six or so? I'd have to check. I made a couple of masks for an indie movie. It was for children, so the face had a permanent smile. We don't usually make our masks with a smile. It's too limiting."

My stomach flipped. "Could you look it up, please?"

"Of course." He walked across to a table which held a variety of computers, large-screen monitors and equipment. I followed him over.

He tapped at a computer, bringing up lists of items, each item with a small photograph beside it. Clicking on one of the photographs, he enlarged it.

"So, there it is," he said.

I realised I was holding onto a gulp of air. The mask looked as close to the drawings of Bear as it could possibly get. I asked him who had bought the mask.

He looked at the monitor again. "I'm sorry. There isn't much information entered. It says here we bought the mask back from the film director half-price, to use as a demo. And then a year later we sold it. We didn't record who bought it."

"How long ago?" I asked.

"Okay, we do have that information. It was in November 2016."

The date was certainly right.

"Could I take a couple of photographs?" I asked.

"Go for it." Sanjay moved back a little from the screen.

"I just need to send this to some people." I stepped away a short distance. I sent the picture to Lori, Sean, Nick, Marcy, Penny, Roxanne and Rhys. Then I dashed off a text:

URGENT. *Need to know if Charlotte, Elijah, Max or Olivia recognises this face. Show it and ask. Please say nothing. Need unbiased answers.*

After a second, I added: *No calls please. Just text.*

I waited in the showroom, my heart racing. The multiple animatronic beings and eyeless masks watched me silently.

My phone began buzzing with replies.

Nick texted just one word: *Bear.*

Lori replied next with: *Charlotte says it's Bear. What's going on?*

My knees weakened and I had to grab the bench for support.

"Detective?" called Sanjay from behind me. "Are you alright?"

I turned, nodding. I almost lost my voice when I spoke. "Thank you incredibly much for your assistance. You've been more helpful than you know."

He grinned. "Happy to help."

Leaving the theatrical supply store, I began running, startling the people in the hall—Sanjay had called the people in this tech quarter *geeks*. But I didn't slow my pace. It seemed like the race had begun. And for once, I knew what direction in which to run.

A third message came through. This one from Roxanne: *She says it's Bear.*

I hurried back down to the bottom floor and then across to the retail sector of Close Quarters.

It was five minutes to five. Many of the shops closed at that hour.

Panting hard, I increased my pace, charging up the escalators. I arrived on the same level as the camera superstore just as the store was shuffling the last customers out. I saw Blair closing the bifold doors across the store front.

"Blair!" I called. "Blair! Wait."

He looked at me in open-mouthed shock.

I sprinted over to him, gasping. "I need to see that footage again."

An older man came out, aged in his forties. "I'm afraid we're closed."

I showed my badge, taking a breath. "Detective Wakeland. Homicide."

"I showed her the footage of the camera robbery that happened years ago, Dad," Blair told the man.

I nodded. "I need to see it again. It's important."

"Okay, no problem." The man reached to shake my hand. "I'm Danny Ableman."

Blair finished closing up while his father took me into the interior office.

Danny began playing the films in sequence. The first one was of the thief walking towards the store, taken by the thermal imaging camera on a foggy night.

"Danny," I said, "the person—the thief—who is approaching your store, he practically looks headless." I gestured towards the image. "Parts of the body that are exposed should look the warmest. That's the face, right? The guy is wearing a jacket and pants. Only his face and hands are exposed. But his hands are showing up as warm and his face as cold."

"Yeah, it's odd," he said. "At the time, I thought the camera was glitching."

"Could he have been wearing a mask?"

He exhaled, eyes widening dubiously. "I don't know about that. What kind? When you see him inside, it doesn't look like a mask."

"It would explain the difference in temperature, right?"

He moved the footage forward a few frames, watching intently. "Well, damn... I never picked up on that before. The police didn't, either." He scratched his chin. "But wouldn't a mask heat to the temperature of the skin?"

"Maybe," I said. "But not immediately. If the thief put this on just before entering the building, it could still have been cold. It wouldn't be warm like skin."

Danny nodded. "So, we were duped by a mask...."

I glanced from the footage to him. "I need to see the next film."

The second film was taken inside, by a normal CCTV camera. I watched the face of the thief closely. There was only one shot in which the face was somewhat close up. My back chilled. It was the same face as the mask from Sanjay's theatrical supplies store. It was Bear's face. I was certain of that.

I asked Danny to play the third film. The third film showed the exterior again, switching back to the thermal imaging display.

We both watched closely as eight employees—or spouses of employees —of the retail stores left via the back entrances and out to the parking bay.

Four men and four women. I couldn't make out their faces. One of them unchained a bicycle and rode away on it.

"Do you have a list of who those people are?" I asked.

He nodded and went to look it up in a file. "The men are Martin Chan, Sean Hinton, Rhys Crane and my son, Blair—he's the one on the bike. The women are Josephine Mills, Roxanne Crane, Penny Foster and Lori Hinton."

"Thank you." Privately, I was shocked to hear so many names of parents of the missing children. I knew that Lori, Sean, Rhys and Penny had been working here back then and that most of them still did. But surely the thief wasn't any of them? And I'd cringed when Danny mentioned his son's name. Danny had no idea how determined I was to discover the identity of the thief. And if the thief ended up being his son, everything would change overnight for his family.

I watched the film again. "The thief leaves this way"—I pointed to the screen—"but then vanishes. All the people have gotten into their cars and left by this time, except for two. There are now two cars left."

"Yeah," he said. "I've looked at this footage so many times. The thief takes off on foot with the stolen goods."

I frowned. "Why did this woman walk straight past her car and then come back to it a minute later? Where did she go? What's around that corner?"

"Uh, just the cardboard compactors and industrial waste bins."

"So, she had no good reason to go around there?"

"Some employees might toss their personal rubbish in the bins, I guess."

"Let's rewind and watch again, from when the thief left the back entrance."

The thief appeared to walk straight past the area with the compactors and waste. But did he? That was the point at which he vanished.

"From what distance can your cameras pick up body heat?" I asked Danny.

"About 1000 feet. Ah, 300 metres, that is."

"So, is the thief too far away for your thermal imaging camera to pick him up?"

"Yeah, probably. There was a camera outside the sports footwear store at the time. Their footage showed nothing. The guy vanished."

"Right. So, it's possible he went into the alcove where the compactors and waste are. And then, straight after he vanishes, this woman is the only one around." I pointed at the screen. The woman was tall, streamlined.

"You think the thief is her?" he said surprised. "And you think she was wearing a mask earlier? But she's wearing women's clothing."

"She could have left them in a waste container."

His forehead rippled in a frown. "She's got no backpack with her."

"That could be around the corner, too. Do you have later footage of that night?"

"Yep, but no one turned up."

I sighed in frustration. "What about the next day? Do you still have that footage?"

"Yeah, I kept the whole week."

He looked up the footage and then played it. Early in the morning, employees were arriving. One woman carried a large black, plastic bag to a car and then drove away."

"Her," I said. "Can we backtrack to where she first entered the parking bay?"

He took the footage back a bit.

"She got the bag from where the compactors are," I said.

He shook his head, whistling. "You're right."

Nerves raced up and down the length of my body. Whoever that woman was, she was the thief. And if she was the thief, she was the kidnapper.

Mentally, I noted the licence plate number of the woman's car. I wouldn't run the licence number until I had left the store. I didn't want Danny knowing who she was.

"Danny," I said, "do you have some storage I can borrow? A USB stick? I'd like to copy the footage from that night and the next morning."

"No problem at all." He copied the footage I'd asked for onto a USB and then handed it to me. He had a look of anticipation on his face. "So, what happens now? Will the police be going after this person?"

"Yes," I told him. "Most definitely. For the moment, can I ask that you keep a lid? I need to do some further investigations and then I'll get back to you."

Danny shook his head, grimacing. "I've been waiting a long time for this person to get caught."

Me, too, Danny.

67

KATE

Sprinting to my car, blood roared at my temples, heart galloping in my chest.

I ran the licence plate number.

The name came up.

Shock twisted up inside me.

How could it be *her*?

Every interaction I'd had with her over the past years dashed through my mind. Everything she'd said, every look and gesture.

God, how had I missed this?

Why? Why did she do it? It made no sense. No rhyme. No reason.

I drove over to her house and screeched the car to a stop. Her car wasn't in the driveway. There were no lights on in the house. There was no answer as I banged and rattled on her front door and then ran around to the back and checked the garage.

I raced back to my car and placed her licence plate number on ANPR —the auto number plate recognition system. Any police car passing by her would receive the alert, even from a good distance away. I just needed to wait for a patrol car to pick up her location, and I'd be off and running.

Gathering my breath, I plugged Danny's USB stick into the outlet on my car's onboard computer. I sent it through to Grimshaw and then I called her.

"Wakeland? What's up?"

"I need you to look at the footage I just sent through. I'll talk you through it."

"Now?"

"Yeah. Right now."

Alarms came through on the police ANPR. Patrol cars had passed the suspect in Katoomba. Good, she wasn't far away. *Yet.*

Grimshaw downloaded the footage at her end and began playing it. At my end, I watched the footage on my car's computer screen and pointed out the relevant scenes.

At the end, Grimshaw exhaled a long, heavy breath. "Okay, you've really got something there."

"It's her, right? Undeniable." My voice shook.

"I'd say so. But for the life of me, I can't figure out why she'd do it."

"No, me either. We have to go get her."

"Hold the bus, Wakeland. We need to conduct a proper investigation before we move on this. Give ourselves time to gather more evidence."

"What if we don't have time? What if she just disappears on us?"

"It's almost night. We'll move in first thing in the morning. Just give leave us tonight to look into it further. I know you've lost a granddaughter, Wakeland. But you can't let that affect proper procedure—"

The ANPR pinged again. The suspect had been spotted at Good Forest.

I pulled my car off the road and began heading in that direction.

"The ANPR just pinged her at Good Forest," I told Grimshaw. "I think she's taking the back roads to the highway. We have to get patrol cars onto this. Helicopters. Everything at our disposal."

"We can't do that. She's probably just going for a drive somewhere. And there's a chance that all that we saw on the footage can be explained away."

"Is that what you really think?"

"No, but you have to admit it's not a hundred percent certain. And *who* is her accomplice? Who is Polly?"

"I can't answer that. I don't know. But what I do know is that she's gone, and every second we delay, she's getting further away."

Her sigh was dry and heavy, but also with a distinct note of trepidation. "This could go very wrong. You know that, right?"

"One helicopter. We can do that."

"Okay, I'll get you your patrol cars. I'll contact PolAir. I'll coordinate the live stream. Go find her."

The phone went dead.

I stared at the darkening road ahead, my mind a whirlwind.

Where are you going, Penny Foster?

All this time, it was you. You with your sad eyes and nervous voice and words of sympathy. I'd seen you many times working at the baby goods store, when I went in to buy things when Ivy was a baby. I remember now that you knew all about nanny cams and nursery cameras and streaming devices. I don't know if it was you or Polly who killed Ivy. But whichever way, I'm coming for you.

If she got away, she could disappear. For years if not forever. She'd hidden five children away for three and a half years. She could find a way to hide herself and Max.

The police radio crackled. Penny's car was seen on Mckanes Falls Road, headed north. Okay, so she was headed for the Great Western Highway now. Another alarm sounded. She was now on the highway.

I kept driving towards her location, sending out a message to highway patrol cars to be on the lookout for her. I wouldn't be able to catch her up. That would have to be up to highway patrol.

Ten minutes later, there'd been no more alerts.

There were at least two police patrol cars on the highway who should have passed her. But neither of them had.

Had she turned off the highway? She must have.

I studied the map.

Magpie Hollow Road sat to the west. I made a flying guess she'd exited the highway and taken that road.

Where to now, Penny? Where now?

If I was right about her turning off the highway, then she was currently headed west towards Hampton Road. Hampton Road ran north back to the highway or south where it joined up with Jenolan Caves Road. If she continued going west, she might head onto Hampton and then Sodwalls, and drive towards Bathurst.

They were a set of lonely country back roads in that area. And she'd be a sitting duck. Because she could be fairly easily spotted from the air—as long as we knew her general location. But we didn't know her location. I was just making guesses. I was on the edge of losing her.

She might have simply gotten spooked on the highway and was intending on heading back there within a few minutes. Perhaps she'd spotted one of the patrol cars. If that was true, she should be heading back to the highway now. Otherwise, she would now be driving in a loop, back past Good Forest again.

I heard the thrum of the PolAir helicopter overhead.

"Detective Wakeland," came the voice of the PolAir pilot. "This is Sergeant Hakeem, NSW Aviation."

The police helicopter was about to live stream the traffic footage back to Blue Mountains Police Area Command. Grimshaw was currently monitoring the stream from her end. Hakeem would also be keeping in contact with police officers who came across Penny on the road. Hakeem had been unable to spot Penny's car on the highway and was asking for her current location. But I couldn't answer that with any certainty.

I watched the police helicopter fly overhead.

Did the helicopter spook you, Penny?

There were no more pings coming through. We'd lost her.

I suspected she was taking the back roads in the hope of avoiding police. But she was visible on the back roads, too. I knew for certain that she had at least a basic understanding of thermal imaging. Perhaps she knew or guessed that the helicopter had the thermal imaging capabilities to find her quickly on a lonely back road. And if that was the case, then she would try to hide.

I attempted to form a triangle in my mind, between where I suspected

Penny was now and where she might be headed. She could head north, back to the highway. She could head west, along Sodwalls Road, and enter some pretty open countryside. She could backtrack east along Magpie Hollow Road, but she'd be going back towards Katoomba—and I thought she'd be feeling like a rat in a trap right now and wanting to get away.

That left south. Along Hampton Road. Lots of tree cover, especially where it joined Jenolan Caves Road. But, if she kept going, that would mean a steep climb up a narrow mountain road and then down again to the caves—and almost no way out along that road for her.

I kept coming back to the imagery in my mind of a scared animal seeking cover. Penny had done terrible things. But she was still the person who I'd known. Police often didn't know the character of a person they were pursuing. But I did. I'd known her now for over three years. She was a nervous, highly skittish kind of person. She hadn't been faking that—not entirely. She was probably terrified of being caught.

I guessed that she wasn't thinking clearly. She wanted to disappear. She'd lost her chance to get out on the highway. We'd come after her too soon. I was certain she hadn't expected anyone to come after her.

But where would she go?

The PolAir helicopter would be able to spot her on the country roads. All it would take would be a police vehicle on the ground to read her licence plate number. Penny would know this. She and Polly had been clever enough to evade detection when they'd kidnapped the children and when they'd returned them.

If Penny was running scared, she could be taking the road to the caves. Once she'd reached a certain point, no one could cut her off or stop her—no one from this side of the caves, anyway.

But the fact that there was only one road was also to her disadvantage. The road went to a natural tourist attraction, the Jenolan Caves. There was a rock tunnel to travel through—the Grand Arch, 180 metres long, with a soaring high roof. Cave systems led off the tunnel. Beyond the tunnel, sat the historical Caves House—a sprawling, four-storey Sussex Wealden style hotel built in the mid-1800s.

Could Penny be thinking of stopping there and renting a room? There was no underground parking. Nowhere for Penny to hide her car. Unless she thought she'd outwitted us, and we didn't have a trace on her vehicle—which we certainly didn't.

The hotel ground and the small, surrounding village had only one way out, a road of hairpin turns through bushland and up Mount Trickett. And then into Oberon. But it was snowing towards Oberon. I looked up the weather report. Yes, thick snow cover.

I traced a finger back along the roads. If she'd intended heading to Oberon, she would have peeled off from Jenolan Caves Road onto Duckmaloi Road back when she had the chance.

It was all guesswork on my part. She could have gone in any of a number of directions. She could be waiting somewhere, trying to hide out.

I rubbed my forehead, trying to get my thinking clear. Then made calls to the police helicopter and the police vehicles that had picked up on her vehicle when she'd been on the highway.

I had to make a decision, one way or another.

Penny wasn't silly. She wouldn't have headed towards the snow where her vehicle would get bogged. At least, I hoped she wouldn't. I assumed she had a little boy in her car. Max. If snow began falling, her car would soon get covered, and if she ran out of petrol to run the car's heater or if she tried to run with Max somewhere through the snow, they'd freeze.

An insane thought came to me.

If Penny was running as scared as I imagined she was, she could try to hide somewhere dark and enclosed—somewhere her car couldn't be seen by even the best-equipped PolAir helicopter. It was crazy, but she could be thinking that the best place to wait us out was in the Grand Arch—the rock tunnel right at the Jenolan Caves. There wasn't much wriggle room in the tunnel road, but there was an area inside and to the right that she could conceivably park. She could claim to have car trouble if she were questioned by the tourist operators there. When she felt safe enough, she could attempt to head back to the highway again.

Grimshaw called. "Talk to me, Wakeland."

"We lost her."

"Tell me something I don't know."

"I have an idea."

"Oh?"

"I can't be certain of this, but I have a hunch she's going to try to hide at the caves. Under the arch."

A band of silence stretched thin between us. "You think *what?*"

"Look... I'm going to ask that police block the other side—if it's safe. I don't know if there's snowfall on that side of the caves right now. Or at least, get the 'copter to keep watch while I get there."

"That's kind of crazy."

"I know. *It is.*"

"She'd have to be pretty scattered to attempt that."

It was my turn for a moment of silence. "Is it my imagination, or have you stopped questioning that Penny abducted the kids?"

She exhaled a low grunt. "I just watched that footage of the camera robbery. The guy walked like a dude on the way in. Had a different tilt to his hips on the way out. Like the way a woman would walk. It looked like the person was scared and wanted to make off with their haul and forgot to keep up the act."

"I didn't notice that. I don't think anyone else did, either. We were all too busy trying to get a clear look at his face."

"Yeah, well, I notice things like that. And Penny has that walk. I've seen her stride. I remember it."

"What do you think of my tunnel hideout idea?"

"It's as good as any. Let's go for it."

She kept me on the phone while she directed PolAir and the police pursuit vehicles. There were to be no police sirens. The helicopter was to stay at a distance away.

Within two minutes, we had everything in place.

"Good luck," she said to me finally. "But, remember, no heroic chases. She's probably got the kid in her car. And that's a dangerous road for a chase. We'd never hear the end of it from the public if something happened."

"I know." I steered onto Jenolan Caves Road.

"And there's still room for error," she warned me. "Despite everything.

That one percent chance that she had nothing to do with the kidnappings, after all."

"Got it."

The phone went dead. She was gone. For the first time—*ever*—her voice had been of comfort. I almost wished she'd stayed on the line.

Drifts of fog accompanied me on the drive up the mountain. Twilight crawled from the dark spaces between the trees, spilling onto the road.

There was something about this road and where it led. Its caves were ancient and the birthplace of legends and stories of ghosts. The local indigenous Gundungurra tribes called the area *Binoomea*, meaning *Dark Places*.

Exhaustion steam-trained through me, to the tips of my toes and fingers and making my head heavy as a bowling ball. There had been days of no sleep, of running ragged, of desolation at finding the Megalong Valley house. The day of not finding my mother outside on the grounds of the hospice and thinking the worst. The day of feeling such deep sorrow when holding Harper Rawlings's mother.

This wasn't a place for driving in mental and physical exhaustion. I had to focus. I sensed that I had a deep well of energy to draw upon if I needed it. I was fuelled by the desire to see this through to the end.

You and me, Penny, we have something in common right now. Both of us feeling the same kind of intense drive. You wanting escape and me wanting to stop you.

On the left-hand side of me, the land fell away into a valley of trees. The higher I ascended, the deeper the valley. Until even the treetops sat far below the road, half-shrouded in mist. It was eerie looking down from the cliff edge at the ghostly tree tops.

The barrier along the side of the narrow two-way road was a kind of wire-mesh that seemed just a couple of feet tall, the short wooden posts that it was nailed to following the sharp bends of the road, a few of the posts fallen down. A high rock wall loomed on the right-hand side.

A line of fog tumbled down from the higher altitude.

It was not a road to lose concentration on.

An alert sounded on my dash board.

My focus had been captured by my immediate surroundings. But my car's ANPR system had picked up on the vehicle ahead.

Penny's car.

She was not far away.

Mentally, I readjusted my plan. I no longer had to wonder whether I was right or wrong about her location and what I'd do if I didn't find her. I just had to ensure nothing went wrong from here.

I called Grimshaw. "Penny is on Jenolan Caves Road, proceeding to the caves. Request police blockade be in place on the other side."

"Well done, Wakeland. Take it easy from here."

I could scarcely breathe. "Will do."

I lost Penny again around the bend. But she couldn't go anywhere else. There was just this road and no side streets now. Just the rock wall to the right and the cliff edge to the left.

We continued along the road, me behind her. The slowest *police pursuit* of my career.

Hanging back, I kept out of Penny's sight. It was unlikely she'd spot me in the car behind her in this dark light and mist. But she might guess. And if she was in the state of mind I suspected she was, she could do something extreme and try to drive off the road. Or she could careen into an oncoming car.

If she died, I'd never have the answers I so desperately wanted. I'd never know what happened to Ivy and what she'd done with her. I might never find out who Polly was. And Max could die, too, and he didn't deserve for that to happen.

When I came around the corner, my car's headlights hit the back of her SUV. She must have slowed to a crawl.

I stopped, breathing hard. Why was she going so slow?

I caught a split-second glimpse of the interior.

A set of tiny hands were planted against the back window. Max's small face stared back at me.

The window went dark again as Penny moved off.

If you saw me, Max, don't tell your mother. Please.

The road began its descent now.

I was light-headed. Not enough oxygen in the air. Too much damned mist.

I continued the crawl along the road as it dropped lower and lower. I gave Penny plenty of room. If she now knew I was behind her, she gave no indication. No speeding up or driving erratically. That was good, because new hazards lay head. *People.* Tourists would be staying at the Victorian-age hotel that lay just beyond the tunnel. People might still be walking about.

We were about to cross the tiny stone bridge that stood over Blue River.

The Grand Arch rock tunnel loomed ahead, enormous and soaring in scale.

I entered the tunnel.

Penny's car was just up ahead. She'd driven off to the side and stopped.

I slowed.

Was she baiting me? Waiting to see if I'd park and get out of the car, and then she'd drive off?

Another thought flashed in my mind.

What if she'd already gotten out and fled?

There were a dozen or so caves here that she could run into with Max, some of them leading directly off The Grand Arch. I'd been through them all—*The Ribbon Cave, the Orient, The Temple of Baal, The Devil's Coach House* and others. There were certainly places to go off the tourist path within the cave systems.

She'd have to get past the barriers of the caves that had paid tours, which was almost all of them. But if she were motivated enough, she could find a way to slip in unnoticed.

There was nothing to do except to park and to go and confront her—if she was indeed still in her car.

I parked near the entrance and jumped out. Fog crept inside the cave, curling around the edges of the opening and veiling the view ahead.

The Grand Arch was vastly high and eerily empty in the way that a cathedral with no parishioners inside would be. Perhaps the mist had scared tourists away and into their warm hotel rooms tonight. Or perhaps no night tours were running—I thought I remembered they only ran on weekends.

"Penny," I called before reaching the car. "It's Kate. I want to talk to you."

My voice echoed in hollow staccato, my throat tightening around each word. My attempt to sound calm and reassuring had failed.

"Penny?" I stepped up to the driver's window.

A figure sat rigidly upright in the seat, hands still gripping the wheel. Penny. The engine was off.

She stared ahead, eyes unfocused. Her hair brushed back tightly in a ponytail and her face colourless.

I tried the door handle. It was unlocked.

"Penny, I'm glad you stopped." I glanced over her head. Max sat in the backseat, a blanket around his shoulders and a stack of blankets beside him. I shot him a smile.

Reaching gently across Penny's arm, I slipped the key from the ignition. "I'm going to come around and sit here beside you, while we wait for help. Okay?"

She still didn't look at me.

Stepping away slightly, I made a call to Grimshaw. "I'm with Penny now. I'm going to wait with her until help arrives."

"Is her son unharmed?"

"Yes. As far as I can see."

"Good work. I'll have backup there within minutes."

"Thank you."

I walked around and sat myself in the front passenger seat.

"Are you alright, Penny?" I asked.

In response, she slightly turned her face away.

A desperate wish rose inside me, rattling me to the core. I wanted to shake her violently and demand to know how she could have hurt Ivy and what she did with her. I wanted to punch her head until she spoke. The sudden, white-hot rage frightened me.

But I couldn't even attempt to question her. Even if Penny did answer me, her answers wouldn't be anything Max should have to hear.

If I couldn't keep a lid on it, I'd have to get out of the car.

Whitish streams of air passed between my lips. The air was freezing in the car. Penny hadn't had the heater on.

"Are you cold, Max?" I asked, turning my head.

He shook his head. But he seemed scared.

Did he know that his mother was one of the kidnappers? Or was she able to keep that hidden from him for over three years? I suspected that he'd been clueless. She'd always worn the mask when showing herself to the kids. But he must be aware that something was terribly wrong with his mother tonight.

"Some police are going to come here in a minute," I told Max. "It'll be okay. You'll be warm and have something to eat, and you'll soon be with people who you know."

I hoped that the Parrish family might be able to take him, while things were being sorted. Max and Elijah had been good friends. I'd ask them, anyway.

A distant sound of car engines rumbled in the air. The backup was approaching. They were from Oberon Police Command, but they were very familiar with the case of the five missing children.

The Oberon police vehicles drove in from the opposite end of the tunnel, emerging from the darkness.

I stepped from the car.

"Detective Wakeland?" said an officer. "I'm Senior Constable McMulland. We've got a paramedic with us and an ambulance. In case you needed it." He had a vaguely Irish accent.

"Great. Thank you. I think Penny might need looking at. She seems to be in shock." I indicated towards her SUV. "Max needs checking over, just in case. He's scared, poor little guy."

Suddenly, police were everywhere. Setting up bright lights. Taking photographs and video of the car—of Penny inside the car, and of Max looking out at them from the window. Even of me. An officer helped Penny from her seat, wrapping a silver thermal blanket around her.

As the police took the footage, I realised that as well as being the usual police procedure, this footage would one day provide evidence of a historic event. Part of the lore of the land, just like every strange case that had ever occurred in these mountains.

I had to step away and be alone for a minute. This hadn't been just a strange case. It was part of the story of my family. A tragic story. There was no celebration inside me, no closure. I faced the tunnel entrance, looking directly into darkness.

"Detective," McMulland called. "We didn't realise there was a second child?"

I spun around, not comprehending his words.

"The little girl," he said.

My legs were dead wood as I made my way back to Penny's car. The entire world had slowed.

A girl was sitting beside Max in the back seat of the SUV, her eyes heavy with sleep, dark hair long and tousled around her large eyes and pointed chin.

Everything compressed itself to a single point, a single word.

Ivy.

The child looked like a mini-Abby.

She was undeniably Ivy. *Alive and in front of me.*

All breath left my lungs. Silently, I mouthed her name.

She'd been under what I'd thought was just a stack of blankets. My gaze dropped to her small hands, in which she was clutching a wooden airplane.

An officer brought Max out from his seat, wrapping him up in a thermal blanket.

Someone handed me one of the blankets. Taking it, I helped Ivy from the car and then wrapped her snugly. I felt her small body in my arms, real and solid.

"*You're okay, now,*" I whispered in a breaking voice. "*You're okay, Ivy.*"

68

KATE

Abby rushed towards me in the hospital waiting room—in faded jeans and a white cotton hoodie that was far too thin to guard against the chilly night.

A young man walked in behind her. Logan. Jasper was in his arms. All I could see of the baby was the peak of his tiny knit hat.

Abby grabbed my arms, trembling and gasping. "Mum. Is it really true? You found Ivy?" Her voice rose to a shriek.

I hugged her tightly. "Yes, honey. She's here."

She dissolved into tears, her hand reaching across her mouth. "Where is she? Oh God, I can't believe I'm going to see her again."

"She's sleeping. She's exhausted. Of course you can see her. I'll take you in."

Abby reached for Logan's hand.

He shook his head. "This is your moment. Between mother and daughter."

"No, you're coming with me," Abby insisted tearfully. "You're my family. I want her to see you both."

Logan gave a small smile. "Plenty of time for that. Besides, Ivy might get confused if she wakes and the first thing she sees is a strange, hairy dude and a baby." He thumbed his goatee. "Now, go. I'll be out here waiting."

I smiled gratefully at Logan. The first encounters I'd had with him had been plagued by dire circumstances. I'd been wrong about him in every way, and somehow, I had to atone for that.

Abby seemed uncertain as she walked with me, turning back to look at him and Jasper. "Mum," she said in a half-whisper, "what if she doesn't remember me?"

"She will, given time. It's been hard for all the kids. They were practically babies when they were taken. It'll take lots of love, but it'll be fine. I promise."

We headed down the hospital corridor, to the hospital room where Ivy slept. Pete sat in a chair next to the curtain. Standing, he stepped over to hug Abby.

In that moment, I was terrified that when we pulled the curtain back, Ivy would be gone. Like a dandelion in the wind.

But when Pete slid the curtain away, my fears were groundless. A little girl in a hospital gown slept peacefully on her pillow.

Abby burst into tears, then covered her mouth so as not to wake Ivy.

She bent low, examining Ivy's profile. "*Oh, God...* it's her. It really is. It's Ivy. Look how she's grown. She's... beautiful. Absolutely beautiful."

Ivy's eyelids fluttered and opened.

Abby looked panicked. "I woke her...."

Ivy half-sat, shrinking back at first, looking around at the hospital equipment next to her and then focusing on Abby.

"This is your mummy, Ivy," I said gently.

Ivy glanced from me to Abby, her expression so unsure I knew it must be breaking Abby's heart.

Reaching below the covers, Ivy brought out her wooden airplane. Half-sitting, she ran a tiny finger over the painted, smooth surfaces and then spun one of the landing wheels.

"I love your plane." Abby smiled through her tears. "You always loved planes. You had one, at home. You would take it everywhere. And you'd run about flying it through the air. I told you once that we would go on a big airplane, to somewhere nice. If you like, we'll do that one day soon."

A small, uncertain smile played on Ivy's lips.

Moving closer, Abby put her arms around her little girl.

Ivy didn't lean into the hug, but she didn't resist.

It was the first step.

Lots of time. Lots of love. We'd get there.

69

KATE

Over the next three days, Ivy underwent medical assessments and DNA swabs, just as the other children had. The authorities had to be certain that she was indeed Ivy Wakeland.

Abby, Pete, and I didn't need convincing. She was our Ivy.

Penny had kept Ivy locked away in her garage ever since the day the other four children had been returned. She'd kept Ivy drugged. That was all we knew so far. We now guessed that Ivy had been drugged when the children had seen her lying on the grass at the Megalong Valley house. And we guessed that covering her with sticks and telling the children that she'd died had been a ruse, something Penny and Polly knew the other children would tell on their return.

It'd stung me hard to discover that Ivy had been at Penny's garage for days, including when the birthday parties were held. Ivy should have been blowing out her birthday candles herself.

Ivy was disoriented and unsure in those first days in the hospital. The effects of Penny's drugs would take time to wear off, doctors advised us. We had lots of hugs and played little games with her, gently bringing her back into the world. Dr Zhang was there to guide us every step of the way.

On the third day, Abby introduced Jasper to her. Ivy loved him on sight but couldn't accept that he was her brother. She'd found that concept too strange.

Early days.

Penny had been taken to a psychiatric hospital. She'd been undergoing treatment for shock. So far, she wasn't speaking. And we desperately needed her to. We'd been unable to track down the mysterious Polly.

A week passed before a doctor cleared Penny to talk with us. Even then, she was under suicide watch and had to remain in the hospital.

I met Grimshaw and Booth outside the psychiatric facility.

"How are we tackling this, ladies?" Booth had a grimmer set to her mouth than I'd ever seen before.

"Good guys," replied Grimshaw without hesitation.

I nodded. "She's fragile, from what I've seen."

"She stole five kids and kept them stashed for over three years," Booth remarked. "She's not that fragile. She'd have to have a core of steel. I say we apply some heat."

"You do you," Grimshaw told her. "Wakeland and I will tread more gently. Especially Wakeland. She knows why."

Booth's gaze tracked over my face. "You've got to hold back because of the family connection, yes?"

I nodded. "Yeah. Plus, I just want to find out who Polly is. I don't want Penny clamming up."

My rage had gone on simmer when Ivy had come back to us alive. Still, the raw sense of loss remained. Penny and Polly had stolen years from my family.

We walked inside the hospital and were shown to an office by a psychiatrist. He briefly explained what we had already been told. Penny was of sane mind and fully aware of what she'd done. So far, she'd said nothing except to agree that she'd been behind the kidnapping plot.

Penny sat inside the room, alone. She was even more gaunt than the last time I'd seen her, with dark hollows beneath her eyes. She wore a white cardigan with pearl buttons and had a thick grey scarf bundled around her neck. Her pants were a charcoal colour. She kept her ash-blonde hair back in its customary severe ponytail. The entire effect was almost monochrome, as if she were a figure of yesteryear sitting in a room that was in full colour.

The surrounding walls and furnishings were decorated in shades of green and yellow. Six plush armchairs were arranged in a semi-circle. Sun shone in from the large window. I couldn't imagine a less intimidating setting for a police interview.

Grimshaw, Booth and I sat on seats facing Penny.

"Penny," Grimshaw began. "How are you?"

"The way I look might sum that up, Detective," she answered.

Grimshaw proceeded to read out her rights and tell her that the interview would be recorded. Penny raised her face to gaze at the spots of sunlight on the ceiling. For one heart stopping moment I thought she would tell us she wanted to keep her silence. Just as one last nose-thumbing at the police. But she didn't. She agreed to talk.

Grimshaw began the recording.

Booth tapped the end of her pencil on her notepad. "I'm going to come right out and ask. Who is Polly?"

Penny stretched each side of her cardigan around her thin body. "I suppose you have the right to know," she said, but she didn't elaborate.

"Yes, we do," I said. "Can you tell us her real name?"

"Her name really is Polly. Polly Mulden." She toyed with a button of her cardigan as she spoke.

My spirits leapt. Penny had given us a name, practically right off the bat. It was a good start.

Grimshaw's brow indented furiously as she looked up the name on her phone.

I followed up fast with, "Where can we find her, Penny?"

"She left town on the day we returned the children," Penny told me. "I don't know where she went. She didn't want me to know."

Frustrated, I raked my bottom lip through my teeth. "And what is her connection to you?"

"Sister," Penny answered simply.

Grimshaw's lips fell open. "Your sister? I thought you didn't have any siblings?"

Penny studied the pearl button that she held between her thumb and forefinger, seeming to watch how it reflected the light. "I know everyone is going crazy speculating about me. But they don't understand anything about me."

"Then help us to understand," I said, attempting to keep my tone neutral.

"No one can understand," Penny told me in an admonishing voice. "Ever. They didn't have the life that I've had."

"How about you tell us?" I said. "We're here to listen." The words grated on my tongue. I didn't want to know her life story. We weren't her psychiatrists. We were here to know what happened just before and during the past three and a half years.

Penny kept her focus on the tiny spherical button, as if it held secrets. "Oh yes, of course you are. I'm not silly, Kate. Nothing that I say can possibly help me. Your job is to set up a case for the courts to lock me away for as many years as possible. And for you it's also personal. Because of Ivy."

I noticed Booth was like a loaded gun, impatient to fire off another of her direct questions. Grimshaw glanced her way, giving a discreet shake of her head.

Taking a steadying breath, I tried to remember my notes about Penny. "You grew up in Sydney, right? You attended an independent school in Vaucluse?"

Penny shook her head. "All that was an invention. Well, not entirely. I attended that school for a period of nine weeks, while I stayed with a temporary foster carer." She raised her face to me. "I grew up in the upper mountains."

I frowned. "Upper *Blue* Mountains?"

Penny nodded.

"I can't find a Polly Mulden," Grimshaw remarked.

"Oh, you won't," said Penny. "Polly's name is Madeline Brightwaters now. All our names were changed. Due to the family scandal. There were eleven of us. Different fathers, different mothers." A sad laugh rose from her throat. "I still don't know which ones were my biological parents. Nor do I care. Not anymore. It was a cult, you see. The adults considered the nuclear family to be passé and bourgeois. In those exact words."

"Hang on," said Grimshaw. "I've read about this. A family of kids and adults who lived at the old Mulden property. It was before my time. I wasn't even in the police force then."

Penny began examining her buttons again. "That's right. The Mulden farm. We were wild. No showers. Perhaps a bath once a month, except in winter. Always dirt under the fingernails."

"Refresh me on what went on there," said Grimshaw.

"I was about seven years old when the scandal broke us apart," Penny began. "That was thirty years ago. What happened is that one of my brothers was found in a cave. Tied up, dirty and half-starved. He was fourteen. At first, authorities blamed a homeless person, saying he'd kept my brother a prisoner in that cave. But we knew better. It was one of my fathers... One of the mean ones. Most of them were mean. And the mothers just drank all the time and didn't care. The police started investigating, asking which kid belonged to who. And no one knew. Even the mothers said they'd forgotten whose child was whose."

I listened closely. I'd been working in Sydney thirty years ago, for the state homicide squad. I'd briefly heard about the family, but it hadn't been my area of interest. It had been a matter for child protection.

"That sounds awful. About the beatings and starvation," I said. "So, Polly is one of your sisters?"

"Yes," she answered. "She's a similar age to me. There were no official birth certificates. So, none of us were certain exactly how old we were."

Grimshaw threaded her fingers together, forming a steeple. "Whose idea was it to take the children? Yours or Polly's?"

Penny sighed deeply. "Mine."

Booth leaned in. "Why did you take the kids, Penny?"

Penny's shoulders quivered. "I tried hard to put my past all behind me. It was when I had Max that it all rose up inside me again. I couldn't be the parent he needed. Nothing came naturally to me. He was a standoffish baby from the start. He had allergies. He whined and cried a lot. And then my husband left me. Of course he did. No one could love me. Not even

Max." She stopped, looking squarely at each of us. "On the night that Max was returned, the reason he took so long to come home was because he didn't want to. I thought Polly must have run into a problem with dropping Max off. I didn't know what to do. But when Max finally came home, I discovered that he stalled so long because he wanted to stay with Polly and the other children, at the Megalong Valley house. He remembered me, his own mother, and he didn't want to come back. Do you know how hurtful that is?"

I was beginning to realise that Max must have had a very difficult time with Penny when he was small.

"I never had a perfect, loving family," Penny continued. "And then I'd go into the nursery school and see all these perfect families, who would never know what I'd been through. It began to twist my mind. Other families had children who would never be starved or beaten or made to sleep on the dirt under the house."

I winced at her words. A young child forced to go and sleep on the dirt beneath a house at night was unthinkable.

Grimshaw hooked her eyebrows upwards at Penny. "You're saying you were jealous?"

Penny nodded. "I couldn't turn those thoughts off...."

The next question came from a deep place within me. "Why did you choose Ivy, then, Penny? Abby was a young, single mother with lots of problems. You can't have been jealous of her, surely?"

Penny's shoulders curled inward. "Because she had *you*. I'd see you coming into the preschool to pick Ivy up. I'd see you in the park with her or taking her shopping. Ivy had you as her protector from the day she was born. I've never had anyone protecting *me*. I was always just something to kick around and abuse."

To an extent, I understood her pain. But there were undercurrents of confusion. "How did you think taking the children would help you?"

She seemed to deliberate on her answer, eyes darting around the room. "I told you that none of you would understand. You can't. You've never had my pain. It was stupid, of course it was. But the pain just grew intolerable. It hounded me. It was a thousand birds chattering in my head. Relentlessly.

And then I had the idea that I could snatch away the comfort from other people's lives." Her fingers trembled, and she clenched one hand over the other in an attempt to quell the shakes.

I watched Booth straighten her back, about to launch into another question. Grimshaw gave her another small shake of her head. This was the second interview I'd been in with Grimshaw and I'd realised she was all about timing.

Turning my attention back to Penny, I noticed what Grimshaw had noticed. Penny had more to say, but she was assembling her thoughts. I felt impatience climbing inside me. But I waited.

Penny twisted her fingers around each other, as if she had dirt she needed to wipe off them. "I took the children because I had to. I always intended to give them back. I'm not a monster."

"Did you always intend keeping them for years?" I said.

Penny shook her head, sighing heavily. "It was only meant to be a few months, at first. But I guess... I fed on your pain. On the pain of all of you. It made me feel better. And then there was so much attention on all of us—the parents. For the first time in my life, people were acknowledging my pain, my hurt. They felt sorry for me. It made me feel... loved."

"I've seen your blog," I told her. "I saw the last poem you wrote, the night Max was returned."

"It was to be the last poem," she said in a sorry tone. "Because I intended to disappear. I'd given everyone their children back and soon Max was coming home. And then I'd have to leave."

"You didn't give Ivy back. Why?" My throat felt as if it were stuffed with cotton like a rag doll. I'd had to push the words out.

"I couldn't," Penny told me. "I intended to. But on the day I was to return the children, Ivy happened to see me without my mask. She unexpectedly came into the bedroom when I was talking with my sister. She'd come in to ask what her mother's name was. I'd taken the mask off for a minute, as I was itching underneath it. I told Ivy her mother's name was Abby, without realising the mask was off, without realising I wasn't using the voice modulator."

It was immensely difficult to hear the account of what really happened that day. "And then what?" I asked in a hoarse voice.

"We locked her in the bedroom," Penny replied, "and then my sister and I went out to the kitchen and had a fast, frantic discussion. We couldn't let her go back to her family. Polly got her sleeping pills, and we crushed them up and we got Ivy to drink it. Then we carried her out to the lawn and laid her out on the grass. It was Polly's idea to place sticks all over her and to get me to dig a hole. Polly always was the creative one. We told the children Ivy had been sick, that she'd died."

"Why..." I started, but my voice went to a whisper. I cleared my throat and regained control over myself. "Why was it important to have the children think that Ivy had died?"

She blinked nervously. "Because I hoped you'd stop looking for her as intently. I hoped you'd leave the task force, or better still, leave the police force altogether. And also, people wouldn't be looking for Ivy anymore if they thought she was dead...."

Her thinking was so disordered, so desperate. Believing that Ivy had died hadn't dampened my desire to find her. All it had done was to turn my attention more acutely onto her kidnappers.

"What did you intend doing with Ivy... the day I found you? Where were you going?"

She took a full thirty seconds or more to answer, her face drawing taut. "I don't know... it was supposed to be a new life for Max and me. Somewhere else. But Ivy ruined it. I didn't know what to do. I didn't know where to go. This wasn't supposed to happen...."

I sat back in my seat, flexing my back and shoulders and trying to relieve the tension. She was telling the truth. She really had no plan that day. She'd been running scared, just like I'd thought.

"Going back to the day you returned the children," said Liz Booth to Penny, "tell us how that was planned?"

Penny swallowed, nodding. Her words tumbled over each other when she spoke. "It was a rush... A huge rush, as you can imagine. Polly and I had been getting rid of everything from the house for days. We got rid of it all. So much work. The kids slept on sleeping bags in the play barn on the last three nights—while Polly and I cleaned and bleached the house from floor to ceiling. It was exhausting. *So* exhausting. And then on the day of the returns, we had to get the children ready and also figure out how to do it without being seen... We decided I would wait at my house, and Polly would return the children. We watched the parents online and found out where they all were."

"And Ivy?" inquired Booth. "What did you do with her?"

Penny dropped her head, taking deep, quick breaths. "Don't judge me harshly. It was all last minute. The children were assembled outside and then blindfolded. We put four of the children into Polly's van and Polly drove away. And then I put Ivy into my car. She was sleeping, of course. I drove her to my house, straight into the garage, and made a comfortable bed for her in there. She was being cared for. I did what I had to do...."

She grew increasingly anxious, fiddling with her cardigan buttons again and breathing faster.

Grimshaw, Booth and I exchanged quick glances with each other.

Penny was fast unravelling. The interview might have to end. But we might not get another chance with her before this went to trial—which could be months or even years away.

Grimshaw took control. "Can we get you a drink, Penny? A coffee or tea?"

Penny nodded. "Coffee. Strong. Black."

Booth rose from her seat. "I'll go grab one. Anyone else?"

"Get us all a coffee, thanks Liz," Grimshaw told her. "Actually, tea for me. Coffee makes me a little hyper."

It was the right call. Penny might relax a little if we took a break.

70

KATE

Liz Booth returned with a tray of coffee and biscuits, and we recommenced.

"There's something I'm curious about," said Grimshaw, nibbling at a biscuit, as if this were just a chat among friends. "What happened, exactly, the day the kids went missing? How did you manage it?"

Penny gulped a mouthful of coffee, refusing the biscuits that Booth offered her. "It wasn't the first attempt... I'd had everything set up three times previously. But things didn't go right. There wasn't a moment in which I could do it without being seen. But then I had a lucky break."

Grimshaw dipped her biscuit in her tea. "What was the break?"

"Nola," she answered.

"Oh?" Grimshaw raised her eyebrows.

Penny nodded, setting her gaze on her cup of coffee. "I heard at the nursery school that she was to join the Flying Fox group. I also knew, from watching the children's picnic on three earlier occasions that the ice-cream van stopped there at a certain time. And... I knew something about Nola."

"What did you know?" Grimshaw grabbed another biscuit from the tray.

"I knew that Nola had a phobia about ice-cream vans. She must have had a terrible experience as a young girl." She paused, lifting her shoulders in a sigh. "And I know that because her mother is one of my sisters."

I stopped myself from gasping. "Nola's mother is one of your sisters? Do you mean that she's Polly?"

"She's not Polly." Penny said. "Her name was Maude when I was a child. She has a different name now. She's nine years older than me, and she's my least favourite sibling. Always so cruel."

"How does this connect to Nola and her phobia?" I asked.

"I saw the phobia for myself," Penny replied. "One year, when I was about twenty-six, I swallowed my pride and went to see her. I needed money. I was completely broke and desperate. She got me work doing... well, you know, nude videos. I saw Nola at the house a few of those times. She was still a kid. About thirteen, I think."

"So, Nola knows you are her aunt?" Grimshaw asked.

Penny shook her head. "No, she has no idea. She just thought I was a friend of her mother's. My family... none of us acknowledge each other. We're basically strangers to each other."

Grimshaw kept her tone casual but her eyes were intent. "And how exactly did you discover that Nola has a phobia?"

Penny sipped her coffee. "One day, I was sitting on Maude's front porch with her and Nola, when an ice-cream van went by. I asked Nola if she wanted some money to buy an ice-cream. But she just started humming weirdly and went into a kind of trance. Maude laughed and said that she had a phobia about the vans. She didn't explain why. And then... about four years ago, I saw Nola in the street. She was doing the same weird thing. Standing there and zoning out. When I heard the *Greensleeves* tune in the distance, then I remembered."

Booth frowned. "So, you're telling us that you used this phobia of Nola's on the day that you took the kids?"

Penny bent her head in a nod.

"And then what?" asked Booth. "Did it work?"

"Yes," Penny told her. "When the van came along, it worked much better than I anticipated. Nola actually left the kids to walk up the hill. That left one teacher and an inexperienced teenager looking after the kids.

And both of them were busy setting up the picnic. I was hiding between the trees, at the entrance to the boardwalk. I had my mask on and the voice modulator microphone in place. I wore men's clothing. And I had a basket of treats. They're not allowed to have chocolates at the nursery school, so my basket was fairly enticing. I was all ready." She breathed deeply, seeming almost proud of how well she'd planned it.

Booth pulled her eyebrows into a line of vertical creases. "But, how did you manage to take the five kids that you wanted?"

"It wasn't that difficult," Penny said. "Nola was gone. Justine was busy breaking up a fight between a couple of the kids. And Kaylee had stopped setting up the picnic to film some of the kids. Kaylee was only filming what was happening directly in front of her. She had no idea what was happening just out of her view. I tossed a ball towards Max. The ball was on a string. Max came running for the ball. I stepped out a little and told him that I had special picnic treats for the children who'd behaved the best and I told him which children to get. But he had to whisper it to each of them so that no one else heard. He rounded the kids up quickly. Max is obedient like that."

"And the kids came over to you?" Grimshaw asked, listening closely.

"Yes, they did," Penny confirmed. "It wasn't difficult from that point. I told them it was a big surprise, and we hurried along the boardwalk to the van."

Grimshaw, Booth and I sat in silence for a moment. We finally knew how that day had played out.

"And you took them straight back to the house?" Grimshaw asked.

"Yes," said Penny.

Booth drank down the last of her coffee. "Was Polly already there waiting?"

"Yes, she was." Penny bit her lip. "They were well-looked after, right from the start. Don't think they were mistreated. Polly made them cakes and played games with them. Of course, they cried that first night, and perhaps a few nights after that. But it didn't take long for them to settle in. I didn't go there much, but I watched every night from my computer screen. I put them to bed every night—on the screen. I'd wear the mask with the bear ears every single night and sing them songs and make sure they brushed their teeth."

A musing look came over Penny's face. "It was easier, in many ways, than having Max at home. I didn't know how to love him. I don't like... *physical contact.*" She shuddered, nursing her now-empty coffee cup. "But Max and the children loved me when they saw me on screen. It was like I was there."

"You were everywhere... and nowhere...." Grimshaw remarked.

Penny blinked, glancing over at Grimshaw and looking shaken. "I see that the children told you that."

"Naturally," said Grimshaw.

"Who set the cameras up that you stole?" said Booth bluntly. "You or Polly?"

Penny recoiled. "You know that I stole them?"

"Uh huh," Booth replied.

"Well," said Penny, composing herself. "I needed the cameras. For the children's sake. I couldn't afford to buy them all, so I had to steal some extras. They're *expensive.* I was already paying for the rent and quite a lot of food and things for the children."

Grimshaw flicked biscuit crumbs from her trouser knees then levelled her gaze at Penny. "What made you decide to give the kiddies back when you did?"

Penny gestured in my direction. "*Kate.* It was when Kate was put on the strike force team. I was afraid that I'd be found out. Every time she looked at me, I felt as if she could see straight through me, even though, of course, she couldn't. She was worse than the rest of the police. She was Ivy's *protector,* you know? And when I read in the news that she'd found out about Nola and her phobia, I started to panic. It felt as if she were closing in. I decided it was time... to bring the children back."

"I have a question for you," said Liz Booth to Penny. "Why did Polly agree to any of this?"

"Polly was just drifting through life," Penny said. "She'd spent most of her years in therapy. Doing this gave her a purpose, maybe for the first time ever. It wasn't hard to convince her."

Swallowing, she turned to face me. Her top lip quivered. "I didn't do anything too wrong... not really. The children had a good time... at the house. Polly and I kept them just the way they were when they first came to live there. They stayed age three. Innocent. There were no disappointments for them. No changes. Everyone will see. I'm not a terrible person." She shook her head rigidly. "I'm not."

71

KATE

We found Polly, aka Madeline Brightwaters, two days later. She'd made it all the way to New Zealand.

In a police interview, Polly confirmed everything Penny had said. She sounded regretful to have had to give the children back. She came across like a simple, pleasant sort of person, the type that would be easy to manipulate. She'd enjoyed baking, growing vegetables and caring for the children. She'd lived a directionless life after being rescued from the Mulden farm as a child. Unlike Penny, she hadn't wanted to talk about her childhood at all, becoming disturbed by the mere mention of it. Penny had laid out the exact plan for her to follow on the day she'd returned the children—what to do and where to park to remain undetected.

Would Penny and Polly have returned the children if they hadn't become scared they'd be exposed? I didn't think so. They might have kept them until they'd become teenagers, fleeing from place to place with them.

If life at the Mulden farm had been as awful as Penny said it was, then she and Polly might get a much lighter jail sentence than I'd anticipated. The thought of that terrified me. But I'd cross that bridge when I came to it.

After all the events of the past week, I felt entirely depleted, but also lifted to the peak of the mountains. The joy of having Ivy back cancelled everything else out.

I'd dropped in to see Nola earlier this morning. She was still in the psychiatric hospital, but she'd come out of shock and was now resting. She was doing well, all considering.

Bryce had been refused bail by a magistrate. He'd be sitting in a cell until his first court appearance. He was still refusing to talk to the police. He knew that nothing he could say would help him. In the weeks ahead, Franco and I would be building up the case against him.

After writing up case notes about Penny and Polly, I headed downtown to sit down and eat a quiet lunch a Katoomba café. Just to be alone and recharge my batteries. It felt as if I hadn't sat down to eat a relaxed lunch in forever. I ended up ordering so much food I doubted I'd eat it all.

From my seat, I watched Lori walk down the street with Charlotte. The two of them looked like any other mother and daughter who were out window-shopping. Except they weren't. Both were forever changed by what had happened to them.

I'd heard that Sean had moved out to his own place. The relationship between him and Roxanne hadn't lasted though. I'd also heard that Roxanne and Rhys had split up. Rhys was keeping the kids with him. I was sorry for Charlotte and Olivia to have returned to such fragmented families.

My phone rang.

It was Justine Farina.

"Detective Kate Wakeland," I answered, then sipped my coffee.

"Oh, hello, Kate. I don't normally watch the news, but the news about the kidnappers is everywhere. Congratulations on a job well done."

"Thank you, Justine." I bit into my bagel.

"I couldn't believe it when I found out it was Max's mother behind it all. Oh... and you finding Ivy... in the cave and all. My heart was in my mouth when I watched the video of it on TV. It's just wonderful."

"Yes, it really is." Something about the hesitation in her voice told me there was something on her mind. She hadn't just rung to congratulate me. What could it be? I waited for more.

"I'm guessing Penny told you all about how she managed to kidnap the children that day?" Justine said.

I chewed on my bagel. "Yes. She's told us everything."

The line went silent for a second.

"I... ah, there's something I should tell you," she stated.

"I'm listening."

"Ivy's button. The one shaped like a bee that I found on the hill. I... I didn't find it on the hill. I actually found it... just on the ground in the picnic area. I pretended that I found it on the hill. I wasn't thinking straight that day. I thought that I'd be blamed for letting the children out of my sight, and I'd lose my job. Or even go to jail or something. I... I thought that I could make it look like it was kind of Nola's fault—that the kids had followed her and then she'd let them get past her."

I swallowed the chunk in my mouth. "Oh... Justine. That really did lead the investigation the wrong way, you know."

"I know. I'm so sorry. But Nola *did* zone out that day, so it seemed to me that the most likely scenario was that the kids really did go up the hill." She stalled. "Is... is anything going to happen to me, now that you know?"

"I'll get back to you on that. Thank you for telling me."

I ate the rest of my lunch feeling a little stunned. Something as small as the location of a lost button had indeed affected the investigation. There'd been so little else to go on.

It also occurred to me that Justine had only rung and told me about the button because the kidnappers had been found and she knew we'd interviewed them. Perhaps she worried that we would work out that she was lying, and she wanted to make it easier on herself by contacting us first.

People never failed to surprise me, often in the worst ways. No, that wasn't true. Most of the time, they surprised me in the best of ways. It was easy to become negative in this job.

72

KATE

One month later

The morning was crisp, bright. A peach-coloured light tinted the soft clouds and the grassy hills.

Pete stood beside me, his hand on mine. Ivy held fast to my other hand. Abby, Logan and the baby were close by.

Mum always loved the mornings best. She'd been an early riser all her life. It'd seemed right to hold her funeral close to dawn.

Mourners stood in a semi-circle. Mum had known a lot of people. Still, many were missing from the circle—family and friends who'd already passed away. A couple of the patients from the hospice had made it along, but the majority of them were far too unwell. The Tallman's Valley Hospice had sent me one of Harry Grenville's pictures. A picture of a swan flying. The staff weren't entirely certain that he'd drawn it for Mum, but he'd taken unusual care with it, they said. Regardless, it had made me cry fresh tears when I'd seen it.

Franco, Grimshaw, Ella and Cameron had come, too. Even Inspector Zimmerman had made it, walking on unsteady legs with the aid of a cane.

Liz Booth had told me that she didn't do funerals—I didn't blame her. Funerals were not the kind of events that anyone wanted to attend.

The parents of Harper Rawlings had stepped in to pay their respects but hadn't stayed long. I hadn't expected to see them here at all.

The whole Parrish family stood together. The rest of the families were here, too, but not all of the parents. There was Lori and Charlotte but not Sean. There was Rhys and the kids but not Roxanne.

Penny and her sister had been denied bail. They wouldn't be going to trial for months. It would be a long wait until we knew their fate. Max was the one I felt sorriest for in all of this. He'd been left with no one. Almost. At first, the Parrish family had taken him in. That arrangement couldn't last though, as they'd soon be returning to America. And then Nola had surprised us by offering to take Max. DNA testing had found her to be a blood relative of his—his cousin. She and Max were taking things one day at a time, to see if things would work out. The two of them didn't know each other yet.

Nola glanced over at me, her chin dimpling in a small smile. I smiled back. I hoped that in time she'd let me investigate the offences her mother and others had committed. She deserved to find peace.

My gaze swept over the heads of all five of the returned children. Ivy, Max, Elijah, Olivia and Charlotte. Seeing them all in the one place and under the sunshine was a vision of hope that I clung to. Just a little over a month ago, almost everyone believed we'd never discover what had happened to the children, or if we did, it had seemed that we'd be attending their funerals. But there hadn't been any funerals for the children. Not one. Which was as it should be.

The priest began speaking the last rites.

Abby and Ivy laid flowers down on Mum's coffin.

I tried to listen to the words, but my mind kept drifting away, back to the last weeks that she was alive.

After Ivy had come home from the hospital, my family had spent every last day with my mother. Every day, we'd bring a little picnic. Abby and Ivy and Jasper—who'd just begun sitting up unaided—would sit on the picnic rug, while Pete and I sat next to Mum on chairs. Logan often joined us.

Abby and Ivy would bake blueberry muffins together and bring them. Mum loved those, though she was barely eating.

We talked about old days as a family. About my mother's childhood on the farm, and about me when I was a child. Ivy loved listening to the stories. There was a day when Ivy and Jasper were sitting on Mum's lap and all three fell asleep. And I went to take Ivy, thinking she was too heavy for Mum, and Abby went to take Jasper. And then Mum's eyes flew open and she protested the kids being moved. She wanted them to stay sleeping right where they were.

At one picnic, we were surprised by Lori, Marcy, Nick and Rhys turning up with their children. They'd wanted to thank the woman who'd provided the vital clue about the Maremmas. Mum was grateful but puzzled that her little suggestion could have meant so much.

The parents also wanted to see Harry Grenville, with his pictures and his binoculars. Harry, in his typical fashion, ignored them all.

Pete had his own surprise. He'd been looking at a small property to buy at Katoomba. An acreage with the kind of cottage that I adored, and with more than enough land for Ivy and Jasper to run around on when they came to visit. And large enough that Abby and Logan could build a house on, too, if they wanted. For now, Abby and Logan could have the house we now lived in.

Ivy had jumped up and down with excitement when Pete got to the last item on his list—that the two Maremma dogs could come and live with us, too.

Amid all of that, I'd tried not to see how much Mum was fading.

She'd never quite recovered from her flu. The nurses tried to prepare me. But you can never see your way to the end. You can only see your way from the beginning of your time with a person until the present.

The funeral ceremony ended.

It was time to go.

Abby linked arms with me on my way over to the cars. Her eyes were glazed with tears and the tip of her nose red. Regardless, she looked beautiful, with her translucent skin and dark hair so like her grandmother's.

"Where are the kids?" I asked.

"It's okay, Dad and Logan have got them."

We stepped out of the sunlight into dappled shade. The morning was already warming up. Winter hadn't lasted long this year.

Abby stalled, biting down on her lip. "I need to tell you that I'm sorry. For everything."

I began shaking my head before she was even finished. "Honey, you don't need to be. Don't be sorry."

"No... I do need to be. I wasn't fair on you. I was angry for a long time. With the whole world. I dug the pain down deep. But I shouldn't have."

Tears pricked my eyes. "I wasn't there for you enough. My job took so much out of me. Mum warned me... and she was right."

Abby drew a breath, her shoulders rising and falling. "It wasn't that. There's something I've never told you. I've never told anyone. Not Logan either."

I eyed her in confusion. "Honey, what do you mean?"

She hesitated. "Back when I was fourteen. I did something I'm not proud of."

"When you were *fourteen?*"

That was the year of Abby's life when she and I had fallen apart. When she'd become like a stranger to me.

She nodded. "Instead of telling you, I started hating you. Because it was easier to blame you than blame myself. Which was wrong."

I inhaled the warm air, my mind running with a dozen different things. I told myself to stop, not to play the detective. "Whatever it is, you know you can tell me. We'll get through it. And I want to tell you, I'm proud of you. Nothing can change that."

"I won't tell you right now. It's not the right time. We've just lost Nanna. And we've just gotten Ivy back. This is their time. Not mine. But I needed to tell you that the way I've been behaving isn't your fault. And I wanted to say it *now*, because..." She swallowed, her eyes glistening wet. "Because people die, and then you lose your chance. What if you or me had an accident on the way home from the funeral? Then you'd never know."

"Abby, nothing's going to happen to us. We're okay. You're okay. But you're right. Now's the time to remember your Nanna and think about Ivy and just... enjoy her being back with us."

She hugged me.

Her body relaxed into the hug in a way that it hadn't since forever. Since she was a little girl and I was important in her life. I hugged her back tightly.

So many things melted away in that embrace. Years of heartache.

In the distance, I watched people walking from the cemetery. And there was Pete, with Jasper in his arms, and Logan walking beside him, holding Ivy's hand.

What I had, right here, now, was everything.

Everything else could wait.

ABOUT ONE LAST CHILD

I hope you enjoyed ONE LAST CHILD.

There will be a follow-up book to ONE LAST CHILD, again featuring Detective Kate Wakeland as the main character. The next book will follow the story of the secret that Abby Wakeland has been hiding from her mother since she was fourteen. And the secret will be compelling enough to make Kate decide to stay on in her role as a detective.

When I was developing the story of ONE LAST CHILD, I wanted to write Kate Wakeland as a gutsy, talented detective who finds herself up against the most difficult, heartbreaking case of her life.

My initial idea involved a detective who'd been prevented from joining an investigation into a crime committed against one of her family members. I conducted careful research into the rules and guidelines in relation to detectives taking on such cases or conducting their own personal investigations. And I found the idea so intriguing, I wrote a story based on it.

BOOKS BY ANNI TAYLOR

Find out more about my books here:

annitaylor.me

Domestic psychological thrillers
THE GAME YOU PLAYED
STRANGER IN THE WOODS
ONE LAST CHILD

Dark psychological thriller/horror fiction
THE SIX
POISON ORCHIDS

ABOUT ANNI TAYLOR

Anni Taylor lives on the Central Coast north of Sydney, Australia, with her wonderful partner, amazing sons and a little treats-wrangler dog named Wookie.

Her first thriller, THE GAME YOU PLAYED, and her subsequent thrillers, have all been chart-toppers in their categories. Anni enjoys nothing more than diving into writing the next dark story!

Find out more about her books here:

annitaylor.me

THANK YOU

Much thanks to the Blue Mountains community group who very kindly gave me their insights into the Blue Mountains area, including the lore and myths. I was bowled over by the amazing feedback and discussion they provided. They are a vibrant, passionate community who hold a deep love of the area in which they live.

The Blue Mountains was hit very hard by the recent, devastating fires in New South Wales, and the community spirit was there in spades.

Thank you also to Veronica of Windradyne Boutique Bed & Breakfast, who helpfully answered all of my questions about the Blue Mountains and its history. My partner and I stayed at Windradyne as a base while I conducted my research.

Windradyne has magical, sweeping views and is across the road from the main tourist viewing platforms for the Three Sisters. All while sitting at the dining table and enjoying Veronica's wonderful home-cooked breakfasts, and enjoying the company of other guests. (A lovely American couple and a lovely English couple joined us at the breakfasts.)

Made in the USA
San Bernardino, CA
30 January 2020